RUGGED WATER

BY

JOSEPH C. LINCOLN

AUTHOR OF "DOCTOR NYE," "SHAVINGS," ETC.

D. APPLETON AND COMPANY
NEW YORK :: 1924 :: LONDON

RUGGED WATER

RUGGED WATER

CHAPTER I

A DARK night, but a clear one. No clouds, no fog, and the wind but a light southwesterly breeze. Warm, too, for November. The little room in the tower of the Setuckit Life-Saving Station was chilly, of course—a landsman might have considered it decidedly cold—but to Seleucus Gammon, the member of the Setuckit crew on watch in the tower, it was warm, noticeably and surprisingly so. Seleucus, who had come on duty dressed for the ordinary November temperature, had unbuttoned the heavy jacket which he wore over his sweater and had hung his cap on the hook on the wall, beside the round, brass ship's clock. The brass of the clock was polished to a mirror-like glisten. So, too, was the metal of the telescope on its stand in the middle of the room. So, also, was every particle of brass or nickel in that room. There was no light to render these things visible, and no stove or other heating apparatus. Heat within and cold without meant frost-covered window panes and consequent difficulty in looking through and from those windows, in keeping watch up and down the beaches and over the stretches of sea and shoal. In many stations at this period it was not customary to keep a man on watch in the tower at night; the regulations did not require it and the matter was left to the discretion of the keeper. At Setuckit, however, night watch in the tower was a part of the regular routine; at least, since Captain Oswald Myrick had been in charge there.

Seleucus strolled slowly about the glass-inclosed room, stopping to peer from each window in turn. He was a huge, bulky man, with a salt sea roll in his walk, and as he lumbered from window to window in the darkness, a seeker for comparisons might have been reminded of a walrus wallowing about in an undersized tank. A bald head and a tremendous sweep of shaggy mustache were distinct aids to the walrus suggestion.

The views from each window were made up solely of blackness, spotted with fiery points. To Seleucus, however, the blackness was underlaid with the familiarity of long acquaintance, and every pin prick of fire a punctuation on a page he knew by heart. For example, to the east, ten miles away, the steady white spark was the Orham light-house shining out from the high sand bluffs fronting the Atlantic. Far out, and more to the south, another brilliant point marked the position of the lightship at Sand Hill Shoal, and still farther to the southeast and fainter, because of distance, were the lanterns of the Broad Rip lightship. Swinging to the south he noted two more lightships, those marking respectively the edges of the Tarpaulin and Hog's Back, smaller shoals but quite as dangerous as their bigger brothers. To the west was still another, that moored by Midchannel Shoal, and, eight miles beyond, and flashing at minute intervals, was the lighthouse on Crow Ledge, unique because, like the house in the Scriptural story, it was founded upon a rock, and rocks are distinct novelties along the Cape Cod coast.

On this night—or morning, for it was almost that—and visible because of the unwonted clearness of the atmosphere, one more spark pricked the southern horizon, the light at Long Point, on Nonscusset Island. Between these were scattered others, much less brilliant, and these the watcher knew to be the lights of vessels—schooners for the most part—taking advantage of the fair weather to make safe passage between ports south of "Down East." From the tower of the Setuckit Life-Saving Station in the later years of the nineteenth century—the years before the United States Life-Saving Service was taken over by the Naval Department and rechristened the Coast Guard, before the era of wireless stations and the Cape Cod Canal—on a clear night from Setuckit tower one might count no less than six lighthouses and six lightships, not including that of Setuckit lighthouse itself, which reared its blazing head two miles up the beach, and was, therefore, a next-door neighbor.

A beautiful coast in summer; in winter a wicked, cruel coast, where, so the records show, there were more wrecks during a period of fifty years than at any other spot, except one, from Key West to Eastport, Maine.

These matters, statistical and picturesque, were not, of course, in the thoughts of Mr. Gammon as he stood, hands in pockets, gazing through the tower window facing west. His mental speculations were engaged with matters much more personal and intimate. The little ship's clock on the wall had just struck twice, so he knew that the time was two bells, or five o'clock, therefore it would soon be daybreak, and, later, sunrise, when his watch would end. He knew also that, down below, in the kitchen of the station, Ellis Badger, who happened to be cook that week, was preparing breakfast. Breakfast, the first meal of the four in the station routine of those days, was served before daylight. Dinner was at eleven, supper at four, and there was an extra meal about eight in the evening.

Seleucus thought of breakfast and his always present and enthusiastic appetite hailed the thought joyfully. Then he remembered the sort of cook Badger was, and the joy was chilled with a dash of foreboding. It was Ellis Badger who had accidentally dropped the kitchen cake of soap into the bean pot on a Saturday of the previous winter. The comments of his comrade were expressed with feeling.

"You ain't mad, be you, Seleucus?" queried Mr. Badger solicitously. Gammon's reply was noncommittal.

"I don't know's I'm so mad that they'll have to shoot me, Ellis," he observed. "I ain't bit nobody yet. But I am beginnin' to show signs—I'm frothin' at the mouth."

It was he, also, who suggested that the soap be put into the Badger coffee. "So's it'll be strong enough to wash with," he explained, referring to the coffee.

His anticipations concerning breakfast were not, therefore, entirely free from misgiving, but forty-nine years of a life spent amid storms—meteorological always and matrimonial for the latter half—had endowed Seleucus with a sort of amphibious philosophy, and made him more or less weatherproof. The most savage northeaster blew itself out eventually, and Mrs. Gammon—her Christian name was Jemima—stopped talking if one had sufficient fortitude to endure to the end. The sane procedure during both trials was patiently to wait for that end, and think of something else while waiting.

So, true to his code, and reflecting that, after all, a poor breakfast was better than no breakfast, Mr. Gammon shifted his thought, also his position, and, walking to the eastern window, looked out from that. As he stood there the eastern horizon turned from black to gray, the low-hanging stars above it began to dim; and below him the sand dunes and the cluster of shanties and fish houses of the little settlement at Setuckit Point slowly emerged from the gloom, separated, and assumed individual shape and proportions.

A step sounded on the stair leading to the tower, the door opened and Calvin Homer entered the little room. Homer was Number One man at the Setuckit Station; that is, his was, next to Captain Oswald Myrick's, the position of greatest responsibility and command. On board a ship, he would have ranked as mate and his associates would have added a "sir" to their remarks when addressing him. On the station records he was "Surfman Number One," but his comrades called him Calvin or "Cal," just as they called their commander "Cap'n Oz" or "Ozzie." The keeper of a Cape Cod Life-Saving Station, at that time, had absolute and autocratic control of his crew while the latter were on duty, and the crew recognized and obeyed that authority. But, being independent Yankees, they remained democrats so far as verbal homage to rank and title was concerned.

Homer came into the tower room, closing the door behind him. He was twenty-six, lean, square shouldered, smooth faced, gray eyed, and sunburned to a deep brick red. He had just come up from his cot in the sleeping quarters on the second floor, and was wearing his blue uniform suit, with "NO. I" in white upon the coat sleeves. Gammon noticed the uniform immediately.

"Hello, Cal," he drawled. "Up airly, ain't you? And all togged out, too. Practicin' up to show off afore the girls next summer?"

Homer smiled. "Next summer is a long way off, Seleucus," he said.

"Huh! Maybe 'tis when a feller is as young as you be. I'll be fifty next June, and I can smell Mayflowers already. How's Cap'n Ozzie this mornin'?"

"I don't know. His door is shut, so I hope he's asleep, and his wife, too. I didn't hear anybody moving as I came by. It was a quiet night, so maybe they both slept. I hope so. The cap'n needs all the rest he can get. He starts for home this morning."

"Um-hum. I know he does. Peleg Myrick's goin' to take him over, they tell me. Good thing there's a smooth sea. That old craft of Peleg's is as sloppy as a dish pan if there's more'n a hatful of water stirrin.' I went up to Orham along of Peleg my last liberty day but one, and—crimustee!—I give you my word I thought I'd be drownded afore we made Baker's beach. I told Peleg so. 'What's the matter with ye?' says Peleg. 'This boat of mine 'll weather anything!' he says; 'and this ain't nothin' but a moderate blow. You won't get overboard this trip.' 'I know it,' I told him, 'and that's the trouble. When I'm overboard I can cal'late to make out to swim, but aboard here all I can do is set still and wait for the tide to go over my head. That last sea we shipped filled my ileskins full to the waist. Let me take your hand pump so I can see how bad my boots leak.' He, he! Crimus! Peleg named that boat of his *The Wild Duck*. I told him he'd ought to named her *The Loon*. 'A loon spends half his time under water,' I says. He, he! . . . Humph! Wonder to me Ozzie didn't have a hoss 'n' team to come down over the beach to fetch him and his wife. Don't see why he didn't, do you?"

Homer shook his head. "It's a rough road and a long one," he said. "I guess his wife thought it would be easier for a sick man to travel to West Harniss by water. And it's almost a flat calm just now."

"Just now? Do you mean 'tain't likely to last?"

"I'm afraid not—all day. The glass has fallen a good deal since ten o'clock and it's still going down. . . . Well, has anything happened since you came on watch?"

"Nothin' but watchin', and plenty of that. But you ain't told me why you've got your dress-up clothes on? Don't expect no summer boarders down to watch beach drill this time of year, do you?"

"Hardly. I put the uniform on to please the skipper. He told me he wished I would. Said it would make him feel a little more as if he was leaving somebody in command here when he quit. He's pretty blue at going, but I tell him he'll be back here as well as ever in a fortnight or so."

Mr. Gammon shook his head, sighed, and reached into his pocket for his chewing tobacco.

"That's what you told him, was it?" he observed. "Humph! Ain't you ever been to prayer meetin'?"

"I guess I have. What's that got to do with it?"

Seleucus inserted the plug of tobacco between his teeth and bit and tugged until he separated a section, which he tucked into his cheek.

"I used to go to Methodist vestry meetin' myself about thirty year ago or such a matter," he observed. "Used to go consider'ble in them days, I did, when I was home from fishin'. I was young and my morals wan't settled in the straight and narrer channel, same as they be now. . . . Eh? What did you say?"

"I didn't say anything."

"Didn't you? Then it must have been what you looked that I heard. I went to meetin' Friday nights pretty reg'lar. I was always the churchy kind. . . . Didn't you say nothin' *then?*"

"No."

"Humph! You're missin' chances. I did go, for a fact.

You see, there was a girl that—well, never mind that part. But at them meetin's, time and again, I've heard your great-uncle, Zebedee Ryder, him that kept grocery store, rant and rave about the sin of lyin'. He wouldn't tell a lie for nothin', your Uncle Zeb wouldn't. Used to make his brags about it right out loud."

"Well, it was something to brag about—if it was true."

"Oh, I guess likely 'twas true enough. Nigh as I ever heard Zeb Ryder *wouldn't* tell a lie—for nothin'. If there was five cents to be got a holt of then things might be different. . . . But, anyhow, what I'm tryin' to say is that I can't understand how you, one of Uncle Zeb's own—er—ancestors, can sit in the skipper's room down below there and tell Ozzie that he'll be back here in a fortni't. You know plaguy well he'll never come back."

The younger man did not answer immediately. When he did he said, "I surely hope he will."

"So do I—in one way. In another I don't. Oz Myrick has been life-savin' for twenty-odd year. He was one of the first surfmen on one of the fust reg'lar crews ever set patrollin' a Cape Cod beach. Afore that he was fishin' on the Banks, and swabbin' decks aboard a square rigger when he wan't more'n a kid. He's pretty night as much of a veteran as Superintendent Kellogg, down to Provincetown. It's time he give up and took a rest. Yes, and his check is about ready to be handed in for keeps. He's sick and it's the kind of sickness folks his age don't get over."

Homer nodded. "He knows it," he said, briefly.

"Course he knows it. Cap'n Oz ain't anybody's fool. Told you he was cal'latin' to try and have you appointed keeper in his place, didn't he?"

Homer looked at him sharply. "What makes you say that?" he demanded.

"'Cause he told me he was cal'latin' to. Good notion, too."

His companion shook his head. "I'm not so sure that the notion is good," he said. "There are at least five men here,

and one of 'em is yourself, who have been in the service
longer than I have."

"Humph! I cal'late you could find plenty of fellers up
to Charlestown jail that have been in there long enough, but
'twouldn't be one of them that would be picked out for
warden. It takes more'n a kag of salt mackerel on legs to
handle this job down here. It takes a man—with brains.
We've got a good crew, there's no doubt about that."

"You bet there isn't!"

"I shouldn't take no such bet. They're all right, for this
Setuckit crew. But what are they? Why, the heft of 'em
are fellers like me, that have been in and on and around salt
water so long the pickle drips off 'em when they walk. They
ain't scared of nothin'. I give in to that, but that ain't because
they don't know enough to be. They're too stubborn to let
anything scare 'em, that's why. But they're as independent
and cranky as a parcel of washtubs afloat. A man they know
and have confidence in, he can handle 'em. But you let
somebody try it that ain't that kind and then see. Would
I take the job of keeper down here? I, nor Hez Rogers, nor
Ed Bloomer, nor Sam Bearse, nor any of 'em? You bet we
wouldn't!"

"Why not?"

" 'Cause we've got sense enough to realize the kind of
sense we ain't got. A good fo'mast hand don't necessary
make a good skipper. Takes more'n rubber muscles and
codline hair, that does. Takes brains, I tell you. You've got
brains, Cal, along with nerve and the rest of it. You can
handle a schooner in a shoal, or a surfman that's been on
liberty, and has come back full of pepper tea, and do it
judgmatically. When you get through the wreck's afloat,
if she's floatable, and the man's ready and willin' to go to
work again. And all hands are satisfied the right thing's
been done. This crew here—the heft of 'em—would row you
to hell over bilin' water if you give the word to launch.
They've seen you go there and back again more'n once since
Cap'n Oz was took sick. They'd be glad to have you for
skipper. And Ozzie wants you to be, and so does District

Superintendent Kellogg, for the matter of that. There's only one man I know that hadn't ought to want it."

"Who is that?"

"You yourself. You ain't a Scrabbletown lobscouser, like the most of us. Your old man was a square-rig cap'n, in his day, and your mother was a Baker and time was when her folks was counted high toned and worth money, so I've heard tell. You're smart. You've been to high school. You could get a job up to Boston, and have vessels of your own runnin' ashore afore you died, if you'd mind to set out for it. What in the nation you want to waste your time chasin' other folks's wrecks is more'n I can make out. If you want to be keeper of Setuckit Life-Savin' Station I cal'late you can. But *why* you want to, that I don't know. Why do you, Cal? What makes you stay here?"

The young man shook his head. "I don't know," he replied. "I guess it's because—because—well, you could have had a good job ashore last winter, Seleucus. I know of at least one that was offered you. Why do *you* stay here?"

Gammon grinned. "'Cause I was born a darn fool, and ain't growed out of the habit, I cal'late," he said. "I swear off every fall and vow I'm through life-savin'. Then I turn to and swear on again. There's somethin' about this—this crazy job that gets a feller, same as rum. I like it."

Homer nodded. "I know," he said. "And it's the same way with me. I like it—and I can't give it up—yet. I went into the service just as a time-filler four years ago. I had been at home up in the village for three months with mother; she was sick, and I had to be there. Then she died and—well, there was nothing else in the way of work in sight, and here was sixty-five a month, and a good deal of fun. I meant to stay six months, perhaps. I'm here yet."

"Yes, so you be. But you don't have to stay here, twelve mile from nowhere, do you?"

"No-o. But—well, I seem to be married to the job."

Seleucus shivered. "Boy," he said solemnly, "don't talk that way at your age. If you was married you'd have an excuse for the twelve mile—yes, or fifty. . . . There, there!

Let's talk about somethin' cheerful. There was a Swede
drownded off a schooner down along Race Point last week,
so Wallie Oaks was tellin' me. He see it in the Boston
paper day afore yesterday when he was over to Harniss."

The clock struck three bells and, later, four. The gray
streak along the eastern horizon broadened, turned to rose
and then crimson. Over the edge of the Atlantic, seen beyond the distant roofs of Orham, rolled the winter sun.
Seleucus yawned, stretched and took his cap from the hook.

"And that's over," he observed thankfully, referring to
his term on watch. "One more night nigher the graveyard,
as my grandmother used to say, by way of brightenin' up
breakfast. Well, I don't need no brightenin' up for my
breakfast. And you ain't had yours neither, have you?
Here's Sam. Cal, let's you and me go down and mug
up."

Sam Bearse, raw boned, tanned and mustached, had entered the room while his fellow surfman was speaking. He
grunted a "How be you, Seleucus? Hello, Cal," and, hanging his cap up on the hook, prepared to take over the tower
watch. Homer and Gammon descended to the kitchen.
Then they "mugged up," that is, they ate breakfast together.
The other men, having already breakfasted and washed the
dishes—each washing his own—were now smoking and skylarking outside the station in the sunshine. It being clear
weather, no one was on beach patrol that morning.

Homer finished first, and, leaving his comrade still busy
with coffee and doughnuts, rose from the table and prepared
to go out.

"I'll attend to my dishes when I come in, Seleucus," he
said. "I'm going to look around a minute or two."

Seleucus nodded. "Heave ahead," he observed, his mouth
full. "I'll be done after a spell. Cal'latin' to have another
cup of Ellis's coffee."

"That'll be the fourth, won't it?"

"Um-hum. But it takes about five of this slumgullion to
make one of reg'lar coffee. If I didn't have no more body
to me than this coffee's got, I'd have to hire help to find

myself on a dark night. Like drinkin' fog, 'tis. Every doughnut I eat sinks right down through to the bottom."

There was a chill in the air in spite of the sunshine, but to Calvin Homer and his associates the morning was astonishingly mild and balmy. A little breeze had sprung up, and had shifted more toward the north; the beach grass in the hollows between the dunes and on their crests was waving, the water of the bay was blue and sparkling. Over all, as always at Setuckit, sounded the surge and hiss and thunder of the surf along the beach on the ocean side.

Hezekiah Rogers, surfman Number Four, hailed Homer as the latter passed.

"Wind's breezin' on a little mite, Cal," he said. "And cantin' round more to the no'th. Have you noticed the glass? Fallin', ain't it?"

"Yes. It has been falling all night."

"I bet you! Never see a day like this, this time of year, but it turned out to be a weather breeder. We'll have one old bird of a no'theaster by nighttime, see if we don't. And I have to turn out on patrol at twelve. Godfreys! Who wouldn't sell the farm and go to sea?"

Homer smiled, but did not answer, and, turning the corner of the station, walked toward the buildings at its rear. Two cats and a weather-beaten terrier, the latter a survivor from a wrecked schooner, came trotting to meet him. In a lath inclosure adjoining the barn, a half dozen hens and a rooster with most of his tail feathers blown or pecked away were scratching—presumably for exercise—at the sand. In the barn itself, the station horses—a pair of sturdy animals, named respectively, "Port" and "Starboard"—were standing in their stalls. The horses were almost as valuable members of the Setuckit life-saving outfit as the humans. They pulled the boat wagons to the shore, hauled the heavy car bearing the beach apparatus—the latter comprising the Lyle gun, the breeches buoy, the life car, and all their paraphernalia—on the rare occasions when the apparatus was used, and were respected, pampered and better fed than their two-legged comrades. Homer patted their heads, made sure that they had been given their morning rations, and turned to go out. Hez Rogers met him at the barn door.

"Olive's lookin' for you, Cal," he announced. "She says Ozzie's up and rigged and ready to leave, and wants to see you."

Olive Myrick was the captain's wife. Her home was at West Harniss, nine miles distant across the bay, but she had come down to the station when her husband was taken ill, and had been living there for three weeks. The keeper was permitted, under the regulations, to have his wife with him. In some stations she acted as cook and general housekeeper, receiving a small allowance for the work.

Homer found her waiting for him in the kitchen. She looked tired and worn and anxious, as she had reason to be.

"Oswald wants to see you, Calvin," she said. "We're goin' over to the main just as soon as the boat's ready and he's set on talkin' with you afore he leaves. Go right in."

The skipper's room at Setuckit was on the first floor, leading from the mess room. Entering, Homer found Captain Myrick, dressed and sitting in a rocking chair. The skipper was pale and haggard and his clothes hung loosely on his body. He had lost weight during his illness. Calvin hailed him cheerfully.

"Good morning, Cap'n," he said. "Well, well! you look fit as a fiddle. All taut and rigged and ready to put to sea, eh? We're going to miss you, but we'll be all the more glad when you come back. And you couldn't have better weather for the trip."

Myrick ignored the reference to his appearance, and the weather. He motioned to the only other chair in the room.

"Sit down, Cal," he ordered. "I've got a word or so to say to you."

Homer took the other chair. Captain Myrick drew a long breath.

"Calvin," he went on, "I'm startin' on my last cruise, and I know it."

His subordinate hastened to protest. "No, no!" he exclaimed. "You shouldn't talk that way. What you need is rest. You'll be all right in—"

"Sshh! We ain't young ones, you and I, and there's no sense in makin' believe. I'm never comin' back. I've got my orders and I'm bound in. I know it—although I try to let Olive think I don't. But I do, and so does she, and so do you and all hands. I'm through."

"But, Cap'n—"

"Sshh! You're wastin' time, and I ain't got much more to waste, down here. There'll be a new skipper at the Setuckit Station inside of a month—inside of a week, if my say-so counts—and you're the man that'll have the job, if you want it. What I want to make sure of is that you do want it. Do you?"

Homer hesitated. He did want the appointment, wanted it more than he had ever wanted anything in his life, but he liked and admired the man before him, and his sense of loyalty was strong.

"I don't see any use in talking about that," he declared stubbornly. "You're the keeper here, and there never was a better one. I've enjoyed working under you and I'd like nothing better than to keep on doing it, as long as I stay in the service."

"Um-hum. Well, what I'm asking you is if you're figgerin' on stayin' in the service. Are you?"

"Yes. I guess so. For the present, anyway."

"You guess so? Ain't you sure?"

"Yes, I'm sure. But—"

"Never mind the buts. What do you want to stay for? It ain't the pay. I've been chasin' wrecks for twenty-odd year, and all I'm gettin' is seventy-five a month. You could earn more'n that—a smart young feller like you—at almost anything ashore. What are you wastin' your time life-savin' for?"

It was the same question Seleucus Gammon had asked that very morning. And Homer had asked himself that question many times during the past months. And the answer, however unsatisfactory, was always the same.

"I like the work, Cap'n," he replied. "I realize the pay amounts to nothing. It isn't that. It is just—well, there is something about it that—that—"

"I know. And I know what 'tis, too. It's the same thing that makes a feller go out codfishin' right along, winter and summer, when he could earn more money sawin' wood at home."

"Yes. But, you see—well, it's a man's job."

"So's sawin' wood. But I know what you mean. This life-savin' game *is* a man's job—for a boy's wages. And it's more'n that; there's the gamble in it. You kind of gamble against all outdoors for your life and the other man's. I know—Lord, don't I! It's that, and the salt in your blood and mine, that makes us stick to it. And there's a kind of pride, too. Cal, the average man would call me a fool, and I guess I am, but I've took more pride in keepin' this station the way it ought to be than I would bein' President of the United States."

"I understand. And you've kept it well, too."

"Yes, I cal'late I can say I have. And that's another thing I wanted to say to you. If you're sure you want to be keeper here, I'm goin' to recommend you and my word ought to carry some heft with the superintendent. But, if you *are* skipper of this station, I want you to promise me you'll keep up the Setuckit record. Since I've been here we've handled I don't know how many wrecks, some of 'em we got afloat again and lots of 'em we didn't, but we never lost one life. I'm kind of proud of that."

"You ought to be."

"Maybe so; I am, anyhow. And there's another thing I've took pride in. There's never been a call come to this station yet that we ain't answered. There never was a vessel in distress off our section—and some that weren't ours— that we ain't gone out to her, no matter how much of a gale of wind was blowin' nor what kind of a sea was runnin'. And we never started and then give up and turned back. There ain't so many stations can say that."

"There aren't any others 'round here that I know of."

"Um-um-hum. Well, I've took some pride in that, too. And I want you to promise me you'll try to keep up that record."

"I'll promise you that I'll do my best."

"That ain't quite enough, not at Setuckit, 'tain't. You've got to do a little mite more than your best. You'll have to do things that ain't possible, if you understand what I mean. That's what makes it worth while, this gamblin' game of ours. A feller has to look off to wind'ard and sort of grin and say, 'Well, by thunder, we'll see!' And then *go* and see—and see it through. Do you get my meanin'?"

Calvin nodded. "I ought to, I've watched you," he said, grimly. "Look here, Cap'n Oz: I don't want to brag, but I think—I *think* you can count on me. I like the—the gamble, as you call it."

"All right, boy! All right. I ain't afraid of you, and I haven't been. Just wanted to tell you how the old man was feelin' when he got his clearance papers, that's all. I'm backin' you and I'm bettin' on you, too. . . . Now one thing more. You know this crew pretty well."

"There's none better."

"No, there ain't. They'll go anywheres and do anything, with the right man to lead 'em. But with the wrong man. . . . You know, a crew like ours is made up of kind of rough stuff. That's why they're here. There's some hellions amongst 'em—bound to be. You've got to handle 'em easy. They'll get drunk, some of 'em, if they have a chance, and they'll come back from liberty ready to take charge and run things—some of 'em, as I say. Well, you've got to use judgment. You've got to see some things and put your foot down on 'em hard. And you've got to forget to see some other things. A parcel of husky men all alone down here on the beach, with not so much to do a good deal of the time, is like a school full of young ones. If a new teacher comes on deck, the first thing the young ones do is to find out whether he's boss or they are. If he is they're for him; he can handle 'em like a breeze. But if they find he ain't sure whether he's boss or not—then look out. You know this

crew of ours well as I do. Give 'em a pretty free helm, but
don't let 'em come up into the wind on you. See?"

"I see."

"Well, I cal'late that's about all. Good luck to you, Cal.
Don't forget your old skipper altogether, and, if you can
find a chance to run over to Harniss and see me, do it. . . .
Only don't put it off too long or I may not be there."

"Now, Cap'n, what makes you talk like that? You
know—"

"Yes, I do. So do you, boy. . . . Whew! I wouldn't
believe talkin' would make me so tuckered. I've rowed five
mile through a head wind and sea, and had more breath left
than I've got now. . . . Well, Olive, what is it?"

His wife had entered the room. "You must get your
things on, Oswald," she said. "Peleg is here, and the boat's
ready."

"So? Then I cal'late I'll be ready in a couple of shakes.
So long, Cal. See you outside. Tell the boys to stand by
so's I can say good-by to 'em."

That good-by was a short ceremony. Peleg Myrick's
catboat, the *Wild Duck,* was anchored in the little cove on
the bay side, near the station. Peleg's dory was hauled up
on the beach, and its owner was standing beside it, ready for
his passengers. Mr. Myrick—he was not related to Captain
Oz—was a stubby specimen of marine architecture, the skin
of his hands and face tanned to the color of mahogany and
looking more like leather than a human cuticle. The skin
of his feet and his legs from the knees down was of similar
shade and consistency, a fact perfectly obvious during spring,
summer and fall, when he was accustomed to "go barefoot."
Now, as it was winter, he wore a mammoth pair of high
rubber boots. The remainder of his attire was a hit or miss
jumble of black shirt, sou'wester, faded sweater and patched
trousers. His eyes were small and blue, his nose big and
red, and his mouth and most of his chin hidden beneath a
tousled heap of mustache, which, as Seleucus Gammon described it, looked like "a mess of dry seaweed that had blowed
up under the lee of his face and stuck fast." He lived alone

in a shanty four miles up the beach, and the summer visitors called him the "hermit." In his youth he had played the fiddle at the Orham dances. He had that fiddle yet and lonely surfmen on evening beach patrol heard it wailing as they passed his shanty. He earned the few dollars he needed by clamming and fishing. Between times he prophesied concerning the weather.

He stood by his dory's bow, and about him stood the off-duty members of the Setuckit life-saving crew, Calvin Homer and Seleucus among them. Captain Oswald, leaning on his wife's arm, walked slowly from the station to the shore. Peleg got the dory afloat and stood, knee deep in the water, waiting. Captain Myrick turned to his crew.

"Well, boys," he said, with a one-sided attempt at a grin, "I'm goin' ashore on a little mite of a spree. First liberty I've had for quite a spell. I leave you and Cal to run things. Take care of yourselves."

"We will. . . ." "Sure thing. . . ." "Keep sober as you can, skipper. . . ." "See you back again pretty soon. . . ." "Give my regards to the girls."

These were some of the responses. Peleg helped his passengers into the dory. Then, giving the boat a final shove, he swung over the side and took up the oars. Gammon hailed him.

"Say, Peleg," he drawled, "what's the matter with your prophesyin' factory? Broke down, has it? This is about as good a day as we've had for a month, and, last time you and me talked, you was cal'latin' on one of them East Injy typhoons. Said 'twas goin' to blow the lighthouse out to sea, or somethin' like that."

Peleg's retort was a repetition of the soothsayer's reply to Cæsar.

"Day ain't done yit," he snorted. "You'd have to tie your hair on afore to-morrer mornin'—if you had any to tie."

He swung forward and back with the oars.

"So long, boys," called Captain Oz. "Good luck, Calvin."

The dory moved off, drew abreast of the stubby broad-beamed catboat, and, a few minutes later, the *Wild Duck* stood out into the bay. The life-savers watched her go. Then they turned back to the station. Seleucus made the only remark.

"There goes a good man, Cal," he observed, sententiously. Homer did not answer.

All that forenoon the breeze continued to freshen and to pull more and more from the north to the dreaded northeast. Beach drill that afternoon was held beneath a lowering sky, and in the face of what was already a young gale. The car containing the Lyle gun and accompanying apparatus was dragged out by the horses, and the men went through the maneuvers of shooting the line over the drill mast set in the sand, rigging the breeches buoy and pulling one of their comrades from the crosstrees to the dune which represented dry land and safety. Ordinarily the drill was a matter of routine, but to-day there was a sort of grim prophecy in its details. The glass was still falling and the thermometer was falling also. From a morning phenomenally warm for the time of year the temperature had changed until, at three o'clock, it was so cold that every gust was a broadside of icy needles penetrating oilskins and sweaters and causing the life-savers to slap their mittened hands and kick the heels of their rubber boots together to stir reluctant circulation.

As they put the car back in its house again Gammon turned to Homer with a shrug.

"I'm goin' to bow down and make reverence to Peleg next time I see him," he declared. "The old skate knew what he was talkin' about when he give out his proclamations about dirty weather comin'. It's mean enough now, but it'll be a snorter afore mornin', or I miss my guess. Feels like snow, too. Figgerin' to give the new skipper a reg'lar break in, ain't they, eh?"

Homer nodded. He did not feel like talking. The responsibility of absolute command was heavy upon him. If mistakes were made now, they would be his; if blame came he must take it all. And the Setuckit Station had never lost a life.

He was not afraid, in the ordinary sense. Gales and seas,

and the dangers that come with them, he had experienced often enough. But always before he had been under the command of another man. During Captain Myrick's illness he had led the crew in many rescues, but upon the return to the station he had made his report to his superior, and there his responsibility ended. Now, as temporary skipper, it was different; he was not there to obey orders, but to give them. And he knew the crew would be watching to see how he bore himself on trial.

They were watching him already. He caught sly glances and was conscious of whispers behind his back. Those that he heard were not unkindly in tone—the men liked him—but they were noncommittal. They were waiting for him to prove himself, and, if he did, well and good. If he did not—if he faltered or hesitated, or for one moment showed that he doubted or was not certain—then, like the school children with the new teacher, his rule was forever ended. He might as well resign at once, for they would force him out of the service sooner or later.

Walter Oaks, the newest member of the crew, and the one that Homer liked least, drew alongside as they walked to the station.

"Well, Cap'n Cal," he observed, in a tone loud enough for the others to hear, "how does it seem to be boss of the ship? Ain't goin' to be too stuck-up in your new job to speak to common folks, are you?"

Calvin smiled. "I haven't got any new job yet, Wallie," he replied.

"That's so; so you ain't. Only just a try-out, as you might say. Well, it looks as if you'd have somethin' to try you pretty soon. It's goin' to blow a little mite afore mornin', they tell me. Don't get scared, Cal. If we have to go out and you upset the boat we'll all hang on to Seleucus and drift ashore. Fat'll always keep afloat, so they say, and Seleucus has got enough of that. Ha, ha!"

Gammon himself made answer.

"Hot air's what they fill balloons with," he observed. "You're consider'ble of a gas bag, Wallie. If we capsize

I'm cal'latin' to grab aholt of you and rise right up out of the water."

By supper time snow had begun to fall and when, at ten o'clock, the order was given for those not on watch to turn in, the station was trembling in the grip of a northeast blizzard such as seldom visited even that storm-whipped locality. The hurricane shrieked and howled, the snow and flying sand thrashed against the windows, and above the swish and clatter and scream sounded the eternal bellowing boom of the great rollers beating the outer beach.

Calvin Homer went to his room, the keeper's room just vacated by Captain Myrick. He went there, but he did not undress or go to bed. He left the room at frequent intervals to visit the watchman in the tower, to speak with the returning beach patrols, to attempt to peer through the windows at the chaos outside. This last procedure was wholly useless, the flying snow and sand were jumping back from the panes like fine shot, and more than once he momentarily expected those panes to be beaten in.

At four in the morning he was in the kitchen when Joshua Phinney came in from patrol. The man was muffled to the eyes, but the lashes of those eyes were fringed with icicles and his frozen oilskins cracked and split as Homer helped him to remove them. Phinney's first move, after being taken out of his shell, was to seize the huge coffee pot, kept hot and full always at the back of the range, and pour and drink three cups of its scalding contents.

"Nothing in sight, Josh?" queried Calvin, anxiously.

Phinney was picking the ice from his brows.

"In sight?" he growled. "Lord A'mighty! there ain't any sight. You can't see three feet ahead of your jib boom. All you can do is feel—if you ain't too numb even to do that."

"The telephone's gone, so Hez tells me."

"Gone! I fell over two poles myself on the way up. I don't know's the halfway house ain't blowed flat by this time."

The halfway house was the little hut on the beach two

and a half miles below the station. It contained a stove—
the fire in which the patrolmen were supposed to keep alight
and replenished—a telephone instrument, and the keys to the
time clocks carried by those on patrol. At the halfway house
the patrolman from Setuckit met the patrolman from the
Orham Station, the latter building another two and a half
miles further on.

"Did you meet the fellow from Orham?" inquired Homer.

"Yep. He fell in just as I was tryin' to pick up spunk
enough to crawl out."

"Did he say anything? Was there any news?"

"News! No. He was so froze he couldn't say nothin'
at first, and when he thawed out all he did was swear at the
weather. 'Twas Ezry Cooper, so you can know that the
swearin' was done proper, nothin' left out."

"Sea is over the beach, I suppose?"

"You suppose right. Down abreast that pint where the
Sarah Matthews come ashore it was runnin' five foot deep
and a hundred foot wide. I had to go half a mile out of
my way to get around it."

"You didn't hear anything from outside? No guns, or
anything?"

"Hear! I had to grit my teeth afore I could hear myself
think. If the whole United States Navy was off the Sand
Hill and every ship blowed up to once you couldn't hear
it to-night, I tell you. . . . Well, anything else, Cal? If
there ain't I'm goin' aloft to turn in. Got to roust out Sam
first, of course," with a grin. "He'll be real thankful to me,
won't he, when he finds what he's got to go out into?"

He went up the stairs to the sleeping quarters. Three
minutes later Sam Bearse, muffled, booted, sou'westered and
oilskinned, his Coston signal at his belt, came stumbling
sleepily down.

"Dirty morning, Sam," was Homer's greeting. "There'll
be something doing as soon as it is light enough to see, I
shouldn't wonder. Keep a sharp lookout. Use your Coston, of course; the telephone is down."

Bearse was filling himself with hot coffee and merely

grunted. Then, pulling on his mittens and buttoning his sou'wester beneath his chin, he pushed open the door and went out into the churning blackness. It took all of Homer's strength to pull that door shut.

At half-past five the call came. Calvin was on his way up to the tower when he met Oaks, the man on watch, coming down.

"Sam's burnin' his Coston, Cal," Oaks blurted, excitedly. "He must see somethin'! Lord! it's an awful mess to go off in, ain't it? Cal, do you think you'd better—"

Homer did not stop to hear the rest. He hurried to the tower room. The window toward the southeast was open and banging in the gale. Leaning out, he peered down the beach. The wind was as strong as ever and the cold intense, but it had stopped snowing. A mile or more away a brilliant glow of red light with an intensely blazing core spotted the black background.

Homer sprang to the stairs, ran down the first flight and into the room where the crew, each on his cot, were sleeping the sleep of the entirely healthy.

"Turn out, boys!" he called, briskly.

CHAPTER II

THEY were ready in three minutes. Beside each cot stood its occupant's rubber boots, their tops folded down, and socks, underclothes and trousers stuffed inside, ready for instant donning. Before Homer turned from the door, the men were on their feet and dressing. He went down to the skipper's room—his own now—and hurriedly scrambled into woolen jacket, oilskins and sou'wester. Pulling on a pair of mammoth mittens and taking the lantern from its hook and lighting it, he pushed open the door and went out.

The gale struck him as he turned the corner on his way to the barn. Its force was tremendous. Like a giant's hand it pushed against him and the blown sand cut his face as he leaned forward and fought on. The door of the stable was closed, but not locked, and the horses, awakened by the lantern light, turned to look at him as he entered. He backed them out of their stalls and began harnessing. In a few moments others of the crew joined him. In less than ten minutes from the time of his leaving the tower room the cart, bearing the lifeboat, was on its way down the beach.

It was a fight all the way. The sand was deep and the wheels cut into it. The horses did their best, but they, unaided, could never have made the trip that morning. The men helped, each tugging at the ropes attached to the sides of the cart. No one spoke. Breath was a necessity not to be wasted, and conversation in the midst of that screeching whirlwind would have been unheard. Each head was bent, each foot planted doggedly in the sand, and every muscle strained. The panting horses pulled like the humans. Animals and men had been through it all many times before and each knew what was expected of him.

In clear weather, under ordinary conditions, they would have covered the distance in a short time. As it was, almost half an hour had elapsed before they reached the foot of the high dune from which the spot where Bearse's signal burned was visible. There Bearse himself met them.

He plowed close to Calvin and bellowed in the latter's ear.

" 'Tain't any use to try to get down any further," he panted. "Surf's runnin' clean over the beach just below here. I got in pretty nigh to my waist comin' up. Might's well launch her right abreast here, Cal. . . . Whew! Did you ever see such a blow in your life! And cold! My Godfreys!"

Homer did not reply. Instead he asked a question.

"Where is she?" he shouted.

"On the south end of the Sand Hill. Pretty well out. Two master, looks like. She was sendin' up rockets a while ago, but not now. Come up yonder; I cal'late it's light enough to make her out—a little of her, anyhow."

He led the way to the top of the dune and Homer followed. At this elevation the extreme force of the hurricane was most evident and for the moment Calvin was conscious of nothing else. Then, after he had caught his breath and mopped the sand and spray from his eyes, he looked seaward. It was a gray-and-white upheaval over which he looked. In the dim light of early morning he saw the huge breakers running, in creaming ridges, out, out, out, one behind the other. Immediately before him they fell in frothing, leaping tumult, to surge up the shelving shore to the very base of the dune. The middle distance was obscured by driving scud. He turned to his companion. Bearse pointed a mittened hand.

"There she is," he roared, and above the thunder of the sea his words came only as a faint whisper. "Off yonder. You can sight her once in a while between squalls. . . . There! Look!"

Homer looked—and saw. A mass of crazy wave, a huddle of jumping froth, and, at one spot above it, two black masts slanted against a slaty background. He nodded and turned back.

As they stumbled down the sheltered side of the dune Bearse laid a hand on his own.

"Goin' to try it?" he queried. . . . "Oh, all right!" with a one-sided grin. "Just as you say. I always did like exercise."

Back at the cart Calvin shouted brief orders. Once more the men and horses bent to the tugs and the cart and its burden emerged from between the dunes and came out at the top of the sloping beach.

"Man the surf boat!" shouted Homer.

Each man took his position. The cart was turned broadside to the sea.

"Unload. . . . Take out bolts. . . ."

The bolts which held the vehicle were removed, and the rear and forward wheels of the boat carriage separated.

"Set."

The boat was lowered to the sand.

"Haul out wheels."

The wheels were pulled out of the way. With the lifting bar under her the boat was skidded bow on to the surf.

"Take life belts."

Each man took a life belt from the racks inside the boat and strapped it over his shoulders and about his waist. The only one who did not do this was Badger, the cook, who, according to rule, would be left ashore in charge of the station during his commander's absence.

"Ship rowlocks. . . . Take oars."

Each man at his place—a place fixed by regulation and confirmed by constant drill—put his rowlock in position, and laid his oar crosswise on the boat. Homer gave the outfit a hurried glance of inspection.

"Shove her down," he ordered.

With a rush they slid the boat down the slope and into the surge. The men at the bow were knee-deep in water. Seleucus Gammon found time to shout a comment.

"Crimus! that feels nice and cool," he bellowed. "Come in, boys, the water's fine. What's the matter, Wallie; tired? This'll freshen you up."

Oaks, the comparatively new member of the crew, did not answer. He was looking at the walls of white water just ahead.

"In bow," ordered Calvin.

Seleucus and his opposite surfman sprang over the gunwale and seized their oars.

"Down with her."

As she moved out the other men scrambled in.

"Start rowing. . . . *Go!*"

The boat leaped forward into the breakers. As she did so Homer, the last man to leave shore, swung over the stern and took up the heavy steering oar. A long stroke, another, a moment's wait as a wave broke just before them, and swept beneath. Then another mighty pull, and a rise that lifted them up and up. Flying foam, a deluge of icy water, a series of strokes, and then a coast. They were over the first breaker. The men settled to their long pull. Homer, again swabbing his dripping face with a drenched mitten, peered ahead and bent his strength to the steering oar. A good launch and a lucky one, conditions considered. They were off. So far, so good.

But the launch was only the beginning, a fact which every man realized—the new skipper most of all. There remained a row of at least three miles, through a sea which was establishing a record even for that coast, and with weather conditions about as bad as they could be. Even as exacting a disciplinarian as Superintendent Kellogg, the hardy veteran in charge of the district, would have excused a keeper for not risking the lives of his crew that day. Homer knew this and knew that the men knew it. Surely, as Oaks had intimated, his first "try-out" as temporary head of the Setuckit Station was a tough one.

He was not afraid—for himself. The excitement of the battle was too keen for that. There was a fierce joy in it. But the sense of responsibility was always there, when he permitted himself to think of it. Responsibility, not only for those lives aboard the stranded schooner, but for the safety of his comrades, and the clean record to which Myrick had referred. He set his teeth, and when Gammon, tugging at the bow oar, caught his eyes and grimly grinned, he smiled in return.

The seas were enormous. Only from their crests could he see ahead. Each time the boat swung up to the top of one of those hills of water he peered apprehensively out, fearing that the two black marks, the masts of the wrecked craft, might no longer be in sight. But they were there— they still stood.

He looked into the faces under the sou'westers. Every face was set, and every man was pulling with all his might. No one spoke, they were too busy for that. Even Seleucus, the loquacious, was silent, and no ordinary combination of wind and wave could have prevented him from shouting a profane joke occasionally. The boat moved on, slowly, but doggedly; the spray shot over it in sheets, and froze when it struck. Men, oars, and rigging were covered with ice.

The cold, that was the worst of all. Oilskins glistened like suits of armor. Mittens cracked at the knuckles. Eyebrows and mustaches hung with icicles. But they were gaining; with every stroke they drew nearer to Sand Hill Shoal and the wreck at its southern extremity.

Suddenly Oaks, at Number Six, stopped rowing. Homer, watching the expressions of his men, had of late watched his in particular. He had seen it change. And so he was, in a measure, prepared.

"Go on, Wallie," he shouted. "Row. What's the matter with you?"

Oaks tried to rise from the thwart, would have risen, had not Sam Bearse, at Number Seven, freed one hand and jerked him down again.

"Row, you fool!" growled Sam.

But Oaks did not obey. His chin was quivering, and, in spite of the cold, there were beads of perspiration on his cheeks.

"Put me ashore, Cal Homer," he shrieked. "I—I— Put me ashore! I can't stand this. For God's sake, Cap'n, put me ashore!"

The other men kept on rowing—it was mechanical with them—but their looks expressed the wildest astonishment. This was something new in their experience, brand new.

Calvin was as astonished as the rest.

"Put you *ashore!*" he gasped.

"Yes—yes. Put me ashore. My God, we—we can't make it! We'll be drownded. I—I've got a—a wife to home. She—she— Turn round, Cal Homer, you're crazy! We can't make it. We'll drown, I tell you! You put me ashore."

The man's nerve was completely gone. He let go of his oar entirely and shook both fists in the air. Bearse pulled the oar into the boat.

Oaks's threats changed to pleadings.

. "Oh, Cap'n, please!" he begged. "I'll pay you for it. My pay check's comin' due next week. I'll give you half of it—I swear I will! I'll give you all. I—I can't stand it, I tell you. Turn around and put me ashore."

There was silence in the boat for an instant, silence broken by a tremendous "Haw! haw!" from Seleucus Gammon. The other men, still rowing as hard as ever, looked at each other, then at Oaks, and then at their skipper *pro tem.* Homer, catching that look, knew they were waiting to see how he would meet this entirely unprecedented emergency. It was another test—a test of his capacity as "boss."

"I'll pay you," shrieked Oaks again. "I'll give you—" But Homer interrupted.

"Sit down," he ordered, savagely. "Sit down and row."

"But, Cal, please—"

Calvin lifted the big steering oar from the water.

"Down!" he roared. "Down, or I'll cave your head in with this. . . . Down! Now row—or I'll brain you first and drown you afterwards."

At that moment he would have done it. The men knew it and, what was more important, Oaks himself seemed to realize it. Sobbing and hysterical he sank back upon the thwart, took up the oar which Bearse pushed into his hands, and began rowing once more. Homer glared at him, swallowed hard—and then laughed aloud. A bellow of laughter came from the boat. What might have been a calamity was now a joke, a joke to be remembered and talked about—when the time for talking came.

"Almost there, boys," shouted Calvin, cheerfully. "Keep her going."

The wreck was in plain sight now, only a quarter of a mile away. A little fore and aft schooner, hard and fast aground, at least every third sea breaking over her from stem to stern. Men were in the rigging, five of them. Calvin waved to them and a hand was waved in return.

The sea was more wicked than ever there at the tail of the shoal. It required judgment and experience and skill to bring the lifeboat up under the lee of the wreck. But this—with the exception of Oaks—was a veteran crew, even if their leader was comparatively new to his job, and, after several trials, it was done. The schooner's deck was aslant, and formed a partial shelter. The grapnels were made fast.

"Come down!" shouted Calvin, addressing the men in the rigging. "We'll look out for you. Hurry!"

One of the men—the captain—shouted a reply. Above the tumult of wind and water only a few words were audible in the boat below, something like "half froze."

"We'll have to go after 'em," called Calvin. "Come on, one of you. You, Seleucus, come with me. The rest of you stay in the boat."

Watching his chance he climbed over the tilted rail, Gammon at his heels. The slant of the deck, and the coating of ice upon it, made each step an effort and a risk. The schooner's crew were in the rigging of the foremast. Their captain, when he realized the danger his craft was in, had ordered the anchors thrown over. They had held, but the wind and tide had not only swung the vessel around until she grounded, but their force had ripped the windlass bodily from the deck and jammed it tight in the bow "in the eyes of her," as a sailor would describe it. And over that bow the breakers poured in icy cascades.

The men in the rigging had managed to cast off the lines with which they had secured themselves there, and, stiffly and slowly, were climbing down to the lee rail. Theirs was now, more than ever, a precarious position. Again and again the flying water poured over them. Plainly the schooner was being beaten to pieces, and the masts, the fore-mast especially, might go by the board at any second.

Homer and Gammon slipped and stumbled forward. Each time a wave went over they were obliged to cling with hands and feet. After one tremendous sea Calvin, brushing the water from his eyes, looked anxiously for his companion.

"All right, are you, Seleucus?" he gasped.

Seleucus's voice, punctuated with coughs, made answer.

"All here, so fur," it panted. "Crimustee! have to do some hangin' on, don't ye? Monkey up a tree ain't got nothin' on us. Yes, he has, too. He's got a tail and that ought to help consider'ble. Wish to the Lord I had one. . . . Here you go—you! Give me your fist."

The first man, a foremast hand, was at the foot of the shrouds. Between them, and aided by the other life-savers, he was lifted over the side into the boat. The other four followed, the captain last of all. He had reached the rail, and was about to jump to the boat when a huge breaker, timed exactly right—or wrong—reared its head above the schooner's bow.

"Look out!" bellowed Gammon, and from the boat came an echoing yell of warning. Homer made a flying leap and a clutch at the oilskin collar of the man at the rail. Then the wave broke and he and the owner of that oilskin were thrown headlong to the slanting deck and over and over— "like a couple of punkins," as Seleucus described it after-wards—until they struck the foot of the lee rail with terrific force.

It was Homer who struck first and for an instant he was stunned. His head had hit a stanchion of the bulwark and, if it had not been for his sou'wester, the latter buttoned tightly under his chin, he would almost certainly have been killed. As it was, his head was cut, and when Gammon dragged him out of the surge of water the blood was run-ning down his face. But he still clutched the collar of the schooner's skipper and the pair scrambled dazedly to their feet. Seleucus, who had saved himself from similar disaster by seizing and holding fast to a rope's end, was clear headed and adequate.

"Over with you," he shouted, pushing the skipper to the rail. "Come, wake up!" with a shake. "Into that boat now. Look out for him, you fellers."

The rescued man was bundled over the side into three pairs of outstretched arms.

"Now, Cal," ordered Gammon.

But Homer was capable of taking care of himself by this time.

"You first," he commanded.

"Why . . . why, you durn fool, this ain't no time to. . . . A-a-ll right, just as you say, Cap'n."

He jumped into the boat. Homer cast a comprehensive glance over the abandoned schooner. She was doomed; there was absolutely no hope of saving her or anything aboard her. He, too, climbed over the side.

"All right, Cal, are you?" asked Bearse, anxiously, as Calvin took his place in the stern.

"Yes. Cast off. Lively now."

The boat swung away from the wreck.

"All set? Row."

He braced himself at the steering oar. The crew began rowing. The men from the schooner crouched between the thwarts.

The row home was longer than the outward trip had been, and, although not quite so hard, was hard enough. Homer's head was throbbing wickedly, and he wiped the blood from his face with his frozen mitten from time to time. He had determined not to attempt, with such a load aboard, a landing in the surf upon the outer beach, but to go around the end of the point to the sheltered waters of the bay side.

On the "rips" at the end of the point the seas were higher than any they had yet encountered. The boat climbed and climbed, and then dipped and slid. The cook of the schooner, a half-breed Portuguese, crouching near the bow directly in front of Gammon, began to pray aloud. Seleucus lost patience.

"Shut up!" he roared. "You can hold meetin' when you get ashore. Sing hymns then and take up collection, if you want to. . . . But now you shut up. Shut up, or I'll step on you! Look at Wallie; see how nice he's behavin'."

Oaks had remained quiet since his outbreak on the way to the wreck. He was white and shaking, but he had not spoken, and he was rowing, after a fashion. The other men laughed. Homer smiled, but he shook his head.

"That'll do, Seleucus," he ordered. "Don't talk—row. We want to get home—where it's warm."

The boat soared and coasted over the huge waves. Midway of the rips, at the crest of a billow, Calvin looked back in the direction of the Sand Hill. The two black marks no longer slanted against the sky. The sea had swallowed its prey, the schooner had gone.

Landing in the cove at the back of the point was an easy matter. They beached the boat, and the rescued men—the cook's prayers now turned to profane thanksgivings—staggered through the sand to the station. Homer drew a long breath.

"Leave her where she is," he commanded, referring to the lifeboat. "We'll attend to her later. I don't know how you boys feel, but I want a cup of coffee."

Gammon, as usual, was the first to answer.

"Coffee!" he repeated. "I'm so fur gone I want about another hogshead of that stuff Ellis *calls* coffee. That shows the state *I'm* in."

As they walked up the beach he came close to his commanding officer.

"How's your head, Cal?" he asked

"Oh, it's achin' a little, but it's all right. A bump, that's all."

"Bump! Crimus! If that's a bump then a man with his head cut off has been scratched. . . . Cal," he added, under his breath, "you done a good job this mornin'. You'll make out as skipper at Setuckit. I said you would, and now I know it."

A moment later he was inquiring solicitously concerning Oaks.

"That wife of yours ashore, Wallie," he observed, "she ain't lost you yet, I'm afraid. Don't have no luck, does she?"

Oaks, sullen and downcast, made no reply. He was the first to enter the station and, after swallowing a cup of red-hot coffee, went up to the sleeping room to change his clothes. His immediate future was destined to be unpleasant, and he knew it.

Calvin, too, drank coffee—or Badger's substitute for it—and ate a few mouthfuls. But there was too much to be done—and done at once—to permit of rest. Dry clothes and warmth were restorers in themselves, and water and a bandage helped his cut head. He treated himself to these luxuries and then set about the duties to follow. The men from the schooner had been fed and warmed and dried, and were now stretched on the cots in the room provided for such waifs. There were cases of frostbite among them, and the skipper—his name was Leary—had a badly bruised knee. All this had to be seen to and the regulation entries concerning the wreck made in the log of the station.

Badger reported that nothing of importance had happened during his comrades' absence. Telephone poles and wires were down and there was no communication with other stations or with the main. The glass was still very low, the gale had abated but little, and it was beginning to snow once more. Homer went down to the mess room where the men were sprawled about the stove, smoking and joking. Wallie Oaks was not among them and Calvin asked concerning him. A general grin was his only answer at first, and then Seleucus spoke.

"Wallie's gone out to the barn," he explained. "He ain't comf'table, Wallie ain't. Don't seem to be satisfied nowhere. When he was off yonder he wanted to be put ashore and now he is ashore he acts kind of as if he wished he was to sea

again. I cal'late he's tellin' the horses about his havin' a
wife to home. Seems to me I heard old Port laughin' a
minute or two ago."

The men chuckled. Josh Phinney winked at his companions.

"The heft of us have got wives, fur's that's concerned,"
he observed. "You've got one, ain't you, Seleucus?"

Mr. Gammon regarded him gravely. "I've got a number
eleven boot, too," he announced; "but I ain't makin' any
brags about it. I'm just keepin' it to use on folks that get
too smart and fresh in their talk."

Phinney swung round in his chair.

"I wouldn't keep it too long," he said, cheerfully. "It
might spile. If you ain't had enough exercise this mornin',
and want more, I cal'late maybe I can accommodate you."

Homer raised a hand. "I can give you all the exercise you
need," he said. "It's snowing again and as thick as mud
outside. Seleucus, you'd better go up to the tower and
relieve Ellis on watch for a while. He's been there, off and
on, all the forenoon. Ed, you can get ready to go out on
patrol."

Ed Bloomer's freckled face lengthened.

"Lord A'mighty!" he groaned. "Ain't you got *no* heart,
Cal? I'm so stiffened up now that my jints snap like a
bunch of firecrackers. I've got a wife up to Orham myself."

"Well, when you get to the halfway house you'll be two
miles nearer to her. Think of that, and be happy. I'm
sorry, boys, but it's the dirtiest weather I've seen since
I came here. Make the most of what rest you can
get. We're likely to have another job before this storm is
over."

Leaving Bloomer to lament and don his spare suit of
oilskins, Calvin went out to the barn. In that chilly, gloomy
shed he found Oaks seated on an empty mackerel keg, his
elbows on his knees and his head in his hands. He looked
up, recognized his skipper, and sank back again.

"What's the matter, Wallie?" queried Homer. "What are
you doing out here?"

Oaks did not answer, and the question was repeated.

"What are you doing out here alone?" asked Calvin.

"Nothin'. I want to be alone. Let me be. I wish I was dead. I'd be better off if I was."

"Oh, I guess not."

"Yes, I would, too. I'm goin' to quit. I'm goin' to quit right now. Them fellers'll never give me any peace. I—I wish I'd drownded. Yes," savagely, "and I wish they'd drownded first—so's I could see 'em doin' it."

"Look here, Wallie—"

"Aw, shut up. I've quit this job. I'm through. You haven't got any more say over me, Cal Homer."

"Yes, I have. So long as you're here I've got a lot to say. You lost your nerve out there this morning, and you made a fool of yourself, but that's nothing."

"Nothin'! If you heard all that gang guyin' me you'd think 'twas somethin'. I'll kill that Josh Phinney, I swear to God I will! I'll quit here but I'll kill him and Seleucus Gammon first."

"No, no, you won't. Stop! The boys will guy you for a while, but they'll get over it if you behave like a man and not like a kid. That mess off there scared you—well, it scared all of us. But the rest have been at the work longer than you have, and they didn't let it get the best of 'em. Get up off that keg, and stop playing cry-baby. Go ahead and do your work and behave like a man and they'll forget it by and by."

"Forget it! They'll tell it from one end of Cape Cod to the other. I'll never—"

"If you behave yourself they won't. *I* shan't tell and I'll ask them not to. When they tease you—grin, and keep on grinning. There's no fun in guying a man that laughs. Square yourself with 'em. See here, I'll tell you how you can begin the squaring. Ed Bloomer is pretty well used up, but it's his turn to go on patrol. Go in and offer to go in his place."

"His place! Why, it's his turn, ain't it? 'Tain't mine. I took mine last—"

Homer swung about in disgust. "It looks as if you were getting about what is coming to you," he said.

Nevertheless, when, a little later, he went up to the tower he found Gammon chuckling to himself.

"Crimus!" announced Seleucus gleefully. "What do you suppose has happened, Cal? Josh was up here just now and he says that Ed Bloomer was all rigged and ready to go down the beach when Wallie comes tearin' in and gives out that he's just dyin' to go instead. Ed was so surprised he commenced to holler for a doctor, but Wallie kept sayin' he meant it, and, by crimus, he went, too! What do you think of that?"

Homer nodded. "See here, Seleucus," he said, "I want you fellows to let up on Wallie. He isn't very heavy in the upper story, and he made a fool of himself this morning, but we ought to give him another chance, seems to me. He's new at this game—"

"Ain't much newer than you, is he?"

"Why, yes, a little. And— Well, never mind, I want you and the rest to stop plaguing him about it. Give him his chance. He may make good next time."

Gammon was skeptical.

"Wanted to quit, didn't he?" he asked.

"He hasn't quit."

"Cal, I know them Oakses, knew old man Oaks, and old Caleb Oaks—his uncle—and all the rest of 'em from way back. They're yeller, I tell you. Got a streak of it in 'em and they'd have to be biled afore 'twould come out. Why, old Caleb, one time he—"

"Never mind. You get the crew to let up on Wallie. And I want you and the rest of the boys to keep quiet on this whole business—outside of our own crew. You understand?"

Seleucus turned and looked him over.

"All right, Cap'n," he said, grimly. "They will, I cal'late, if I tell 'em you want 'em to. After the way you handled things this mornin' they'll do 'most anything you ask. But, so fur's Wallie's concerned, 'twon't do much good. He'll

go out patrollin' to make up along with Ed, and he'll suck
around and run errands and wash dishes and all that, to keep
the gang from raggin' him. But he'd do as much for anybody else, if he could get somethin' for himself by doin' it.
He's yeller, like all them Oakses, and he don't belong in a
Setuckit crew. Up to Crooked Hill, or to North End"—
with the contemptuous scorn of one station for a rival—"he
might get on well enough, but not down here to Setuckit—
no, sir! You see if I ain't right."

All that day and the following night the storm raged.
There were no more wrecks, however, and for so much
Setuckit was thankful. By morning, the wind had gone
down and the sun was shining over an icebound coast, with
a tumbling sea visible to the horizon. The mainland of the
Cape was white with snow and, even at wind-swept Setuckit,
there was snow in the hollows between the dunes. The
mercury was climbing in the barometer and there was every
prospect of fair weather for the immediate future.

It was Saturday, house-cleaning day at the station. The
men were washing their clothes, sweeping and scrubbing.
The members of the crew of the *David Cowes* were, most of
them, up and about and helping wherever help was permitted.
Captain Leary, his bruised knee bandaged, and limping with
an improvised cane, was nervous and anxious. He was, of
course, eager to get away and to get word of the loss of his
schooner to his owners, and to send to his family, at Rock-
land, tidings of his own safety and that of his crew. Toward
Homer and the men of the station the feelings of himself and
his shipmates were of sincere gratitude and admiration. He
expressed these feelings in his talks with Calvin.

"Oh, I know you don't want to talk about it, Cap'n," he
said, "but you can't blame us for sayin' 'thank you'! I had
about given up hope when you fellows hove in sight. And
even after we sighted your boat I didn't think there was
one chance in a thousand of your gettin' alongside in time.
'Twas a good job you did, and if anything I can say will
help you or your crew at headquarters, it's going to be said."

Calvin nodded. "Much obliged, Cap'n Leary," he said,

"but don't trouble yourself. It's what we're here for, and what we're paid for. We have got a good crew at this station and they've never laid down yet. I'm sorry about the telephone, and a little anxious, too. That was about the wickedest gale I've ever been through and Gammon and the other men who have been in the service for years say they never saw a worse one. When we do get news it will be pretty serious, I'm afraid. There must have been more wrecks than yours, and we'll hear about 'em in a little while."

"How do you expect to hear?"

"Oh, somebody will be coming down from Orham before long. Some of the fellows up there have shanties and fishing gear down here and they'll be anxious to find out what damage has been done. Superintendent Kellogg will be worried, too, and he'll want to get in touch with us. Maybe they've got some news at the Orham Station by this time. If they have they'll get it to us as soon as they can."

"How soon do you figure I and my men can get off? I don't want to hurry you, but I'm mighty anxious to get word to my owners and home."

"Of course. Well, we'll get you off some time this afternoon if this weather holds. If nobody comes down from Orham we'll get sail on the spare boat and have somebody get you up that way."

By noon, however, word came from the watchman in the tower that a sailboat was in sight, coming from the direction of Harniss. Homer went up to investigate.

"Who is it, Hez?" he asked, of Rogers, then on duty.

"Looks like Peleg," replied Rogers. "That's who I make it out to be."

It was the hermit, sure enough, and he arrived, wet and chilled, but garrulous. The Cape had been storm swept from Race Point to Buzzard's Bay. Telephone and telegraph poles were down all along the line and no trains had been through since Thursday night. Some one had driven over from Bayport in a sleigh just before he left and brought rumors of a wreck at Crooked Hill Shoal.

"Didn't have no particulars, he didn't," declared Peleg. "But from what he heard there was a consider'ble of lives lost. They'd just got a wire through from Trumet to Bayport and that's how he heard about it, so they say. Look here, Cal, how about my weather prophesyin'? Didn't I tell Seleucus Gammon he'd have to tie his hair on afore mornin'? Didn't I, eh? Where is that Gammon critter? I want to preach to him."

He had, so he said, landed Oswald Myrick and wife safely before the storm broke, and they had been driven from the landing place to their home at West Harniss. Peleg departed to crow over Seleucus, leaving Homer more anxious than ever to hear from the mainland.

The next item of news came by way of the beach. One of the crew at the Orham Station had tramped as far as the halfway house to bring it, and Sam Bearse had, on his own initiative, walked down there on the chance of hearing something. What he heard was sufficiently sensational to pay, in Sam's estimation, for the exertion of the trip. The wreck at Crooked Hill Shoal had been that of a three-masted schooner, from New York to Portland, loaded with coal. She had struck on Thursday night and the Crooked Hill Station crew had gone out to her early the next morning. They made the outward trip safely and took off all but two of the schooner's crew, those two having been washed overboard before they reached the vessel.

But the real sensation of Bearse's news was to follow. On the way back to the beach the crowded lifeboat had, somehow or other, been permitted to swing broadside with the trough of the sea. She was overturned and every man, life crew and all, had been drowned. Only one was dragged from the surf with the breath of life in him.

The group of listeners in the kitchen of the Setuckit Station looked at each other aghast. Accidents, and even occasional deaths, were more or less to be expected, they were risks of their trade—but this wholesale killing was staggering.

"Only one saved, you say, Sam?" queried Homer incredulously.

"So they say," declared Sam. "That's the yarn."

"Who was the one?" demanded Phinney.

"Crooked Hill feller name of Bartlett. Number Two man he was, I understand. Anybody here know him?"

Seleucus Gammon nodded. "I do, I cal'late," he said. "If it's the feller I think 'tis it's Benoni Bartlett. He's been in the service for a long spell, 'most as long as I have. 'Bout my age he must be, too. . . . Humph! Benoni, eh? And he's the only one got ashore! Sho! Well, if it's Benoni he'll figger 'twas the A'mighty himself picked him to be hauled out of the wet. Crimus! yes, he'll think that sure."

"Why?" asked Rogers.

"'Cause he's kind of cracked on such things. Reg'lar Bible crank, so some of the Trumet fellers tell me. . . . Sho! Benoni the only one saved out of all that crowd. Some good men gone on that load. . . . Boys, the newspapers 'll make talk about this, won't they? Remember what a fuss there was when the Orham crew was lost? Bartlett 'll be what they call a hero, if he don't look out. . . . Tut, tut, tut! Sho! Crimustee!"

CHAPTER III

THE news of the Crooked Hill disaster reached the Boston papers the moment that telegraphic communication was reopened. It was but one fatal incident of the great storm, but, coming so closely on the heels of a somewhat similar happening at Orham a few years before, it attracted wide notice. The editors, sensing its dramatic qualities, sent their reporters down to investigate. The reporters interviewed the townspeople at Trumet, the fishermen at the little settlement near Crooked Hill, and any one else who seemed likely to furnish details and help to fill space. Bartlett, the sole survivor, was besieged. He was in a state of complete nervous collapse and the doctors permitted him to see no one, but the newspaper men saw the doctors, the longshoremen and the townspeople generally, and made the most of everything they were told.

The first batch of papers brought to Setuckit displayed photographs of the Crooked Hill Station, of the crew—a snapshot taken two years before—of the beach opposite the shoal, of the men who helped Bartlett ashore, of the house where he was being taken care of, of Bartlett himself—another ancient snapshot—and one enterprising sheet exhibited a smudgy and libelous likeness of Miss Norma Bartlett, his daughter. This last was a vague cross-hatching of inky lines, through which one caught glimpses of a young woman apparently not more than sixteen, and as a recognizable likeness was of about as much value as a portrait of a rooster taken through the wires of his coop at twilight on a foggy afternoon.

The life-savers at Setuckit found the papers immensely interesting. The long stories of the reporters were read silently and aloud. The pictures were scrutinized with care. Seleucus, the only Setuckitite who had known Bartlett, was

41

cross-questioned and catechized. Mr. Gammon obligingly remembered everything he could and, when his memory failed, called upon his inventive faculties. Their own exploit, the rescue of the crew of the *David Cowes,* was completely overshadowed and practically ignored, so far as public notice was concerned. There were brief paragraphs mentioning it, but they were but items in a long list of maritime casualties.

Captain Leary and his men had shown no symptoms of forgetting, however. They were taken to Orham the afternoon of the day following the rescue. At the beach, as they were about to leave, Leary again expressed their gratitude and admiration.

"It was the finest job I've ever seen done on salt water, Cap'n Homer," he declared. "I'm going to tell my owners so, and everybody else that asks me. We wouldn't, one of us, be here now if it wasn't for you fellows, and if we can ever get even you bet we'll do it. I'll make it my business to write to headquarters and tell 'em what I think of it. It'll be the first letter I write after I get home, and my whole crew will sign it. They'll be tickled to death at the chance."

Homer thanked him, but urged him not to trouble.

"To tell you the truth, Cap'n," he said, "it was only by mighty good luck that we got to you in time. What happened over at Crooked Hill might just as well have happened here, and we can be thankful our pictures aren't in the papers instead of those poor fellows'."

Gammon and some of the other men were not so magnanimous.

"Humph!" grunted Seleucus, tossing his copy of the Boston *Star* aside; "all this kind of makes you tired, don't it? After all, by crimus, a life-savin' crew's job is to save lives. If the Crooked Hill gang had got their boat to shore with all hands safe and sound 'twould have been somethin' to hurrah about. They didn't, they got upset and drownded, which wa'n't their job at all. Somebody bungled somethin' and all hands paid for it. It's too bad and I'm sorry for 'em, the

Lord knows, but just the same the bunglin' was a fact. Did
you read that piece about Sup'rintendent Kellogg preachin'
what a wonderful critter Bartlett is? Why is he wonderful?
'Cause he was lucky enough to be hove up on the beach and
was snaked out of the wet by the scruff of his neck. He's a
hero, Bartlett is—says so in the paper. Well, why ain't I
a hero? *I* got ashore and nobody else hauled me there
neither. I *am* a hero—I'll bet you on it! Smoke up a piece
of glass and look at me through it. No, no, don't risk your
eyesight without the glass; I'm liable to dazzle you."

Josh Phinney grinned.

"We're all heroes, Seleucus," he declared. "Pretty ones.
Trouble is nobody else believes it and we can't prove it."

"Kellogg knows it," declared Seleucus. "He talks that
way about Bartlett 'cause he has to. He'd 'a' been swimmin'
against the tide if he didn't. But suppose them Crooked
Hillers had lost their boat and all got ashore themselves;
do you cal'late the sup'rintendent would have called 'em
heroes then? Humph! he'd have given 'em blue Tophet
for smashin' up the boat. He ain't any old maid cryin'
over yarns in a newspaper, Kellogg ain't. He's been life-
savin' or bossin' life-savers for twenty-odd year. He knows
what's what."

Ed Bloomer leaned over and scratched a match on Gammon's trouser leg.

"What ails you, Seleucus," he observed, "is that you're
jealous, that's all. If they printed *your* picture you'd be
all set up. I'd like to see *your* picture in the paper. 'Seleucus Gammon, the noble sea—er—sea——' "

"Sea lion," put in Phinney. "I see some of them sea lions
up to Boston at a show one time. One of 'em stuck his head
up out of the water and hollered, and I swear I thought
'twas Seleucus in swimmin'. Yes, I did. I was just goin'
to answer him."

Seleucus rose. "Wa'n't goin' to tell him dinner was ready,
was you, Josh?" he queried. "If you was I bet he was glad
to hear it. You're cook this week, I've heard tell, but I
should be glad to have a little mite of proof of it."

"Proof 'll be on the table in about ten minutes now. Keep your patience bilin', hero."

"Huh! Takes a hero to keep patient when you're cook, Josh. . . . Hello! speakin' of heroes, here comes Wallie. I understand Wallie's favorite hymn up to prayer meetin' is 'Pull for the shore, sailor.' Let's sing it for him. What d'ye say?"

They sang a verse with gravity and gusto. Oaks pretended not to notice. Generally speaking, he had been tormented less than he expected, a fact due entirely to Homer's request that the crew "let up on him."

If the papers and the public paid little attention to the Setuckit exploit, Calvin and his men received gratifying acknowledgment from other sources. Oswald Myrick wrote expressing congratulations in no stinted phrase. Superintendent Kellogg sent a commendatory letter and notified Homer that he was coming down to see him as soon as he could get away. "Partly on business and partly on pleasure," the letter ended, "although I am hoping the business may be pleasant for us both."

From this hint Calvin inferred that his appointment as keeper at Setuckit was assured. The crew seemed to take it for granted and to be thoroughly satisfied at the prospect. In a dozen ways they made it quite plain that their commander's handling of the *David Cowes* affair had proved his case, so far as they were concerned.

But the Crooked Hill sensation was destined to be more than a nine days' wonder. The stories in the Boston dailies were copied elsewhere. In New York, in Philadelphia— even as far away as Chicago—the tale of the loss of the life crew was given columns of space and editorials were written praising "the gallant fellows who had died in the performance of their duty." Benoni Bartlett, the only one who had not died, was invariably given more space than any one else. Even in the halls of Congress he was talked about, for the newest representative from Massachusetts used his name and the loss of his fellow surfmen as texts for his maiden speech, a speech in which he attacked the administration for shameful neglect of the public service and general misbehavior.

The speech—the small portion of it which was reported— was gleefully read in the mess room at Setuckit.

"Seleucus, we're getting talked about," declared Phinney. "Listen to this: 'And I say to you, gentlemen, that the neglect which causes men like these to die on the storm-eaten'—no— 'beaten—shores of the old Bay State is but another instance of the disregard of the common people, a disregard of the worker and a panderin' to the interests which is makin' the name of the party in power a stench in the nostrils of decent men and women.' Hear that, do you? Now, will you keep on votin' the Republican ticket?"

Seleucus, whose political adherence had remained fixed since the candidacy of Rutherford B. Hayes, snorted defiance.

"Bah!" he exclaimed. "Didn't say nothin' about raisin' no wages down in this section, did he? I presume likely not. Who was it saved this country in '61 and has been savin' it ever since? 'Twan't no copperhead Democrat, I'll tell you that."

"Ho, ho! You're a stench, Seleucus. Says so right here in the paper. Burn some sugar, somebody."

In Boston they were raising a fund to present Bartlett with a watch and a chain, a gold medal, or a house and lot; the exact nature of the reward was not yet determined, and there seemed to be marked differences of opinion on that point, but they were bound to give him something.

The good weather continued and the days and nights at Setuckit were singularly free from incident. Jupiter Pluvius, or old Boreas, or whoever was responsible, seemed to have exhausted all his efforts in the record-breaking storm, and to be willing to rest for the time being.

On a Thursday, about a fortnight after the *Cowes* wreck, District Superintendent Kellogg made his promised visit. He was a square-shouldered, burly man, whose sixty years and gray hairs had not diminished his vigor to any appreciable extent and who knew the life-saving game from the first deal to the final bet. The men in the service respected and liked him. He was strict, but just. He did not overpraise and he was prompt to punish, but his punishments were always deserved, and the culprit usually grinned in public, even if he swore in private. He called each one of his men by his first name and knew all about them and their records.

Calvin Homer was very fond of him, and felt sure that the liking was reciprocated. Remembering the hint in the superintendent's letter he could not help feeling a bit excited when his superior officer's boat was sighted coming down the bay.

But the excitement proved to be unjustified. Nothing whatever was said about the appointment of a keeper. Kellogg inspected the station, watched the drill, expressed himself as satisfied, and offered almost no suggestions. He was not as talkative as usual, and seemed to have something on his mind, something not altogether pleasant, which was troubling him a good deal.

Only during the last few minutes, as he was about to sail away again, did he even remotely hint at the appointment.

"You're doing first rate, Calvin," he said. "I knew you would. The men are all back of you and are contented and satisfied. If I had my way—"

He paused, and then repeated the last words.

"If I had my way—" he said again, and again paused.

Calvin thought he must be waiting for him to speak.

"Well, don't you have it, sir?" he suggested. "It always seemed to me that if anybody did about as he liked it was you, Cap'n Kellogg."

Kellogg sniffed.

"I generally cal'late to, that's a fact," he replied. "I generally figure that I know my business and expect to be left alone to mind it. Sometimes, though, other folks try to mind it for me. There's a lot of interfering damn fools in this world; did you know it?"

Homer did not know exactly how he was expected to reply to this statement.

"Why—yes—so I've heard," he agreed.

"You've heard right. And most of 'em have been elected

somethin' or other. Politics are all right in town meeting or up to the State House, but, by holy, they don't belong on the beach. Cal, if—if things don't turn out exactly as—as you and I know they ought to—why . . . but, there, maybe they will. I'll see you again pretty soon. You'll hear from me before long, anyhow. Good-by."

He went away, leaving Homer disappointed and apprehensive. Apparently his appointment was by no means a certainty. Something had interfered—politics presumably—but what politician would care to bother with a seventy-five-dollar-a-month job in the life-saving service? Politics made men postmasters, of course, but so far it had let the life-savers alone.

He worried about the matter for a time and then determined to put it from his mind. He had not taken a day from the beach for nearly six weeks and, the good weather continuing, decided to go up to Orham for an afternoon and perhaps part of an evening. There were some errands to be done in the village and—well, there were other reasons which tempted him.

Peleg Myrick took him up in the *Wild Duck*. Peleg was still boastful concerning the accuracy of his prophecy in the matter of the big gale.

"What did them Weather Bureau folks at Washin'ton give out the day afore she landed on us?" he wanted to know. "Did *they* say 'twas goin' to blow hard enough to lift the scales off a mackerel? No, siree, they never! 'Twas old Peleg said that. *They* said, 'No'therly winds and cloudy,' that's what *they* said. All right as fur as it went, I give in; but 'twas like sayin' a young one was freckled when he had smallpox. *I* said, 'It's goin' to tear loose and let her rip and you want to stand from under.' Folks laughed. Seleucus Gammon, he laughed; but thinks I, 'Them that laughs last laughs later on.' Well, I was right, wa'n't I? I cal'late I was. I don't make out to call myself a weather bureau—no, nor a weather washstand neither—but when I—"

And so on, most of the way up the bay. Calvin paid little attention; he had heard Mr. Myrick before. The sole ques-

tion he asked was the usual one asked by all acquainted with
the hermit, the question asked by every summer boarder, and
the answer to which was a byword in Orham and its vicinity.
Homer knew that answer by heart, but he asked the question
merely because answering it pleased Peleg.

"Let's see," he observed, "how is it you get your points
on the weather? Something in your bones, isn't it?"

"That's it, that's it. It's a gift, way I look at it. My
grandmother she had some of it, too, but not so strong as I
have. Her bones used to ache consid'rable 'cordin' to the
way the wind was, but she never studied of it out, she never
systemated it, the way I have. I get a—a—snitch in my
starboard elbow, we'll say. That means, gener'lly speakin',
sou'west wind, more or less of it 'cordin' to the ache. If she
keeps on a-runnin' till she gets fur as the wrist, then says I,
'Look out! It's goin' blow hard. Smoky sou'wester, maybe.'
Now, when my knee gets tunin' up—"

His passenger interrupted. "Say, Peleg," he broke in,
"you must have been a sort of all-over jumping toothache
week before last."

Peleg groaned at the recollection.

"Man alive!" he declared. "I was just one twistin' titter
from jibboom to rudder."

Safely landed at the Orham wharf, Homer strolled up to
the village, did his few errands at the stores, exchanged
casual comments with acquaintances and then walked briskly
away. The acquaintances would have been glad to talk
longer, had he given them the opportunity. The wreck and
the stories in the papers were, so to speak, dispensations of
Providence to the gossips. This was the dull season for them
and topics were scarce. All sorts of rumors were flying about,
rumors intimately connected with the life-saving service and
the Setuckit crew in particular. Calvin Homer might have
confirmed or denied some of these rumors had he been
persuaded to talk, but, apparently, he could not be so persuaded. They tried, they threw out hints, they asked leading
questions, but received no satisfaction. He was pleasant and
willing to chat on subjects of no particular importance, but

when the one absorbing topic was broached, he, as one of them described it, "shut up like a quahaug."

The gossips at the post office watched him as he walked out, and one or two of them followed him as far as the door and peered after him, as long as he was in sight.

"Headed to the south'ard, ain't he?" queried Obed Halleck, who, occupying the most comfortable seat by the stove, had prudently resisted temptation and remained where he was. Seth Burgess, one of the pair who had gone out to the platform, nodded significantly. "South'ard it is," he answered. "Course it ain't none of my business, but if anybody offered to bet he was bound down in the latitude of the Neck Road *I* wouldn't take 'em up."

Gaius Cahoon, his comrade on the platform committee, grinned.

"Cal don't tell much more'n he figgers to, does he?" he observed.

Mr. Halleck winked. "Not to us, he don't," he admitted. "If you was better lookin', Gaius, and had red hair, you might be talked to more, I shouldn't wonder."

"If his name was Myra he would, sartin," observed Seth. "He'll tell Myra all there is to tell—she'll make him. Myra generally makes out to get what she sets out after."

"And she's set out to get him," concurred Gaius. "Well, she's some girl, Myra is, and smart, too. I don't know's I blame him for hangin' round down there. If I was younger I might be cruisin' down the Neck Road myself. I was some cruiser in my day," he added, complacently.

Burgess chuckled. "Yes, you was, Gaius," he declared. "And so was I. He, he! You and me was a team in them times. Do you remember that night when we went over to the Thanksgivin' ball at Denboro? There was a couple of girls over there that—"

The reminiscence was lengthy and given in detail. Whenever the narrator omitted a remark or incident Mr. Cahoon broke in to supply it.

Meanwhile Calvin Homer was walking down the Neck Road. It was nearly six o'clock, Orham's supper time. Windows in the rear of the houses were alight and smoke was rising from the kitchen chimneys. It was a crisp, fine winter evening, a snap in the air and the early stars like electrically lighted pin holes in the blue-black canopy of a cloudless sky. There was almost no wind. Calvin's conscience was as clear as the weather, so far as absence from his post was concerned. He had, while at the post office, telephoned Setuckit, and learned from Gammon, who had been left in charge, that all was well at the station.

"Stay as long as you want to, Cal," Seleucus had said over the phone. "Cal'late we can manage to keep house while you're gone. . . . Eh? Wait a minute. . . . Well, never mind. Thought maybe Wallie'd want you to see his wife and find out if she was still ashore, but seems he ain't partic'lar. So long."

The Neck Road was not in those days—nor is it even yet— a populous thoroughfare. The dwellings along it are scattered and placed well back from the street. The house occupied by Mrs. Serepta Fuller and her daughter was one of the largest, of a type of architecture inflicted upon this country in the early 'fifties, and displaying much jig-saw ornamentation.

Calvin turned in at the gate and walked up the path to the side door. Before he could knock, the door was opened by Mrs. Fuller herself, who had heard his step. She resembled the house in some respects, being rather large, and, for her age, still ornamental. She welcomed the visitor warmly.

"We're so glad to see you, Cap'n Homer," she declared. "We've been counting on it ever since we got your letter. Myra is as excited as can be. I declare you'd think it was a year since you were here. And it *is* a long time; and we see so few people—of the right kind, I mean. Come right in. Take off your things. Supper will be ready in just a few minutes. Shan't I get you a cup of hot tea or something? It's real wintry out, isn't it?"

Homer declined the tea. While he was removing his hat and coat Myra Fuller came hurrying to greet him. She was a striking-looking young woman, her hair that "certain shade of red" which so many like and each one describes differently, a pair of large and most expressive blue eyes, red lips and a determined chin. Her figure was what her mother's had been twenty years before—in fact, Mrs. Fuller often said that Myra was the image of herself when she was a girl. Those who remembered the lady when she was Sarepta Townsend were satisfied to agree with this statement, just as they had been satisfied with Sarepta in her day. A great many young fellows—and older ones, too—found Myra perfectly satisfactory. She herself seemed less easy to suit.

She was, owing to what her mother often referred to as their "reduced circumstances," teaching in the Orham high school. She was a satisfactory teacher and a remarkably good disciplinarian. She sang a little and played a little more and danced very well indeed. Why she was, at twenty-five, still single, was one of Orham's mysteries. The men, most of them, were certain it was not because of the lack of opportunities; the women, practically all of them, seemed less sure, although they expressed little discontent with the fact itself.

Calvin Homer had, of course, known the Fullers all his life. He had known Myra when a schoolgirl. Then she went away to study at Bridgewater and he had not seen her for a long time. After her return he met her infrequently at dances and parties. Rumors of her engagement to this fellow or that had been spread about the town, but they were always denied. Of late he had seen her more frequently, had called—when on liberty—and was always asked to call again. People wondered why Myra Fuller—an ambitious young woman with aspirations, inherited and cultivated— should care to bother with one as humble as a member of the life-saving service. Captain Ziba Snow, one of Orham's influential citizens, who lived in the big house at the corner of the Neck Road and the West Main Road, expressed that wonder one evening at the supper table.

"I noticed Calvin Homer up street this afternoon," said the captain. "He's ashore on liberty—I presume likely. And, later on, I noticed him and Myra Fuller walking along together, sweet and sociable as a couple of rats in a sugar hogs-head. I don't blame him—she's a mighty good-lookin' girl; but why Sarepta Fuller's child should be wasting time with an ordinary young chap life-saving along shore I can't make out."

Nellie Snow, his seventeen-year-old daughter, answered his remark.

"Because he isn't a bit ordinary," she declared, with conviction. "He is one of the handsomest and nicest fellows in Orham, all the girls say so—and smart, too, even if he is a life-saver. If Myra Fuller gets him she'll be lucky. I hope she doesn't."

Her father turned to regard her with sudden and significant scrutiny.

"Humph!" he said, after a moment. That was all, but a "humph" may express much.

Miss Fuller's welcome was as cordial as her mother's. The supper was a distinctly pleasant meal. Since his own mother's death Calvin had learned to appreciate and look forward to the comparatively few home meals which came his way. Life at the station was interesting—tremendously interesting to him, or he would not have remained there—but there was a flavor of rest and homely comfort and domesticity about a supper like this one which awakened memories and gratified senses which, at other times, he was scarcely aware he possessed. The shaded light, the table linen, the polished knives and forks and spoons, the quiet ease of it all—he found himself contrasting these with the bare mess room at Setuckit, the glare of the bracket lamps and their reflectors, the hit or miss service and the noisy jokes. He liked his work, he was tremendously fond of his crew, enjoyed being with them and was proud to consider himself one of them—but this, this was different and he liked this, too. This supper was like the old-time suppers at home. It was good to hear feminine voices once more, a pleasant change from Seleucus Gammon's gruff sallies and Josh Phinney's strident rejoinders.

The Fullers did their best to make him feel at home. The

Miss Fuller tossed her head.

"*I* could make him," she declared. "I only wish I had the chance."

"How? What do you mean?"

Another toss of the head, a droop of the eyelids, and a little smile.

"Oh, I could," repeated the young lady.

Her mother smiled indulgently. "Myra's got a real convincing way with her," she said. "And she is so cross when she talks about what she calls your wrongs, Calvin. I never saw her so put out before. She has talked about nobody but you ever since those newspaper stories began. I don't know what does ail her."

Miss Fuller was prettily confused. "Oh, mother, stop!" she commanded. "Don't be so silly. . . . Now, let's forget the old papers and talk about something else."

So they did, to their guest's relief. Mrs. Fuller spoke feelingly concerning bygone days, when her husband was alive and they were "able to have things." This led, by tortuous paths, to the present, its inconveniences, and her daughter's capabilities as a teacher and household manager. After a time Myra again felt called upon to protest.

"Oh, mother, do stop talking about me," she begged. Sarepta bridled.

"Why shouldn't I talk about you?" she wished to know. "You're all the child I've got and nobody ever had a smarter or better one. . . . Do have another cup of tea, Cap'n Calvin."

When they rose from the table Mrs. Fuller insisted upon doing the clearing away unassisted.

"Myra," she said, "you and the cap'n go right into the sitting room and talk. He'll be having to go back to the station pretty soon and goodness knows when he'll be able to come again. There are only a few dishes—we never have anything but an everyday supper when *you* come, Calvin; treat you just like one of the family, you see—and I'd just as soon do them as not."

So Calvin and Myra went into the sitting room, the big

square room with the square piano and the black walnut
set, and on the walls the oil portraits of Sarepta's father and
mother, portraits painted by an unknown artist who should
have been an undertaker. The hanging lamp in that sitting
room gave but a dim light—Myra declared she did not know
what was the matter with the old thing—and so, when they
sat together upon the haircloth sofa to look over the scrapbook which Miss Fuller had kept since she was a girl, they
were obliged to bend low in order to see.

The scrapbook she had brought down from her own room
at Calvin's request. How he came to make the request he
could scarcely have told. Miss Fuller had, for some reason,
happened to mention it, had casually spoken of her pos-
session of such a book, soon after they came into the sitting
room. Then they had talked about it, just why he was not
sure, for he had not at first been greatly interested. But
the young lady said it was her chief treasure. There were
things in it she would not show to any one—oh, not for
worlds and worlds! That is, to hardly any one. Didn't he
wish *he* might see it? Being thus challenged, he, of course,
declared he wanted to see it. Miss Fuller at first laughed,
was provokingly obdurate, and then flutteringly hesitant.
Would he promise not to tell if she showed it to him? He
would. And promise not to read anything in it unless she gave
permission? Yes, he would promise that. So, after more
hesitation—becoming and pretty hesitation—the scrapbook
was brought and they bent over it, sitting close together upon
the old sofa.

And, as they bent, strands of her hair brushed his cheek,
he could hear her soft breathing. He was conscious—increasingly and peculiarly conscious—of her nearness to him
and of the perfume she had used, of the full curve of her
neck and the touch of her hands as they turned the pages
together.

There were many of these pages, some with schoolgirl
pictures and clippings from normal-school magazines and in-
vitations to parties and the like. All these Miss Fuller passed
by quickly, some of them very quickly, but over the pages in

the latter portion of the book she seemed to linger just a little. And suddenly Calvin, bending beside her, became aware that these recent pages were filled with clippings dealing with the exploits of the Setuckit crew, his own crew.

There was a picture of the crew, with himself as Number One man, prominent in the foreground. There were long stories of wrecks and, in each—he could not help noting—his own name was mentioned. In two or three instances, the name was underscored in pencil. He felt an odd thrill. She must be very much interested in him, this attractive young woman beside him, to keep and treasure all these. And why had she penciled his name more than those of his comrades? It was flattering—yes; but to him it was more than that. A sophisticated person might have felt it a trifle obvious, but Calvin was anything but sophisticated, so far as the opposite sex was concerned. He had been a shy boy, and he was now a man's man. Women were scarce at Setuckit, even in the summer months, and when they visited the station he had made it a rule to keep out of their way. He turned again to look at the rich gold of the head beside him and the thrill returned—and lingered. The rustle of the pages ceased, the book remained open. There was silence in the room, a significant, dangerous silence.

It was Calvin who broke that silence, and his voice trembled a little as he spoke.

"Why have you kept all those, Myra?" he asked, in a low tone.

She did not answer immediately, and when she did her tone, too, was almost a whisper.

"Oh, I—I don't know," she faltered. "I—I wanted to keep them."

"Have you read them all?"

"Yes, I—I think I know them about by heart."

"But—why?"

"I don't know. . . . Please don't ask me!"

So of course he did ask her. His hand moved toward hers, clasped it. She did not withdraw her own.

"Why have you kept all these?" he repeated.

"I don't know, Calvin."

"But you say you know them by heart. Do you, really?"

"Yes."

"Myra—I—was it because you—you liked to read about—about me?"

The golden head turned, the big blue eyes looked up into his. As has already been said, they were expressive eyes.

"Oh—oh, Calvin!" she breathed.

The inevitable followed as, time, place and personalities considered, it was bound to follow. He kissed her. A few minutes—or more than a few—later he came out of a giddy sort of daze to find himself seated there upon the haircloth sofa, holding a handsome young woman in his arms, and stammering various things—he was not quite sure what.

But the young woman seemed to be sure. If she also had been in a daze there was little trace of it remaining. She snuggled comfortably in his arms and looked up at him again.

"Oh, Calvin," she murmured, "isn't it wonderful?"

It was wonderful, certainly, so far as he was concerned, so wonderful that he scarcely realized what it was all about, least of all what it really meant. And then, at that psychological moment, the door from the dining room opened and Mrs. Fuller entered. If she had been listening at the other side of that door the moment could not have been more psychological.

She uttered a little scream. So did Myra. Calvin said nothing—words were not among his possessions just then.

"*Well!* Why, I never!" gasped Sarepta. Her daughter gently disengaged her waist from the partially paralyzed arms encircling it, and rose.

"Mother," she said, "Calvin and I are engaged to be married. Isn't it *wonderful?* . . . Calvin dear, it is only mother. Can't you speak to her?"

He could not, of course, but it really made little difference, for Mrs. Fuller did sufficient speaking for the two. At first she declared she believed she should faint right straight away; but it was an erroneous belief—she did not faint. She ex-

claimed, and choked, and wept a little, and then kissed
Myra over and over again, after which she threw her arms
about Mr. Homer's neck and kissed him. Calvin, whose
kissing experiences, outside of his own family, had been
pretty closely limited to games at boy-and-girl parties and a
few casual flirtations on straw rides or returns from dances,
was overwhelmed with guilty embarrassment. There was no
reason why he should feel guilty, but somehow he did. And
even yet he could scarcely comprehend the situation; the
after effects of the daze were still with him.

Mrs. Fuller wept and hugged him, and she and Myra
hugged each other, and then the former declared she was so
glad she did not know what to do.

"If I had had the picking of a son-in-law," she vowed,
"I couldn't have found a better one. And, oh, Calvin, I
don't believe even you realize what a dear, lovely, smart wife
you're going to have. She is a blessing. We'll all be so
happy together, won't we?"

And so on, for a time. Then Sarepta turned to the door.
"I must run back to my dishes," she said, and added archly,
"I guess likely you can spare me. Engaged folks aren't very
particular about having other company around. At least, I
know *I* wasn't when *I* was engaged. Of course I'll see you
again, Calvin dear, before you go. Oh, I'm *so* glad, for all
our sakes!"

She went away, carefully closing the door after her. Myra
sat down again upon the sofa and Calvin, still giddy, sat
down beside her. It was nearly ten when he rose to go.
He had told Peleg that he would meet him at the wharf at
nine, and his odd sense of guilt was not lessened by this
knowledge. He and Myra had said many things since her
mother left them; Miss Fuller said most of them.

She had spoken of the future—their future together—but
she had spoken of his own even more. She was very ambitious for him, she declared. He was going to get that appointment as keeper, that was sure already, but that was to
be only the beginning.

"You are going right on," she said with confidence, "right

on up and up. My husband isn't going to be just a life-saver, he is going to be more than that. Superintendent Kellogg is getting pretty old for such a place as he has. He won't be there very much longer; he'll make some mistake or other, and then some one else will be appointed district super-intendent."

Calvin protested. "Oh, no," he said. "Cap'n Kellogg is a fine man and—"

She put her fingers on his lips. "He's an old man," she insisted. "And he's an old fool, too."

"Now, Myra—"

"He is, or he would have appointed you keeper two weeks ago. And he wouldn't have allowed those idiots of newspaper men to print all those lies about that Bartlett and the rest. I hate that Bartlett."

"Why? You don't know him, do you?"

"No, but I know his daughter, or I did know her over at Bridgewater. She was there for a little while, a freshy when I was in my senior year. I met her three or four times and I didn't like her a bit. She is a silly, goody-goody thing, pretending to be too honorable to have any fun, or— Oh, I hate hypocrites, don't you? . . . But there, dearest, we won't talk about her, will we? We'll talk about you. I want you to promise you'll do everything you can after you are keeper to push yourself forward. I'll help you—oh, I can! There are ways. I know lots of people, and some of them—the men especially—like me pretty well. We'll make you superintendent some day. But we won't stop there. You're not going to stay in the life-saving service, you know."

"Well, I don't suppose I shall, always. There isn't much future in it. But I shall hate to give it up. I do like it. The fellows in it are—"

"They aren't your kind and you don't belong with them. You're going to be a rich man some day. I always said I should marry a rich man, and I'll make you one before I'm forty. You just promise me to push yourself forward all you can, and we'll show some of those narrow, self-satisfied

Orham ninnies a few things. . . . Now, don't look so frightened, dear. . . . Kiss me, Calvin."

They said good night at the side door, an affectionate, lingering farewell it was, on Miss Fuller's part especially. He was to write her every day and she would write him. And he must not forget his promise.

"Keep yourself in the front of things all the time," she urged. "If the reporters come down there don't let them talk to any one but you. And I shall be helping and contriving here. You'll be surprised at what I can do to help. A girl that—well, that isn't *too* homely and that knows a thing or two can help a lot. Good night, you dear boy. Remember the promise."

Homer, walking briskly along the deserted sidewalks on his way to the wharf, was in a curious state of mind. If there was one thing certain it was that, when he came to the Fuller home that evening, he had no intention of leaving it an engaged man. He had given little thought to marriage. His plans for the future had been indefinite enough; they had centered about his work and the new responsibilities of command which seemed likely to be his, and women had no part in them. And now—why, now one woman had taken charge of them, would—and ought to—monopolize them. Myra Fuller was a pretty girl, an attractive and very clever girl, but—

There should be no "buts," he realized that keenly, and his conscience smote him. It was wonderful to think that such a girl loved him; he did not understand it. And yet she did love him; she had said so and he must believe it. He should be very proud. She was one of the most popular girls in Orham. When other girls had been neglected by masculine followers Myra had always had at least one hanging about. He remembered rumors of her engagement—or rumors that she was "just as good as engaged"—to this fellow or that. And now, of all the list, she had chosen him. As his wife—the word smote him almost like a chill. He was to take a wife. He was engaged to be married. *He* was!

She herself had suggested that the engagement be kept

a secret for the present. He had agreed to this—had, in fact, felt a sort of relief in agreeing. He did not quite understand why she wished to delay the announcement; the delay, apparently, had something to do with those ambitious plans for his future which she talked so much about. It was fine of her to be so interested in him. She had said he was to become a rich man; she was to make him one. He had never dreamed of riches; the acquiring of money had never attracted him greatly. But it attracted her; she meant to make him rich in spite of himself. And she would do it— yes, when a girl like that set out to do a thing, she would and could achieve her object. He felt perfectly certain of that, and with the certainty came a sense of helplessness, almost as if he were in a trap with no way out.

His walk to the landing was not the path of glory which a triumphant lover is supposed to tread. The loom of the sail of Peleg's boat at the end of the wharf brought him out of his mental maze and Mr. Myrick's voice impatiently hailing him awoke him from the future to the immediate reality.

"Well, so here you be at last," vouchsafed the skipper of the *Wild Duck*. "I began to think you'd got lost in the dark somewhere. Been roostin' here over an hour, I have. I don't know's you realize it, but it's beginnin' to breeze on and I've got a couple of aches in my port knee jint that means blow, if they don't mean more'n that. Where you been cruisin' to, anyhow? I'm pretty nigh froze to a crisp. This ain't no Fourth of July night; didn't you know it? Good thing I had comp'ny or I'd a lost my grip on to myself and swore a few. Climb aboard! Lively! My fingers are so numb I don't know's I can unlimber 'em enough to cast off."

To most of this tirade Homer paid no attention. He swung over the stringpiece of the wharf and dropped into the cockpit of the catboat. Then he became aware that he and Myrick were not the only persons aboard the *Wild Duck*. Some one else was seated there in the stern near the tiller. This individual rose to his feet. A heavy, bulky man he was and, against the background of starlit sky and water, Calvin caught sight of the fringes of a thick beard stirring in the wind.

He did not recognize the man, but he took it for granted that the latter must be some one he knew.

"Why, hello!" he said.

The man held out a mittened hand. His voice, when he spoke, was deep and his method of speech what Cape Codders describe as "moderate."

"How are you, Mr. Homer?" he said. "Glad to know you."

Calvin shook the proffered hand, but he was puzzled. The man was a stranger. Myrick grinned the grin of superior knowledge.

"Don't know who 'tis, do ye, Cal?" he observed. "Well, it's somebody that we've all heard consider'ble tell of lately. Cal, let me make you acquainted to Mr. Benoni Bartlett. Crooked Hill Shoals—*you* know, Cal. He's cal'latin' to sail down to the pint along with us, Mr. Bartlett is. Ain't ye, Mr. Bartlett?"

Bartlett bowed, gravely and deliberately, as he seemed to do everything.

"Goin' to ask you to take care of me at the station for a little while, Homer," he said. "I'm goin' down there to— well, to kind of look things over, the Lord willin'."

Calvin stared at him. Why was Bartlett going to Setuckit Station to look things over? What on earth did it mean? What *might* it mean?

The catboat swung away from the wharf. Myrick came aft to the tiller.

"All set, be ye?" inquired Peleg. "Um-hum. And time enough, too, I'd say. Let 'er go."

CHAPTER IV

DURING the sail down to Setuckit Peleg did most of the talking. Bartlett seemed disinclined to converse, and his answers to Myrick's questions were monosyllabic. These questions dealt with almost every conceivable topic, but centered, naturally enough, about the great storm and the disaster at Crooked Hill Shoal, the tragic happening of which the *Wild Duck's* unexpected passenger was the sole survivor. And of this particular subject it was increasingly plain that Bartlett was determined not to speak.

"You've had a turrible time, ain't you, Mr. Bartlett?" observed Peleg, hopefully.

Silence. Myrick tried again.

"I say, you and the Crooked Hill crew had a turrible time," he repeated. Still no acknowledgment.

"Eh?" persisted the hermit, by no means discouraged. "What did you say, Mr. Bartlett?"

"When?"

"Why, just now."

"I didn't say anything."

"No, I don't know's you did, come to think of it. I was sayin' that you Crooked Hill fellers had a turrible time in that wreck scrape of yours. . . . I guess likely you didn't hear me."

"I heard you."

"Oh! Oh, I want to know! . . . Well—er—well—?"

"What?"

"Why—why, I thought you was just goin' to say somethin' about it."

"I wasn't."

Mr. Myrick swallowed hard, opened his mouth, closed it, and then attempted another attack, strategical this time and addressed by way of his other passenger.

"Me and Calvin and all the boys down to Setuckit, we've been talkin' about you Crooked Hill folks a lot lately," he observed. "Been readin' the papers every chance we could get, ain't we, Calvin?"

But this move, too, was a failure. Homer was as sparing of speech as Bartlett. He had no wish to talk. He was doing a vast amount of thinking and his thoughts were speculative and distrusting. Benoni Bartlett, the newspaper sensation, was on his way to the Setuckit station to "look things over." Why? Again he remembered his recent talk with Superintendent Kellogg and the latter's evident ill humor and his hint at interference in high places. The hint had made him uneasy at the time, but he had tried to forget it. Now it came back to him, with all its possible implications, including one of which he had never dreamed as a possibility. Even the mental disturbance following realization of the fact that he was engaged to be married was crowded out of his mind. So he, too, snubbed the garrulous Myrick.

Peleg, however, was not the type to accept a snub. If the others refused to talk to him, he, at least, could talk to them, and he continued to do so. The wind was so far but a mild and steady breeze, and the weather, in spite of the prognostications of his various "joints," as fine as could be wished. His task as skipper and pilot was, therefore, an easy one and his mind and tongue were free. He used the latter unsparingly. It was not every night—or day, for that matter— that the *Wild Duck* carried a real live hero, one whose name and photograph were published abroad. Once, years before, he had acted as cook for a party a member of which was an ex-governor of the state. Peleg had talked of that happy week ever since. The subject was, except with strangers, utterly worn out; his Setuckit acquaintances hailed the least reference to it with derisive jeers. Now, by good luck, he was thrown in contact with another celebrity, some one else to furnish floods of embellished reminiscence in the months to come. So Mr. Myrick's exultant tongue wagged alone.

Neither of his passengers paid the least attention to him. They sat, one on each side of the cockpit, each engrossed in

his own musings. Bartlett, his heavy beard blown by the
wind and his cap pulled down over his eyes, was a bulky
shadow, mysterious, silent and, in Homer's eyes, increasingly
ominous. Calvin, his knees crossed and one arm resting upon
the rail, stared ahead over the water. He lit his pipe and
then, remembering that he had bought some cigars at the
store in the village, offered them to his fellow voyagers.
Peleg seized his with enthusiasm. Bartlett refused.

"I don't smoke," he said gravely. "Much obliged."

Myrick thought he saw a possible crack in the social ice
and jumped at it.

"Don't care about terbacker, Mr. Bartlett?" he asked.
"Don't like it, eh?"

"Yes."

"Eh? What? Oh, you do? But you don't smoke? Hum.
. . . Well, some folks had ruther chew, I know. And some
of 'em had ruther do both to once. I knew a man one time
—used to play the bass fiddle, he did, along with me, up to
Thanksgivin' and Fourth of July balls; that man—"

The heavy beard lifted. "I don't chew and I don't smoke,"
said Bartlett, slowly. "And I don't go to dancin' times,
either."

"Humph! Sho! Don't you believe in dancin'?"

The reply was prompt this time. "Believe!" scornfully.
"I believe in the devil—so far as that goes."

Even Mr. Myrick was stumped for the moment. The
stumping was but momentary, however, and, although he
changed the subject, he continued to talk. The next time
he struck fire was with what should have been a much less
inflammable topic than tobacco. He had wandered, by circuitous ways, back to the Crooked Hill wreck.

"Well, Mr. Bartlett," he observed, "I presume likely you
ain't feelin' quite yourself even yet, be you?"

His passenger straightened in his seat.

"What do you mean by that?" he demanded, sharply.

"Eh? Why—why, nothin' special. I was just thinkin'
that, considerin' all you'd been through, you couldn't scurcely
be what you'd call fit yet awhile, so—"

Bartlett lifted a big hand. "Fit!" he repeated. "Did any-body tell you I wasn't fit?"

"Tell me? Why, no, nobody told me. I just thought—"

"I'm as fit to-day as ever I was. As ever I was. Do you understand?"

"Why—why, sartin I understand. I only—well, all I meant was that, considerin' how you'd been next door to drownded—just saved by luck, as you might say—"

"It wasn't luck that saved me."

"No? No-o, of course 'twasn't, not really. Them fellers on the beach they—"

"They didn't save me, either."

Peleg was surprised; so was Homer.

"They didn't?" cried Myrick. "Why, do tell! Is that so! The newspapers, they said— Why, who did save you, Mr. Bartlett?"

The answer was solemnly given, there was a tremendous earnestness in it.

"God A'mighty saved me," declared Bartlett. "Him—and nobody else."

Mr. Myrick gasped. "Eh? Sho! Why—I never thought of *Him*," he stammered.

The big beard nodded.

"Most folks don't," declared Bartlett. "It would be better for 'em if they did."

He did not speak again until the end of the trip was at hand. Then occurred an incident which, in the light of after events, was prophetic. At the time, however, it seemed odd—that was all. The *Wild Duck* had drawn up to her moorings in the sheltered cove in the bay side of the point. Peleg's dory was anchored there and he had picked up her anchor rope with the boat hook and drawn the dory alongside.

"All ashore that's goin' ashore," he announced. "Hop in, Cal. Git right aboard, Mr. Bartlett."

Homer swung over the side into the dory. His fellow pas-senger followed suit, but more slowly and carefully, and seated himself on the after thwart. Myrick, having lowered the sail of the catboat and anchored her, tumbled after them with the ease and lightness of a hippopotamus. The dory heeled down until her rail touched the water. Calvin laughed.

"Great Scott, Peleg!" he exclaimed. "You're as spry and handy as a ton of coal, aren't you?"

Bartlett did not laugh. He, too, uttered an exclamation, but it was more like that of a nervous woman.

"Careful!" he cried, sharply. "Look *out!*"

It was not so much the words as the tone which was odd. Homer stared at him in surprise. Even Myrick seemed to share the surprise, for he, too, stared.

"Sit still, you!" snapped Bartlett.

Peleg grinned as he fitted the oars between the thole pins.

"Sartin sure, Mr. Bartlett," he agreed. "Settin' still is my job for a few minutes now. Think I was goin' to upset ye, did ye? Well, I ain't. This old dory of mine is kind of a crank, if you aren't used to her, but she'll stay right side up, give her her own way. Strangers, though, she makes 'em kind of fidgety sometimes and I don't know's I blame 'em."

The passenger in the stern laughed then, and in an uneasy and embarrassed fashion. It was the first time Homer had heard him laugh, and even now he seemed to do it with an effort.

"I began to think I was in for another spill," he explained. "So this is Setuckit, eh? I haven't been here for over en years."

They landed on the beach, said good night to Myrick, who was booked for another long sail before reaching his home moorings opposite his shanty, and walked together through the heavy sand up to the station. The mess room was untenanted, all the crew, except the man on beach patrol and the watchman in the tower, having turned in hours before. Bartlett looked about the room with interest.

"Keep things taut and shipshape aboard here, don't you?" he observed. "Well, I cal'late I'll go aloft and turn in myself. I presume likely you've got an empty berth up in the spare room, haven't you?"

Homer told him that the room was empty; it had been

unoccupied since the departure of the men from the *David Cowes*.

Bartlett nodded. "First rate," he said. "Well, I'll sleep there, then—for to-night, anyhow. I'm goin' to stay here for a day or so and er—well, look around, same as I said. You and I'll have some talks together to-morrow or next day."

Homer offered to go up with him and light the lamps, but the offer was declined.

"I guess likely I know the ropes aboard here," was the answer. "I've been in the service long enough to know 'em. Thank you just the same. Good night."

Slowly and heavily the bulky figure climbed the stairs. Calvin watched it go. Then he sat down by the stove to think. His thoughts were more bewildering than ever and no more pleasant. When, a half hour later, he passed the door of the spare room—the quarters for wrecked sailors—on his way to the tower, he noticed that the door of that room was ajar and that the lamp was still burning. Glancing in as he passed, he saw Benoni Bartlett seated beneath the bracket lamp reading a book. It was a small, leather-bound book, and Homer judged it to be either a pocket Bible or a Testament.

Next morning the appearance of the unexpected guest at the breakfast table aroused tremendous interest and much speculative gossip among the men. The guest himself was as uncommunicative as Myrick and Homer had found him the previous night. He was agreeable enough in his solemn way and answered when spoken to—on all subjects except those dealing with the Crooked Hill tragedy and his own narrow escape. Of these he simply would not talk. He inspected the station and its surroundings thoroughly and without waiting for an invitation. The barn, the horses, the boats and their appurtenances, all these he seemed to find most interesting. This interest, considering the fact that he had spent years of his life in the life-saving service, was deemed peculiar, to say the least.

Seleucus Gammon, watching his chance, spoke to Homer concerning it.

"What in the nation is he loafin' down here at Setuckit for, Cal?" demanded Seleucus. "Just now I caught him in the boat room pawin' over the breeches buoy gear. 'How do you like the looks of 'em?' says I, lookin' to see him squirm a little mite; 'most anybody would, you know, bein' caught nosin' around where 'twan't any of his partic'lar business. But no, sir-ee! Crimustee! Nary a squirm did *he* squirm. Just said everything 'peared to be all right, fur's he could see; and that's all he said. I swear if he didn't seem to be waitin' for me to clear out so's he could do some more pawin'. I said one or two more things and he never said nothin', so after a spell I had to go. But what's it all mean? What's he here for? Who told him to come?"

Calvin shook his head. "I don't know any more about it than you do, Seleucus," he said. "He's here—to look things over, that's what he told me. And that's all he told. Of course he wouldn't have come on his own accord. Probably we shall know more by and by."

"Humph! Maybe. But what do you cal'late it means?"

"Don't know, Seleucus. And there isn't much use guessing."

"I cal'late not. . . . But say, Cal, he's a queer critter, ain't he? I'd heard he was, and maybe this narrer squeak of his has made him queerer. Don't talk much, and don't laugh once in a dog's age. Only time I see him get the least mite stirred up was when Josh Phinney hove out some joke or other about Noah and the ark. Josh was sayin' he cal'lated old Noah must have took some of the animals aboard in the breeches buoy, 'long towards the last of the high water. 'Twan't much of a joke, but 'twas as good as most of Josh's reg'lar run. The rest of us laughed, but old Bologny—that's what the gang is beginnin' to call him behind his back; Bologny sausage, you know—Bologny never laughed; no sir! Phinney winked at us fellers, and asked him if he didn't think 'twas prob'le that Noah shot a line over the tree where the monkeys was and took 'em off that way. Now if it had been me I'd have said that one thing was sartin, he got 'em aboard somehow, because one of their great, great

grandchildren was settin' right in front of me. But all
Bologny done was get up and go out. Well, I always heard
he was pious as Jabez Lothrop's dog that wouldn't eat his
Sunday dinner nowheres but on the meetin'-house back steps.
Humph! . . . What did you say, Cal?"

"Nothing."

"Ain't much use of sayin' anything, is there? The boys
are sayin' it, though. Josh vows he cal'lates Bologny must
have been one of Noah's fo'mast hands. Says his whiskers
remind him of some of the pictures in the Sunday-school
books. . . . Say, Cal—"

"Well? What is it?"

"Cal," Seleucus was serious enough now, "you don't s'pose
it's possible that—that Superintendent Kellogg's gone crazy,
do you?"

"What do you mean?"

"I shouldn't wonder if you know what I mean. Don't
you?"

Homer hesitated. "I don't know anything," he answered
after a moment. "And if I did it wouldn't be my business
—or yours—to talk about it."

"Humph! Well, all we can do is wait and see, I s'pose
likely, same as the old woman waited for the pullet to lay so's
to make sure the critter wa'n't a rooster. . . . Ah hum! I
always knew there was a lot of plaguy fools in this world,
but it don't hardly seem as if the plaguiest ones could be
plaguy enough to— All right, *a-all* right; I'm through. But
don't worry, Cal; this crew's behind you."

All that day Calvin waited, expecting one of the promised
"talks" with his visitor. But the latter made no move toward
a confidential interview. He was, as always, quiet, solemn
and for the most part gentle of speech and mild in demeanor.
He treated Homer with marked politeness, but he made no
explanation concerning the real reason for his visit.

And on the following forenoon, the mystery was solved.
Kellogg drove down the beach in the buggy behind a sturdy
little bay horse. It needed but a glance at his superior's face
to show Calvin that the district superintendent was not in a

pleasant frame of mind. His first question was concerning Bartlett's whereabouts. The latter was, at that moment, in the boat room and thither went Kellogg, closing the door behind him. The two men remained there for more than half an hour. When the superintendent emerged he looked more gloomy than when he entered. He laid a hand upon Homer's arm and motioned toward the keeper's room.

"Come along with me, Calvin," he said. "I want to talk with you."

They entered the bedroom and sat down. Homer upon the bed and Kellogg on the only chair. There they looked at each other. Kellogg seemed to find it hard to begin the conversation, but as his companion remained silent he was obliged to begin. He drew a long breath and spoke.

"Calvin," he said, "I've got some bad news for you. I never found that it did any good to mope around and growl when I had the toothache; better have the thing out and be done with it. Benoni Bartlett is going to be keeper of this station. He's got the appointment and the only question was whether, after he'd come down here and looked the place over, he'd want to take it. He does want to take it—fact is, he's just told me that he has made up his mind to take it— so that's settled. He's the new keeper here at Setuckit."

Calvin did not answer; at the moment he had no comment to make. It was what he had feared, what he had increasingly expected ever since his meeting with Bartlett aboard the *Wild Duck*. The confirmation of his forebodings, however, was not the less a shock. The injustice of it and the bitter disappointment were overwhelming. He did not trust himself to speak—yet. There were many things to say, and he intended to say them, but he would let Kellogg finish first.

His feelings showed in his face and the superintendent needed no words to understand them. He leaned forward and laid a hand upon the young man's knee.

"I don't want you to blame me for this, Cal," he said, earnestly. "Speaking between ourselves here, with the door shut, I don't mind telling you that you can't feel any worse about it than I do. It's a shame and, if it would do any good, I'd write those fellows at Washington a letter that would blister the paper, and finish up by handing in my resignation. I'm district superintendent down here and I generally figure to know what's what and who's who a whole lot better than a parcel of politicians. I recommended you as high as I ever recommended any man for any job. You were in line for keeper here. You were fit for it; you'd earned it; the men wanted you and I wanted you. As a general thing the department lets me have my way and my word goes. But here was a case where, for once, it didn't go. 'Twas the papers and the politicians that did us both. Bartlett's been played up as a hero from Dan to Beersheba. He's been preached about and speeched about every since he was lucky enough to be hauled out of the surf there at Crooked Hill. He'd got to be rewarded—that's all there was to it. And some smart Aleck decided that the fitting reward for him was to make him skipper of the newest and best station on this section of the coast. So they shoved you and me to one side and made him that. And now he *is* keeper. See how it was, don't you?"

Calvin nodded. "I see," he said, shortly. "I don't blame you, Cap'n Kellogg."

"I don't want you to. But let me say this much more: Last time I talked with you I could see what was in the offing and I did my level best to steer it off on another tack. They were bound to make Bartlett cap'n of something and I suggested making him keeper of his old station, at Crooked Hill Shoal. Nothing doing. Crooked Hill was a smaller station than this one, not so new nor so well found. And, for some reason or other, Bartlett himself didn't want to go there. Just why he didn't I'm not sure. He was always queer and cranky, but since his narrow squeak he's been queerer and crankier still. He won't talk about Crooked Hill, won't go near the place, acts—well, if you asked me, I'd say he acted scared of the very name of it. He wouldn't hear of being captain of a Crooked Hill crew, that was that. But when the dumb fools at Washington—is that door shut tight?—when they nosed in and began to talk of Setuckit

he pricked up his ears. And now it's gone through. . . .
Calvin, what are you going to do about it?"

Homer smiled. "I'm going to look for another job," he
said.

"Meaning you're going to quit the service?"

"Of course."

"I expected to hear you say so, but I'm hoping you'll
change your mind."

"Why should I? Look here, Cap'n Kellogg. I hope I'm
not a quitter, generally speaking, but here is a case where
quitting is the only sensible thing for me to do. I like this
job here. I don't know why I do, but I do, and if I had
been made cap'n of this crew I should have stayed on and
done my darndest to make good. How long I should have
stayed I don't know, for of course I realize that there is
mighty little future in it, but I'd have stayed for a good
while; until I decided I must make the move that I shall
have to make some time. But now—well, this looks like the
time, doesn't it?"

"Maybe it does—maybe it does, Cal, in a way. But you
know what all hands will say, don't you? They'll say that,
when you couldn't play the game your own way, you took
your dolls and went home. You won't call it that; maybe I
won't; but about everybody else will."

"Let them; I shan't care."

"Oh, yes, you will, you'll care a lot. It's no fun to be
misjudged and lied about. You might lick some of the liars,
but you couldn't lick 'em all, and two thirds of the lying will
be done behind your back. You say you like the service, and
I know you do; you and I are made that way—we can't help
liking it. You tell me you were bound to quit it some time.
Well, I guess likely that's pretty good judgment, for an ambitious young fellow. But when you do quit you'll find
considerable satisfaction in doing it just when you want to,
not when other folks expect you to. . . . Eh? What is it?"

Calvin had smiled again, a sudden and bitter smile. Kellogg was talking to him much as he—Homer—had talked to
Wallie Oaks that day of the big storm. The irony in the

situation was, in its way, funny. But the smile lasted only a moment.

"I suppose you're right, Cap'n," he admitted. "All you say is true enough, but the fact is that this business—oh, I guessed it when Bartlett came here; even before that, when you were here last—this business has made me sick of the whole game. I thought the United States Life-Saving Service was one line that was out of politics. I'm no politician. I don't belong with 'em. I'm going to try for a job ashore. I ought to be getting on in this world, if I'm ever going to. It is high time I did, I guess. . . . There are reasons why I must."

Kellogg regarded him with interest. "Special reasons? he asked. "What do you mean?"

Homer had said more than he meant to say. He had been thinking aloud and the last sentence had slipped by his guard. He hastened to protest.

"Oh, nothing, nothing," he evaded. "I guess I didn't mean anything in particular, Cap'n."

"Humph! . . . Well, here's another thing for you to consider before you hand in your papers. This isn't the only open job in my district. Maybe I've got a little influence left, in spite of politics. Somebody's got to be keeper at Crooked Hill. How would you like to go down there, Cal?"

Calvin's reply was prompt and decisive.

"I don't know how I should like it," he said. "I do know I wouldn't take it if it was offered me. This was my station —and the only one I care about."

Kellogg nodded. "I understand," he said. "I thought likely you'd feel that way. I didn't think you'd be interested in 'seconds.' I shouldn't if I was in your shoes. But, Homer, there is one thing you ought to care about. Something that, knowing you, I honestly believe you do care about, same as I care—it's the good of this service."

He had lighted a cigar. Now, tossing it, still alight and smoldering, upon the little table, he leaned forward once more and tapped his friend's knee with his forefinger.

"The good of the United States Life-Saving Service," he

repeated. "That service you was talking about a minute ago. I'm not much a hand to preach sermons—I ain't a minister, and you know it, boy—but sometimes I do feel like climbing into the pulpit and letting her go. What keeps men like you and me on the jobs we've got? It isn't the pay—God knows we don't get any pay worth talking about. We get into the work, first because of the—of the—well, of the kind of risk and snap and fun there always is in taking chances, and then we stay in it because we like it better than anything else. And pretty soon we don't think of anything *but* the work and shoving it through. Don't think of our own selves hardly at all, do we? Course that don't hold with the bulk of surf-men, lots of them are here to-day and gone to-morrow; but it does hold with fellows like Oswald Myrick, and me—and you, unless I'm mighty mistaken. That being the case, when things don't go as we want 'em to, it looks to me as if we didn't have any right to jump overboard and wade ashore. We ought to stick by the boat closer than ever. Calvin, you've got to stay down here at Setuckit, a spell anyhow, on just one account—the good of the service. . . . Where did I heave that cigar?"

He found the cigar, which had fallen to the floor, re-lighted it, and gazed intently at his friend, plainly anxious to see what impression his "sermon" had made. And it was just as plain that it had made little or none. It did resemble the preachment Calvin had delivered to Oaks—Calvin him-self was obliged to admit that—but this—this was different. He was still stubborn.

"I can't see that my staying here will help the service," he said. "And, honestly, Cap'n, I think it is time I thought about myself a little."

"Maybe it is, in a way, but in another way it isn't. The service—"

Homer interrupted.

"The service hasn't thought much about me, I should say," he broke in impatiently. "Why should I think of it?"

"Because you should. Hang it all, Cal, you know you ought to. It hasn't thought of me—much. It has turned down the strongest recommendation I ever made. Turned it down flat. I'm as mad over this thing as you are and, just like you, I was all for resigning. But I've made it a habit to think a spell before I act and, after I had thought, I decided I couldn't resign. 'Twas my job to stay and keep the craft off the shoals. And it's yours, too. You're going to be needed, or I miss my guess."

Calvin looked at him and the look was returned, intently and earnestly.

"Just what do you mean by that?" demanded Homer.

"What I say. Cal, how much have you seen of this Bartlett?"

"Seen of him? Why, I sailed down with him in Myrick's boat, and I have talked with him a dozen times since. What do you—"

"Wait! I'm going to tell you. Have you noticed anything funny about him?"

"Why, I don't know. He is a sort of crank on the Bible. The men have noticed that. Any one would notice it."

"I know. He's that, and always was; but more so since the wreck scrape. But have you noticed anything else? Pretty—er—well, nervous sometimes, isn't he?"

"Nervous?"

"Yes. I ran across Peleg Myrick driving down just now and Peleg told me how Bartlett yelled at him to be careful when you fellows got aboard the dory. Course he told me a lot more than that—he'd have been talking yet, if I'd stopped to listen—but he did tell that about the dory. You noticed it, of course?"

"Why—yes, I noticed that he did seem rather—er—nervous then, as you say."

"Um-hum. And he's been as nervous as that every time we have talked about the wreck and the upsetting of the lifeboat. He doesn't want to speak of that, and when he and I drove down to Crooked Hill from Trumet a little while ago he acted so queer that I couldn't keep my eyes off him. I caught him standing staring off at the breakers where the schooner went to pieces—and it was a cold day, but I give you my word the sweat was standing out on his forehead like melting frost on a window."

"I don't know that that was so queer, considering how near he came to being drowned with the rest in those very breakers."

"Maybe not. Maybe not; but there was a look in his eyes that I didn't like. I've seen that look in a man's eyes before, and—Cal, sometimes a close shave same as Benoni Bartlett has been through has an effect that you wouldn't expect. Particularly where the man is as high strung and odd as this fellow has been ever since I've known him—yes, and getting more so every year. Sometimes—and I've seen cases —a thing like that gets a man—'gets his goat,' as the boys tell about. If it does get it, get it good, he—well, that man isn't liable to be the right one to take out a Setuckit life crew in gales such as we have down here. . . . There! I shouldn't say this to anybody but you. And of course you'll keep it under your hat."

"Of course. But, see here, Cap'n, you don't think—"

"I don't think anything—special. The appointment wasn't mine, and I've told you so. But this district is mine, and this station is under me, and I'm responsible for it. Calvin Homer, I want you to stay here, for a while anyhow, as Number One man of this crew. I can depend on you and the crew depend on you, too. Will you stay on?"

Homer was silent. Kellogg waited a moment and then made another attempt.

"There's one thing more I might say," he went on. "Politics or not, the skipper of one of my crews has got to make good. There'll be no favorites played while I'm district superintendent. Now Bartlett will probably make good enough. But if he doesn't—well, then I *will* have the say as to who takes his place. And you know who that will be."

This move was a mistake. Calvin frowned.

"Never mind that," he said. "I shouldn't stay anywhere with the idea of taking another man's place."

"Nobody expects you to," sharply. "Leave yourself out

of it for a minute, can't you? Your own concerns don't count a mite. Neither do mine, in one way. What does count is what I've been preaching at you for half an hour— the good of the service. *I* tell you the good of the service calls for a man down here just now that this crew knows and likes and will stand by. They don't know Bartlett yet. They do know you. If you've *got* to have something personal in it—why, I'll be the person. *I* want you to promise me you'll hang on here as Number One man for three months, anyhow. *I* need you. You can cuss the service if you want to, but stick by it for three months—and stick by me. Come—will you?"

For the first time Homer's determination was really shaken. He liked and respected his superintendent; every man in the service did that. Kellogg he counted as a firm friend, and, in spite of his assumed indifference, the appeal to his loyalty to the service was effective also. He hesitated.

Kellogg grinned, and sighed in relief.

"You will," he said. "I thought you would. And I don't believe you'll lose out in the long run. You stay the three months and then we'll see."

"But—er—how do you know Bartlett will want me as his Number One?"

"'Cause he said he did just now. Told me he liked what he'd seen of you first rate and did hope you'd stay. But if he didn't it wouldn't make any difference. I want you as Number One, don't I? Damn it all, man! do you think the politicians have taken *all* the backbone out of me? My name is Cyrus G. Kellogg, by holy! When I change it to Mush and Skim Milk I'll let you know."

Even then the matter was by no means settled. The most that Calvin would concede was that he would think matters over and give his decision to his superior before the latter's departure. Kellogg, however, seemed satisfied.

"That's all right," he declared. "I'll be here till after dinner. You can say yes then, just as well as now, if you'd rather. . . . There! I feel considerable better. Now we'll go and give Bartlett a few points. He's going to ride up to the main along with me. He'll be down to-morrow or next day to take charge."

His optimism concerning the decision was justified. When dinner was over Calvin took his friend aside and gave the latter his promise to remain at Setuckit as Number One man until the first of March. It was now the middle of December.

"But I tell you, Cap'n," he added, "I still don't like the idea a bit. The way you argued it I don't see how I can do anything else, but I don't like it. And you didn't say so, but I realize that you have another reason, besides those you mentioned, for wanting me to stay a while. You figure the crew—some of them—will flare up a little at having an out-sider rung in as skipper, and you're hoping I can smooth them down. I'll do what I can, of course. But I do think it puts me in a rotten position."

Kellogg slapped him on the shoulder. "It puts you in just the right position—for now," he vowed. "And I'll put you in a better one the first chance I get. And, meantime, I shall sleep a little better nights. Thanks, Calvin. . . . And now—here's another tooth to be hauled—we'll collect Benoni and break the news to the boys."

The crew—even the man in the tower was called down for the moment—were brought into the mess room and there the superintendent told them of the new appointment.

"Cap'n Bartlett is to be your skipper now," he said, in conclusion. "The rest of you will keep your rankings just as they are, with Homer as Number One. I shall count on every one of you to do your best for the new keeper and for me. Anybody that doesn't will hear from me in a hurry. Now maybe Cap'n Bartlett would like to say a word."

Bartlett, thus appealed to, stepped forward. He was as grave and unsmiling as ever, and his eyes, beneath their heavy, grizzled brows, regarded the group before him.

"Men," he said, "I didn't take this appointment without a whole lot of prayerful thinkin'. It does seem to be a call on me that I hadn't ought to put by. I've got a daughter and she seems anxious to have me get on, and I'm takin' it full as much for her sake as my own. Course I realize that, same as Cap'n Kellogg says, I've got to count on you to help. You'll find me, I cal'late, a just man to them that do justly by me and their work. I ain't liable to be very strict —it ain't my way to be—but of course I can't stand for any rum drinkin' or nothin' like that. Rum's a curse—one of the worst on earth—and sailors and men alongshore suffer from it full as much or more 'n anybody. I've been life-savin' a long spell and I tell you I've seen—"

He had raised his hand in a gesture, but Kellogg touched his shoulder and, with a start, he dropped it and turned. The superintendent whispered and Bartlett nodded.

"Yes—yes, that's so," he said, in acknowledgment of the whisper. "Cap'n Kellogg says he and I have got to be goin'," he added, turning to the men. "So I sha'n't say any more now—nor any other time," with an apologetic smile. "I cal'late we'll all be too busy to make speeches or listen to 'em. I'll do my best to be square with you, and you will with me, I know. And, with the good Lord's help, we'll make a go of it. . . . Er—I guess that's about all."

A few minutes later he and the superintendent climbed into the buggy and moved away up the beach. The men, silent so far, watched them go. But Homer was quite aware —and the expressions on their faces proved it—that they would not remain silent long. There would be talk enough as soon as they recovered from their astonishment. Would it be talk and nothing more serious? That was the question which troubled him most. His foot was on the threshold of his own room—the room which, in a day or two, he must relinquish to another man—but he turned back.

"See here, boys," he said, earnestly, "I want you to listen to me a minute. We're going to have a new skipper here and when he comes I'll be Number One man again; but until he shows up I'm in charge. And I don't want any growling or fool business. Now get to your work. Rogers, you're on watch in the lookout, aren't you? Tumble up there, lively. Peleg says we're going to have a blow before night. He may be right—he is sometimes. On the job, all hands."

He did not wait to see what effect his orders may have

had, but went into the skipper's room. As he closed the door
he heard one word, it was Josh Phinney who uttered it.

"*Hell!*" exclaimed Josh. That was all, but no more, and
no deeper disgust could have been expressed in a volume.

All the rest of that day a gunpowdery atmosphere pervaded
the Setuckit Life-Saving Station. It was apparent always;
wherever Calvin happened to be he was aware of it. In the
mess room, in the kitchen, on the beach during signal drill
—wherever a group of the crew were gathered, there was
always that air of sullen rebellion and obstinate discontent.
During supper, usually the jolliest of station meals, the jokes
were few and most of these Homer himself supplied. The
men ate in silence, with occasional mutterings or sidelong
whispers. But when they were alone, when he was not of
the company, he knew they talked much. Seleucus Gammon
admitted it, under cross-examination. Calvin called Seleucus
into his room and there the admission was made.

"Of course the fellers are sore," grumbled Gammon. "Why
wouldn't they be? The heft of 'em are like me, they've been
at Setuckit a long time. Oaks is the only new one and he
ain't much account and shouldn't ought to be here, by rights.
We had Oz Myrick as skipper for years. He was a good
man, one of our own crowd and the boys liked him and was
for him. They like you, too, Cal—you're one of the gang
they know—and all hands figgered you'd be made keeper, and
they wanted you to be. But now they've put this Bartlett
over us, a feller from outside. What for? That's what all
hands are askin'. What for? Kellogg—"

Homer interrupted. "You mustn't blame Kellogg," he
said. "Not a bit. He is under orders, same as the rest of
us, and he obeys those orders and keeps his mouth shut.
That's what you fellows are expected to do, and you will—
as long as I am in charge, anyhow."

Seleucus flapped an enormous paw in protest. "Who said
we wouldn't, Cal?" he demanded. "*You* won't have no
trouble. It's this draggin' in a whisker-faced, Bible-backed
outsider that makes the row. And shovin' an able man like
you to one side. Why—"

"Hold on there! I'm the one who was shoved aside, as you call it. And that is my business and not yours nor Josh Phinney's. You say you're for me. That's what you said, wasn't it?"

"You bet, Calvin!" with enthusiasm. "We're on your side, every man Jack."

"All right. Then do what I tell you to do, and go to work and shut up. And when Cap'n Bartlett gets here give him as fair a show as you would have given me. If you want to prove you are on my side prove it that way."

Seleucus pulled his mustache. "I don't blame you for bein' touchy, Cal," he said, with an air of sympathetic tolerance which was exasperating. "Heave ahead and lay into me all you want to. I can stand it; I feel just the same as you do."

Calvin's patience was on a hair trigger that afternoon. "Oh, get out, you idiot!" he ordered. "But if you or any one else shirks on his job and I find it out I'll make him step lively. And if you take my advice you'll stop growling and whispering and behave yourselves. As for the skipper's appointment, do as I'm going to do—forget it."

Which was comparatively easy as advice to give others, but tremendously hard for the adviser to live up to. Calvin could not forget; he thought of little else during his waking moments, and they were many, that night. Myrick's prophesied "blow" amounted to little or nothing. The fair weather continued and the crew were not called out. Homer devoutly wished they might be. A risky launching and a hard, strenuous adventure in the line of duty would be heaven-sent distractions just then. Disappointment, resentment—yes, and discouragement, were his and he could not shake them off. A dozen times he repented of his promise to Kellogg. How could he hang on here, wasting his time, for another three months?

And what would Myra Fuller say when she heard the news? She had promised to marry him—he had promised to marry her. The thought of that promise and what it meant was more overwhelming than all else. Myra was ambitious; she had boasted of it. She was, most of all, ambitious for him. He was to make good—in the service first and in larger fields of endeavor afterward. She had declared that she would make him successful—and the first step toward that success was to have been his captaincy at Setuckit. He groaned at the thought of her disappointment. She was a wonderful girl—so clever and handsome, and so greatly sought after. Why she should have chosen him he could not comprehend, had given up trying to do so. But she had so chosen and he ought already to be proving himself worthy of his luck. And now, within a few hours of their betrothal, she would learn that he had been passed over and the appointment upon which they had both counted had gone to another. If it had happened before—if Kellogg had told him the truth when he came to Setuckit on his former visit, if he had spoken out instead of hinting—then— why, then he and Myra might not have become engaged. He might not have called at the Fuller house, would not have felt like calling anywhere, and the disappointment would have been his alone and, therefore, so very much easier to bear. Almost he found himself wishing that he had not made that call. Then he realized that such a wish was ungrateful and disloyal—even dishonorable.

It was a pretty bad night, and he was glad when morning came. A clear, bright morning it was, so the distraction of hard work for him and the discontented crew was not likely to come that day. The discontent and undercurrent of rebellion were just as evident at breakfast. His pointed counsel to Gammon had had apparently no effect.

Yet a distraction did come that forenoon and in an unexpected way. A distraction not so much for him as for the crew and, in particular, for Seleucus. The latter's brother-in-law, a man named Philander Jarvis, was what Cape Codders call a "boat fisherman." He owned a catboat and went off to the fishing banks along Orham's borders after cod. He made his trips daily, except on Sundays, winter and summer, and it took more than an ordinary gale to keep Philander on shore. He owned a shanty, a tiny four-room house at Setuckit, within a few hundred yards of the station. This particular fall, and thus far into December, he had been making his daily voyages from South Orham, and living with his sister Jemima—Seleucus's wife—at the Gammon home in that village.

It has been already noted in this chronicle that Seleucus was a married man. The casual stranger, seeing how closely he stuck to his work at the Setuckit Station, how seldom he visited the mainland, and how infrequently he availed himself of the one day in nine, the "shore liberty" allotted each surfman under the regulations, might never have suspected the fact that he possessed a wife. But he did—or she possessed him—and all Orham knew it and had talked and chuckled over it for years. Seleucus was quite aware of the gossip and the chuckles, but he never joined in them. The jibes which he failed to appreciate were those dealing with matrimony. The surest way to stir him to wrath was to hint that his excuses for remaining at the station when he might be at home were rather flimsy. One sly reference to that effect and Seleucus was ready to fight. He boasted loudly of Jemima's smartness as a money-saver and housekeeper; he often remarked that he missed her "like fury," and when the first of July came and the crew—the keeper excepted—left Setuckit for their month's vacation, he was loud in proclaiming joy at the prospect of getting back to the society of his life partner. But when, at the beginning of August, the rest of the crew returned to duty, they usually found that Mr. Gammon had arrived there a day ahead, and with a more or less plausible excuse for so doing.

Never, except on rare occasions, and then only to particular friends like Calvin Homer, did he even intimate that his married life was not a dream of bliss. Once—during Captain Myrick's illness, when the latter's wife was at the station—Homer had found him, an open letter in his hand, gazing dolefully from the tower window.

"What's the matter, Seleucus?" Calvin asked. "You look as if you had given up hope. Bad news from home?"

Seleucus stuffed the letter into his pocket and turned away from the window.

"Cal," he demanded, with apparent irrelevance, "do I look like a fellow that would be liable to try to be shinin' up to an old married woman with a sick husband?"

Calvin laughed. "I shouldn't say that you did—no," he replied.

"I guess not. And there ain't no other females—except hens and cats—down in this neighborhood this time of year, is there?"

"Not many."

"Many? There ain't nary one. Then what's the use of heavin' out hints about not knowin' what I may be up to, and the like of that? And all on account of my not writin' no letters for three weeks. Crimus! One letter a month ought to be enough for anybody—anybody that's married, anyhow. And 'why don't you get liberty days same as the other men? —It looks pretty suspicious to me.' Why don't I? With all I have to do down here, now Cap'n Ozzie's laid up! Crimustee!"

On the forenoon of the day following the announcement of Bartlett's appointment, Homer happened to be in the keeper's room, writing a letter to Myra. It was a letter he dreaded to write, for in it he would be obliged to tell her of the dashing of their hopes. It was a hard task, but he had rather she learned the news from him than from any one else, so he settled himself to it. The letter was scarcely begun when he heard a commotion outside the station. Some one was running up the beach, shouting as he came.

The men in the mess room heard the shouts and Calvin heard them rising and moving to the door. Then that door was flung open and Hezekiah Rogers's voice was raised in delighted announcement.

"Oh, boys!" yelled Rogers. "Boys, here's the best fun since they killed the pig. Haw, haw, haw! Who do you think's just come—come here to Setuckit to stay the rest of the winter? Haw, haw! If it ain't rich, then *I* don't know!"

They demanded, in concert, to be told what he was talking about. Who had come?

Hezekiah's joy made him scarcely articulate, but he did his best.

"Philander Jarvis has just landed," he proclaimed, "come down in his catboat, he did. He's goin' to open up his shanty and go coddin' from here, 'stead of South Orham. . . . Oh, hold on a minute! that ain't nothin'; the rich part's astern. Who do you cal'late's come to keep house for him? Come to live right next door? Haw, haw, haw! Jemima Gammon, that's who. Seleucus spied 'em from the tower and he was down to the beach when they landed. You'd ought to see his face. He's there now, helpin' get the dunnage ashore. Come on, fellows, quick!"

There was a howl of ecstasy from the mess room and a tumultuous exit. Calvin, leaving his letter, rose and followed. In the cove the Jarvis fishing boat was anchored, a dory was pulled up on the beach, and from that dory Mr. Gammon and a stolid individual whom Homer recognized as Philander Jarvis were lifting bundles and a battered trunk. Superintending the trunk's transfer was a little, sharp-featured woman, with a protruding chin, and lips which snapped together like the spring lid of a tin tobacco box. Surrounding the trio was the group of delighted life savers.

The little woman's lips were shut only occasionally. For the most part they were open and words—many words—issued from between them.

"For mercy sakes be careful of that trunk!" she commanded, shrilly. "Look out! Look *out,* you'll drop it right souse into the water. Seleucus Gammon, if you get them things of mine wet I declare I'll make you go in swimmin' after 'em. Be *careful!* Of course," with some sarcasm, "a lady might think there was grown men enough standin' around here to bear a hand, but it appears everybody's too busy. I've heard," the sarcasm more emphatic, "about how busy *some* folks are down here, but— Oh, how d'ye do, Mr. Homer? I'm havin' a time, ain't I? Seleucus, you be careful of that box! It's got my—well, never mind what's in it;

I don't want it wet, anyhow. Nice day, ain't it, Mr. Homer?"

She and Calvin shook hands. Some of the men, apparently a bit abashed by the lady's hint, stepped forward and assisted with the luggage. Mrs. Gammon continued to talk.

"I guess likely you're surprised to see me comin' here to live," she said. "Well, I'm kind of surprised to be here, myself. But when a person's got a brother who's set on livin' in such a Lord-forsaken place, and a husband that just seems to *love* that place a good sight better than he does his civilized home and them that's in it—*well,* then maybe it's time that husband's wife came to find out what there is makes him love it so much. One letter in six weeks, and no sight nor sound of the man you're married to, may do for some folks, but it don't for me. Thinks I'll— Now, Ph-lander, you and Seleucus take them things right up to that shanty of yours quick 's ever you can. And then you get a fire agoin'. I'm as nigh to bein' froze as I want to be in *this* world."

Philander and Seleucus took up the trunk. Phinney and Bloomer followed carrying packages. Mrs. Gammon, carrying nothing but an umbrella, brought up the rear. The little procession was suggestive of a funeral, so Homer thought. Then he caught a glimpse of Seleucus's face and the suggestion changed; it was much more like a march to the scaffold. Jemima, of course, was the sheriff and there was no doubt whatever as to the identity of the condemned.

CHAPTER V

THE joyful surprise of Mrs. Gammon's arrival—joyful to every one with one possible, even probable, exception—furnished the distraction for which Homer had been hoping. The surfmen at Setuckit Station forgot for the time their discontent and incipient rebellion and laughed and joked and behaved more than ever like school children. Their treatment of Seleucus was that of a group of sympathetic friends congratulating a comrade upon his good fortune. They were so kind and thoughtful and so ready to suggest opportunities for him to be with his wife. If he happened to be busy at some task not immediately in the line of duty one of them was certain to offer to take it off his hands. For example:

"Now, now, Seleucus," urged Phinney, "there ain't any need for you to be stayin' in here paintin' that door. Let me do it for you. You run over and see Jemima. She's lonesome, I'll bet. You cruise right along and cheer her up."

Mr. Gammon, dripping paint brush in hand, was not as grateful as he should have been.

"She knows I've got this door to do," he growled. "It'll take me half the mornin' to finish it. I told her so. You've done your part, Josh. 'Tain't likely I'll shove mine off on to you."

Phinney's generosity was touching.

"No shovin' about it," he declared. "If I couldn't oblige an old chum that much I'd be ashamed. Give me that brush. Yes, yes; you will too. Jemima's expectin' you. I told her I could do the paintin's well as not and that you could come right over."

Seleucus turned. "You did!" he exclaimed. "What are you interferin' with my affairs for?"

"Interferin'? Why, how you talk! I'm doin' you a favor, if you only knew it. Philander's off coddin' and she says she wants you to chop up some kindlin' wood. Said you promised to do it this mornin', afore you left, but you never done it. She says she can't understand why 'tis you have so much work to keep you here at the station; said the rest of us seem to have loafin' time enough. Seemed to think 'twas kind of mysterious. I told her you was a whale of a feller for workin', was doin' odd jobs about all the time since Olive Myrick went; kind of takin' up your mind, seemed so."

Mr. Gammon started and frowned. He deposited the brush in the paint pot.

"What in time did you tell her that for?" he snapped. "What's Oz Myrick's wife got to do with my mind, I want to know?"

"She wanted to know that, too,—Jemima did," confided Josh solemnly. "I told her nothin', of course—only that when there was a nice pleasant woman around lots of odd jobs got done of themselves, as you might say. I said you was a great hand to help Olive when she was here, and probably you kind of got in the habit of it."

Seleucus rose and slammed out of the room. At the door he turned, as if to speak, but meeting Mr. Phinney's gaze of kindly solicitude he changed his mind and said nothing.

The mess room now was minus his society during the off hours of the day or evening, but his comrades called on him at the Jarvis shanty quite frequently and seemed to find happiness in so doing. During these calls Seleucus said little, but his conversation was not missed. Wherever Mrs. Gammon was there was sure to be talk sufficient.

Calvin had written Myra Fuller the fateful letter telling her the bad news of his loss of the captaincy, and was now awaiting her still more fateful reply. He and she had had two conversations over the phone since the evening of their betrothal, but these talks were brief and necessarily not intimate. The telephone instrument was on the wall of the mess room where the men spent much of their time, and, as the engagement was to be kept a secret, no word of it or other closely personal subjects could be mentioned. He told her, during the most recent of these talks, that he had written an important letter, but she had not then received it. He promised to come up to Orham just as soon as he could get away, but added that that was not likely to be for some time. She would understand why when she read his letter. She must have received and read it before this, but he had not heard from her again.

And, three days after his first visit, Benoni Bartlett came again to Setuckit and took formal charge of the station. Homer vacated the skipper's room and stepped back into his old place as Number One. The newspapers—Peleg Myrick brought them down—gave columns to the Bartlett appointment and much praise to the department for its wisdom in fitly rewarding the hero of Crooked Hill Shoal. These praises were read by all at the station and its vicinity —which included the Jarvis shanty and the home of the lightkeeper two miles up the beach. There was lively comment concerning those praises, comment which might have burned the ears of the new skipper, had it reached them. Calvin took care that it did not. Nor would he listen to any of the sympathy which his fellow surfmen were eager to hand him. The thing was done—it was settled and over—forget it and attend to business, these were his orders. And, in a way, the men did appear to be forgetting it. Nevertheless, he was quite aware that they were watching Bartlett and waiting to see what sort of leader he was. Prejudice was still there, plenty of it, but the new skipper could overcome that, if he proved himself.

He was a peculiar man; that had been his reputation and of its truth there was no doubt. Big, strong, and, to all outward appearance, experienced and adequate; but as odd and moody an individual as Homer had ever seen. In all matters pertaining to the station routine he was alert and exacting. The daily drills, beach, boat, signal, or the practice in resuscitating the nearly drowned, went on under his eye precisely as they should. The watch and the patrols were not permitted to shirk. He was likely to be up and about at any hour of the night, and this the crew learned.

It was in his manner and habits that the peculiarities showed. The men commented on them.

"He's the queerest old skate I ever come across," declared Phinney. "Talk with you sociable and folksey as can be one minute, and the next march right by you and not see you at all. Talks to himself, too, he does. Have you noticed that? And he has the Bible right along his bed, so's he can gaffle into it night or day. Takes a dose of that Bible a mighty sight more regular than he does his meals. I've found out one way to start him goin'. Tell him you think rum is a cuss to creation and he'll tune up like a hand organ. Grind away on that hymn for a week, he would, I cal'late. Wallie Oaks has found that out. Wallie's beginnin' to pull a strong oar with him already. Never mind, he'll tumble to Wallie pretty soon—if there's any tumble to him."

"It's his eyes I notice 'special," observed Seleucus, who —because it was his turn to go out on the next patrol—was temporarily free from the apron-string tether. "He's got the funniest eyes ever I see. One minute they're blazin' under them big eyebrows of his like a clam-bake fire under a heap of seaweed. And, next time you see him, they're as flat and fishy as them in the head of a dead haddock. Seems to know his work, he does, too; but if he ain't cracked some-wheres then he's liable to crack afore he dies. We ain't had a wreck to go off to yet since he's been here. We can tell better about him after we see how he handles one of them jobs."

The opportunity to watch the new skipper under stress of active duty came the very next day. A thick fog, compli-cated with a light snowstorm, decoyed a lumber schooner off her course early that morning and daylight found her aground on the lower end of the Hog's Back, with distress signals set. The fog had cleared and Bearse sighted her from the tower. There was but a moderate sea running and the job looked like an easy one.

Bearse called Homer and the latter notified Bartlett. The

two men went up to the lookout and each gazed at the stranded vessel through the spyglass. Calvin expected a prompt order to get out the boat, but that order was not given immediately. Bartlett turned away from the telescope and stood there, pulling at his beard.

"Come down to my room, mate," he said, after a moment. Homer followed him down the stairs to the skipper's room. There he waited, wondering at the delay. Benoni walked the floor, his hands in his pockets and—so it seemed to his companion—a peculiar expression on his face. Then he turned.

"What do you think of it, Homer?" he demanded.

Calvin did not understand. "Think of what?" he asked.

"Her—that schooner? I suppose we better go off to her, hadn't we?"

If he had asked whether or not the crew should be fed that day the question, to Homer's mind, could not have been more extraordinary.

"Why—why, she is signaling for us, isn't she?" he stammered in amazement.

"Yes, yes, looks's if she was. You think—you think, then —Hum! . . . All right. Turn out the crew. Go ahead. I'll be right with you."

Calvin hurried out to give the orders. At the door he happened to look back. The skipper was standing by the little table, his eyes closed, his head bent and his lips moving. Was he praying? It certainly looked so.

But he was businesslike enough during the next few hours. The boat was dragged to the shore, launched and headed for the Hog's Back. Calvin, tugging at the oar in his place as Number One, could see the skipper's face as he stood in the stern and he watched it keenly. Bartlett, except for the necessary orders, said not a word. He steered well, he gave his orders crisply and in a voice that carried command. His gaze was fixed on the vessel ahead and his lips, except when he issued those orders, were shut in a grim line. Homer could find no fault with his actions or manner. He seemed to know what to do and how to do it, as of course he should, considering his long experience. The only possible criticism might have been that, for such an ordinary expedition, with conditions as favorable as these, he appeared to be under an unnecessary mental strain. But it was his first trip as captain of a crew and Calvin, realizing this, found it sufficient excuse. In fact, he never would have noticed it—or fancied that he did—had it not been for Superintendent Kellogg's hints and forebodings. And, doubtless, Kellogg's words were founded on prejudice and his own suspicions merely imaginative.

He was more than ever convinced of this by Bartlett's behavior when they boarded the schooner. She was in no pressing danger, lying easily on the very edge of the shoal, and on an even keel. Moreover, the tide was rising and the wind moderate and favorable. She could be floated at high water, and this Benoni plainly realized and set about bringing to pass. Her anchors were carried off to deep water, her deck load of boards were cast overboard or shifted, and her jib and foresail made ready for hoisting when the time came. In all this—and it deepened Calvin's favorable impression—Bartlett was in absolute command and permitted no interference. The vessel's captain was anxious and irritable, but his suggestions and protests were ignored and, when the schooner did swing off the shoal and started on her course once more, the profuse thanks were ignored also.

"All right, all right," said Bartlett, gruffly. "You needn't thank us—we ain't nothin' but the Lord's instruments. Thank Him; He's the one to thank. . . . And keep a sharper lookout when you come over these shoals next time."

Altogether the new keeper's first salt-water test was a personal success. The crew—even the most exacting and anxious to find fault—were obliged to admit that he had come through satisfactorily. Gammon and Phinney, of course, admitted it grudgingly.

"He handled everything all right enough," agreed the latter; "but he'd ought to. 'Twas a cinch. Only I wish he wouldn't be so everlastin' solemn about everything. Every time I looked aft while we was rowin' out, there was his old owl face starin' at me. Never cracked a joke nor so much as a grin. Don't make things any easier, that don't. Look how jolly Cal Homer was when we went off to the *David Cowes*. And that cruise was somethin' to be solemn about. I don't mind ownin' up I didn't feel much like grinnin' *that* day. But Cal was singin' out his funny sayin's half the time. That's the kind of skipper I like to ship along with."

This was, of course, mild exaggeration. Homer's jokes on that strenuous trip had been few and these few limited to its start and finish. During the rest of the time the uproar of wind and wave would have prevented the hearing of his witticisms, even if he felt like uttering them—which he most decidedly did not. But the crew remembered the one or two, and willing imagination supplied the rest.

Seleucus chimed in.

"That's so," he declared. "I like to laugh when I get my orders. Ain't any preachin' against laughin' in the Scriptur's that I know of."

Just here the door opened and the diminutive figure of Mrs. Gammon bounced in. As Bloomer described it afterward, her feathers were all on end.

"Oh, there you are!" she snapped, addressing her husband. "Settin' here spinnin' yarns and I not knowin' whether you'd got back safe or had been drownded off to that schooner. Wonder you wouldn't come far's the door and holler, anyhow. Long's I've got a husband I wouldn't mind bein' sure that he was alive."

Seleucus stared at her in bewildered amazement.

"Why, Jemima," he protested, "how you talk! If I'd been drownded I guess likely you'd have heard of it afore this. I was comin' acrost in a minute. I was just settin' here warmin' my feet; they got kind of chilly off yonder."

It seemed a reasonable excuse, but the lady's reception of it was as frigid as her husband's toes.

"You can bake your feet just as well over to my cookstove," she announced. "That is, after you do what you promised to the very first thing this forenoon—fix it so's a body can build a fire in it without bein' choked to death with

smoke. Come right along now. I'll keep you busy enough
to stay warm, if that's all that ails you."

She bounced out again—most of her movements were
bounces. Mr. Gammon slowly rose from his comfortable
chair. His expression was of funereal gravity.

"Well, Seleucus," drawled Bloomer, "it looks to me as if
you'd got your orders. Why don't you laugh?"

Mr. Gammon did not laugh; perhaps he thought that,
under the circumstances, more hilarity would be superfluous.

Homer, naturally, was more in the company of the new
keeper than any one else. Bartlett consulted him on various
points of station routine and, little by little, the pair grew
better acquainted. The acquaintanceship never developed
into anything closer. Benoni Bartlett's peculiar character
was not one to make friends easily. His moods were much
more variable than the weather which, in spite of Peleg
Myrick's dire predictions, continued surprisingly good for the
beginning of the week before Christmas. There were hours
during which the new keeper scarcely spoke to his Number
One man and others when he was almost confidential and
mentioned intimate matters not connected with work. He
told of his religious experiences, how he had been a "mighty
tough customer" in days gone by and how, later, at a revival
meeting in Trumet he had "seen the great light."

"I tell you, boy," he said, his eyes smoldering beneath the
shaggy brows, "I never knew what comfort of mind was till
I found the Lord. Since then I've cast my burdens on to Him
and He's hauled me through. Why was I the one picked out
to be saved over yonder on Crooked Hill—the only one of a
dozen men?"

It was the first time Calvin had ever heard him mention
his recent harrowing experience, and he looked at him curi-
ously. Bartlett was quite unconscious of the look.

"Why was I saved?" repeated the keeper. "I know why
—know it just as well as I know you and I are standin' here
this minute. 'Twas because the Almighty was provin' to me
that He looked out for His own. In all that mess over there
—when the boat capsized, and they was drownin' all around

me—hollerin' for help and—and screamin'—Lord above! I—I hear that screechin' yet—nights I hear it. I—I—"

He stopped abruptly. Homer spoke to him but he paid no attention. Nor did he say more at the time. Instead he walked away, his head bent and his lips moving.

These were the times when Calvin was inclined to be doubtful of his complete sanity. But there were others when he was chatty and reminiscent and even likable. This was especially true when he spoke of his daughter, Norma, who was, he said, a librarian in a mid-Massachusetts city. He was tremendously proud of her. Here the sternly literal follower of the Scriptures had broken the law and set up an idol to be worshiped.

"She's an awful smart girl, Norma is," he confided. "I don't care if she is my daughter and I say it—she is, and you'll say so, too, when you see her. She'll be comin' down here to see me some of these days, she says so in her letters. Writes me every twice a week, she does, and I write her full as often. I don't know's I'd have felt like takin' this job here at Setuckit if she hadn't been so set on my doin' it. I—I didn't seem to have any hankerin' for any more life-savin'. I've been around boats and on salt water 'bout all my life, but after that—that Crooked Hill business, I—I—"

He stopped again, just as he had in their former conversation. This time, however, Calvin brought him back by a reference to his daughter.

"She wanted you to take it, did she?" he suggested.

"Hey? . . . Oh, yes! yes, she did. All those pieces in the paper they seemed to—well," with an odd air of shy apology, "they seemed to make her kind of proud of her old papa. That's what she calls me—'papa'—same as she used to when she was little. You see, she ain't like me, she's like her mother. I'm rough and tough and onedicated—never had much chance for schoolin', I didn't—but her mother, now, she was pretty and smart, and knew everything. A school-teacher, she was—yes, sir, a school-teacher. And she married me! . . . I never could understand it—or I never used to. Now, of course, I realize that 'twas the Lord's doin'. He had reasons of His own, same as He always does. Same as He see fit to take her away when Norma wa'n't much more'n a baby. 'He moves in a mysterious way His wonders to perform.' That's poetry, boy. A hymn tune. Did you ever read it? Mary—that was my wife's name— she used to read it to me. I get Norma to read it sometimes. And it's true, too. It ain't for us to go pryin' into God A'mighty's affairs. He knows—"

And so on. He was off again, his eyes alight. But this little glimpse into his heart and of the love he bore his daughter made Homer like him better and feel more charitable toward him. He was eccentric—almost unbalanced on some subjects—but he was human and rather pitiable. Calvin was still sore at the loss of the appointment which should have been his, but he could not hold a grudge against the man who had received it.

Myra Fuller could hold that grudge, however. Her letter, when at last it did come, proved that. Badger, returning from his "liberty day," brought down the station mail, and the letter which Calvin had been expecting was there with the others. He opened the envelope with fingers which trembled a little. Considering that it was the first written word he had received from the girl who was to be his wife his feelings were strange—there was more dread than eagerness in them. He feared to read what she had written.

Yet, in a way, the fear was unjustified. Myra did not blame him in the least. She said so, and more than once. The manner in which he had been treated was mean and wicked, but it was not his fault, of course. Superintendent Kellogg was to blame, he and the idiots at Washington, and the newspapers. She hated that Kellogg, never did like him, and Calvin was to remember that she had said he was an old fool. "But he *is* old, Calvin dear," she wrote, "and that is what we mustn't forget. He can't keep that position of his much longer and when he resigns—or is forced out— you and I know who should have the superintendency, don't we? And *I* know a few men in politics, myself. Perhaps you think I am only a girl and can't do anything to help.

There are some things a girl can do—with men—better than men can do them. Wait and see. Just wait and see."

It was upon Bartlett that her resentment seemed to center most fiercely. "I hate him, hate him, *hate* him," she declared. "I never met him, of course, but I have met that daughter of his and so I know what the family is like. We'll get even with them, though, you and I. And it may not take so very long, either. He is captain there at Setuckit, but he is only on trial and you are Number One man under him and the men all like you. It will depend on you and them whether he makes good or not, after all. I mustn't write any more about what I mean—you understand why—but you must make an excuse for coming to Orham very soon and when you come we will have a long talk. But I am sure you understand how to act and what to do every minute of the time until then. You must not miss a chance, and for my sake you won't, will you, dearest. . . ?"

There was more, but the remainder was very intimate indeed, and dealt not at all with Benoni Bartlett nor the captaincy. And, after the signature, was an underscored P. S.

"Burn this letter just as soon as you have read it."

Homer followed instructions, so far as the burning was concerned. He read the letter through twice and then put it carefully upon the hot coals in the kitchen stove, not replacing the lid until he had seen the closely written sheets crumble to ashes. Then he went out and took a walk up and down the beach, thinking.

Myra had not blamed him—even in her great disappointment she had not done that—and so much was—or should be—comforting. She still trusted in him and believed in him. But it was evident that she was by no means resigned to the situation. She considered it to be but temporary and more than hinted that, at least, it could be made so. She was going to help and she expected him to do so. But how? If the meaning between her lines was what it seemed to be he—well, but, of course, after all, she did not mean that. But she was absolutely wrong about Kellogg. Kellogg

was not at fault. He was a fine fellow and a friend and
any scheme which involved forcing him out of the superintendency must not be considered for a moment. He must
make her see that. He must contrive an excuse for getting
to Orham for that "long talk."

And on the second day before Christmas the excuse came.
There were supplies, in the way of holiday "extras," to be
brought down from the village, and there were also presents
and Christmas boxes waiting there at the express office and
post office. Josh Phinney was the lucky man who was to
have liberty on Christmas day, but Josh had received permission from Bartlett to remain overnight. An expected
baby in the Phinney household was the reason for the ex-
tension of time and the happy father played that reason for
all it was worth. Possibly a little more than it was worth,
according to some of the skeptics.

"What's the matter with you, Hez?" demanded the exultant Mr. Phinney. "Don't blame Bologny for lettin' me
have a few hours extry, I hope. He see the right thing,
Bologny did, and done it. He'd ought to. Don't have a baby
every day."

"Humph! Some folks have one every year. And the
last couple or so I've heard you do more growlin' than
hurrahin' over. Didn't know what you was goin' to pay for
their board and clothes with, you didn't."

"That's all right. I haven't got to worry about this one's
board yet awhile. It's provided for. Go on, Hez! you're
jealous, that's what ails you."

But the men expected their Christmas mail and boxes
before the holiday and, as Peleg was not going to Orham at
the time, some one else, they felt, should go. So Calvin,
seizing the opportunity, intimated to Bartlett that he had a
few necessary errands which should be done and the keeper
gave him permission to make the trip, provided he got back
before supper that same afternoon. Philander Jarvis was
laid up with an attack of lumbago and his catboat was idle,
so Homer and Phinney borrowed it.

The morning was mild and hazy, and the wind light but

fair. The pair got an early start and landed at the Orham wharf before ten. Josh wished his comrade a merry Christmas and hurried up to the shops to buy small presents for a large family. Calvin waited until he was out of sight and then walked away in the general direction of the Main Road. He, too, intended visiting those shops, but his errand was entirely personal to himself—and one other.

After a perplexing half hour in the store of Laban Bassett, "Jewelery, Silver, Notions and Fancy Articles, Watches and Clocks Repaired," he at last, bought a ring which cost more than he could afford but which Laban assured him was "the newest and most stylish thing out." With this, neatly boxed and in his pocket—a pocket now otherwise very nearly empty —he left the Main Road and, walking across the fields, came out upon the West Main Road close to its juncture with the Neck Road. Into the latter he turned, and, a few minutes later, into the gateway of the Fuller home. He fondly imagined himself unobserved. But he was not; Nellie Snow was watching him, so also was her mother. To be unobserved in Orham was then, as it is now, almost an impossibility, especially in the winter months.

Mrs. Fuller answered his knock. She was in her morning wrapper and her hair was somewhat disarranged. Altogether her appearance was in marked contrast to what it had been on the occasion of his former visit, and she seemed quite aware of the fact. If Calvin had been of a critical turn of mind he might have considered her expression, when she opened the door, and saw him standing there on the step, not one of overwhelming joy. She colored, frowned, and was evidently embarrassed. But he, too, was embarrassed so he did not notice these things. And her confusion was but momentary.

She was *so* glad to see him. And so surprised. Myra had not told her he was coming. He explained that his visit was unpremeditated and asked if Myra was in. Why no, she was not; she was at school. The vacation did not begin until the following day; he had forgotten that? He had, of course, and apologized. Oh, that was all right. It didn't make a bit of difference. Myra would be at home for dinner, and he must come right in and visit. Oh yes, he must. And he would dine with them? She wouldn't take no for an answer—that is, provided he wasn't *too* particular and would be satisfied with just an everyday, picked up meal. You see, having to do her own housework, they lived *very* simply, and just got along with as little as possible. Myra insisted on that. She would *not* let her mother work *too* hard. She was the most thoughtful daughter that ever lived, so Mrs. Fuller really did believe. It was a good deal of a come-down for them both, for in the old days, when the captain was living, everything was *so* different. Then, when company came unexpectedly it was all right. They kept help then, of course, and—

Homer, more embarrassed than ever, interrupted when the lady paused for breath, and said that he guessed he would not wait, but would come back later. He had not intended to stay for dinner anyway, and—

But Sarepta would not hear of his going. He must come right in. And he wouldn't mind if the dinner wasn't much, would he?

"After all, you're one of the family now, Calvin," she announced, with a smile, the archness of which was a sort of faded reminder of her daughter's. "And home folks aren't fussy, are they?"

So he entered the house and Mrs. Fuller, still protesting her pleasure in seeing him and lamenting over the dinner and begging his pardon for "looking so like fury" because she had not had a minute to change her clothes, relieved him of his hat and coat, ushered him into the sitting room and departed, tucking up the stray fringes of her hair as she went. Calvin was vaguely conscious that that hair did not seem to be as plentiful as when he last saw it.

Left alone in the sitting room, with the haircloth set and the portraits of the departed, he waited. His hostess bobbed in and out occasionally, to ask questions concerning affairs at the station, or to deliver an item of local gossip. She would have talked much concerning the Bartlett appoint-

ment, but he was discouragingly silent on that point. She
declared it to be a sin and a shame, and that everybody was
saying so—"Everybody that amounts to anything, that is,"
she added, with a somewhat tart emphasis. "There's a few
that pretend to believe Kellogg did the best he could, but
they don't say it when *we're* around. Cap'n Ziba, here at
the corner, was standing up for the Kellogg man the other
day and Myra heard him. She told him what she thought
of it, you better be sure of that. Myra says Cap'n Ziba's
all right enough—she and the cap'n are nice and friendly—
but it's that daughter of his—that Nellie Snow—she can't
bear. So many of the girls here in Orham are jealous of
Myra. She gets along real well with the men—the school
committee now, she can do anything she wants to with them,
but some of the women and girls are hateful as they can be.
Just jealousy, that's all it is. They can't stand superiority,
and Myra is superior. I guess *you* think she is, don't you,
Calvin? Ha, ha!"

With each appearance she was a trifle more ornamental.
The wrapper vanished, and was replaced by a becoming
gown. Her hair was neatly arranged, and it must have been
Homer's fancy which had deemed it scanty, for now there
was an abundance.

He was alone when he heard Myra's step on the walk.
The sitting room door was slightly ajar, and he heard her
enter—also her mother's greeting.

"Why, Myra, where have you been?" cried Mrs. Fuller.
"You're much as ten minutes late."

Myra's reply was tart in its impatience.

"Oh, I had to stop and listen to that ninny of a Ezra
Blodgett," she explained. "He didn't really have a thing to
say, but he is rich and is going to be on the committee next
year, so I had to look sweet and pretend I liked it. Silly
thing! Deliver me from soft-headed old men. And the
married ones or the widowers are the worst. I only wish
that old-maid sister of his could have seen the way he looked
at me. . . . Well, what are you making signs about? What's
the matter with you?"

Then followed a brief silence—silence as far as the visitor in the sitting room was concerned. Then Miss Fuller said, "Oh!" and followed it with, "My goodness!"

But there were no traces of ill temper when she ran in to greet her lover. And she was so pretty and so vivacious, and her expressions of joyful surprise were so flattering, her welcoming hug and kiss so intoxicating, that Calvin—whose opinion of Mr. Blodgett—an opinion founded upon the latter's local reputation—was anything but favorable—forgot his momentary resentment. She closed the door, with elaborate and playful carefulness, and they sat together once more upon that ancient sofa.

There was so much to say, so Myra declared, and such a provokingly short time to say it in. Wasn't he going to stay for supper and the evening? Oh, he must! She had to go back to that horrid school right after dinner and—just think—they hadn't seen each other for ages. And so on. It was pleasant, and as wonderful as ever. But when he explained that he had promised Captain Bartlett to be back at the station by supper time, the young lady's smile vanished.

"Promise!" she repeated, scornfully. "You don't have to keep a promise to that man, I hope. What right has he got to ask favors of you?"

It was not a favor asked, but an order given, so Homer explained. The explanation did not help greatly.

"The idea of his giving you orders! He! *You* ought to be the one to give orders down there. And you will be giving them before long. Tell me, how is he getting on with the men? They hate him, I know that."

Calvin turned to look at her. "You know they hate him?" he repeated. "Why, who said they did?"

"Ellis Badger for one. He told me lots of things. He was up here on liberty, you know, a little while ago, and I made it my business to see him. At first he wouldn't say much, he was afraid to, I guess; the poor thing doesn't dare call his soul his own when he is within a mile of home. But I was ever so nice to him"—she laughed at the recollection—"and before we finished our talk he told me all he knew.

That wasn't too much, for he doesn't know more than enough to get out of his own way, but he told me how mad the crew were because you had been slighted and Bartlett made keeper. He said every man was on your side, and would do anything to help you. Of course I couldn't speak plainly—I wouldn't have him guess what I was up to for the world—but I think I dropped some hints that will do good. From what he said I don't imagine that Bartlett will have the smoothest time that ever was. We'll see that he doesn't, won't we? And now tell me; what have *you* done. . . . ? Why do you look at me like that? What is it?"

He was regarding her uneasily. All this sounded like confirmation of the meaning he had at first fancied lay between the lines of her letter, and which he had dismissed as impossible. Even now he could not believe she really meant it. She could not expect him to—

Then came a discreet knock at the door and Mrs. Fuller called to announce that dinner was ready. The meal was by no means a bad one, in spite of Sarepta's profuse apologies for its "picked-upness." Homer would not have noticed if it had been. His appetite was not hearty just then. Myra had not said much, it is true, but she had said enough to trouble him greatly. The consciousness of impending crisis was strong upon him.

And back once more in the sitting room, with the door closed, she repeated her question. What had he done at the station since the new keeper came?

He hesitated. "Done?" he said. "Why, I have done my regular work, of course."

"Oh, I know," impatiently. "You have to do that, or pretend to. But what else have you done—to help our plan?"

He looked at her and then looked away again.

"I'm not sure that I know just what you mean," he said. This was not true; he was beginning to fear that he did know only too well.

She laughed incredulously and tossed her head.

"Rubbish!" she exclaimed. "Of course you know. I

mean what are you doing to help yourself—to help us—
down there? I haven't done much yet, I haven't really begun, but I have done something. I gave Ellis Badger—
oh, if he wasn't such a fool!—as broad hints as I dared about
Bartlett's being unfit to be keeper, and how people felt
about it, and how no one expected him to get on with the
crew, and that no one blamed them for not paying attention to what he said. I told him—I said he mustn't breathe
a word to any one, but of course he will and I meant him to
—that everybody worth while here in Orham expected Bartlett to fail, and was only waiting to see it happen. And I
praised you to the skies—not out and out, I had too much
sense for that—but in a roundabout way, and he agreed with
every bit of it. Oh, he will tell the others. You see if he
doesn't. And it will help a lot. Now I want to know about
you. Are you keeping yourself in the front of everything
as you promised me you would?"

"I am doing my work as Number One. . . . And I am
making the men do theirs."

She cried out, sharply. "But you mustn't," she protested.
"That is the very thing. Never mind the men. If they
don't do as they should that isn't your affair—now. It is
his—that Bartlett's. Don't you see? If he can't keep order,
and if things don't go right, as they used to go when Oswald Myrick was keeper—or when you took his place—then
there will be no one to blame but Bartlett. And everything
that goes wrong will be so much the worse for him and so
much better for you. Don't you see, dear? Oh, you must
see!"

He saw. The crisis had arrived. He drew a long breath.

"You mean," he asked, slowly, "that you don't *want* things
at the station to go right?"

"Why, of course! The worse they go the sooner there
will be a change. Kellogg will have to put him out and you
will get the appointment. That is what we both want, what
we are both working for, isn't it?"

He did not answer. She was regarding him now and she
leaned forward to see his face.

"Well? What ails you?" she demanded, crisply. "Why don't you say something? Look at me."

He turned then and looked, but his look did not please her.

"Calvin," she cried, "what is the matter with you? What are you thinking. . . ? Has something happened that you haven't told me about?"

He shook his head. "No," he answered. "Nothing has happened. I—I— See here, Myra, you don't expect me not to play straight with Cap'n Bartlett, do you?"

"Captain! For mercy's sake, don't *you* call him captain. And what do you mean by playing straight?"

"Why—why, working against him, behind his back, with —with the men, and all that. You wouldn't want me to do that?"

"Why wouldn't I? Has he played straight, as you call it, with you?"

"Yes, I guess he has. It isn't his fault that they made him keeper—not really, it isn't."

"Nonsense! Of course it is. He knew well enough that you should have the place. But he schemed and planned until he sneaked in. The miserable, contriving—"

"Now, now, Myra. He isn't contriving. He wouldn't know how to be. He's just—well, simple, sort of. And queer. I kind of pity him, sometimes. Honestly, I do."

Miss Fuller moved away from him on the sofa. Her eyes were sparkling now, but the sparkle could hardly be called a love light.

"Pity him!" she cried shrilly. "Pity *him!* Calvin Homer, are you crazy?"

"No-o, I guess not. No more crazy than usual. But, you see, Myra, I do pity him. He's so—so all alone. He must know the men don't like him. I think he realizes, in a way, that he wouldn't be liked by most people. He talks to me more than he does the rest. I don't know why, unless it is because—because—"

"Because he is trying to keep you friendly, of course. He knows you could make trouble for him—and ought to—and he is smart enough to make up to you and head that trouble off. If he can soft soap you, why, he thinks you will help him with the men—and the superintendent. It is plain enough. I should think any fool could see that."

Calvin shifted uneasily. "It isn't that, Myra," he declared. "You haven't seen him. You haven't heard him talk. If you had you would know that he couldn't soft soap anybody. . . . Oh, I don't like him, especially—"

"I should hope *not!*"

"But I don't hate him, or anything like that. And— and, honest, Myra, I don't like the idea of working under-hand against him while he is my skipper. It doesn't seem fair to me."

"It is just as fair as he has been to you—yes, and fairer. Can't you see this is a fight for your rights? Are you going to knuckle down and let him walk all over you? What ails you? Haven't you any fight in you?"

"I guess I have. But that kind of fight isn't square. Men —decent men—don't fight that way. If it was a fair, stand-up scrap I could—"

"Oh, *don't* be so ridiculous! And how about being fair to me? You are going to be my husband some day. I tell you here and now, I don't intend to marry a man who is contented to play second fiddle in a life-saving station. You and I promised each other to work ever and ever so hard for each other. You were going to try in every way to push yourself forward and I was going to help you. And I am doing my part. What have you done? Nothing—except make friends with the very person who stands most in our way. Is that fair to me?"

Calvin hesitated. His resolution was as strong as ever, but the question made a certain appeal to his sense of justice. After all, she had been planning and working to help him. And they had promised to work and plan for each other. At the time when the promise was made he had had no clear idea of its meaning—surely not of any such meaning as hers must have been—but she, perhaps, thought he had. And, always with him, was the conviction of her superiority, her beauty, her popularity, the incomprehensibility of her choosing him from her list of suitors. He shook his head.

"No," he admitted. "Maybe you're right, Myra—from your way of looking at it. Perhaps it isn't just fair to you. . . . I guess it isn't. . . . But—"

"But what? . . . Go on!"

"But I—I can't—it seems as if I couldn't play politics down there at Setuckit. And such dirty back-door politics, too."

"Thank you for the compliment, I'm sure."

"Oh, I don't mean you see it that way. I know you don't. But I can't see it any other. . . . And I can't do it, that's all. . . . I just can't."

She rose from the sofa. The fire in her eyes was ominous.

"You can't?" she sneered. "That means you won't, I take it."

He nodded, wretchedly. "I hate to have you put it that way," he said. "But I can't do what you want me to, Myra."

"Indeed! . . . Then I suppose you understand what that means, so far as you and I are concerned?"

"Yes. . . . I suppose I do. . . . I am sorry. It isn't your fault. It's mine, I guess. . . . I'm afraid it was all a mistake, anyway, your taking a fellow like me."

She made no answer to this confession. He, too, rose from the sofa and stood there, waiting for his dismissal. But that dismissal was not given. There was a long moment of silence and then, to his amazement, she came to him, put her arms about his neck and looked up into his face.

"Calvin," she breathed.

Were there tears in those expressive eyes of hers? There must be, for her voice trembled as she spoke his name.

"Calvin—oh, Calvin, dearest!" she whispered.

He groaned, in conscience-stricken misery.

"I— It isn't fair to you, Myra," he stammered, chokingly. "I know it isn't. You're doing everything for me, but—but I can't help it. I'm made stubborn, I guess. . . . Oh, I don't know what is the matter with me."

She kissed him. "I do," she declared. "You're just a

dear, sweet innocent boy, who is so honest himself that he
thinks every one else is the same. And he needs some one
to look after him, doesn't he? Yes, he does. And he has
some one, only he mustn't be cross to her and he must pay
attention when she tries to help him, because she knows best.
. . . And now we won't quarrel any more, will we? We
won't say another word about the old life-saving station.
We'll sit here on the sofa and talk about no one but just our
very selves."

And they did, Miss Fuller doing most of the talking. The
station, nor Bartlett, nor her plans, nor the sharp difference
of opinion concerning them, were mentioned at all. And
when he attempted to mention them she would not let him
do so, but whispered that he must not be naughty any more—
and wasn't he ever and ever so happy? Of course he said
he was—but even as he said it, a disturbing doubt returned
to trouble him.

When the time came for her to go back to the school he
walked with her as far as the turn of the Main Road. There
they separated. The real farewells had, of course, been said
in the Fuller sitting room; this public parting was but a casual
handshake and good-by, for the benefit of watchful Orham.

He called at the post office, the express office and the
grocery store. The various boxes and heavy packages he
arranged to have sent to the wharf in the grocer's delivery
wagon. And toward that wharf he strolled, meditating
deeply. He took the longest way, over the fields and around
the two-mile curve of the Shell Road. There was plenty of
time—he must wait until the grocer's boy came—and meanwhile he did not care to meet acquaintances. He wanted to
be alone—and think.

He had foreseen a crisis and that crisis had come—and
burst—and then apparently was not. But had it gone, defi-
nitely and forever, or was it merely waiting around the next
corner, ready to jump at him later on? Had Myra been convinced that she was wrong and he was right, and would she
hereafter be contented to let matters at Setuckit take their
regular course, trusting to luck and his own hard work to

bring him promotion and advancement, there or elsewhere? Knowing her and her ambitions he could scarcely believe it. She had yielded for the time—or, at least, had refused to let him go—but had she actually given up one iota of her schemes for ousting Bartlett—and Kellogg? And wouldn't she continue to "play politics" and do her best to make him play them, too? He would not play them—he was as resolute as ever on that point—but would she understand that and not keep trying? He went over their recent disagreement and reconciliation word for word and he could not remember that she had said anything which indicated relinquishment of her designs. If she meant to go on, then the final settlement between them had been only postponed. Nothing at all was really settled.

He almost wished it had been. If she had bade him go and never speak to her again—well, then at least, his trouble would have been present and tangible. He would have known the worst and could face it, whereas now it was clouding his whole future, like a fog bank, with all sorts of possible perils behind it. He wished it was cver and done with.

He wished—

Then he awoke to a realization of what he was wishing and felt ashamed of himself. He swore aloud, jammed his hands into his pockets and one of them came in contact with a small, square package.

It was the package containing the ring he had bought of Laban Bassett that forenoon. He had meant it as an engagement ring and a Christmas present combined. The distressed scene in the Fuller sitting room had driven all thought of it from his mind. He had actually forgotten to give it to her. Now he *knew* there was something the matter with him.

CHAPTER VI

HIS first move, after realization of his criminal forgetfulness, was to look at his watch. Was there
time in which to return to the Fuller home and
leave the ring? Scarcely—and yet he could do it if he hurried. But Myra would not be there, she was at school, and
Sarepta had said something about going to sewing circle.
If he ran he might reach there before she left, but what would
the neighbors think if they saw him galloping up to the door
as if he were going to a fire? The idea of visiting the school-
house and facing a brigade of sniggering youngsters was not
tenable. He could not present the ring in person, he must
send it by a messenger—if he could find one.

Wide awake now and with the thought of that messenger
foremost in his mind, he walked briskly on. As he climbed
the hill where the Shell Road emerges from the pines beyond
the big swamp, and came in sight of the bay, he realized that
he had lingered too long. The morning haze—a haze more
befitting a day in May than December—had become something more definite and disturbing. The whole western horizon was piled high with fog. The mainland of the Cape
beyond Denboro was gone, the beach ended just past Harniss.
Setuckit was still visible—that is, he could see the speck which
he knew was the tower of the life-saving station above the
last low-lying dune—but behind it was but a gray curtain.
The breeze had died almost entirely; there was scarcely
enough left to give steerage way. If he was to make good
his promise to Bartlett and get back to the station before
supper he must start at once. Even then, unless the wind
freshened, he would barely make it.

He heard the rattle of a cart on the road below and to his
left and, turning, saw the grocer's wagon approaching. That
was good; he would not be kept waiting for his Christmas

freight. The cart was a covered affair and he could not see the packages and boxes, but of course they were there. There seemed to be two persons on the driver's seat. He did not stop to look longer; it was the contents of the vehicle, not its passengers, which interested him. He left the road, vaulted the rail fence, and hurried down through the bayberry and beach-plum bushes to the landing.

The cart reached there before he did and was drawn up at the outer end of the wharf, only its rear showing beyond the walls of the fish house. Jimmie Kelley, the grocer's boy, a chubby youth of seventeen, was unloading the bundles and boxes and piling them on the planks at his feet. Among them, to Homer's surprise, was a leather suit case. Jimmie heard his approach and greeted him with a grin.

"Hello, Cap'n Cal," hailed Jimmie. "Beat you to it, didn't I? Here's your stuff. Want me should help you stow it aboard?"

Calvin shook his head. "I guess I can handle it," he said. Then, mindful of his determination not to do any more forgetting, he added, "I'd rather you took the time to go back by way of the Neck Road and do an errand for me. Can you?"

Jimmie's grin widened. "Sure thing," he declared. "Where's the errand to; up to Myra's?"

Homer's hand was in his pocket and the package containing the ring was in the hand. But there it stayed. He hesitated.

"Take it just as well as not," urged Jimmie. "Glad to. Myra ain't to home now, though; she's up to school."

The hand was removed from the pocket—empty. Its owner frowned.

"Who said anything about—about her?" he demanded tartly. Was it absolutely impossible to keep a secret in Orham?

"Why—why, nobody did, as I know of. Only you said the Neck Road—and she lives there—and of course—well, everybody says—I just thought—"

Calvin interrupted. "Never mind," he snapped. "Let the

errand go. You can help me with these things here. Whose suit case is that?"

But Jimmie was troubled. "Ain't mad, are you, Cap'n Cal?" he queried. "I didn't mean nothin'. I was just—"

"Oh, forget it! What is that suit case doing here?"

Young Kelley's grin returned. He winked, and pointed over his shoulder.

"It's hers," he said.

"Hers? Whose?"

"Sshh! She'll hear you. She's right here on the wharf. Gee, she's a pippin, too! You won't be mad when you see *her,* Cap'n Cal. She's goin' down to Setuckit along with you. Her old man don't know it; it's his Christmas surprise."

Homer stepped forward and peered around the corner of the fish house. At the further edge of the wharf a girl was standing. Her back was toward them and she was looking out over the water. He stepped back again.

"Who is it?" he whispered. Jimmie was eager to supply the information.

"It's that—er—what's-her-name—Normal Bartlett. 'Tain't Normal, but it's something like it. Old man Bartlett's girl, you know; the one they put the picture of in the paper; the one that 'tends libr'y up to Fairborough. She came down on to-day's train and wanted to be took to Setuckit right off. Nobody didn't know how they was goin' to get her there, until Mr. Eldridge at the store, he recollected you was up to town and was goin' back this afternoon. He cal'lated you'd just as soon take her down as not. Old Seth Burgess, he was hangin' 'round as usual, and he says— He, he!—he said, 'Cal won't mind takin' her. Judas!' he says, 'I'd be willin' to take her 'most anywheres, myself. . . .' And he was dead right, too. Say, she's a peach, Cap'n. Honest she is! Wait till you see her."

Calvin did not speak. At that moment he was profoundly irritated. In his present state of mind solitude and his own thoughts were unpleasant enough, but they were far preferable to the society of any one else, least of all a stranger—and a girl.

Young Kelley chattered on. He was an impressionable youth, and enthusiastic.

"She said she'd ride down to the wharf along of me in the team," he confided, "and she done it. Asked me a lot of questions about things down to the station, and the like of that. Gee, she's all right! Not a mite stuck up, lots of fun to her. And you ought to hear her laugh—and see her do it! . . . Gee!"

Homer could not help smiling. "She hit *you* hard, didn't she, Jim?" he observed.

Jimmie blushed under his freckles, but he stuck to his guns.

"I don't care; she's all *right,*" he declared. "I ain't the only one. You'd ought to seen old Ezra Blodgett stare at her when she came out of the store. He was goin' by and he stopped dead still and just gawped. He—"

But Calvin had no more time to waste. "Come, pick up some of this stuff and put it aboard," he ordered. "I'll take the rest. Hurry up!"

Jimmie made a grab for the handle of the suit case.

"I might's well take this," he said quickly. "It's handy to lug. Come on, Cap'n."

The girl turned to meet them as they came out from behind the wagon. Calvin, although in no mood to receive favorable impressions, was nevertheless willing to concede that Jimmie's enthusiasm was not altogether unwarranted. A pair of clear gray eyes, a provoking nose, a wide mouth parted in a smile which seemed not at all forced, and a firm little chin. She wore a heavy coat of rough cloth, with the collar turned up, and a neat and becoming turban. Under the edges of the hat and against the background of her coat collar her brown hair was bunched in rebellious masses. She was a good-looking girl—there was no doubt of that—not handsome and statuesque like Myra Fuller—no, not at all like Myra. And least of all like what he had expected Benoni Bartlett's daughter to be. Benoni had spoken of his daughter, and more than once, but if he possessed her photograph, he had never shown it to his Number One man.

She came to meet them, smiling and unembarrassed.

"I suppose you are Mr. Homer," she said. "I am Norma Bartlett. How do you do. . . .? Oh, please don't trouble to shake hands—now. Your hands are full."

They were, both of them. And Calvin *was* embarrassed, as he usually was when meeting strange young women. He started to put down his load of boxes and bundles, then decided not to do so, and immediately wished he had.

"How do you do, Miss Bartlett?" he stammered, inanely. "I—I—"

She saw that he was embarrassed, and helped him out.

"You are surprised, of course," she said. "I don't wonder. But I hope I am not making you a lot of trouble. I came to spend Christmas week with father. I didn't write I was coming, for I wanted to surprise him. It never occurred to me that the station might be such an out-of-the-way place to get to. When they told me you were going down there I— well—I invited myself. If there isn't room—"

He assured her there was plenty of room.

"Get the dunnage aboard, Jim," he ordered. "We'll have to hustle, with no more wind than this."

The packages and the suit case were stowed in the little cabin of the catboat. Jimmie personally attended to the stowing of the case; he refused any assistance so far as that was concerned. He would have helped Miss Bartlett into the boat, but she did not appear to need help, catching a halyard and leaping lightly from the stringpiece to the deck as if she were used to boats. Homer lingered a moment before following her. Young Kelley reluctantly clambered up and stood beside him.

"How about that errand, Cap'n Cal?" he queried.

Calvin frowned. Then he took the ring box from his pocket.

"Leave this at the Fullers'," he said. "Tell Mrs. Fuller it is something I meant to—well, something I forgot. Tell her I'll write, or telephone, and explain."

Jimmie regarded the little parcel with consuming curiosity.

" 'Tain't for Sarepta, is it?" he queried. "Shall I say it's for her?"

"No, no," sharply. "You tell her what I told you. She'll understand."

Jimmie winked. "I'm on, Cap'n," he declared. "I know what to say, I guess likely. And I guess likely you don't want me to say nothin' to nobody else neither. Eh? Ain't that so?"

Homer did not answer. His passenger did not appear to be listening, but she must have overheard the dialogue. Not that that made any difference, but the whole business was vexing. He had a feeling that Myra would not like the idea of his having forgotten to give her the ring. She might not like his sending it in this offhand fashion. He was tempted to change his mind for the third time and wait and deliver his gift in person later on. But Jimmie's next remark decided the matter.

"I understand, Cap'n," he whispered. "Day after to-morrow's Christmas, eh? I'll fix things all right for you. I'm used to doin' errands and things for folks. Why, one time old man Blodgett give me a quarter for takin' a letter to—well, never mind who 'twas to. I told him I'd never tell, and I ain't—so far."

It was apparent that he wanted to tell very much, but he received no encouragement. Calvin took a coin from his pocket—it happened to be a half dollar—and gave it to him.

"There! take that," he commanded. "And clear out."

He jumped aboard the catboat and set about hoisting the sail and casting off. As the boat swung lazily away from the wharf Jimmie called after them.

"Merry Christmas, Cap'n," he shouted. "Merry Christmas, Miss Bartlett."

The young lady returned the wish. She laughed merrily. "He isn't exactly a shy boy, is he?" she observed.

Calvin grunted. He was busy with the wheel and the sheet.

"He talked steadily all the way to the wharf," continued the passenger. "I asked him one or two questions and he answered at least twenty. He likes you, Mr. Homer. He told me ever so many things about you."

Homer glowered at her. He wondered just exactly what had been told. Jimmie Kelley, in his opinion, was altogether too wise for his age.

The breeze had freshened a little by the time they reached the harbor entrance, but there was no promise of constancy in it. The fog was drawing nearer.

Miss Bartlett gazed ahead over the smooth, oily waves of the bay.

"Where is it we are going?" she asked. "Where is Setuckit?"

Homer pointed. "About ten miles off yonder," he replied. "If it was clear you could see the lighthouse and the tower of the station."

"But you can't see them now. That is fog ahead, isn't it?"

"Yes. It is coming in fast. It will be thick enough in half an hour."

"Really?"

"Yes. But there is nothing to worry about. We'll get there all right, and before supper, if the wind holds."

"Oh, I'm not worried. I suppose you will steer by compass when the fog comes."

"Yes. You're used to boats, I guess."

"I ought to be. I lived in Trumet until I was fifteen, before I went away to school. I was in a boat, or about boats, a great deal of the time. I love all this—the salt water and the sand and the gulls—yes, even the fog. You don't, I imagine—the fog part, at least?"

"No. I've seen too much trouble come from the stuff."

"Of course. Father hates it, too. So do all the men in the life-saving service. . . . Tell me a little about father, Mr. Homer. How is he?"

"Why—he is all right, I guess. He is well—or he was this morning."

"Do you think he is quite himself? Does he seem nervous or anxious? Oh, you know what I mean! Does he eat and sleep as he should?"

"Yes, I should say so. He is—of course he is new to his

job there at Setuckit and new to the station. Naturally, getting used to things may worry him a little at first."

"So you think he does worry? I was afraid of it."

"I don't know that he worries any more than any other man would. There is a good deal of care about the keeper's job and—well, Cap'n Bartlett has been through a lot lately. It was enough to upset any man's nerves, that Crooked Hill business."

She shuddered. "I know," she said. "It was terrible— terrible! I knew all the men who were drowned. Some of them I had known since I was a baby. I went down there, you see, just after it happened, and stayed with father until he was well enough for me to leave. I was there when they picked up the bodies, and I met some of the widows and— But I don't want to talk about that. I won't. I dream about it even now. I *must* get it out of my mind."

She paused. Homer remembered her father's confession concerning his own dreams.

"You said something about upset nerves," she went on. "Do you mean you think father's nerves are upset?"

"Why—why, no, not especially. I mean—I meant it wouldn't be surprising if they were."

"I'm afraid his are. Mr. Homer, I suppose you think my father is a very odd man. You do think that, don't you?"

It was not at all the question he expected, and he was not ready with an answer. She noticed his hesitancy and drew her own conclusions. Her tone changed.

"I can see you do," she said quickly. "Most people do. They don't know him, that's all. There is no better man in this world than my father."

"Why—why, I don't doubt it, Miss Bartlett. I didn't say—"

"It doesn't make any difference what any one says. I know him—and they don't, that's all. He is very religious, and that is unusual, goodness knows, in the life-saving service; and those that don't understand him call him a crank, behind his back. They never call him one before his face— or mine," with a defiant toss of her head.

Homer had—in thought at least—more than once called his new keeper a "crank." He did not know what to say.

"How is he getting on with his work?" she persisted. "Do the men like him?"

Here was another embarrassing question.

"Why—why, yes, sure," he answered, with almost too much emphasis. "He's doing first rate. We haven't had but one call since he has been there. That was a lumber schooner aground on the Hog's Back and he got her off in no time. I never saw a job handled better. Didn't he write you about that?"

"Yes." She turned and looked at him, and again her expression had changed. "He writes me every day," she said. "Sometimes I don't get the letters for three or four days, but then I get them together. He writes me everything. He has written me often about you."

"Oh—has he?"

"Yes. He says you are as dependable a mate as he ever signed with. That is a good deal for father to say. You ought to be proud, Mr. Homer."

He did not feel particularly proud. He was rather glad to know that Bartlett had seen fit to praise him in those letters. And undeniably thankful that, in his own conversations with Kellogg and the men, while they had hinted and criticized, he had said nothing. It made him feel less like a hypocrite. A girl as straightforward and outspoken as this one seemed to be would have little use for hypocrites. Not that her opinion was of great importance to him, but his own was.

"Father says you obey orders and he thinks he can trust you," she went on. "Loyalty is a strong point in his religion. He is a crank on *that,* if you want to call him so. So am I, for that matter."

Calvin murmured that loyalty was a fine thing. He was thinking of Myra Fuller and the after-dinner scene in the sitting room.

"The fog is almost on top of us now," he observed.

But she would not look at the fog. "I want to ask you a

little more about father," she said. "I may not have as good
a chance as this again. Mr. Homer, please tell me the exact
truth; do you think his taking this place at Setuckit was a
mistake?"

This girl should be a lawyer. She certainly had a talent
for cross-examination.

"Why—I don't know what you mean," he said.

"I mean just that. Do you think it would be better—for
him—if he had not accepted the appointment?"

"Why shouldn't he accept it? He wanted it, didn't he?"

"He didn't apply for it. Of course you know that. It was
offered to him and I think no one was more surprised than
he when the offer was made. And he wasn't sure that he
ought to take it. Neither was I."

This statement was surprising. Calvin looked at her.

"He told me—yes, and he told the men—that he took the
place on your account," he said bluntly. "He said you wanted
him to do it."

She was troubled. "Did he say that?" she asked. "I'm
sorry. And yet it is true, in a way. If I had said no, he
would have refused. He would do anything to please me.
But of course I wouldn't say it. He had been in the service
for years and it was time he got some recognition. And he
certainly deserved the appointment—or anything they could
do for him. Didn't he?"

"Why—why, yes."

"What makes you say it that way? Don't you *know* he
deserved it? Can you think of any one who should have
had it rather than he?"

He could, but he could not tell her so. And he was growing tired of the witness stand.

"Look here, Miss Bartlett," he said in good-natured desperation, "I don't just see what you are trying to get at.
I didn't say Cap'n Bartlett shouldn't be keeper at Setuckit.
I didn't say anything like it. You were the one who started
this thing. You asked me if I thought his taking the job
was a mistake."

She caught the change in his tone instantly. She, too,

smiled, and then burst into a laugh. That laugh was all that
Jimmie Kelley had said of it—pleasant to hear—and see.

"I'm sorry, Mr. Homer," she cried. "I beg your pardon.
You and I haven't known each other but a few minutes and
I have been scolding at you like a schoolma'am. I am sure
you must think that, no matter whether father is a crank
or not, there isn't a bit of doubt about his daughter. You
see, I am very anxious about him. That is what I meant
by a mistake. I am, I suppose, in a way responsible for his
staying on in the service and taking those new cares. Perhaps he shouldn't have done it. Perhaps I should have insisted on his getting away from the Cape and the sea and
everything connected with them. It might have been better
for his health—and happiness. That is why I flew at you
so. I have been flying at myself in just the same way. It is
my conscience. Don't you wish sometimes you didn't have
any—any conscience, I mean?"

Here was something to be answered without the least
equivocation.

"You bet!" he exclaimed devoutly.

She laughed again. "And now I'll try to behave," she
declared. "Oh, my! here *is* the fog."

It was—plenty of it. It dropped upon them like a blanket,
but with none of the blanket's warmth. Heavy, wet and raw
it swept over the boat and the sea. The moment before all
astern had been pleasant and, for the season, almost warm.
Now there was nothing—astern, ahead, and at the sides—
nothing. They were cut off from the rest of creation,
wrapped in a salty, soggy stillness. And the raw chill pene-
trated through wraps and underclothing to the skin. Fog
at any time is likely to be cold, but this was a December fog.

Miss Bartlett buttoned her coat and drew the collar more
closely about her face. Homer was looking up at the sail.
There were flabby bulges in its surfaces.

"Is anything wrong?" she asked.

"Nothing but the wind. And the only thing wrong with
that is that there isn't any worth talking about. It's next
door to a flat calm."

"You'll have to use the compass now, won't you?"

"Yes. The compass box is in the cabin, I suppose. Could you take this wheel just a minute?"

She took his place beside the wheel. There was no hesitancy in her manner.

"It seems like old times," she said. "I used to love to steer."

He disappeared in the cabin, the interior of which was a conglomerate of oilskins, rubber boots, nautical odds and ends, semidarkness, bad air and odors. She heard him rummaging.

"Have you found it?" she asked.

"Not yet. I've found about everything else. Phew! Smells like a codfish graveyard. Here! here's something for you."

His head and shoulders appeared through the hatchway and he tossed a stained and crumpled oilskin "slicker" in her direction.

"Put that on over your other things," he said. "That is, if you don't mind fish scales. There's nothing like oilclothes for keeping out cold."

She donned the slicker. It engulfed her from ears to toes. She was obliged to turn back several inches of sleeves in order to free her hands.

"Now I do feel like a sailor," she announced.

"Might as well make a clean job of it. Better give me your hat. The fog will turn it into a dishrag in no time."

"Never mind. It isn't a new one—not very."

"No use spoiling it. There's half a barrel of sou'westers down here, more or less. Try that one."

He threw out an ancient sou'wester, creased and sticky, and, like everything else aboard Mr. Jarvis's boat, decidedly odoriferous. He watched as she, in seamanlike fashion, steadied the wheel with her body, and then used both hands to remove her hat. She caught his look and laughed.

"I know I'm a sight," she said, the eternal feminine prompting the eternal observation. "But I don't care. This is fun."

He could have told her what sort of sight she was, bareheaded and laughing, against the gray background. But complimenting young ladies was not one of his accomplishments. And the thought was but momentary and casual. What did cross his mind, as it had crossed it more than once before during their very brief acquaintance, was the incredulity of the fact that the grumpy rough old fanatic who commanded at Setuckit should have a daughter like this. Benoni had said she was like her mother. It must be true—certainly she was not like him.

She pulled the sou'wester down upon her head and buttoned it beneath her chin.

"There!" she exclaimed, leaning forward to hand him the discarded hat. "Now I'm ready for anything. But how about you? Are there more things like these in that place?"

"Enough to fit out a Banks schooner—if the hands weren't particular. There is everything here except money—and that compass. I haven't found that yet."

Nor did he find it. Ten minutes of rummaging and overhauling the contents of that cabin resulted only in absolute proof that the compass was not there.

"By George!" he exclaimed emerging. "I remember now. Philander said that he had got to make himself a new compass box. Said it last week. I'll bet he took the old one, compass and all, ashore with him and it's in his shanty now. . . . Humph!"

"Then you can't tell how to steer, can you?"

"Not very well, so long as this fog holds. . . . Oh, we'll be all right. There is nothing to be frightened about."

"I'm not frightened." Indeed she did not look as if she were. He struggled into another of the Jarvis slickers and, after several trials, found a sou'wester which fitted well enough.

"I'll take the helm now," he said.

"Do you want to? I don't mind steering, if you have anything else to do. I like it—really I do. . . . But there isn't anything to steer for."

"No, not much. The foghorns ought to help a little, but

unless the wind breezes on we shan't make any headway.
The tide is about full. When it begins to go out it'll carry
us along some."

"Then there really isn't anything to do but wait. . . . And
there are so many foghorns, aren't there?"

There were, a dozen of them. Some faint and distant,
others nearer. They sounded from aft, ahead and to port.
And their tones varied from thunderous bass to querulous
treble.

"Those little ones are aboard vessels off yonder," he explained. "The big one astern is at Orham. There! hear
that? That's the one we want to head for, if we can. It's at
Setuckit light, a couple of miles this side of the station. Two
long toots and then a short. Get it?"

She listened. "I think I do," she said, doubtfully, "but
they're awfully mixed up. There is hardly *any* wind now.
How far away is Setuckit?"

"About five—no, about six miles."

"It will take us a long time to get there at this rate."

"Take forever if we don't get a breeze. . . . But don't
worry. There isn't any danger."

"I'm not worried about *that*," scornfully. "I'm not a landlubber. But I know you feel you ought to be there. I suppose they know we're on the way—know you are, at any
rate. They must have seen us through the glass before the
fog came, don't you think?"

He smiled. "You do know the ropes, don't you?" he
observed.

"I ought to. I've looked through the Crooked Hill glass
ever so many times. It was a treat I used to tease for when
I was a little girl. Oh!" suddenly. "You don't suppose they
saw me, do you? If father knew I was coming it would
spoil the surprise. And *he* might worry."

"Nobody down there knows you but Cap'n Bartlett. And
the fog hit Setuckit long before it did us. No, they may
have seen the boat, but they couldn't tell who was aboard of
her. One thing we've got to look out for, and that is not to
get aground. There isn't too much water around here. If

you don't mind hanging on to that wheel I'll go for'ard and watch for shoals. Every chance you get keep her in towards that foghorn."

He left her and going forward stood there, in the little space between the mast and the catboat's bow, peering into the fog, or, stooping, tried to see the sand or weeds on the bottom. This, easy enough in the sunshine, was practically impossible now. An hour passed. The breeze was as light as ever.

Once she called to him. "Do you think that foghorn sounds any nearer?" she asked.

"Precious little. The tide is setting out and it may have carried us further out into the bay."

At last he gave up his task as lookout and came aft again.

"This is too bad, Miss Bartlett," he declared. "It looks as if we might be here all night. It is half past four and getting dark already. Are you frozen?"

Her laugh was reassuring. "Frozen!" she repeated. "With these things on? I'm roasted—or boiled. A roast doesn't drip. Look at me."

The fog was hanging in drops on her sou'wester and slicker and her cheeks were beaded with it. He knew she must be uncomfortable, because—toughened by experience as he was—he was chilled. And even as she spoke he saw her shiver.

"Here!" he exclaimed. "This won't do. We've got to get ashore somehow."

"I don't mind, except on your account. I'm having a real adventure. This is a change from handing out books in the Fairborough library. But I know you feel you should be back on duty. If the Setuckit people saw us don't you suppose they might send a boat . . . ? Oh, I beg pardon! That *was* a landlubber's question, wasn't it?"

He grinned. "If they sent a boat for me," he said, "in Orham Bay, in a flat calm—well, I'd jump overboard when I saw it coming. It would be better than waiting to hear what the men said when they got here. If Cap'n Bartlett knew you were aboard he might send for you, but not for his Number One man. Well, hardly."

"Of course. It was stupid of me. When I was ten or twelve I knew better than to dream such a thing. So we'll just keep on waiting and hoping for less fog and more wind. We ought to whistle for a breeze, hadn't we? I wonder if I could whistle. I used to."

She tried and succeeded remarkably well. The effort, too, was becoming, particularly when the whistle changed to a laugh.

"I was thinking how father used to scold me for whistling," she said. "He was forever quoting the proverb about 'whistling girls and crowing hens.' Mr. Homer, you brought him down to Setuckit on his first trip, didn't you? I remember now, he wrote me you did. And now you are bringing me. That's an odd coincidence. Father will say it is the workings of Providence. He sees special acts of Providence in everything. But he means it; he is absolutely sincere," she added, loyally.

Calvin sniffed. "If it is Providence that got us into this scrape, it must have a grudge against me," he vowed. Then, realizing that the speech was not altogether gracious, he added, "Of course I don't mean that I wasn't glad to bring you down, Miss Bartlett. But I don't see how sticking us out here in a fog is going to help anything much. Do you?"

"Well, it makes us better acquainted."

"Yes. Yes, I—"

He could not think of anything to add to the affirmative. And she did not wait for more. She changed the subject.

"I know what is the matter with me," she exclaimed. "I'm actually hungry. And it isn't five o'clock. It must be the sea air. I'm ashamed of myself."

He looked at her. "Where did you get your dinner?" he asked.

She hesitated. "Oh, that was all right," she replied hurriedly. "My dinner was all right."

"Did you have any?"

She colored slightly. "Well, no, I didn't," she confessed,

after a moment. "But that doesn't make any difference. I quite often go without lunch. It is good for me. And I just know I shall eat too much down here. . . . Why, what is it?"

He had been sitting on the wheel box. Now he rose, briskly and with determination.

"There's a little more breeze," he announced. "We're going ashore."

"You mean we can get to Setuckit?"

"I don't know about that—how soon we'll get to the station; but we're going ashore as straight as we can and without any more fooling."

He put the wheel over and the sail swung lazily across.

"Here, Miss Bartlett," he ordered, "you take the helm and keep her just as she is. I'm going forward again."

For another twenty minutes he peered over the bow. Then he came back.

"I'll take her now," he said. "And would you mind going up there and keeping a lookout? We ought to be getting in close by this time and I don't want to run on a flat. If you see anything either ahead or underneath, sing out."

She obeyed. "It seems to me that big foghorn sounds nearer than it did," she said, pausing a moment and listening.

"It ought to. We must be pretty close to the beach."

"But I don't see how you can tell where the beach—or anything else—is now."

"It's all beach—miles of it—on this side. We'll hit it somewhere."

"And then? When we do hit it?"

"Then we'll anchor this craft and go ashore. Unless I'm completely turned around we can't be far from Halfway Point and there are some shanties there. Somebody lives in one of 'em—an old fellow named Myrick. He'll give us a cup of coffee and maybe something more substantial. After that—well, we'll see."

"Mr. Homer, you're not doing this just because I was silly enough not to eat any lunch?"

His answer was emphatic. "I'm doing it," he declared,

"because I'm sick of roosting out here in this ice chest. Keep a sharp lookout and be sure and sing out if you see anything."

Seeing anything was next to an impossibility, for, between the fog and the lateness of the hour, it was almost dark. The boat moved slowly on before the fitful breeze.

"Sighted anything yet?" he called, after an interval.

"No."

A few moments later she spoke.

"Mr. Homer," she said, eagerly, "look! Look off there—there to the right. Isn't there something there? Something tall like—like a tree—or a pole? Yes—yes. It's a mast, isn't it?"

He peered under the sail.

"It's a boat," she cried. "It's another boat, with the sail down."

It was a boat, at anchor. He steered close by its stern.

"Good!" he exclaimed. "It's the *Wild Duck*. She belongs to the old fellow I was telling you about. We're luckier than we have any right to be. We've hit Halfway Point right in the bull's-eye. Come aft now. I'm going to anchor."

A minute more and their catboat, its anchor over the side, swung lazily in the tideway. The sail lay in a crumpled heap on the deck.

"And now what?" asked Miss Bartlett excitedly.

"Now I'm going to yell. You can help, if you want to." Leaning over the rail he began to shout.

"Peleg!" he roared. "Peleg Myrick! Ahoy there, Peleg!" She called, too, but stopped, breathless and laughing.

"All I can think of to scream is 'Fire!'" she declared.

"That'll do as well as anything. Oh, Peleg! Peleg Myrick! Here! Turn out! Pe-leg!"

From the darkness came the sound of a door banging open. Then a hoarse voice made answer.

"Here I be," it bellowed. "Who is it? What's the matter with ye?"

"It's me, Cal Homer. We want to come ashore. Got your dory there?"

"Eh? Yes, I've got her. Hold on a minute and I'll come off to ye. Keep ahollerin'."

They kept "ahollerin'." Then followed the clatter of oars, grunts and profane ejaculations. Then the measured click and squeak of those oars moving between thole pins. Out of the darkness emerged the dory and Mr. Myrick.

"Hello, Cal," observed the latter, bringing the dory scraping along the catboat's side. "What's the matter with ye? Kind of off your course, looks like to me. Ain't took sick, be ye? Eh? Who's that? Anybody I know?"

"No. I'll tell you all about it when you get us up to that shanty of yours. Now, Miss Bartlett. Easy does it."

The caution was unnecessary. She was in the dory even as he spoke. And, once in, she showed none of her father's nervousness. Calvin followed. Peleg pushed off.

"I don't see how you can tell where to go," observed the young lady. "It all looks alike to me."

Myrick grunted. "Chuck me overboard anywheres in Orham Bay and I'd guarantee to drift here or hereabouts," he declared. "It comes natural to me, I cal'late. I can smell home, same as a cat."

By way of proof he jammed the dory's bow hard and fast on the slope of the beach. Above, on the crest of that beach, a blur of yellow lamplight showed.

" 'And see, amid the darkness,
   Shine out the lights of home,' "

quoted Miss Bartlett joyfully.

"Eh?" said Peleg. "Yus-yus. And it's nine chances to one the durn lamp's smokin', too, 'Twas startin' out to when you folks hollered. I've got to buy a new wick next time I go up to the main. The robbers charge six cents apiece for 'em, too, they do. Livin's expensive these days, Cal, did you know it? I wisht I was rich, then I might be wuth money."

CHAPTER VII

"AND now what?" asked the young lady. She and Homer were seated at the oilcloth-covered table in Mr. Myrick's combined parlor, dining room and kitchen. Peleg had played the hospitable host so far as in him lay. He had set before them warmed-over baked beans, pilot crackers, half of an "evaporated apple" pie and a decoction which he called coffee. There was more of the latter left than of anything else. Miss Bartlett had eaten until, as she said, she was thoroughly ashamed but thoroughly happy.

"Have another cup, won't you, Cal?" begged Peleg, flourishing the by no means glittering coffee pot.

Calvin declined. His fellow voyager had refused already.

"What's the matter? Good and hot, ain't it?" demanded Peleg.

"Yes, it's hot."

It was the only good thing he could truthfully say concerning it.

"Flavored right, too, ain't it? . . . Hey? Ain't it?"

"It is flavored."

"I bet ye! That's good coffee. You came just the right time for it. I made that potful fresh day afore yesterday. Well, if you won't you won't. Git down, you Sou'west! Think I set table for you to eat off'n? Beats the divil what dumb animals know, don't it? Got sense same as a human, that cat has. Leave anything to eat around and he'll locate it inside of ten minutes. Seems to *know*—he does."

The cat, a huge gray and white one, was anything but dumb just then. He made another attempt to jump on the table. His master caught him just in time.

"Sshh!" he ordered. "There, there! I'll put you outdoors if you don't stop bellerin'. Make more noise than the Setuckit foghorn. There's another thing about that cat;

when he's hungry he'll ask for his grub just same as a Christian. Smartest cat as ever I owned, that Sou'west is."

"Is that his name—Southwest?" asked Miss Bartlett.

"Um-hum. I named him that 'cause he's so nice and pleasant, same as a sou'west wind is liable to be. I had one one time and I labeled him No'theaster. He was cranky— don't talk! Brush past him with your breeches' laig and he was just as liable as not to haul off and fetch you a scratch that would make you hop to Jericho. Had claws on to him like the teeth on a clam hoe. I don't wear no shoes and stockin's 'long in summer—don't need 'em down here, you understand—and I give you my word that critter made my underpinnin' look like a piece of plowed ground. I got tired of it after a spell and give him away—to a friend of mine."

"That dog of yours died, didn't he, Peleg?" inquired Homer. "Let's see; what was his name?"

"Skeezicks? Yes, he died. The weather down here kind of worked through and killed him finally, seemed so. He was one of them Mexican Chinee dogs, them kind that don't have no fur on 'em, you understand. Bald all over, like—like an egg. A feller off an English ship that was wrecked abreast here give him to me one time. He was a good dog, too, but he couldn't seem to stand the winters. He'd set there back of the cookstove and shake and shiver and shiver and shake till I cal'lated he'd come apart. And the worst of it was the kind of sad, blamin' sort of way he'd look at me with them big pop eyes of his—as if 'twas my fault 'twas so cold."

Calvin laughed. "Probably he thought it was," he said. "He knew you were the boss weather prophet in these latitudes."

Myrick shook his head reminiscently. "I don't know about that," he observed. "All I know is he just shook himself to death, as you might say. Got thinner and thinner— Say, Cal, you know how sort of—er—loose the hide is on one of them kind of dogs; hangs slack, and slats like a sail in a calm? Um-hum. . . . What is it, ma'am?"

Miss Bartlett, whose eyes were sparkling, chokingly declared that she had not spoken. Peleg nodded.

"Oh, I thought I heard you say somethin'," he said. "Well, the skin on that Skeezicks dog was slack enough to begin with, but it kept gettin' slacker and slacker till I snum if he didn't look like somethin' sewed up in a bag. Finally he hauled down the flag and died. I was sorry enough to lose him, poor thing; but 'twas a kind of relief, in a way, to have him quit shiverin'. Yes, 'twas. I've stuck to cats ever since. The colder it gets the more hair a cat gets on, seems so. And the warmer it gets the more comes off onto everything else," he added, regretfully. . . . "Well, Cal, to change the subject, what you figgerin' to do now? That was what you was askin' a minute ago, wan't it, Miss What's-name?"

The young lady answered that it was. "I wondered what the next part of your plan might be, Mr. Homer," she said. "I am on dry land, thanks to you; and, thanks to Mr. Myrick, I'm not a bit hungry. But what am I to do next, please?"

Calvin was ready with an answer. "You'd better stay right here for a while," he said. "I've been thinking it over and I guess the quickest way to get things moving is for me to go across the beach and up to the halfway shanty. I can telephone from there to the station and probably your father will get one of the men to come down here with the horse and cart after you. That is, if you don't mind riding in a cart. It's too dark for anybody to see you—and, anyway, we aren't very fussy around here; are we, Peleg?"

But Miss Bartlett was not entirely satisfied with this arrangement. It was not riding in the cart to which she objected—it was riding at all.

"All this telephoning and harnessing, and everything will take time and make a lot of trouble," she declared. "*You* are not going to wait for any cart, I suppose, Mr. Homer?"

"Oh, no, I'm going to walk. It is only three miles or so."

"That is what I thought. Well, I am going to walk, too. And we'll start this very minute."

Calvin protested. It would be difficult walking, part of it, at least. And it was wet and pitch dark and—

"And you think I'm a city girl and might collapse and have to be carried, I suppose. Well, I'm not, and I shan't.

I walk more than three miles every day of my life, for exercise. As for the wet—do you think it will be any wetter
than it was aboard that boat? And we can borrow those
oilskins, can't we? Or keep on borrowing them?"

She had her way, of course. Homer left the Jarvis catboat in Myrick's charge; he would come after it in the morning, or send some one. He borrowed a lantern of Peleg, a
battered and smelly affair, which even its owner confessed
gave "about as much light as a white bean."

"It's liable to go out on you," he explained; "the wick's
kind of short in the reach. And you can't see much by it,
the glass is so smurry. But you better take it, Cal. It'll
be kind of company for ye."

So, arrayed once more in the oilskins, they started, Myrick
and Sou'west whooping farewells from the door of the
shanty. Into the dripping, soggy blackness they trudged, he
leading the way with the lantern and she following. Up and
over and down dunes, sometimes through sand more than
ankle deep, then through tangles of blackberry vines and
stunted bayberry bushes; or stretches of coarse beach grass
amid which bits of driftwood and sun-bleached wreckage were
scattered like the white bones of long-drowned sailors. After
one particularly trying ascent she stopped.

"What is it?" he asked, turning. "Are you tired? Shall
we rest a while?"

"No-no, I'm all right," she panted, "I'm out of breath,
that's all. These oilskins are so dreadfully long. I try to
hold them up, but I can't seem to do it."

"I told you you shouldn't try the walk," he said anxiously.
"We might go back, you know. We haven't got very
far yet."

"Go back!" indignantly. "I guess *not!* I was just wondering if—if—"

"What?"

"Why, I thought perhaps if I took your arm we might
get ahead faster. I—you see, I should be nearer the lantern
and I could see where to step. But it would tire you, I'm
afraid."

He was angry at himself for not having thought of it.
As a matter of fact, his thoughts had wandered from Setuckit beach and were hovering about the Neck Road in
Orham. He was again wondering what Myra would think
of his having forgotten to give her the ring, and then sending
it by the Kelley boy. And the scene in the sitting room; he
went over it once more. No, it had not settled anything.
Why hadn't it? It should have. He should have gone on
with it to the finish. If he had not been a coward—

His musings had brought him to this unpleasant conviction when Miss Bartlett's breathless appeal shook him out
of them and back to her and the present. He turned hastily.

"I—I'm sorry," he stammered. "I don't know what—
Pshaw! What ails me, anyhow?"

He went back to where she was standing and offered his
arm. She hesitated.

"You're sure it won't tire you?" she asked. "I'll try not
to hang too heavily."

"No, no. The only thing that makes me tired is that I
didn't have sense enough to think of it. Cruising on ahead
there and leaving you to get along on your own hook in the
dark! I don't know what your father will say to me for
getting you into this scrape."

"But you didn't get me into it. I invited myself into your
boat and you couldn't get me out of it. Besides, it has
been a lot of fun."

"Fun!"

"Why, yes. I'm enjoying every minute of it. It is just
what I told you it was—the whole of it—an adventure. Of
course adventures don't mean anything to a life-saver, but
they do to librarians. Now I've got my breath again. Shall
we go?"

They floundered on, but now Calvin was not thinking of
Myra Fuller and the late unpleasantness. How could he, with
this girl clinging to his arm, stumbling occasionally, but never
complaining, treating it all as a joke and making light of
briers and bushes and holes and hummocks? Another half
mile of this and they came over a high dune and down upon

hard, sloping sand. Before them—and close to them—were
the surge and boom and liquid hiss of great waves in tumultuous advance and retreat.

"There!" he exclaimed. "Here is the outer beach. We're
across, thank goodness! Now it will be plainer sailing for
you. Are you tired to death?"

She was breathing quickly, but she could still laugh.

"Of course not," she declared. "Why should I be? What
do you think I am?"

His reply was involuntarily uttered, but it was emphatic.
"You're a good sport," he declared. "I'll say that for you."

The way thereafter was, as he said, almost plain sailing.
The tightly-packed sand uncovered by the ebbing tide was
easy to walk upon and they could really hurry. The fog
was as thick as ever and the darkness as pitchy, but the
exercise and the oilskins kept them warm and the knowledge—on Homer's part, at least—that the anxiety of their
adventure was happily past, brought a care-free sense of
relief much more stimulating than the Myrick coffee. Miss
Bartlett chatted and questioned and, without realizing it, he
began to speak of himself, to tell her of his early life, his
father's death and his boyhood with his mother at Orham.
This led, naturally enough, to his entering the service, and
then to the Setuckit crew and what fine fellows they were.
He told of the life down there, the jokes and gossip, of
Seleucus Gammon and of Mrs. Gammon's unexpected arrival. As he thought it over afterward, it seemed to him
he had told this comparative stranger, this girl, everything
even remotely connected with himself or those associated
with him. But he had not; he had never mentioned his hopes
and disappointment in the matter of the keeper's appointment; nor had he so much as hinted at the existence of
Myra Fuller.

Peleg's lantern had sputtered itself out long before, but they
did not need it now. They passed the lighthouse, its beacon
a yellow smudge high up in the fog an eighth of a mile
from the beach; and the clamorous screech of the foghorn
vibrated against their eardrums. They made a wide circle

where the shore curved inward and began to mount a high dune which, so Homer told her, was only a little way from the station. And, as they climbed, a new sound made itself heard, a whistle and dry rush and rustle quite different from the tumult of the sea.

"Hello!" cried Calvin. "Hear that? That's wind through the grass and bushes. Here comes a good breeze at last. That ought to blow things clear."

It was a true prophecy. The wind met them at the top of the dune, crisp, sharp and piercing. It whipped the light sand against their faces. And, in another minute, the fog had gone. They stepped from wet blackness out into the clear cold of a starlit night. Below them, and only a little way off, was Setuckit Station, its lighted windows agleam.

"Oh, how lovely!" exclaimed Miss Bartlett. "It is—it is like getting home, isn't it?"

"It is home," declared Calvin. "And here's the patrol going out."

The patrolman was Sam Bearse, oilskinned, sou'westered, Coston signal at his belt and lantern in hand. He met them at the foot of the dune and raised the lantern to peer into their faces.

"Why, hello, Cal!" hailed Sam in surprise. "What in time you doin' out here on the beach? We cal'lated you was becalmed off in the bay somewheres. Hez spied you from the tower just after you left Orham and we didn't know but you'd anchored to wait till it blew clear. The old man's havin' a conniption fit. A body'd think you'd never been to sea afore. Of all the fuss—"

Homer hastily interrupted. He explained the situation. Bearse nodded. "I see—yes, yes," he said. "Hez said it looked to him as if you had a passenger aboard. So 'twas the cap'n's daughter, eh? Pleased to meet you, ma'am. Your father'll be glad enough to see you both, I guess likely. So long."

Five minutes more—minutes during which both were silent —they opened the door of the station mess room. The men there, off duty, greeted their associate with a shout and then, seeing his companion, stopped abashed.

"Where's Cap'n Bartlett?" asked Calvin.

He was in his room, they told him.

"In there, through that door," he said. "Go right in, Miss Bartlett."

She did so. They heard a gasp of surprise and then a choking exclamation. The door closed and Homer turned to face the eager questions of his fellow surfmen. His romantic adventure as squire of dames was over, but the talk concerning the unexpected visitor had only begun.

She occupied her father's room that night, as, in fact, she did during the nights to follow, Bartlett sleeping in the spare room on one of the cots. She did not join the crew at their five o'clock breakfast, but she came to the table for the eleven o'clock dinner and that meal was more decorous and orderly in consequence. Not that she "put on airs" or was unduly dignified, but the men themselves were bashful and quiet. She insisted on helping with the cooking—and the results of the latter were apparent and welcome. After the dishwashing she called Homer to one side and announced that she was going to try to make the place look a little more "Christmassy."

"I don't suppose there is a bit of evergreen on this beach, is there?" she asked.

He shook his head. "Not a bit nearer than the Orham woods, so far as I know," he said.

"Oh, why didn't I think to bring some holly or something from Boston? I could have just as well as not. Doesn't *anything* grow around here—anything that stays green all winter, I mean?"

He thought it over. "Well," he said, doubtfully, "seems to me there's a little patch of hog cranberry in the hollow up back of the lighthouse. That might be better than nothing."

"It would be splendid. Now tell me just where to find it."

"Some of the men would be glad to get it for you, I know. I'll ask 'em to."

"Indeed you won't! They are busy and I haven't anything to do. I'll get it myself."

And she did, returning from her quest with an oat sack full of the glistening vines of the wild cranberry.

"Now," she said, this time addressing her remark to Mr. Gammon, who happened to be in the mess room, "I wish I had some of those bayberry plums—or the branches with the plums on them. There must be lots around here."

Seleucus snorted. "Them bayberry balls, you mean?" he queried. "Crimus! if that's all you want I can get you a bushel in no time. Bayberries ain't no more good to nobody than miskeeters and hoptoads; that's why there's so many of all of 'em runnin' wild in these latitudes."

He brought a huge armful of the fragrant bayberry limbs, with their clusters of gray berries. She looped the windows and the lamp brackets with the green vines and tucked the bayberry sprays among them. Seleucus and Ed Bloomer and Ellis Badger watched the decorating and expressed approval.

"There!" vowed Gammon. "Ain't that pretty? Ed, you and me and Ellis never'd thought of that. If anybody'd told me that hog cranberry vines was good for anything but to catch your feet in and trip you and set you to swearin' I'd have laughed at 'em."

"And all I ever cal'lated bayberry balls was for," said Badger, "was to load a young one's blowgun with and shoot around in school when teacher wan't lookin'. You never can tell, can you?"

"Not till you try. I'm standin' here larnin'. Next summer I'm goin' to hang some strings of hoptoads and wood ticks up around and see how *they* look. I'll let you catch 'em for me, Ed."

Mr. Bloomer grunted. "Won't be any trouble to catch the ticks," he declared. "All I'd have to do is cruise a little ways through the beach grass yonder and then brush off my pant laigs."

Hez Rogers had walked up to Myrick's after breakfast and the Jarvis catboat was now at anchor before its owner's shanty. Its cargo of bundles and boxes, and Miss Bartlett's

suit case, was brought ashore. As Sam Bearse said, they
were now "all sot" for Christmas.

"Be our luck though," he added, "to have it blow a howlin'
no'theaster and snow like a busted feather bed by to-morrer
mornin'. 'Member last Christmas, fellers? We spent two
thirds of the day tryin' to haul a three-master off the Sand
Hill. And we had to give her up finally, at that, and be
satisfied to get the crew ashore. We've been luckier this
year, so fur's weather's consarned, than I can remember since
I've been at the station. We'll make up for it by and by;
maybe to-morrer'll be the beginnin'. Course the Gov'ment
signals are set for fair, but they ain't final. Peleg Myrick's
the real thing. Pity old Peleg ain't here so's we could hear
from his port elbow."

Apparently, however, the Myrick joints were in normal
condition and the Government's weather prophets right, for
Christmas day was, although much colder, clear and fine.
After breakfast the various bundles were opened. There
were the presents from home; every man had some, inex-
pensive always, homemade very often; but down there at
Setuckit the value of home or gifts was not judged by price
or quality.

"Look at that!" shouted Rogers, proudly exhibiting a
mysterious casket, gorgeous in crimson and blue silk tufting.
"My Emeline made that all herself, out of a cigar box and
a shirtwaist of her mother's—yes, and a piece of her grandmother's weddin' dress. And only nine year old, too."

"Which is nine year old?" demanded Badger. "Her
grandmother or the weddin' dress?"

"What's your wife doin' with a cigar box?" asked Bearse.
"Gettin' kind of extravagant, ain't she? If I was you I'd
tell her to stick to a pipe and save money. . . . There, there,
Hez, keep your hair on. Can't you take a little foolin'?
It's real kind of cute and pretty, though, ain't it?" examin-
ing the gift, and sniffing at the tufting. "All dolled up with
smell-um-sweet, too. What's it for, Hez?"

The proud parent looked a trifle foolish.

"She got the receipt for makin' it out of a magazine or

somethin'," he explained with a grin. "She says it's for me
to keep my neckties in. Ha, ha! Yes, neckties is what she
says. All right, I'll keep all I've got there, except on liberty
days—then I'll have to wear it."

There was an abundance of this sort of thing; the jokes,
like the presents, were crude and homemade, but nobody
was overcritical. Seleucus was on tower watch that morning,
but had breakfasted at the Jarvis shanty. He returned to
duty looking rather glum and Homer, noticing this, tried
to cheer him up.

"How is Philander this morning?" he asked.

"He's all right again, pretty nigh. Him and—and *her*'ll
be over for dinner."

There was no doubt as to the identity of the "her"; the
gloomy emphasis was unmistakable. Mr. Gammon seemed
inclined to say more, but hesitated.

"What is it?" queried Calvin. "Nobody can hear you
—they're making too much noise. What have you got
on your mind?"

"Say, Cal, look here. You know that crazy bed-com-
forter I won up to the Harniss Odd Fellers' Fair; the one
Cap'n Ozzie took a ten-cent chance for me on?"

"Yes."

"Well, I've had it down here, you know, ever since Olive
fetched it for me. I was cal'latin' to take it home some one
of my liberty days, but I ain't had but one since, and then
I forgot it. So, after Jemimy come, thinks I, 'I'll give it to
her for Christmas.' 'Twas sort of bright and—er—gay,
Cal; I'll leave it to you if 'twan't."

"It was gay, all right. Did your wife like it?"

"Like it!" Seleucus groaned. "Say, Cal, when she found
it 'twas Olive fetched it down she—she— Oh, crimustee!
I *told* her Olive never made it nor give it to me, neither. I
told her I won it in a ten-cent raffle."

"Well, that ought to have settled it, I should say."

"Settled it! She switched round and laid into me for
givin' her a ten-cent present."

"What did she give you?"

"Eh? All she give me was the divil—but I got plenty of that."

Bartlett took his Number One man aside and showed the latter a sweater and a pair of fur-lined gloves which his daughter had brought. He was overflowing with pride.

"She didn't forget the old man, Calvin," he boasted. "Course those gloves are too good for me to use, but I don't tell her so. I'll keep 'em to look at and for goin' ashore. And here's somethin' else she brought. I haven't showed it to anybody and I don't want you to say anything about it. Those men out yonder are wanderin', in darkness, most of 'em, and they wouldn't understand. But you—well, I shouldn't be surprised if the Lord had put his mark on you, boy, and he'll lead you to the fold some day. . . . That's the way I feel about her—Norma. It troubles me sometimes, when I realize that she ain't found salvation yet, and what might happen if she was took away sudden afore she done it. Yet—and yet"—he seemed to be arguing the matter with himself—"I can't think she'd go to hell. Seem's if the Almighty'd make allowances. Don't you think he would?"

Homer stared at him. "What are you talking about?" he exclaimed, in amazement.

"Eh? . . . Oh, nothin', nothin'. Was I sayin' somethin' I hadn't ought to? I—I—humph! I get to thinkin' too hard, I guess. Comes over me by spells, lately, it does, seems so. Well, this is what else she brought me. Look at it, boy."

It was a leather-bound Bible with his name on the cover. He held it in his big hands and patted it reverently.

"I opened it when I was alone in my room just now," he went on, "and what do you suppose 'twas I found? Hadn't been readin' but a little ways afore I come to it. Listen. 'Many daughters have done virtuously, but thou excellest them all.' 'Thou excellest 'em all.' That's what I found, boy. Those are the words He sent to me. And they're right to the point. She does excel 'em all. . . . Amen! Praise the Lord!"

Calvin made no comment. His mind was in a state between pity and foreboding. And yet Benoni's next speech was rational enough.

"She tells me—Norma does," he went on, "that you was mighty kind and accommodatin' to her the other afternoon. She says nobody could have been nicer and more thoughtful than you was, gettin' her down here. She's much obliged and so am I. I tell her that I've come to count on you a whole lot, Calvin. You're straight with me, and—and I ain't so sure about some of the rest of 'em."

The interview ended there, before Homer could ask what he meant. But the concluding sentence was surprising, for it showed a degree of perspicacity which he had not believed his eccentric commander possessed.

The Christmas dinner was an elaborate affair. Its materials had been ordered in Orham and, of course, brought down in the Jarvis catboat with the presents. They—the turkey and canned plum pudding and the rest—were paid for with the contents of the station "kitty." This was a time-honored institution in the service. On the mantel in the mess room stood a battered earthen bean pot. Each pay day every member of the crew—keeper included—put a certain very small percentage of his wage into this pot. Sometimes extra dimes and nickels were added—as, for instance, if some one had had a windfall or happened to be "flush." This accumulation was the kitty and was to be spent to provide the wherewithal for special celebrations, such as Thanksgiving, Washington's Birthday, or Christmas.

Mrs. Gammon and Philander Jarvis joined them at dinner. It was the first time the former had met Norma Bartlett, and her gimlet eyes looked as if they might bore holes in the young woman. Norma and her apparel were scrutinized and itemized from head to foot. If a vote of the rest of the assemblage had been taken it would have been unanimous in the opinion that she was worth any amount of scrutiny. The men's gaze followed her as she bustled about, clear eyed, laughing, self-possessed and unaffected. Ed Bloomer tapped Wallie Oaks on the knee beneath the tablecloth.

"Steady, Wallie, steady," he whispered. "Remember that wife of yours ashore."

Oaks started and grinned sheepishly.

"For thunder sakes, Ed," he whispered in return, "how did old Bologny come to have a girl like that?"

It was the question Calvin Homer had asked himself during the voyage down in the Jarvis catboat—and which, at that moment, he was asking again. It is possible that Seleucus Gammon also was asking it, for he, like the rest, watched Miss Bartlett intently, and then, turning, caught his wife's eye. Jemima, evidently, had been watching him. Seleucus was a large man and he filled his clothes well, but, under the influence of that searching glare, he seemed to shrink into them. As Hezekiah Rogers described it, he "puckered up like a baked apple."

At five o'clock was performed a ceremony which, ordinarily, was a part of the Sunday routine. The keeper was supposed to be the principal performer—Captain Myrick had always filled that position—but, as Benoni Bartlett was a newcomer and unacquainted with the families of his surfmen, Homer had by request taken charge and kept it. He did so now. Standing before the telephone instrument in the living-room wall, he called up, one after the other, the houses of his comrades, in Orham, in South or West Harniss, wherever they might be. Some of the men had no telephones of their own, but these had arranged by letter for some representative of the family to be at the house of a neighbor possessing one, to receive and exchange news and gossip.

Calvin did all the telephoning. The men stood about in an eager circle. They took their turns, according to ranking, and were allowed three minutes each—no more.

"You're next, Hez," announced Homer. "Yes. . . . Is that you, Mrs. Rogers? . . . Yes, he's well and wishes all hands a merry Christmas. . . . No, we haven't been turned out for a week; having an easy time down here just now. . . . Eh? . . . She wants to know how your chilblains are and if you're using the Eureka liniment same as she told you to. . . . Yes, he says they're better and he'll need another bottle pretty soon. . . . Yes, he liked the mittens and they fitted tip-top. . . . He wants to know what's the news? . . . I see. . . . Hez, she says your Willie got into a scrap with the Bearse boy—that's your Ike, Sam—and blacked his eye. She says it was all Ike's fault."

A strenuous protest here from the indignant Mr. Bearse.

"I know a darn sight better. Ikey's as quiet a kid as ever lived. Me and his ma tell him to mind his own business and he does. That young one of yours, Hez, is all the time raisin' hob over in our yard and—"

"Sshh!" this from Homer, at the phone. "Settle that by and by. All right, Mrs. Rogers; I'll tell him what you say. Good-by. . . . Time's up, Hez. . . . Wallie, you're next."

And so on. The after-supper hour was a lively discussion of the telephoned news, spiced with spirited argument between the fathers of the recently-embattled William and Isaac.

Norma was hugely amused by all this. She listened eagerly, her eyes shining. Her father, grave and absent-minded, did not seem to heed, but she was tremendously interested. When she and Calvin happened to be alone for a few moments, she voiced her thought.

"How like children they are, every one of them," she declared. "Just like grown-up boys, that's all. Interested in little childish things, and making so much of them. And yet they are all grown men with families. Isn't it funny—and queer?"

He smiled. "It's funny enough," he admitted. "Sometimes a lot funnier than it was just now. Mrs. Oaks and Josh Phinney's wife got into a row a while ago over a hen that some kid had killed with a sling shot, and Wallie and Josh all but had a mix-up right in the mess room. They didn't speak for ten days and even now it isn't a safe subject to play with. Yes, it's funny, but I don't know that it is so queer. When things do happen around a life-saving station they are big things, but they happen only once in a while. The rest of the time nothing happens and the little things get to look big, that's all. Yes, we are like children. And the longer we stay in the service the more childish we get, I suppose."

She looked at him. "But you are not," she said, with the directness which seemed so essentially a part of her. "You are not childish at all, Mr. Homer. And you aren't like the rest of the men here, either."

"That is because I haven't been here but a year or two. Give me time and I'll develop—backwards."

"I don't know. I don't believe you will. But, at any rate, I am very glad you are here now."

"Why?"

"On father's account. On the way down in the boat you remember I asked if you thought he was worried—if the cares and responsibilities here were troubling him. I can see for myself now, and they are. And I am almost certain that it was a mistake, his accepting the appointment."

There was no "almost" in Calvin's certainty, although he made a pretense of protesting.

"Oh, he's all right," he said. "He'll get along first-rate, I guess."

It was merely a Yankee habit which added the "I guess," but it was an error in addition. Those two words were the ones she pounced upon.

"You guess?" she repeated. "Why do you only guess?" Then, before he could reply, she put out her hand. "Oh, never mind, Mr. Homer," she added. "Of course you didn't mean anything in particular. And please don't think I am going to persecute you with more questions, as I did in that boat. Father is perfectly able to get along as keeper of this station. I never had a doubt of *that*," with a scornful little laugh. "What I started out to say was that I am glad he has a mate like you to relieve him of some of his petty worries. You will help him all you can, won't you?"

"Why—why, I'll do my best, Miss Bartlett."

"He knows you will—and so do I. We are both relying on you, you see. Thank you, Mr. Homer."

She nodded and went away, leaving him in what might

be called a mixed state of mind. It was—yes, it was pleasant to have her say such things, and think them. But they made his position more difficult, and additional difficulties were quite unnecessary. If things went wrong she would blame him. She would think he had failed to give the help he had promised, and he did not wish her to think that. She had said she trusted him. It was quite wonderful—to be selected as a confidant by a girl like Norma Bartlett.

But there was Myra Fuller. She, too, believed in and trusted him. His conscience smote him. Before turning in he wrote Myra a long letter, explaining his forgetfulness in the matter of the ring, and asking her forgiveness. He said nothing concerning their disagreement. That subject he avoided in the letter, but he could not avoid it in his thinking. For both she and Norma were demanding of him loyalty—and a kept faith.

The next morning Josh Phinney should have returned to duty, but he did not. At ten the telephone bell rang and Bloomer answered the call. He chuckled as he hung up the receiver and went to the tower to report to Captain Bartlett. Later he made a more elaborate report to his fellow surfmen.

"Josh just called up," he said. "There's a new Phinney up to his house. A boy—and all hands gettin' along fine. Josh says for us to drink an extry dipperful of water to George Dewey Phinney, that's the young one's name. He'll be down—Josh will—this afternoon. Orrin Hendricks is goin' to drive him down with a horse 'n' team. Say," he added, in a whisper and with a significant wink, "I shouldn't be surprised if Josh had had more'n one dipper of somethin' stronger'n water. He sort of sounded so to me. Hope he don't land here scuppers under. Cal'late old Bologny'd froth up some if he did. Eh?"

As it happened Captain Bartlett and his daughter were not at the station when the missing member returned from his "liberty." The afternoon drill was over and the skipper and his daughter had gone for a walk to the lighthouse. Homer was in the boat room, inspecting some of the gear which he was inclined to think needed replacement. He heard the station dog—"Hard Luck" was the animal's name, and it looked it—barking excitedly, but paid little attention. A few minutes later, however, he heard shouts of laughter in the mess room. Sauntering leisurely in he found a group of surfmen gathered about the stove and firing questions at a man, who, bundled in heavy coat, mittens and sweaters —shore-going togs—was sprawled in a chair, his countenance expressing the most hopeless misery. This was Joshua Phinney. In another chair a person whom Calvin recognized as Orrin Hendricks, an Orham longshoreman, was reclining. Mr. Hendricks, however, was smiling—broadly, even vacuously.

No one noticed Homer's entrance. The crew were enjoying themselves.

"Brace up, Josh," advised Ed Bloomer. "It might be worse, you know."

"If you're goin' to cry, Josh," observed Sam Bearse, "let me fetch the slop bucket to catch the tears. No use splashin' up the clean floor. Look at Orrin. He ain't cryin', be you, Orrin?"

Mr. Hendricks, thus appealed to, declared that he wasn't crying by a considerable sight. To prove it he burst into song. He stridently advised his audience to "Drop the anchor, furl the sail. We are safe within the—within th' jail.ﹳ Haw, haw! Thash good one, ain't it? Eh, Cal? That's stuff, ain't it? Merry Chris'mas 'n' 'appy New Year. Let 'er go!"

Bearse, Bloomer and the others, thus apprised of the presence of their Number One man, looked somewhat abashed and a trifle apprehensive. Hendricks favored the company with another selection. This time his choice was "After the Ball."

Homer turned to Gammon, who was grinning in the doorway.

"When did they get here?" he asked.

"Few minutes ago. Come in Orrin's hors' 'n' buggy. It's outside here now."

"All right. Put Orrin aboard the buggy and one of you drive him down as far as the Orham Station. Seleucus, you do it. Then turn him over to the men there and let them get him home. Hurry up! Lively!"

Seleucus looked peeved. "And then I'll have to hoof it all the way back, I presume likely?" he said.

"Yes."

"Well, say, Cal—"

"You can say it afterwards. Do you want Cap'n Bartlett to see 'em here—like this?"

Seleucus was stirred to instant life.

"You're dead right, I don't," he declared. "Come on, Orrin; come on. You can do the rest of your Moody and Sankyin' outside. Nobody'll have to hear you there but me and the gulls. And the gulls ain't particular. Come on!"

He pulled the protesting vocalist to his feet and piloted those feet to the door. Homer crossed to where Phinney was sitting and laid a hand on his shoulder.

"You better turn in, Josh," he ordered. "The skipper 'll be back pretty soon and he'd better not see you."

To his surprise Mr. Phinney burst into tears. He sobbed bitterly.

"What's the matter with you?" demanded Calvin. "Stop that crying. Stop it."

But Josh did not stop. He lifted up his voice and wept.

"You—you don't know's what's—whash happened up to my house," he sobbed.

Calvin remembered the important event which had called the man home. His tone changed.

"Why, what is it, Josh?" he asked sympathetically. "The baby isn't—nothin's happened to the new baby?"

The tears flowed down the Phinney cheeks, but the Phinney head was shaken.

"Baby's all right," said Josh. "Baby's fine. George Dewey —thash name. Little Georgie Dewey Phinney. Poor little kid!"

"*Poor* little—! Why, what— Is your wife—?"

"My wife's fine. She's fine woman. *She's* all right. But —oh dear!"

Homer's apprehensions were relieved, but his patience was wearing.

"What are you crying about?" he demanded sharply.

Josh raised his head. Then he gave utterance to a remark which was destined to be added to the list of Setuckit Station jokes and to go down in history.

"I—I cal'late you'd cry if—if your mother-in-law had— had burned her foot with a flatiron," he wailed.

Even Calvin was obliged to join in the hilarious howl which greeted this touching disclosure. But he was the first to recover.

"Get him to bed," he commanded. "And hurry up. Keep him quiet there, if you can, and he'll feel better in the morning. . . . And, look here," he added gravely, "don't say anything about this. If Cap'n Bartlett hears of it—well, you know how he feels about drinking."

The grief-stricken son-in-law of a scorched parent was dragged up to the sleeping quarters. When the Bartletts returned all was quiet. Calvin reported that Phinney had come back, but that he was pretty well used up and, under orders, had turned in.

"They've got a new baby up there," he added, "and Josh is tired out, I guess."

The explanation was accepted as satisfactory and Homer was relieved. Phinney, when on duty, was a first-class surf-man—his lapses from rectitude were few—and Calvin did not care to have him get into trouble. It looked as if that trouble had been avoided.

But, later on that evening, Wallie Oaks touched his arm, winked, and asked him to step outside for a moment.

"Say, Cal," he whispered, "you know what's happened this afternoon, don't you? About Josh and Orrin, I mean?"

"Happened? They were both drunk; I know that."

"Um-hum. Sure! But that ain't the whole of it. They

fetched down a jug along with 'em. It's hid around here somewheres, too."

Homer turned on him. "How do you know?" he asked, sharply.

"Sshh! Don't talk so loud. I wouldn't want none of 'em to know I was tellin' you. I didn't see the jug myself, but I smelled whisky on Hez Rogers's breath when he went out on patrol just now, and I've seen him and Ed and the rest of 'em whisperin' and laughin' together. They never told *me*—they've got a grudge against me, anyhow—but I tumbled all right, and I thought you ought to know about it. Only," anxiously, "don't let 'em know I give the thing away, will you?"

Calvin hesitated. This was not entirely unexpected. Smuggling liquor to the life-saving stations was done occasionally. Not that the men were drunkards, far from it, but liquor was strictly forbidden—therefore, obtaining it was in the nature of a lark. It was one more instance of the schoolboy's delight in outwitting his teacher, that was all. But the situation must be handled with diplomacy, as the clever teacher handles mischief in the schoolroom. Over-severity would be a fatal mistake. And Benoni Bartlett was a fanatic.

Wallie whispered again.

"You'll tell the cap'n, won't you, Cal?" he asked.

In his eagerness he clutched his companion's arm. Homer shook him off.

"No, I shan't tell him," he said, emphatically. "And don't you do it, either. You keep your mouth shut; do you understand? I'll attend to this thing myself."

Wallie's disappointment was obvious.

"Why, see here, Cal," he protested, "one of the very things Bologny—Cap'n Bartlett, I mean—said when he took this job was that he wouldn't stand for any rum drinkin'! If he knew—"

"He mustn't know. There is no need of his knowing. I'll see there is no more drinking. But as for you, Wallie, you keep still. If the men knew you were telling tales they would—well, it wouldn't help that grudge you were talking about."

"But—but, Cal—good Lord! you ain't goin' to give me away, are you?"

"Not if you keep quiet."

CHAPTER VIII

PHINNEY came to breakfast with the rest. His appetite was far from robust and his spirits were still low. There was a general atmosphere of the "morning after" surrounding him, but he made no reference to the accident which had befallen his wife's mother and Homer was certain that Bartlett would notice nothing unusual in his manner. So far the situation was satisfactory. It remained to be seen, however, what might develop later on. If Oaks's suspicions concerning the jug were founded on fact, developments were to be expected.

The first symptoms of these developments appeared before the forenoon was over. The weather was thick and threatening, so beach patrol was necessary. The spirits of certain members of the crew were unusually high. The skylarking in the mess room became so noisy that Norma remarked it. She was quite unsuspecting.

"They are full of fun this morning, aren't they, Mr. Homer?" she observed. "They were making such a racket just now that father said he was going to tell them to stop; but I wouldn't let him do it. Rogers and Bloomer were teasing Walter Oaks, plaguing him about something he said when you were all off at some wreck or other. Something about his wife. They were shouting so that I couldn't help hearing it. They're boys, just as I've said so many times, but they are more boylike than ever to-day, it seems to me."

Calvin made some sort of excuse for leaving her and went to investigate. Outside, at the rear of the station, he found the two she had mentioned. Badger was there also, an interested spectator. Wallie Oaks, a sullen expression on his face, was backed against the wall, while Hez and Ed were putting him through some sort of exercise.

"Hello there, Cal!" hailed Bloomer. "You're just in time.

It's Wallie's birthday and he's goin' to sing a song for us.
He's goin' to sing 'Nancy Lee.' It's one of his pet songs,
all about his wife ashore.

> " 'And there she stands
> And waves her hands,
> And waits for me—'

Come on, Wallie, now! Go to it! We'll all join in the
chorus."

Oaks puffed sullenly at his pipe. Rogers, a broad grin
on his face, slapped his big hands together.

"Go on, Wal," he ordered. "If you won't sing, then Ed
and I'll walk you Spanish three times around the station. A
man's got to either sing or dance on his birthday. Maybe
Ed and I can't make you sing, but we can make you dance—
and step high, too; eh, Ed? Ho, ho!"

Oaks took his pipe from his mouth. "You lay a hand on
me and you'll wish you hadn't, Hez Rogers," he threatened.
"I can stand foolin' all right, but enough of it's enough. Especially when—"

The remainder of the sentence was an inarticulate mutter.

"Eh? What's the last of that?" demanded Bloomer.
"Say it out loud."

"I'll say it when I get good and ready. And maybe I'll
say it—"

Homer broke in.

"That'll do, Wallie," he snapped. "No, you keep still.
Look here, Hez, you and Ed and Ellis are making more noise
than a camp meeting; did you know it? You'll have the
skipper out after you, first thing you know."

Rogers laughed.

"Let him come," he proclaimed. "We ain't scared of any
Crooked Hill heroes, I guess. Let him come! Maybe he'll
sing a hymn tune for us, after Wallie gets through. Ho, ho!
Good idea; ain't that so, Ed?"

Bloomer joined in the laugh. "Sure thing," he agreed.
"What are you buttin' in for, Cal? You ain't skipper nowa-

days, worse luck. And *you* ain't playin' up to old Bologny
—after the mean trick he worked on you!"

Calvin smiled. "I'm not playing up to anybody and you
know it, Ed," he said. "But we've got a visitor down here.
You don't want her to think we're a gang of rough-necks, do
you? She says you are the finest crew she ever saw.
You've made a hit with her, boys."

Hez grinned. "Say, she's a peach, that girl, even if she
is old Bible-back's daughter," he announced. "We're the
finest crew afloat, eh? Good for her! Good judgment, that
is, and I can lick any man that says we ain't. *You* say we
ain't, will you, Wallie?"

"She won't think so if you start a fight with her father.
If you've got to raise a ruction this morning why not raise
it where she can't hear you? Take your racket somewhere
else."

Badger offered a suggestion. "I tell you what let's do,
boys," he said. "Seleucus is over to the shanty cleanin' fish
for Jemimy's dinner. Let's go over and start him and her
goin'. We'll tell her Seleucus is dead gone on this Bartlett
girl, follers her around like a dog. That ought to raise one
or two sprouts—eh?"

The idea was received with delight. Oaks was forgotten.
"But where's Josh?" asked Hez. "He'll want to be in on
this. Oh, Josh!"

From the door of the stable Phinney himself made answer.
His morning-after depression had mysteriously disappeared.
He appeared to be in high good humor.

"Here I be, fellers," he answered. "Ahh. . . ! I feel
better. . . . Where you bound? I'm with you, wherever
'tis."

He concluded with another "A-ah," expressive, apparently,
of complete satisfaction. Also he smacked his lips. Bloomer
and Rogers explained matters in concert. The trio, accompanied by Badger, moved noisily away in the direction of
the Jarvis shanty. Oaks and Homer were left alone.

"Wallie," said Calvin, "you go on patrol as soon as Bearse
comes off. You'd better go now and get ready. It's my

tower watch. The skipper's up there now, but I'll relieve him in a minute."

Oaks turned toward the door of the station. He was still gloomy and morose.

"I'll stand this kind of thing from those fellers about so far and no farther," he muttered. "I'm gettin' sick of it. You know what's the matter with that gang, don't you, Cal? You know what I told you last night?"

Homer did not answer. As soon as he was alone, however, he walked briskly to the stable, entered, and closed the door carefully behind him. Port and Starboard turned their heads to regard him over the sides of their stalls, and "Slabsides," one of the station cats, in the barn on a mouse hunt, came running to rub against his legs. He and Slabsides were great friends, but just now the latter was not treated to his customary petting. Calvin, too, was on a hunt, and he must locate his prey quickly, if he hoped to do so unobserved.

He sniffed the air in the dark, shut-up stable. There were the usual smells, of course—horse, hay and leather. But— unless his imagination was affecting his nostrils—there was also a faint suspicion of another fragrance, an odor which he had noticed while in conversation with Bloomer and Rogers, and in particular when Josh Phinney passed him as he came out of that barn a minute or two before. He sniffed again. Then he began a systematic search of the lower floor. The mow, according to his experience, was as likely a place as any, but he would try the lower floor first.

The mangers, under the horses' noses, were empty except for the rations of hay which should be there. Leaving them he walked over and threw up the lid of the oat bin. The moment he lifted that lid he knew he had found the hiding place. That bin was redolent less of oats than of rye. His fingers, burrowing amid the grain, encountered a smooth, rounded surface. He dragged from the bin a gallon jug, the contents of which gurgled liquidly.

He thrust the jug beneath his coat, lowered the lid of the bin, and walked to the door, Slabsides galloping playfully before him. His idea was to go somewhere among the dunes at the rear of the barn, pour out the whisky, and then bury the empty jug in the sand. But as he stepped across the threshold he realized that this ceremony must be postponed. Not only was Sam Bearse returning from patrol, approaching the station, but Norma Bartlett was standing by the back door and had seen him. Moreover, she was already walking in his direction.

The morning was raw and damp and, when he left the station, he had hurriedly donned a long oilskin slicker— one which he had borrowed from Philander Jarvis's store in the catboat's cabin and which had not yet been returned. It was hanging by the kitchen door and he had taken it because it was more convenient than his own heavy coat, which was in the sleeping quarters. Now he blessed the luck which had prompted the action. A gallon jug is hard to conceal, but the skirts of a long slicker hide it as well as any garment can.

Nevertheless, a jug doesn't hide itself and it requires support. To cling to the handle beneath one's coat and appear unconscious and casual while carrying on a conversation with a young woman is no easy task. Also, the jug was bulky and, although the slicker was large, Calvin was conscious of a manifest bulge of the garment in its vicinity.

Miss Bartlett, however, did not seem to notice the bulge. Nor, at first, did she appear aware that Homer was ill at ease. She walked briskly to meet him. She was wearing her father's pea jacket, which enveloped her from chin to knees, and above its turned-up collar her hair tossed in the wind, for she was bareheaded. Already the sea air and breeze had replaced the city pallor with a light coat of tan. Her cheeks were crimson and her eyes bright.

"Where are the men?" she asked. "It was so quiet, all at once, that I came out to see what had happened. I hope you didn't take too seriously what I said about their being so noisy. I didn't mind a bit, really. You didn't send them away on my account, did you?"

He shook his head. "No—oh, no," he replied uneasily. "I believe they've gone over to the Jarvises' to see Seleucus. . . . It—it's a nice day, isn't it?"

She laughed. "Is it?" she repeated. "It doesn't seem so very nice to me. Almost as if it were going to rain—or snow. And father has just hoisted the weather signals and they forecast high winds and a storm of some kind. But I suppose Mr. Myrick might give us a real prophecy if he were here. I hope I shall see him again, before I go. He is lots of fun."

Homer agreed, absent-mindedly. The jug was occupying his thoughts.

"And you can't think the weather so very good," she went on. "You are wearing your oilskins. Where have you been?"

"Oh, just—just out to the barn, that's all. To—to see the horses."

"Is it your turn to do that? I understood father to say Mr. Bloomer was stable man this week. But I suppose you, as Number One, have to keep a sort of general eye on everything."

"Yes—er—sort of. Er—going for a walk, were you?"

"No, I just came out, as I said, to see why it was so quiet all at once. . . . What is the matter, Mr. Homer? Has anything gone wrong?"

"Wrong? No, no. Nothing is wrong. Why—what made you ask that?"

"There is nothing wrong with the crew? No trouble of any kind?"

"Trouble? What sort of trouble could there be? Everything is all right. Where is your father?"

"He is in the tower with Walter Oaks."

"Eh? With Wallie? What is Wallie doing there? He ought to be starting on patrol."

"He is going to, I believe. He is dressed for it. But he went up to see father. Said he wanted to see him about something. . . . Are you sure everything is all right, Mr. Homer?"

"Eh? Yes—yes, Miss Bartlett. I'm sure. Yes, indeed."

"Have you hurt your arm? Why do you hold it that way?"

"Eh . . . ? Oh, that's all right. I—er—well, I must be going. It's my watch in the tower."

He walked hastily away. With every step a musical "swash" sounded from beneath the skirt of the slicker. As he turned to enter the station he looked back; she was watching him intently. He felt remarkably like a fool and was quite sure that he must look like one.

He went directly to the crew's quarters—fortunately there was no one else there—for Bearse was warming his hands by the kitchen stove—and, turning back the blankets of his cot, hid the whisky jug beneath them. Then he hastened up to the tower. He met Oaks on the stairs.

"What are you doing up here, Wallie?" he asked, suspiciously. "You're late for patrol, did you know it?"

Oaks scowled. "I don't know's that's any of your business," he said. "You ain't skipper no more, are you?"

Calvin ignored the question. "What are you chasing the cap'n for?" he demanded.

Wallie stopped. "Who said I was chasin' him?" he blurted. "Who said—"

"Miss Bartlett said you told her there was something you wanted to see him about. Look here, Wallie; you remember what I told you about keeping your mouth shut? It was mighty good advice, if I did give it."

The other's face flushed. "I ain't sayin' 'twasn't, am I?" he protested. "I went up to ask Cap'n Bartlett if I couldn't have an extry day off next week. That's all, if you must know."

Bartlett, when Homer reached the tower room, had almost nothing to say to his mate. He seemed, so the latter thought, gloomy and morose, and, a few minutes later, went below.

Rogers returned from the Jarvis cottage a short time afterward and visited Calvin in the tower. It was his week

as cook, so he had left Bloomer, Badger and Phinney and
come back to get dinner. He was full of chuckles.

"They're raisin' heigho over there, them fellers," he declared. "Stringin' Seleucus about this Bartlett girl. You
recollect Norma's readin' that piece out of last week's *Globe*
about the seagull—piece of poetry 'twas? Um-hum. Well,
Josh he sort of hinted that she was readin' it to Seleucus
especial, and that set Jemimy goin'. She wanted to know
if that was all Seleucus had to do in his spare time, set
around and read poetry with women. Well—you know
Seleucus—he got all het up and laid into Josh, and course
that only made things worse so far as his wife's concerned.
How any sane critter can be jealous about a homely old
pickle tub like Seleucus mercy only knows; but Jemimy *ain't*
sane—she's crazy as a loon on them subjects. If *I* was
married to her I'd straighten her out with a tholepin; but
Seleucus he just sets and takes it. And he's big enough to
eat a shrimp like her for breakfast, at that. Only if he did
I cal'late she'd pison him."

"You'd better get down to your cooking, hadn't you,
Hez?" suggested Homer.

"Yes, I cal'late likely I had, but there ain't any rush—not
to-day. I've got a second steward, did you know it?
Norma's making turkey soup out of the Christmas left-
overs. Yes, and she's makin' a sugar cake for us, too. What
do you think of that? We'll live high while she's around,
won't we, Cal? Well, I guess I'll go down and give her a
hand. Ain't a bad job, standin' close alongside of that kind
of steward. I wouldn't mind signin' up for a consider'ble
cruise with a pippin like her. Eh? What do *you* say,
Cal?"

Calvin looked at him. "If I were you, Hez," he observed,
"I wouldn't stand too close to her just now."

"Why not?"

"Because she might notice that you'd been taking something besides coffee."

Rogers's hand moved involuntarily to his lips.

"Sho!" he muttered. "Humph! I'll have to chew a stick

of cinnamon or somethin'. Wouldn't want old Bologny to get on. Say, Cal, how'd you tumble? Josh tell you?"

"Nobody needed to tell me. Stuff like that advertises itself. Don't forget that cinnamon, Hez."

The turkey soup and cake received high praise, but Homer had little appetite. He was awaiting the explosion which he believed was in the air. Benoni Bartlett's behavior was what troubled him most. The skipper was silent and frowning all through the meal. Calvin, remembering Oaks's conference with Bartlett and, putting two and two together, was fearful. There was the incriminating evidence hidden in his bed. He must get rid of it somehow, but opportunities for doing so before nightfall and unobserved were likely to be few. Bartlett, bigoted and fanatical, might do almost anything. His standing with the crew was precarious enough already. If he made a mistake now—if, by some ill-advised action, he changed the men's prejudice to active enmity—then the situation at Setuckit Station would become serious indeed.

For himself, Homer cared little. Nothing that could happen to him was worth consideration. If the worst did happen and the whisky was discovered where he had hidden it, he made up his mind to say nothing and take the consequences. Later he could tell Kellogg the truth and the superintendent, a wise man of long experience, would understand. But the fat would be in the fire, so far as Bartlett's relationship with the crew was concerned. That relationship would become impossible. A life-saving crew that hated its captain could and would—for similar experiences at other stations were matters of service gossip—make the latter's life miserable and, more than all, absolutely wreck the efficiency of the outfit. Tact, tact, and more tact—that was what was required. And Benoni Bartlett, so Calvin Homer believed, possessed no tact whatever. And there was his daughter! *She* would not understand.

The dinner ended without any untoward happenings, but within an hour the trouble came. It was the afternoon set apart by regulation for beach drill, but the keeper gave no

orders to that effect. Instead he left the table and went
away, apparently to the boat room. The surfmen, those off
duty, lounged in the mess room or went outside. Calvin,
anxious and apprehensive, joined the outside group a little
later. Rogers, Bloomer and Phinney were standing near the
back door, whispering excitedly. The whispering ceased
when he appeared. Bloomer turned to him.

"Say, Cal," he queried, "what's the old man doin' out in
the barn?"

Homer looked at him. "Out in the barn?" he repeated,
with as casual an appearance of unconcern as he could mus-
ter. "I don't know. Is he there?"

"Yes. Come out of the front door a few minutes ago
and went straight to the barn. I sung out to him, but he
never answered. What's he up to, anyway?"

"Give it up. Looking things over, I suppose. What
of it?"

"Nothin'. Only what set him—"

He was interrupted. Ellis Badger came hurrying to join
the group.

"Say, boys," he whispered, excitedly, ignoring Calvin altogether, "he's pawin' around in there like a dog chasin' rats.
He's been to the bin."

His comrades stared at him, then at each other. Phinney
spoke.

"To the bin!" he exclaimed. "He has . . . ? Well?"

"That's the funny part of it," went on Badger. "I peeked
in through the side window just as he lifted up the lid. I
see him, with his head and shoulders down inside that bin
for much as five minutes. He took time enough to count
the oats, seemed so to me. And then he just slammed down
the cover again. That's all there was to it."

His comrades continued to stare. "What do you mean—
that's all?" demanded Rogers.

"I mean just that. He never found nothin', or, if he did,
he— Eh? Oh, hello, Cal! Well, what of it, Hez? Cal's
all right; he's no tattletale. Anyhow, Bologny never found
anything. I saw his face when he slammed down that cover

and 'twas sour as last week's milk. He was huntin' and he didn't strike ile, I'll bet on it. He's up in the mow now. Huntin' there, I presume likely."

Bloomer turned to Phinney. "You was the last one in that barn, wasn't you, Josh?" he asked. "Nobody's been there since dinner?"

Josh shook his head. "Nobody that I know of," he declared. "Seleucus came over from his shanty with you and me and Ellis; and, anyhow, he didn't know anything about —we didn't tell him. He relieved you up in the tower, didn't he, Cal?"

Homer nodded.

"Um-hum," grunted Josh. "I thought so; he's up there now. And Sam's inside smokin'; you can see him. And we didn't tell him yet, either. And Wallie— Eh? Where's Wallie?"

Calvin answered. "He is out on patrol," he said. "It's time he was back. You go out next, don't you, Ellis?"

They paid no heed to the question. Phinney was frowning.

"Wallie was on, I guess likely," he observed thoughtfully. "He as much as said so when we was guyin' him a spell ago. And he's always playin' up to the old man, makin' out to us that he ain't got any use for him, but playin' pet dog to him every chance he gets. Say! you don't suppose Wallie—"

Again Homer cut in. It seemed to him high time.

"What are you fellows talking about?" he asked. "Wallie went on patrol just after you went across to Philander's. And he hasn't got back yet. What is all this, anyway?"

Bloomer laughed, sheepishly. "Oh, nothin', Cal," he answered. "Just a little joke, that's all. Tell you some time. Josh, if it wan't Wallie, then who was it? The only one left is Cal here, and *he* didn't know. And Norma—where's she?"

"She's readin' a book in the keeper's room. Sshh here's Bologny. He looks like heavy weather, don't he? Be innocent. All hands."

Bartlett, his hands in his coat pockets, came striding from the barn. His brows were drawn together and his jaw, beneath the beard, was set. He stopped before the group. "Well, Cap'n," observed Rogers cheerfully. "Be gettin' ready for drill pretty soon, I presume likely, won't we?"

The skipper grunted. "Come inside, all hands of you," he ordered. "I've got a word to say."

They followed him into the station. As they did so, Oaks appeared returning from patrol. He joined them in the mess room. Bearse was already there. Seleucus was in the tower, but Bartlett called him down. The men stood or sat. Their captain paced the floor a moment, then he swung about and faced them. He was tugging at his beard and in his eyes was that peculiar glitter which Homer had seen there before when the man was excited.

"Look here," he began, suddenly. "Look here, you. When I first came here to this station, when I took this job, Cap'n Kellogg asked me to say a word and I did it. You was here, all hands of you, and you heard me. You recollect I said I'd act square with you and I expected you to act square by me? That's what I said and I told you that, with the help of the Lord A'mighty, we'd get along together. You heard me say that, didn't you?"

No one answered.

"Eh? Didn't you?" he repeated, raising his voice.

Still no answer. Calvin, glancing at his companions, saw the look of puzzled bewilderment on the faces of Bearse and Gammon, the pair not in the secret. Phinney, Bloomer and Badger were, according to instructions, pictures of bland innocence. Wallie Oaks was the most interesting study. Unless Calvin was very much mistaken, Wallie was frightened.

"Why don't you say somethin'?" demanded Bartlett, almost in a shout. "You heard me say that about actin' square, didn't you?"

Seleucus grinned. "I did, for one," he observed. "I can hear you now, too. You don't need to holler."

The door of the skipper's room opened and Norma came

out. She looked at the men, then at her father, and, coming over, put her hand on his arm.

"Why, father!" she exclaimed. "What is it? What is the matter?"

Bartlett looked at her. Then he shook his arm free.

"Never mind," he growled. "I don't want you to bother me now. I'm talkin' to the crew."

"But, father, what is it?"

"Sshh! Let me alone. I know what it is—and so do they. You—you men—you heard me say that one thing I wouldn't stand for was rum drinkin'. I said I wouldn't have rum around this station. I meant it. Rum is the devil's work. I tell you I know it. I've seen it. I tell you—"

"Father—father! Don't shout so. They hear you."

"They're goin' to hear me. I know somebody has brought liquor down here. I tell you I know it. There's been rum drunk here—to-day. And there's some of it hid somewheres, I ain't found it yet, but I will find it. And I'll find out who brought it and who hid it. I—I—"

He paused, choking and inarticulate, his clenched fists shaking. His daughter again put her hand on his shoulder.

"Father—please don't!" she begged. She looked at the faces of the crew. Her gaze met Calvin's and rested there. There was appeal in the look. He had not meant to speak, but he found himself doing so.

"Cap'n Bartlett," he said, quietly, "don't get excited. Tell us about it. What makes you think—"

Benoni interrupted. "Think!" he shouted. "There's no thinkin' about it. I *know.* I know rum was brought here and I can guess who brought it. I don't know where it is now, but I know where 'twas. 'Twas in the grain box out yonder in the barn. I smelt it. That bin is rank with it. Don't tell me I was mistaken. I know the smell of the devil-ish stuff too well. Too well I know it. When I was a young man, afore I found salvation, I—I—'It biteth like a sarpent and stingeth like an adder.' I won't have it here. I—"

"There, there, father! Hush, hush, you'll make yourself

sick. You frighten me. Please, for my sake. . . ! That's
better. Now tell them quietly."

Bartlett's fist opened. He drew his hand across his forehead.

"Well—well, all right, Norma," he said. "I—I didn't
mean to let the thing run away with me so. And—and I
didn't want you to know about it; I knew 'twould plague
you. Now, you men, listen to me. I won't have liquor
here. I won't have it. I'm a just man—I am—but I won't
stand that. No, and I ain't through with this either. I've
only begun. Somebody took that bottle, or jug, or whatever 'twas, out of that bin and hid it somewheres else. I'll
find it, though. I will if I have to hunt through every man's
kit—every one. And the man that's got it had better look
out, that's all. He better look out. I— Oh, all right,
Norma. What made you mix up in this. . . ? All right,
I'm through for now. But," with an ominous scowl in the
direction of the others, "I ain't through with the man who
fetches rum to this station—or drinks it after it gets here.
I ain't through with him. And I'll find where it's hid. . . .
Now go back to duty. We'll turn out for drill in five minutes."

He drew his hand across his forehead once more and
turned away. His daughter put her arm about him.

"Come in here, into my room, father," she said gently.
"You must rest. And I want to talk to you."

The men looked at each other. Homer led the way to the
back door and the others followed. Once outside, feelings
were expressed, and with fluent emphasis.

"Gosh!" exclaimed Bearse, with contemptuous disgust.
"That was a pretty piece of play actin', wan't it? What the
blue blazes does he mean talkin' to us like that! Say, I'll
tell you one thing; the man that starts overhaulin' *my* kit
is goin' to wake up on the floor with a black eye—no matter
who he is, keeper or not."

"Crimus!" snorted Seleucus. "Don't call *him* a keeper
of no life-savin' station. He's a Sunday-school teacher, and
a loony one at that. Well, I told you he looked like a damn

fool when he come here. Eh? Now didn't I? Crimustee!"

Homer put in a word. "He's cracked on temperance, boys," he observed. "But we knew that before. Now let's take it easy and pay no attention. He'll get over it. He isn't going to search anybody's kit. Besides, his daughter is here, and we don't want a row to spoil her vacation. She's going to-morrow. Think of that cake she made for dinner —and be thankful."

Oaks spoke next.

"Anyhow," he protested, eagerly, "what's he mean by sayin' there's rum hid around the station? *I* ain't heard of none. There ain't any, is there?"

Ed Bloomer's laugh was not entirely humorous. "Maybe that ain't the main question, Wallie," he said. "The thing some of us want to know is who told the skipper there was."

Drill passed without unusual incident. Bartlett conducted it in businesslike fashion. He seemed nervous and shaken —and, or so Homer fancied—rather abashed and self-conscious. Nothing further was said by him during that afternoon or evening in reference to the liquor or his outburst concerning it. But heavily upon Calvin's mind weighed the thought of the jug hidden in his cot. He must get that away, out of the station and out of sight—and soon.

He turned in with the rest of the crew—except those on duty in the tower or on patrol—at ten o'clock. He lay there wide awake, his feet touching the jug, until eleven. Then, certain that his comrades were asleep, he cautiously rose, partially dressed, slipped on the Jarvis slicker once more, and tiptoed downstairs, through the mess room and out at the back door. The jug was clutched tightly in his hand.

Outside, in the raw cold of the winter night, he breathed easier and walked faster. Behind a dune he dug a hole in the sand and, after pouring out the whisky, put the jug in the hole and covered it carefully. Then he walked back to the station. That source of trouble was dead—and buried.

But his self-congratulation was short lived. He was tiptoeing cautiously through the mess room, past the door of the skipper's room—his daughter's room now—when that door opened. Miss Bartlett herself came out. She was fully dressed. Apparently she had not been in bed at all.

He looked at her and she looked at him. He wanted very much to say something, but he did not know what to say. She spoke first.

"Well, Mr. Homer?" she asked, coldly.

"Why—why, Miss Bartlett!" he stammered, inanely. "Are you—are you up?"

"Yes. And so are you. Why?"

"Why—why, I just—I was—"

She motioned toward a chair. "Would you mind sitting down a minute?" she went on. "I want to talk with you. I have been waiting for you. I saw you when you went out."

He hesitated, and then sat down by the table. She sat opposite him.

"I saw you when you went out," she repeated. "I expected to see you. Mr. Homer, I think you and I ought to have a plain understanding. I know what you have been doing—or I can guess."

"You—er—I don't know what you mean."

"Of course you do," impatiently. "You know exactly what I mean. You have been getting rid of that whisky that father is so excited about. And you were the one who took it out of the grain bin. You had it under your coat when I met you coming from the barn this afternoon. . . . Oh, don't deny it, please! I'm not quite an imbecile. I knew then that you were hiding something. When you walked I could hear it. And I didn't need to hear; your face was enough. You looked—but there! we won't waste time arguing over a certainty. I want to hear your explanation—if you have one."

Her tone was coldly sarcastic, and it was a mistake. It helped him to recover from his surprise and chagrin; also it aroused his resentment. After all, why should he answer her questions? And he had done nothing of which to be ashamed.

"I don't know that there is any explanation," he said. "If there is, I—well, why should I make it to you?"

Her eyes flashed. "Why should you make it to me?" she repeated. "Because you owe it to me. I am Captain Bartlett's daughter."

"But you aren't Cap'n Bartlett. If he asks me I shall tell him—perhaps. Or perhaps not. I'm not sure of even that."

She rose and stood facing him. "Indeed!" she exclaimed, scornfully. "I see. You might tell father—perhaps! But you *didn't* tell him. You knew how he felt about—about such things. And how nervous and—and broken he is just now. You knew all this, and yet, instead of helping him, you—you help the *sneaks* that are working against him. Oh, they are! Do you think he doesn't know it? Do you think *I* haven't seen it since I have been here? How some of them hate him—and are jealous of him—and— Oh, it is wicked! Wicked!"

He was silent. She looked down at him, her fiery indignation flaming in her cheeks.

"And he trusts you. You know that. He has told you so, and he has told me. Yes, and I told you that very thing; how he liked you and believed in you. And I trusted you, too. I was going away from here to-morrow believing that, at least, father and I had one loyal friend whom we could count on. You promised me you would help him all you could. You promised—oh, but you are like the rest! You are worse, because you know more than they do. You are different altogether—or I thought you were. And yet, all the time, while you were pretending to him and to me, you have been— Oh, I'm ashamed! I am ashamed of you. But I'm more ashamed of myself for believing in you. . . . There! We have had our understanding. That is all that is necessary. It is quite sufficient."

It might be sufficient for her, but it was not for him. She had turned her back upon him and was on the way to her room, but he sprang after her and caught her arm.

"Miss Bartlett," he said.

She tried to free herself. "Let me be," she commanded.

"No, I won't—not yet."

She tried again to shake off his grip, but he merely tightened it.

"You hurt me," she cried. "Let me be. I shall call father."

"All right, call him. I'm perfectly willing he should hear what I've got to say. But if I were you I should hear it myself first. After that, if you still want to, you may call him and welcome. Now come back here and sit down, please."

She hesitated. She was almost in tears, but, inexperienced with the sex as he was, he did not make the mistake of thinking them tears of grief. Then she drew herself erect.

"Very well," she said icily. "If you will take your hand away I will sit down and listen. I suppose I shall have to. But I shall never speak to you again as long as I live."

"All right. At any rate, I'll do the speaking for a while. All you need do is listen. . . . Now then: Miss Bartlett, I suppose you think, because you caught me with that whisky jug this afternoon and to-night, that I brought the stuff down here and am responsible for the drinking and for your father's trouble with the crew. Well, I'm not."

She kept her word, so far as speaking was concerned. He might have been on a different planet if entire indifference to his existence could be offered as evidence. But he went doggedly on. Mentioning no names, he told of his suspicions concerning the drinking and the liquor smuggling, of his finding the jug, of the recent internment behind the dune. Also he told why he had acted as he did.

"I didn't intend that your father should know anything about it," he said. "I didn't tell him for two or three reasons. One of them is that I knew what a—well, what prejudices he had against drinking, and that, if he found it out, he was likely to act and speak as he did this afternoon. That performance of his was about the worst mistake he could have made—with this kind of a crew. *About* the worst; the very worst would have been to start overhauling their chests and kits as he talked of doing. I was trying to save him—yes, and you—from going on the rocks. Another thing was the crew themselves. They're good fellows; there isn't another bunch alongshore that can match them when it comes to doing the jobs they're put here for. But they have to be handled carefully. They aren't drunkards—not a bit of it. So far as I know there isn't one who really cares a red cent for whisky. But, as you yourself have said a half-dozen times, they are like kids in some ways. Shut off down here they're looking for fun, mischief, skylarking —whatever you want to call it. You can't lick 'em—they won't stand it—and the fellow that tries it had better quit before he begins. To get along smoothly you must pretend not to see some things. To get rid of those things you must use reason, not force. Your father ought to know all this, I say—he has been in the service long enough—but it begins to look as if he didn't know it."

He paused momentarily. She was looking at him now, and her expression had changed. He noticed the change, but he went on.

"Suppose Cap'n Bartlett had found that whisky," he said, "and who brought it here? The regulations are pretty strict. He might, being as cranky as he is— Oh, I know that is pretty plain, but I'm telling the straight truth now—he might start in to fire that man out of this station and out of the service. What then? Well, in the first place, a good man —yes, a *good* man and a mighty good life-saver—is lost to Setuckit, and, more than that, his wife and family lose their bread and butter for a while. All that man needs—really needs—is to have somebody, a fellow he knows and believes in, talk a little common sense to him and ask him to play the game. That was what I was going to do, if I had had a chance."

She spoke then.

"Who was the man?" she asked, impulsively. "Oh, but of course you won't tell. You shouldn't. I beg your pardon."

"That's all right. No, of course I won't tell. And I guess that is about all there is to say, Miss Bartlett. As for my being a sneak and working against your father, that is

—well, it isn't so, that's all. I had an idea I was working for him. I've still got it—the idea. But I tell you, honestly, he has made the job a lot harder by his blow-up this afternoon."

He nodded and walked towards the stairs; but now it was she who interfered.

"Mr. Homer," she cried, "please don't go—yet. I am so sorry. I beg your pardon—oh, I do! And I am really ashamed of myself now. I might have known—yes, I think I did know even when I pretended not to—that you weren't the kind of man I said you were. I understand now. And I thank you for making me understand, and for being such a friend to father—and me. Will you—will you shake hands —and forgive me?"

He took her hand. The look in her eyes now was not one to be avoided. He certainly had no wish to avoid it. And her fingers were like electric points sending a peculiar and entirely unfamiliar shock throughout his system. He forgot everything else except that look and that handclasp. Yet he should not have forgotten; as an engaged man he should have remembered another hand and another pair of eyes. He should, there is no doubt of that; but there is just as little doubt that he did not—at that moment.

It was she who broke the little tableau of reconciliation. She withdrew her fingers from his, and smiled. The smile was a happy one, though there might have been a shade of embarrassment in it. Her eyes, too, were smiling, but there was a mist in them.

"I shall tell father in the morning," she said. "Oh, not what you have told me, of course. But I shall try and make him see that he must be more diplomatic and careful with the men. I shall let him think that the advice is all due to my own brilliant sagacity. Of course it isn't; it is all yours. And I am ever and ever so much obliged to you, Mr. Homer."

"Oh, that is all right. I knew you didn't understand."

"I didn't, but I do now, and try to forgive me for saying those dreadful things. Good night."

They separated. Calvin went up to the sleeping quarters,

cautiously undressed and climbed into bed. For at least an hour the darkness surrounding that cot was decorated with eyes, misty gray eyes, looking at him—looking into his in a way that—that—

Then other thoughts crept in. The eyes disappeared. Before he did fall asleep, which was a good while afterward, he had made up his mind to write Myra Fuller another long letter at once. She had not replied to his recent one, but that should make no difference. He would write her because he ought to—because he wanted to—at any rate, because he ought to want to.

CHAPTER IX

MISS BARTLETT left Setuckit for Fairborough and her work there, the following afternoon. That morning Calvin took Phinney aside and had a straightforward talk with him. He told Josh that it was he who had removed the jug from the grain bin, and got rid of it and its contents. At first Phinney was inclined to be angry and resentful. What did Homer mean by butting in? What business was it of his?

Calvin, keeping his temper, explained carefully.

"I did it mainly on your account, Josh," he said. "You know what a crank the old man is. He might have thrown you out of the service."

"Well? Suppose he had? This ain't such a fancy job, as I know of. Sixty-five a month and find my own grub ain't liable to make a millionaire out of me. I guess likely I could strike somethin' ashore that would fetch me in as much as that—and not wait very long for it, neither."

"Maybe you could. If you had quit here on your own hook, of course you could. But if the whole Cape knew you were fired because you were drunk and were in the habit of carrying a jug of whisky around with you, that might make it harder. And it wouldn't be the nicest piece of news for your wife to hear. Not just now it wouldn't."

Phinney thought it over.

"I guess maybe you're right, Cal," he admitted, after a moment. "But, good land! it ain't such a turrible wicked thing, is it? It has been done as much as once afore, I cal'late. Why, when Oz Myrick was skipper he—"

"He was pretty easy—yes. He knew you fellows and knew you were straight enough—or meant to be—and that you didn't drink because you couldn't get along without it.

But even he would have cut your liberty for three months.
And you remember Frank Jameson? Cap'n Oz sent him
packing."

"Humph! Frankie J. was a reg'lar souse, that's why."

"Yes, and the cap'n knew it. He gave him three or four
chances and then discharged him. He knew him. But
Cap'n Bartlett doesn't know you. If he had seen you the
other night, as the rest of us did—and it is only by luck
that he didn't—and if he had found that jug with Orrin
Hendrick's name on the express tag tied to the handle—
well, wouldn't he have had a pretty fair excuse for thinking
you were as much of a souse as Frank?"

Josh grinned sheepishly. "Maybe so," he agreed. "I'm
glad he didn't. I wouldn't want Sarah and the kids to hear
about it. Much obliged, Cal."

"That's all right. It was your wife and the kids I was
thinking of."

"Um-hum. The whole business was kind of darn foolish
for a man as old as I am. I was all nervous and worked
up on account of Sarah; and then, when 'twas all over,
and she and the baby was doin' well, I—" he stopped and
groaned. "Godfreys, Cal," he confided, "there was a spell
there when even the doctor wan't sure she'd pull through.
When he was sure—that next day—I—I went outdoors and
run acrost Orrin, and he'd had a couple of gallons sent down
for Christmas, and—humph! That's how it started."

"Of course. I understand. But if I were you—I'm no
parson, you know that—"

"Old Bologny is—or worse."

"Never mind him. I'm preaching now. If I were you,
Josh, with a good wife and six smart children, I'd keep out
of Orrin's way when I went on liberty."

"I know I ought to. Guess likely I will. Orrin's lots
of fun, but he ain't much account. All right, Cal. I'm
glad you done what you did. Shall I tell the boys?"

"Yes, tell those that know about the whisky. No need
to say anything to Sam, or Seleucus—or Wallie. It would
only start them talking."

"Well, Wallie— Say, Cal, how did Bologny find out, anyway? You didn't tell him; you say you didn't."

"No, I didn't tell him. He just got on to things, I suppose. It was plain enough. All he had to do was to watch the way you fellows acted, and get near enough to you. But there's one more thing, Josh: I want you to help me keep things running smoothly down here. Don't make any more trouble for the cap'n than you can help."

Phinney stared. "Good Godfreys mighty!" he cried. "*You* ain't playin' pet to Bartlett, are you?"

"I'm not playing to anybody. All I'm thinking of is this Setuckit Life-Station. It's got a reputation. The last thing Cap'n Ozzie asked was for us to keep that reputation where it is. I'm asking you and the rest to help do it."

Josh whistled. "All right, Cal," he said again. "But we'll have one sweet job—with the keeper we've got."

"He hasn't done so badly."

"He hasn't had any chance to do anything—yet. We've only had one craft to go to since he come, and that didn't amount to anything. Let's see how he acts in a February snorter, with a five-mile row and a toss-up between keepin' afloat and goin' to the bottom. Let's see how he handles that."

"Probably he'll handle it all right."

"Perhaps—maybe. But Seleucus Gammon don't think so. Seleucus still sticks to it that he's got a yellow streak. Well, time'll tell, I cal'late. I'll fix you up with the boys, Cal—about the rum jug, I mean."

Norma's good-bys to the crew were said at the dinner table. They were more in the nature of *au revoir* than farewells, for she declared she should see them all again before very long.

"I have had a perfectly lovely time," she said. "You have all been very nice to me and I shan't forget it. Thank you ever and ever so much."

With Calvin Homer she was a little more explicit and confidential.

"I am going to try and come down again next month,"

she said. "I am still troubled about father. I hate to leave him. But I feel better since our talk last night, Mr. Homer. I know that he has one loyal friend here. You will do all you can to make it easy for him, won't you?"

He nodded. "I told you I would do what I could," he said.

"And that is a great deal. No one else could possibly do as much. And you have forgiven me for being so stupid —and hateful—last night? I hope you have, because I haven't forgiven myself. You will just forget it all, won't you? Promise."

He promised, but even as he did so, he knew he was not speaking the whole truth. Forgetting that midnight meeting in the mess room was not going to be easy. He had arisen that morning with the fixed resolve to put certain memories from his mind, to keep them from his thoughts, but even now, as she stood there before him, his thoughts were playing traitor to that resolution. If only she would not look at him like that.

She put out her hand.

"Good-by," she said.

"Good-by, Miss Bartlett. I hope you have a good trip."

She rode away, a few minutes later, in the buggy for which her father had telephoned the night before. Benoni accompanied her. He was going as far as Orham, to see her safely aboard the train, then Peleg Myrick was to bring him down in the *Wild Duck*. The crew, those not on duty, waved to her as the buggy moved off. She waved in return.

"She's a mighty smart, nice girl," declared Seleucus. As his wife was not present he was free to express his opinion. "We're goin' to miss her, I swan if we ain't. Too bad she had to go so soon. Eh, Cal?"

Calvin did not answer. He was inclined to the opinion that, for his peace of mind, it was an extremely good thing that Norma Bartlett had gone. As for missing her—well, that was different. He went in to write the letter to Myra Fuller. It was not a love letter exactly, but it was more intimate and affectionate than it might have been if his conscience had not troubled him so acutely. He could not help feeling guilty. He had promised the Bartlett girl to help her father. Myra expected him to do just the opposite. This last he could not and would not do; he had told Myra so, and there was some comfort in that thought. But, also, there was foreboding concerning the future. Why had he been so foolish as to yield to Kellogg's pleading and remain at Setuckit?

Captain Bartlett returned that evening from his trip to Orham and was, for the next day or two, more than usually silent and noncommunicative. He spent his spare time in his room—that so recently occupied by his daughter—and Homer, visiting that room to report or ask for orders, found him either reading in his new Bible or sitting by the window gazing out at nothing in particular. He was as watchfully strict as ever in matters of daily drill and routine, but he never again alluded to the smuggled whisky. His threat to search the men's belongings had either been forgotten, or, as Calvin was inclined to think, its fulfillment had been abandoned because of Norma's reasoning and persuasion. Josh Phinney had, apparently, kept his promise to help in soothing the ruffled feelings of his comrades, for rebellious murmurings ceased and good nature was the rule. Only Wallie Oaks appeared peevish and discontented. Wallie's popularity, never at summer heat, was now below zero.

Then came the long-expected break in the stretch of good weather. The Government signals, day after day, were set for high winds and cold. Peleg Myrick's elbows and knees were filled with disquieting pangs and his prophecies were gloomy and disturbing. On the first Thursday of the new year the Setuckit crew was called out at four o'clock in the morning to the aid of a coasting schooner in trouble near the Sand Hill. The sea was high and the wind steadily increasing, but there was no danger—as danger was reckoned at Setuckit.

And yet the skipper was nervous—very nervous. For

some minutes after the call came he was in the tower, watching the schooner through the glass, and when Homer ventured to hint that they were losing time he made no answer. At last, however, he gave orders for the launching, and they started.

The job was an easy one. The vessel—a three-masted coaster, on her way down from Nova Scotia with a cargo of lumber and shingles—was badly iced and some of her crew were sick. She was short handed and her skipper, worn out and half sick himself, had lost courage and set distress signals. They boarded her, cleared away the ice as best they could, made hot coffee for all hands and brought her out of the dangerous rips into the comparatively safe waters of the ship channel. There, a revenue cutter happening along, they turned her over to the cutter's protection and pulled back home. "A reg'lar pudd'n," so Seleucus characterized the whole proceeding. "But look at the old man," he added, in an undertone. "Blessed if he don't look as if he'd been through somethin' tough. Solemn as an aowl in a meetin'-house steeple, ain't he? Well, if this gale keeps on to blow he may have somethin' to be solemn about. Ah, hum-a-day! this world's a sea of trouble and them that's got wives ashore better larn how to swim. Eh, Wallie?"

Oaks, this time, was provided with a ready retort. "All right," he observed. "You can start your swimmin' right now. Here comes Jemimy, lookin' for you. Take long strokes, Seleucus."

The signals, flying at the top of the pole, spelled "Easterly winds increasing to gale velocity." By noon the gale had arrived. The sea was pounding and thundering along the outer beach and all to the southeast was a tumbling smother of green and white against an iron-gray sky. Far out, against the horizon, were scattered white dots, vessels making an offing, edging away from the shoals.

Homer, on his way to the tower to relieve Badger, met the latter coming down.

"What are you quitting for, Ellis?" he asked. "I'm ahead of time."

"Sure you are," was the reply. "But the old man told me I needn't stay if I didn't want to. And I knew you'd be right along. He's up there, with his starboard eye glued to that spyglass. And he's all of a twitter, seems so. Uneasy as a tomcat out in a rainstorm. What's the matter with him?"

"Oh, nothing in particular, I guess. He has been down in the dumps ever since his daughter left. We'll all have to make allowances till he gets his bearings. That Crooked Hill business knocked him on his beam ends and he feels the care of this job more than he would if it hadn't. Even an easy thing like that schooner this morning is a good deal of a strain for him. He'll be all right; give him time."

"Humph! Maybe so. But he's liable to be strained again before long. There's a little two-master off back of the Sand Hill that's makin' heavy weather of it. I pointed her out to him and he ain't taken his eye off her since. Keeps talkin' to himself, he does. Gospel talk, too—most of it. Sounds as if he was runnin' a missionary meetin' all on his own hook. I begun to be afraid he'd be askin' me to sign a subscription paper for the heathen next. Say, Cal, do you cal'late he's crazy?"

"Crazy! Do you think Cap'n Kellogg would give that job to a crazy man?"

"Huh! I tell you what I *do* think. I think Kellogg was crazy when he give it to him. But there! I'm goin' below to rest up a little mite. It'll be our luck to have to go off to that two-master afore the day's over. We've had a soft time so far this winter. Now the trouble will come in bunches, same as bananas—see if it don't."

Homer found the skipper at the telescope. He spoke to him, but Bartlett did not answer. Calvin paced back and forth by the windows overlooking the bay and the group of fish shanties on the beach below. There was activity there, centering in the vicinity of the shanty occupied by Philander Jarvis and his sister. Philander and another Orham fisherman named Alvin Crocker had recently purchased a fish weir which had belonged to one Laban Poundberry of Harniss.

Poundberry was dead and the weir was a part of his estate.
It had been—like all the fish traps along Setuckit beach—
taken up when the winter set in, and the poles and nets were
stored in another building a mile or so up the shore. Jarvis
and Crocker intended resetting it in the spring, before the
mackerel began running. They were to work it in partner-
ship.

The weir—its nets and ropes and floats—needed overhauling and mending and Crocker had come down from Orham
that morning, bringing with him four men, longshoremen
like himself, who, being out of work, were glad of the opportunity to earn a few dollars by helping with the mending.
They—Crocker and the men—were planning to sleep and
eat aboard the craft in which they came, an antique but
seaworthy affair, once part of the outfit of a New Bedford
whaler, but now decked over forward and fitted with a mast
and sail. She was anchored in the cove alongside the Jarvis
catboat.

The men, a quartette of tanned and square-shouldered
huskies, were ashore. They had had dinner and were
grouped about the door of the Jarvis shanty, smoking, chatting and apparently awaiting orders. Alvin and Philander,
their employers, were, so Homer guessed, inside, probably
discussing ways and means. Jarvis, although a hard worker,
never did things in a hurry and his partner had the reputation of being "mighty moderate." Calvin, glancing at the
clock on the wall of the tower room, was inclined to think
that little, if any, net mending would be accomplished that
day. The consultation would probably last an hour or two
longer and end in the decision to begin operations bright
and early the next morning.

He stood by the window, looking down at the group by
the Jarvis shanty. It was now augmented by three members
of the Setuckit crew, Gammon among them. There were
shouts of laughter and Calvin surmised that, as usual,
Seleucus was furnishing the cause. The gale was fierce and
the cold penetrating. Ordinary weak mortals would have
found it pleasanter inside by the stove, but these fellows

were weatherproof. And, besides, Philander's domicile was
not planned for the housing of a convention.

"Lord A'mighty!"

It was Bartlett who uttered the exclamation. Homer
turned hastily from the window. The skipper was still peering through the telescope. His right hand steadied the
glass, but his left was outstretched and shaking.

"What's the matter?" demanded Calvin. "What is it,
Cap'n?"

Bartlett turned. His face, beneath its tan, was pale.

"She—she's struck," he gasped. "She's aground. Look!"

Calvin, stepping forward, bent and gazed through the telescope. Its rim framed a dismal circle of tumbling water,
gray and white. In the center of that circle was the little
schooner, reefed fore and mainsails set, the remnant of a
jib whipping, the whole seen through fringes of flying spray.
The masts leaned at an angle, but they did not move. Ellis
Badger was a true prophet. The schooner had not been able
to fight clear of Sand Hill Shoal. She was hard and fast
aground upon it. Here was another job for the Setuckit
crew, the second that day—and the day but half over.

Homer straightened and turned to his commander.

"Shall I order 'em out?" he asked. "All ready, are you,
Cap'n?"

Bartlett did not speak. He was again peering through the
glass. Calvin tried again.

"Shall I get out the boat?" he asked, moving toward the
door. His hand was on the knob when the skipper shouted
at him.

"Where are you goin'?" he demanded.

"Why—why, I thought—don't you want to order out the
crew?"

"No. Not yet. Wait."

Homer waited. What there might be to wait for was
beyond his understanding. The Sand Hill, on a day like
this, was not likely to wait for them; it was already busy
with that schooner.

But he had been ordered to wait and it was his business

to obey orders. Bartlett still stared through the glass. Steps sounded on the stairs and Hezekiah Rogers opened the door.

"Oh, Cal," said Hez. "I want to speak to you just a minute. Nothin' special, only I wanted to ask if you knew whether that box of salt in the kitchen is all we've got. It's runnin' low and, bein's I'm cook, I—"

"Sshh!" ordered Bartlett savagely. He was still at the telescope. Homer motioned to Rogers and stepped out on the landing.

"Never mind the salt now, Hez," he whispered. "Tell the boys to get ready. That two-master is on the Sand Hill and we'll be starting for her in a minute."

Rogers nodded and hurried down. Calvin reëntered the tower room. Bartlett was waiting for him.

"What did you tell him?" he asked sharply.

"Why, nothing except that the men had better get ready. I thought—"

"You thought! You don't have to think, do you? I'm cap'n of this crew, ain't I?"

"Of course you are. But—"

"Never mind then. When I get ready to give my orders I give 'em. You understand that?"

Calvin did not reply. He was furiously angry, and to speak would have been a risky proceeding. He swung on his heel.

"Where are you goin'?" demanded Bartlett.

"Nowhere in particular. Outside, that's all."

"You're on duty here, ain't you?"

"Yes."

"Stay here, then."

Calvin hesitated. Then he walked back to the window. Below, on the beach, he saw Rogers hurrying from the back door toward the group by the Jarvis shanty. He joined that group. There was an instant of eager talk and then Hez, Seleucus and the other two members of the crew—they were Bloomer and Bearse—started on the run for the station. He felt a hand on his arm. Looking over his shoulder he saw

the skipper's face close to his own. It was still pale, but
it wore a feeble, half-apologetic smile.

"Don't mind the way I talked to you, Calvin," stammered
Benoni. "I—I'm nervous and—dreadful worried. I ain't
mad at you, or—or anything like that. I just don't know
what to do about this thing. I don't know what it's my
duty to do."

Homer thought he understood. On other occasions—one
that very morning—he had seen his commander hesitate
when called to the rescue of a stranded vessel. He had seen
him hesitate and linger when waiting seemed quite inexcus-
able. But, when the moments of hesitation were over, he
had carried the rescue work through with adequacy and dis-
patch. No doubt he would do the same now. The man
was not strong; his nerves were in a wretched state. Yes,
as he had told Badger, allowances must be made, irritating
though the making of them might be.

"That's all right, Cap'n," he said. "Don't worry. We'll
be in time. She looks to me as if she was lying fairly easy.
We'll get there before she breaks up. I'll order out the
boat."

Again he started to go and again he was stopped. The
keeper once more caught him by the arm.

"Wait," he commanded. "Wait. I—I've got to think
this out. I've got to."

He stooped again to the telescope. Calvin, his own anxiety increasing, looked out of the window. The four longshoremen—the Jarvis and Crocker quartette—had hastened
to the top of the dune behind the shanty and were standing
there gazing off to sea. Philander and Alvin came out and
joined the watchers. Mrs. Gammon, an apron over her
head, stood in the doorway looking after them.

Bartlett left the glass and began pacing up and down the
floor. He was muttering disjointed phrases and sentences.
They sounded like Scriptural quotations or prayers. Suddenly he stopped.

"What would you do, boy?" he demanded, his voice quav-
ering. "What do you think ought to be done? Speak out.

Say somethin', why don't you? Do you think it's right for us to go off to that schooner?"

"Right? Safe, do you mean?"

"Yes. Have I got a right to risk lives, the lives of them that's dependent on me—risk 'em again, right off like this?"

Homer was thoroughly alarmed now. There was a risk, of course—there was always risk in their work—but no unusual risk.

"Cap'n Bartlett," he began. "I don't see—I don't think you need to worry. We'll make it, easy. And there is time enough if we start now. The longer we wait—"

Bartlett interrupted. "I didn't ask you that," he shouted. "I'm cap'n here, ain't I? I didn't ask you whether we'd wait or not. I asked you if—if— Why don't you answer me?"

"I'm trying to answer you. You asked if it was safe. I say it is."

"*You* say so? What do you know about it? You ain't seen the wrath of God A'mighty movin' over the face of the waters the way I have. You ain't seen the fellers you've lived with and been with for years drownin' alongside you. You ain't—oh, you ain't seen anything! You say go—of course you do. But what does it mean to you? Nothin', except your own chance, and you can take that, same as I'd take mine. But what about the lives of them I'm responsible for? What about them that's put in my charge? Eh? Eh?"

Homer thought he understood at last. It was not personal cowardice, it was the overwhelming sense of responsibility for the safety of his crew which was breaking Benoni Bartlett's nerve. Gently but firmly he shook off the clutch on his sleeve.

"There, there, Cap'n," he said. "It's all right. You're tired and worn out. This morning's job was too much for you. You go and turn in. Leave it to me. I'll attend to everything. We'll get to that schooner and handle her all right. You turn in and leave it to me. I'll tell the boys you are sick."

"Eh? What's that? Who said I was sick?"

"Why—well, you are next door to it. You aren't long out of the doctor's hands and you had a hard strain this morning. I—"

"Quiet—you! I ain't sick. And I won't have any lies told on my account. I ain't responsible to you nor this crew for what I do. I'm responsible to God A'mighty. He's the one. When he tells me what's my duty I'll do it. You can go now. I want to be alone."

"But, Cap'n, we've *got* to go. What shall I tell the crew?"

"Eh. . . ? Well, you tell 'em to get ready to turn out. Then you and they can wait for orders. That's all. . . . That's all. Go below and tell 'em."

Calvin went. The telling was not likely to be an easy task. The truth—the bare truth without attempt at explanation—would never do. The men would not understand and would think—almost anything.

They were in the mess room when he reached there, oil-skinned, sou'westered, booted—ready for work. They greeted him with a yell.

"Well, here you be at last," cried Phinney. "Thought you and Bologny had gone to sleep aloft there. What are we waitin' for?"

"The old man converted you, has he?" queried Badger. "He was holdin' special service when I left. What did you —stop to sing the last hymn?"

Seleucus chimed in. "Wallie here is just chompin' the bit," he declared. "I had to hold him to keep him from swimmin' off to that schooner all on his own hook. He's one of them dare-devils, Wallie is. Shall we start, Cal?"

Homer shook his head. "Not yet, boys," he said. "Cap'n Bartlett isn't—well, he'll be down in a minute. He told me to tell you to be ready when he came."

There was a roar of laughter. "Be ready!" repeated Phinney. "We've been ready for much as ten minutes. All hands are here but Ed and Sam and they're out harnessin'.

Ready—huh! If Bologny'd left it to us we'd have had the boat through the surf by now."

"The orders are to wait," said Calvin.

"But, Cal—"

"Oh, take it easy, Josh! We needn't worry if the skipper doesn't."

Five minutes passed; then five more. Philander Jarvis opened the outer door and looked in.

"What are you fellers hangin' around that stove for?" he demanded. "All dead, are you? That craft 'll go to pieces if you don't get to her some time this week."

The Setuckit crew were sufficiently critical themselves but they did not brook criticism from outsiders.

"Go pick the herrin' scales out of your hair, Phil," ordered Seleucus. "This ain't your funeral."

Jarvis grunted. "There'll be a few funerals if you fellers don't get on to your job," he announced. "And if you don't want that job I cal'late I can find somebody that does. That schooner would pay for her salvage, maybe."

A lump of coal missed his head by an inch or two and he dodged out of the door.

"For crimus sakes where *is* Bologny?" fidgeted Gammon. "Oz Myrick—yes, or any other live man—would have been halfway off there by this time."

Another five minutes elapsed before the skipper made his appearance. And when he did they were amazed to see him in ordinary clothes instead of his rough-weather rig. He was paler than ever, or so it seemed to Calvin, and his glance wavered a little as it surveyed the crew. Yet the hand which he raised for silence was steady enough. His tone was conciliatory; Homer thought it almost pleading.

"Men," he said, "there's a schooner ashore on the Sand Hill. She seems to lay easy and I think there's no present danger. We may most likely have to go off to her, but we'll wait and rest a spell first. There's a rugged sea runnin' and it's blowin' a gale. 'Twould be a hard pull for you, after the one you had this mornin'. I'll go aloft now and

keep an eye on her through the glass.   Stand by till you hear
from me."

He turned and they heard him climbing the stairs.   The
crew stared at each other in silence for a moment.   But
only for a moment; then the silence was broken.   Every one
had something to say and said it.   They crowded about
Homer, demanding to know what it meant, what they were
waiting for.

"It's blowin' harder every minute," protested Phinney.
"She'll break up afore we get to her.   What's the matter
with him, Cal?   Don't he know that?"

"Rest!" snorted Bloomer, who had come in from the
stable.   "Does he think them seas off yonder are restin'?
Is he loony?   What did he say to you, Cal?"

Seleucus was at his eblow.   "Yellow, that's what's the
matter, Cal," he whispered.   "It's the yellow streak showin'.
He's scared, that's what ails him."

Homer tried to quiet the tumult.   He was as perturbed
and as disgusted as the rest, but, as Number One man, he
felt that he must not show his feelings.   He had promised
Kellogg to use his influence for order and obedience.   And
he had promised Norma.   Yes, it was up to him.

"Here, hold on, boys!" he urged.   "Don't go up in the
air.   The old man must know what he's doing.   And it's his
business, not ours."

There was another babel.

"His business!"—"To set around here and rest while that
schooner's goin' to pieces?"—"What do you think Oz
Myrick would say to that?"—"Cal, what's the matter with
you, anyway?"—"Godfreys! it's catchin' and Cal's got it
now"—

These were some of the angry protests.

"Come on, boys!" yelled Phinney.   "This place makes me
sick.   Come on outside.   To hell with Bologny!   Come
on!"

Calvin blocked the doorway.   "Hush!" he shouted.
"Josh, you fool, use your common sense, if you've got any.
What do you want to do; get this whole crew fired?   You've

had your orders. I don't like 'em any better than you do, but they are orders. Shut up! Stay where you are, I tell you!"

They stayed, but only because he was at the door and they could not pass without a fight. He went on talking.

"The skipper's made his plans, I suppose," he said. "He never starts until he thinks it is the right time. He has never backed out yet, has he? He says wait. Well, then, wait. Do you want to be hauled up before the superintendent—every one of you?"

This had some effect; they ceased attempting to push by him, but they were still rebellious.

"Scared," repeated Gammon, aloud this time. "He's scart blue. Couldn't you see it in his eye? He—"

"Shut up, Seleucus! Because a skipper is careful of his men it doesn't follow that he's scared. He orders you to wait. Well, I say it, too. Do any of you think I'm scared? If anybody does let him step out and say it. . . . Come, Seleucus," with a laugh. "You're doing most of that kind of talking; tell me that I'm frightened and see what happens. Come on!"

It was a grand-stand play, and was so intended, but it had an effect. It distracted attention from the main issue and focused it upon Mr. Gammon. The uproar changed to gleeful shouts.

"Go on, Seleucus!"—"That's the boy!"—"Put up your fists; square off!"—"Battlin' Seleucus, the holy terror"—"Look out for the solar plexus punch, Cal."

Seleucus grinned. "I'm a little mite off trainin'," he answered. "Besides, Cal and me ain't in the same class. You wouldn't fight a man that wan't your weight, would you, Cal?"

Calvin was smiling, too, but there was a certain grimness in his smile.

"Anybody else, then?" he inquired, his glance moving from face to face. "How about you, Wallie? You're talking to yourself back there. Say it out loud."

Oaks immediately became the center of interest. An unwilling and much surprised center, but an overwhelmingly popular one. Homer seized the opportunity.

"Go outdoors, if you want to," he suggested, "but hang around and be ready. We'll start any minute now, you can bet on that."

It was Oaks who led the way out and he was pursued by a hectoring crowd. The telephone bell rang. Calvin answered the call. He came away from the instrument more troubled than ever. It was the Orham Station which had called. They were watching the stranded schooner and wanted to know why Setuckit had not started to her rescue. Homer assured them that Setuckit was about to start . . . but was it?

He moved toward the stairs. He was strongly tempted to make another trial at urging prompt action by his skipper. What caused him to hesitate was the habit of obedience which service under Myrick and Kellogg had made part of his nature. Discipline in a life-saving station might be lax enough in minor matters, but, at the final test, the orders of the keeper were not to be questioned nor disputed. Nothing excused disregard of those orders.

So he hesitated. And, as he stood there, suddenly, outside the station, arose a tumult of shouts and excited profanity. He ran to the window. The crew had been standing near the door; now he was just in time to see the last man running in the direction of the Jarvis shanty. He threw open the door and hurried out.

In the cove the Crocker whaleboat, under the merest rag of sail, was moving out into the bay. It was filled with men; Crocker himself was at the tiller, and with him were Jarvis and the four longshoremen from Orham. The boat was headed, not down the beach toward the weir shanty, but in the other direction, toward the point and the open sea.

For a moment Calvin did not understand. Where on earth were they bound—those men in that whaleboat—in such a gale and through such a sea? And then the meaning of it flashed to his mind. He ran headlong down to the beach where his comrades were standing. He seized the nearest—Bearse, as it happened—by the shoulder and swung him violently round.

"Are they going off to that schooner?" he demanded savagely.

Sam Bearse was, ordinarily, a quiet, sober man. Now his answer was decorated with a savage fringe of oaths. Yes, that was just where the whaleboat was going. Crocker and Philander had learned of the orders to "wait" and had stolen a march on them. If they salvaged that schooner they could claim payment from the underwriters. It was a risk, but those fellows were a tough crowd and would risk anything for money.

"And we," bellowed Bearse, "*we* stand here and see 'em go. For God sakes, Cal, what do you think the whole Cape'll say about us when it hears the yarn? We loafin' here and —and that blanked dashed yellow dog up there in that tower—"

Calvin heard no more. He was racing up the slope to the station. Up the stairs he bounded and into the tower room. Bartlett was on his knees, his hands clasped and his head bent. He did not look up when his subordinate entered; apparently he did not hear him.

Homer seized his shoulder and shook him. The skipper's eyes opened and he turned dazedly.

"What—what is it?" he faltered. "What's the matter?"

Calvin told him and wasted no words in the telling. Bartlett rose to his feet.

"Eh? I—I—say that again," he ordered.

Calvin said it again. Benoni did not wait for him to finish. He sprang to the window, stared after the rapidly moving whaleboat, and then whirled back.

"Turn out all hands!" he roared. "What are you standin' here for? Turn 'em out! Lively!"

That was enough. Homer leaped to the stairs.

The boat, on its car, was out of the house before the skipper dashed from the door of the station. He was bareheaded, his oilskin coat unbuttoned. He shouted orders as he came.

"Lively!" he bellowed. "Get her goin'!"

The oars fell into place with a clatter. Homer and Seleucus jumped to their seats in the bow.

"Off with her!" roared the skipper.

He was, of course, the last aboard, and, so reckless was his frenzied disregard of personal safety that Bearse had to literally drag him over the stern out of the boiling surf. The bottom of the boat was awash as they swung up to the crest of the first breaker.

"Row!" ordered Bartlett. "Row! Lay to it, you loafers! Haul, why don't you?"

It was a row—that one. Not that the seas were higher than many they had found, or even as high, nor the gale as strong, nor the cold as punishing. But with every stroke the skipper bullied them, roared at them, drove them on. Seleucus, swinging his great shoulders back and forth, managed to turn his head and gasp a word to his nearest neighbor.

"Plumb crazy, Cal," he panted. "Plumb crazy—if you ask me."

Crazy or not—and Homer was inclined to share Gammon's opinion—the torrent of abuse and bullying was achieving results. They were gaining on the whaleboat. Crocker and his companions had given up trying to make headway with the fragment of sail they could carry, and were also rowing. And they were not novices at the work. The Setuckit boat gained steadily, but it gained slowly. They were perhaps fifty yards apart as they came down the stretch, the Sand Hill Shoal and the stranded schooner a quarter of a mile away.

But the whaleboat made it first. She was drawing under the little vessel's lee, as the lifeboat came leaping up. The schooner's men—there were but four of them—were in the rigging. Crocker and Jarvis were preparing to make fast to the rail.

"Lay to it!" screamed Bartlett. "Haul, you weak-livered swabs! Haul!"

The lifeboat swung on, its bow headed straight for the

little space between the schooner and the whaleboat. A collision was certain, and it meant the staving and perhaps sinking of the Crocker craft. The life-savers gazed at their skipper; their stroke involuntarily slackened. Bartlett noticed it.

"Pull!" he roared. "What are you hangin' back for? Pull!"

The rival crew was growing anxious. Jarvis had not yet made fast to the schooner and unless he did—

Crocker shouted.

"Look out!" he warned. "Keep off!"

Benoni Bartlett, erect in the liftboat's stern, did not move his steering oar one inch.

"Out of my way!" he cried. "Damn your black souls! Get out—or I'll ram straight through you!"

And the whaleboat did get out of the way. The men aboard her were anything but cowardly, but they had no time to think or prepare for resistance. Their boat swung off just in time and that of the Setuckit crew shot into the space it had occupied. Seleucus and Homer seized the schooner's rail. Bartlett, abandoning the steering oar, tumbled on board. Phinney would have followed, but Calvin got ahead of him.

"Hold her, boys!" he shouted. "I'm going."

The skipper had attempted to scramble up the sloping deck, but a sea, breaking over the forequarter, threw him headlong back. Homer caught him as he reeled to the rail, and held him tight.

"Let go of me," gasped Bartlett. "Let go of me, or I'll kill you."

But Calvin did not let go. It was perfectly obvious that nothing could save the schooner. The vessel's crew were climbing down the rigging. Two of them were already in the lifeboat.

"Steady, Cap'n, steady," he pleaded. "We can't do anything here. She'll go any minute. The men are in the boat now. Come on."

Bartlett fought like a wild man. He ordered, begged,

even—to Calvin's amazement—swore. Then, all at once, he seemed to wilt—to collapse completely.

"What do you want?" he panted, feebly. "I—I—what shall we do?"

"We can't do anything. We've got the men. Get back into the boat."

He pushed his commander to the rail. Bearse and Oaks reached up to help. The skipper, passive enough now, was assisted aboard. Homer followed.

"Shove her clear, boys," he ordered. Bartlett had not spoken; he seemed to be in a trance. The lifeboat swung clear of the wreck. Calvin, at his place in the bow, looked anxiously aft. The skipper had taken up the steering oar, but he was not using it.

"Are you all right, Cap'n Bartlett?" shouted Homer. "I'll take her in if you say so?"

Bartlett's shoulders straightened. "Give way," he ordered. The oars dipped, and the pull home began. They had progressed not more than an eighth of a mile when the mainmast of the little vessel they had just left went over the side. Above the bellow of the breakers the crack and crash were audible.

CHAPTER X

THEY passed the whaleboat on the way in. The Crocker and Jarvis crew were taking it easy now and they made no attempt to race with their successful rivals. The dangerous "rips" were navigated safely and the landing in the cove made without trouble. The lifeboat was beached and the schooner's men helped ashore. Homer, busy with the rest, had paid no heed to Bartlett. When he did turn to the latter, to ask for further orders, he found him gone.

"He's up to the station long ago," volunteered Seleucus. "Started just as soon as we made the beach. Didn't get hurt out yonder, did he? He looked pretty sick to me."

Calvin superintended the transfer of the practically helpless sailors from the shore to the station. Then he hurried back to attend to the housing of the boat. The whaleboat had arrived by this time and its recent occupants were exchanging repartee with the life-savers.

"Little mite late on gettin' started, wan't you, Josh?" queried Crocker with a grin. "What was the matter; somebody's feet chilly, or somethin' like that?"

Phinney's retort was prompt, even if the reference to the late start was ignored.

"You ought to learn how to row, Alvin," he declared. "We walked up on you as if you was restin'. Kind of tired, it looked like to me. You're a healthy lot of salvagers, you are. You remind me of Hard Luck, our dog up to the station. You'd think he was goin' to eat a cat alive, judgin' by the way he starts after it. But when the cat turns 'round he slacks up and changes his mind. You fellows started fine, but when the pinch come you changed your mind. Ho, ho!"

Philander Jarvis put in a word. "Well, we started, anyhow," he observed. "We didn't set around the stove waitin' for somebody else to show us the way."

"They was warmin' those cold feet of theirs," explained Crocker. "That's why they stuck so close to the stove. The cold-foot life-savers! Haw, haw!"

"Cal'late Bartlett's warmin' *his* feet now," added one of the longshoremen. "I don't see him around here anywheres."

Sam Bearse smiled serenely. "Looked to me as if you saw him out there," he drawled. "You got out of his way about as spry as any crowd ever I saw. You're lovely bluffers. You talk—talk—talk, but you don't prove much."

Jarvis was on his way to the shanty, but he paused to shout a final word.

"*We* don't have to prove nothin'," he taunted. "You fellers will have to do the provin'. Wait till they hear this yarn up to the village. There'll be talk enough then."

Homer's first question—when the lifeboat was back in the boat room and the shipwrecked men warmed, fed, and stretched on the cots in the spare room—was concerning the whereabouts of his superior. Hezekiah Rogers, who, as cook, had remained ashore while his comrades went off to the schooner, answered the question.

"He's in his room yonder," said Hez. "Come straight in, the minute you fellers landed, and marched by me without sayin' a word. I asked him if he didn't want a cup of coffee, but he never peeped. He was talkin' to himself, seemed so, and, if you could judge by his face, he didn't like to hear what he said. Is he sick, Cal? They tell me he was a reg'lar bucko mate on the way off to the shoal. Swore a blue streak! Godfreys!" with a chuckle, "I didn't think he knew how. Must be more of a man than we give him credit for."

Calvin knocked at the door of the keeper's room. There was no answer to his first knock, nor the one which followed. He bent to the crack of the door and listened. He heard the steady murmur of a voice within. Bartlett obviously was alone. Therefore, just as obviously, he must still be talking to himself.

Calvin opened the door, looked, and then, entering, closed

the door carefully behind him. The skipper was lying halfway across the bed, his legs trailing upon the floor, his head
upon his arms. His sou'wester lay at his feet, and the
water which had run from his dripping oilskins and rubber
boots was in puddles about him. He was groaning and
muttering.

"Oh, Lord, forgive me!" Homer heard him say. "Forgive a poor, weak sinner. Send down your forgiveness upon
him. Be merciful, Lord, and—"

Calvin called his name. "Cap'n Bartlett," he cried sharply.
"Cap'n Bartlett!"

Bartlett ceased to groan and mutter. Slowly he raised his
head, turned, and looked.

"Eh?" he stammered. "Eh? Did somebody— Who is
it? What do you want?"

"It's me—Homer. What's the matter? Are you sick?"

The keeper blinked at him for a moment. Then he raised
himself to his knees.

"What are you doin' in here?" he asked.

"Why—why, I came to see what ailed you. I knocked and
you didn't answer, so—so I thought you were sick, or hurt,
or something. I heard you groan."

Bartlett stood erect; he swayed a little, and caught the
bed's head to steady himself.

"I—I—" he faltered, "I guess maybe I don't feel very
good. I don't know what— Was I groanin', you say?"

"I thought you were." He said nothing concerning what
he had heard after he entered.

"Maybe I was—maybe so. I don't know. My—my head
feels kind of funny. Did any of the rest of 'em out there
hear me?"

"No. I shouldn't if I hadn't listened to make sure you
were in here."

"That's good . . . that's good. They wouldn't understand. . . . Well," after an interval, "do you want me? Is
—is everything attended to?"

"Yes."

"Those men off that schooner? Are they—"

"They're up aloft, and all right. The boat is taken care of. I've seen to everything."

"That's good . . . that's good. I'm much obliged to you. Yes, I am. . . ."

"Don't you think you had better take off your wet clothes and turn in for a rest? And let me get you some coffee? You look pretty well played out."

The skipper's figure stiffened. He shook his head.

"When I get ready to turn in I'll do it," he said gruffly. "I don't need any orders from you—or anybody else. Who's been talkin' about my bein' sick? Who has? I suppose they think I ain't capable of handlin' this job? That's it, eh?"

Calvin ignored the rasping irritation in the tone. The man was swaying on his feet even as he spoke.

"They know better than to think that, Cap'n," he protested, with a smile. "They saw how you handled the job we just finished."

To his surprise the effect of this speech was one of alarm, rather than reassurance. The keeper looked bewildered and frightened. He drew a hand across his forehead.

"Did I do it all right?" he asked anxiously. "Do you— do they think I handled it all right?"

"Why, of course they do. You know you did."

Bartlett drew a long breath. "That's good . . . that's good," he sighed. "Tell me—was I kind of—kind of rough?"

"Rough?"

"Yes. I—boy, I used to be a pretty hard ticket in the old days. Used to act rough—and talk rough. Even now when I get excited—I—I'm liable to lose my temper and do things —and say things—that— Well, never mind, never mind. It's a hard fight for a man like me to keep His commandments—yes, 'tis. We're all poor weak sinners and I'm as weak as the rest. Maybe He'll make allowances for me; don't you cal'late He will?"

Calvin shook his head. "There, there, Cap'n Bartlett," he said, "don't worry. Nobody could have done better than you did. You're tired and you need rest, that's all. Turn in for a while."

Bartlett sat down upon the bed. "Maybe I will," he said feebly. "Maybe I will. I—I do feel sort of beat out. I don't know what's the matter with me these days. I ain't the man I used to be, seems so. That Crooked Hill business took it out of me more'n I thought, I guess. Do you know, boy," he added, looking up, with a pathetic appeal in his eyes, "it's a funny thing to say, but I can't hardly seem to remember much about goin' off to that schooner. I remember startin', but after that it's all sort of—of mixed up. . . . Don't you tell nobody I said that, will you?"

"Of course not."

"No. And I'll be all right, soon's I rest a spell. You attend to things, will you? Not makin' out the reports," sharply. "I'll take care of them. . . . I guess that's all. I'll be all right. I *am* all right. Tell the men so."

Homer did tell the men so. He told them that the skipper was tired after his strenuous exertions and was resting. They accepted the explanation. As a matter of fact, Bartlett had raised himself in their estimation. They were jubilant at having beaten the whaleboat's crew in the race to the wreck and, so far as their skipper's "roughness" was concerned, it had a tendency to make him more popular.

"He's a reg'lar feller, after all, I shouldn't wonder," commented Badger. "Talked to us like a Dutch uncle, didn't he? Cap'n Ozzie couldn't have given it to us any hotter than old Bologny did there for a spell. And when he started blastin' Al Crocker's soul I felt like hollerin' for three cheers. The old man may be a little mite late gettin' on the job, but when he does get on it he's there. He may turn out better'n we thought; eh, Cal?"

Most of the comment was as favorable, but there were a few reservations. Seleucus Gammon crowed over his brother-in-law and exalted Bartlett's behavior as loudly as the rest—except in Jemima's presence—but with Homer he was more pessimistic.

"That's all right, Cal," he observed. "The old man's helped himself with the boys just now. They're so tickled at cheatin' the Crocker gang out of that salvage that they

ain't had time to think things over. But you and I know
that that whole business was queer. Bologny acted like a
man off on the Sand Hill and on the way out—but 'twas like
a crazy man, not a sensible one. He's sane enough now—all
except his prayer-meetin' foolishness—but if he wan't loony
then I never saw anybody that was. And, more'n that, here's
another thing maybe you ain't thought of: We saved that
schooner's crew, by the skin of our teeth, but if we'd started
three quarters of an hour sooner we might have saved the
schooner. The boys have forgot that, but Crocker and
Philander and their bunch haven't forgot it. Wait till they
go up to Orham; they'll do some talkin' and start other folks
talkin', too. There'll be questions asked, you see. Crimustee! Cal, there's trouble comin' from this yet; you mark
my words."

Homer said he guessed not, but his confidence was but
pretense. Seleucus's forebodings were but faint echoes of
his own. He, too, believed there would be talk in Orham,
when the news reached there. Not only would Crocker and
his men spread abroad their version of the Setuckit crew's
delay in starting for the wreck, but the life-savers at the
Orham Station would comment also. They had been watching
and wondering—the telephone message proved that. The tale
would spread and grow. It would reach Kellogg's ears; it
was bound to reach them sooner or later. Myra Fuller
would hear it. And, when she did, what would she say?
What would she expect him to say—and do?

The answer to these last questions he might have learned
if he had been privileged to drop in at the Fuller home on
the Neck Road late in the evening of the following day.
He might have learned other things, too. He might have
found interest in a conversation between Mrs. Fuller and
her daughter which took place at the supper table before the
news from Setuckit came. Sarepta was scolding because
Myra had insisted upon changing her gown before coming
to the table. The young lady was now arrayed in her best
and was quite indifferent to her mother's ill humor.

"Oh, be still, mother!" she said. "You're mad because I'm going out and you're not. I should think you would be glad to have me enjoy myself once in a while. You can't expect me to stick around that everlasting school all day and sit around this poky old house every night. What harm is there in my going to a dance with Ezra Blodgett, I'd like to know? He's an old fool, of course, but he's got lots of money and he isn't afraid to spend it. You used to tell me to get all I could out of him. You know you did."

Mrs. Fuller sniffed. "I'd tell you so now," she declared, "if you wasn't engaged to somebody else. Ezra Blodgett is rich and you could have had him as well as not if you hadn't gone silly over that Calvin Homer. 'Twould have been a good job, too. Then you wouldn't have to teach school and I wouldn't have to stay in this house and make a slave of myself. I'd like to know what your poor dead father would say if he could know that I had to wash the very dishes you eat off of while you go traipsing to Odd Fellows' dances over at Harniss. I guess he'd be some surprised at the way his child treated me."

Myra tossed her head. "I never noticed you were so anxious to find out what he said when he was alive," she observed. "You generally did about what you wanted to."

"Is that so! Well, I guess you never saw me going off with one man when I was engaged to marry another. I guess you never saw me do that."

"Probably not; I wasn't here. Besides, I'm not doing anything out of the way. Calvin would want me to have a good time. He may be having one himself. How do I know what he's doing there at Setuckit?"

"Humph! I don't think he's going to many dancing times out on the beach. And, besides, you know well enough I don't care what you do except for what folks will say. Everybody knows you're keeping company with Calvin and they'll talk—see if they don't. He'll hear it, pretty soon, and then 'twill be just as it's been with every other fellow you've had."

"Oh, no, it won't. I can manage Calvin. He likes me pretty well. Yes, and I like him, too. He's a nice boy."

"Nice boy! He's nice lookin', that's why you are so crazy over him. But all he is is just a common everyday life-saver. I wouldn't care so much for that, though, if you would only marry him and settle down. How in the world he is ever going to support us I can't see—but he'd be *somebody.*"

"He isn't going to be a life-saver all his life. He is smart and he'll get ahead. I'll make him."

"Yes, so I've heard you say; but you haven't made much of him yet."

"I haven't had the chance. It's coming, though. That Bartlett won't last long, and when he goes Calvin will have his place. Cap'n Kellogg told me as much as that—or, if he didn't tell me, he told somebody else who did tell me. *I* know."

"Yes, you always know. I suppose you know that that daughter of Bartlett's has been visitin' down at the station?"

"Of course I know it," sharply. "What of it?"

"Oh, nothing. And you know that your nice Calvin boy took her down in his boat the very night after he left here?"

"Yes, I know that, too. But how did you know?"

"Oh, I heard. I don't miss everything that goes on, even if my own daughter don't tell me. They say the Bartlett girl is awful pretty, too."

Miss Fuller's expressive eyes were becoming very expressive.

"Look here, mother," she snapped, "are you trying to make me jealous? Because if you are you're wasting your time. If I can't take care of myself so far as a namby-pamby kid like that Norma Bartlett is concerned then I'll jump overboard. She couldn't have Calvin Homer, even if she wanted him. I've got him. And I'm going to keep him."

"All right. Then I wouldn't take too many chances, that's all. I see you've got his ring on. Going to let Mr. Blodgett see that?"

"Why not? He doesn't know it is an engagement ring, does he?"

"I don't know why he should. *I* wouldn't guess a thing like that was anybody's engagement ring. Didn't cost *over* thirty-five dollars, if it did that. And if your father had bought *my* engagement ring at Simmons's right here in Orham I'd have had something to say about it. He got *his* ring at Jordan Marsh's, in Boston, and it cost 'most a hundred dollars, too."

"How do you know? He told you so, I suppose? You shouldn't believe all you hear, mother."

Sarepta bounced to her feet. "I don't believe everything I hear from *you*," she announced bitterly. "And I'll tell you something else," she added. "Your father—and I should think you'd be ashamed to talk about him as you do—"

Myra's provoking drawl interrupted. "Oh, but think," she said sweetly, "how I used to hear you talk *to* him, mother dear."

Her mother winced at the shot, but she fired a volley in return.

"I'll tell *you* something, young woman," she repeated. "When your father bought my engagement ring he gave it to me himself. He didn't send it 'round in the grocery cart like—like a quart of onions. If he had I'd—I'd have thrown it at him."

This time she had scored. Miss Fuller's sweetly sarcastic smile disappeared. Her lips closed tightly.

"I'll never forgive him for that," she said, between her teeth. "And I'll make him pay for it, too. See if I don't."

Sarepta nodded in triumph. "Better make sure you get him first," she advised. "And if I wanted him I wouldn't set folks talking too much about you and Ezra Blodgett."

Myra also rose. "You mind your own business, mother," she commanded.

"Oh, I'm minding it. If I was minding yours—or if you had let me mind it—I should have told you to grab Ezra long ago. He is old, and he's kind of soft headed, but he's got lots of money. You could wind him around your finger, and that isn't a bad kind of husband to have. Your life-saver is handsome enough, and he's good enough, but he hasn't got a cent and never will have."

Her daughter regarded her steadily. "You think so, do you?" she said. "Well, I know a man when I see one and I'm smart enough to make him amount to something in the world. I mean to marry Calvin Homer; I like him better than any one I ever saw in my life. As for his getting on— well, wait and see. I'm attending to that part of it."

"Humph! Maybe you are. But, unless you want to spend your honeymoon in a fish shanty down at Setuckit I should attend to it pretty soon. . . . There; see what you've done! Cups cost money. You haven't married your rich life-saver yet, so you can't afford to break dishes in your tantrums. Sshh! here's Ezra now. Take him into the sitting room. I'll clean up the mess you made—*as* usual."

When Myra returned home, at one o'clock the next morning, from the Odd Fellows' "Grand Ball" in the Harniss town hall, she went straight to her mother's room. Sarepta was sleeping soundly and was not too good natured at being wakened. But her irritation vanished as she heard the news her daughter had to tell.

"My sakes alive!" she exclaimed. "Do you suppose it is true?"

Myra nodded. "Of course it is true," she declared. "They were talking about it the whole evening. They say the schooner could have been saved just as well as not, but Bartlett wouldn't let the crew go off to her. Alvin Crocker told Henry Mullett and Henry told Ezra and Ezra told me that Bartlett ordered the Setuckit crew to stay ashore and rest. Just think of it! Rest!"

"But he did order 'em to go, finally?"

"Yes, he did, but not until Crocker and Philander Jarvis and their crowd had started first. And old Blodgett said that Henry said Alvin said—"

"My soul and body! Do stop saying 'said' and tell me *what* they said. It must be pretty close to morning and I want to get a little sleep before I have to get up and get your breakfast. What was it they said?"

"Alvin said he didn't believe Bartlett would have started at all if they hadn't shamed him into doing it. Everybody says there will be an investigation. If Superintendent Kellogg hears of it—"

"Well, do you think he will hear of it?"

Miss Fuller laughed triumphantly. "You just bet he will!" she declared. "I'll see that he does. Oh, yes, he'll hear of it all right."

"Humph! You act pretty sure, seems to me. Who is going to tell him, I want to know? You won't see him, it isn't likely."

"I shan't need to. Ezra Blodgett is going to Provincetown to-morrow or next day and he'll see him. He promised me he would."

Sarepta raised her head from the pillow.

"What!" she exclaimed. "You don't mean to tell me that you've got Ezra Blodgett working to make Calvin Homer keeper at Setuckit? He isn't quite such a numbskull as to help you marry another man, is he?"

Her daughter laughed again. "He doesn't know that he is helping," she announced. "I told him I thought it was his duty as a good citizen to give Cap'n Kellogg a tip as to how things were going down there, that's all."

"I want to know! Well, I never heard anybody brag about Ezra Blodgett's being such a good citizen as all that comes to. He isn't liable to put himself out for anybody but himself. I wouldn't put much trust in that notion, if I were you."

Myra laughed again. "You told me this very evening," she said, "that I could wind him around my finger. He winds beautifully. . . . And he likes it, mother dear—oh, yes, he likes it."

"Well, all I can say is he must be an old fool."

"He is," sweetly, "but I'm not. And I am going to make Calvin Homer keeper of Setuckit Station. Good night, mother."

Mrs. Fuller gave it up in disgust.

"You're bound to marry that life-saver, aren't you?" she sneered.

The sneer was wasted. Myra's certainty of coming triumph was too complete.

"Yes, I am," she said. "Come, mother, what is the matter with you? You were as sweet as syrup when Calvin and I got engaged."

"Maybe I was. I thought 'twas high time you married somebody."

"He's somebody, isn't he?"

"Humph! I'm not so sure. It looks to me as if he was pretty close to being a nobody."

Myra turned quickly. "The man who marries me won't be a nobody long," she declared sharply. "You may as well understand that now. And as for him—"

"Well? What about him?"

The young woman's eyes flashed. "I'll make him understand it, too," she said. "But I'll marry him first."

CHAPTER XI

WHEN Peleg Myrick came down to Setuckit two days after the storm he brought the station mail. In it was a letter addressed to Calvin. He recognized the writing on the envelope and waited until he was alone before opening it. The note was short—for a letter from an engaged young woman to her fiancé it was astonishingly so—but it was urgent. Practically every other word was underscored.

"Dearest [wrote Myra], I must see you *very* soon. I have some *important* things to say to you. Just as soon as you possibly can I want you to take a day off and come up here. I know you wonder why you have not heard from me before. No doubt you are beginning to think I have forgotten my precious boy altogether. *That* is *not* true, you may be sure. Far, far from it. I have been planning and planning for us both every minute since you left me, and that seems ages and ages ago, doesn't it? If I had not had your dear letters to comfort me I don't know what I should have done. Of course I understand how hard it is for you to get away, with the responsibility of the station *entirely* on your shoulders, but now you *must* come. I have heard what has been going on down there—every one is talking about it—and I am as excited as can be. Now is our time. You understand what I mean, Calvin dear, don't you? And we must make the most of it. Come to me at once. I must see you. Write, or get word to me somehow, when you are coming. But make it very soon. In a very little while, if things go as they should—and as we must *make* things—we can announce our engagement. Then I shall be the happiest girl in the world. And you will be happy, too; won't you, dear. . . .?"

The remainder of the letter would not be particularly interesting to the world in general. Nor, to tell the exact truth,

was it as interesting to Calvin as such assurances are assumed
to be to the person most concerned.   If Miss Fuller was on
the verge of becoming the happiest girl in the world he was
by no means the happiest man.   The underscored sentences
in the letter troubled him, not so much by what they expressed
as by what he feared they might imply.   Well, she was right
in one thing—they were in complete agreement there—he
must go to Orham and see her immediately.   He could write,
of course, and make his position perfectly clear, but writing
seemed cowardly.   No, he must see her.

But when he thought of putting this determination into
action difficulties began presenting themselves.   Benoni Bartlett was not well, plainly not at all well.   His exertions and
the mental strain of two wrecks in one day had had an effect
which—to Homer at least—was obvious.   The keeper was
up and about and attending to his duties, but he seemed de-
pressed and more nervous and careworn than ever.   He was
silent, even morose, during the days, and at night the men
on duty were likely to meet him wandering about the station
at any hour.   He talked to himself more than ever and Calvin
noticed that the little Bible which his daughter had given
him was always open upon the table in his room.   He
developed a habit of asking peculiar questions, questions
upon points of religious belief and at the most unexpected
times.

The occasion when Homer first mentioned the "liberty day"
which he desired was one of these times.   Calvin, knowing
that the skipper was alone in his room, visited that room
and stated his case.   He explained that he had not taken a
day off for a long while, that he had some business in Orham
which needed attention, and suggested that he be allowed to
go up to the village the next day.   Bartlett, seated in the
chair by the window and gazing out, did not turn his head.
He heard—or appeared to hear—his subordinate through to
the end, but when he did speak his answer was not an answer
at all; it contained no reference to the matter of the requested
liberty.   He pulled slowly at his beard and asked:

"Boy, do you read the Word reg'lar?"

the men there. Seleucus Gammon, too, heard the story from his brother-in-law. He and Homer talked it over.

"I don't cal'late much'll come of it this time, Cal," confided Seleucus. "If we hadn't beat out Philander and Alvin and their gang and got the men off that vessel there would have been the Old Harry to pay. But we did, you see. Old Bologny was a kind of late starter, but when he got agoin' he sartin did make things hum. Crimustee, how he did lay into Alvin! It done me good to hear him cuss. Proved he was *human,* you understand. It helped him with the boys more'n anything else could. They've been talkin' about it, of course, and we've all made up our minds, if Kellogg should breeze down here askin' questions, to stand by the old man. Give him another chance, anyhow."

"Humph! You've changed your mind about the skipper since the last time we talked, Seleucus. Then, if I remember, you figured that he was crazy."

"I think he is yet. Crazy as a bug on a hot plate—when it comes to prayer-meetin' talk and the like of that. And I own up he acted crazy off to that wreck. But *that* was sensible crazy. That's the kind of craziness that counts for somethin'. The crazier he gets that way the better skipper of Setuckit Life-Savin' Station he'll be. That's the way the boys feel. They want to give him another chance and see how loony he'll be next time. They want to hear him swear some more. Ho, ho! Crimus! I wouldn't have missed that for two months' pay."

"But—remember, you said it yourself, Seleucus—we might have got that schooner afloat if we had started in time."

Gammon stopped laughing and nodded gravely. "You and me know that, Cal," he admitted, "but the boys don't; or, if it did come acrost their minds, they've forgot it. And they won't let Cap'n Kellogg know they ever thought of such a thing. No, we're all agoin' to stand by Bologny, unless— well, unless you want the keeper's job yourself, Cal. If you do—well, *if* you do then we'll talk different."

"I don't. Not that way. You and all hands are not to mention my name. You understand that?"

"Sartin sure. We know how you feel, Cal. We don't blame you for feelin' that way. . . . That Norma Bartlett is a mighty fine girl."

Calvin swung about to glare at him.

"What on earth has she got to do with it?" he demanded hotly.

"Eh? Why, nothin'. Who said she had? I was just sayin' what a nice girl she was, that's all. No need for you to get red faced and foam up over that, as I know of. But the boys like her first-rate and they're more for Bologny right now than they've been afore since he was wished on to us. If you doubt it you notice how Wallie Oaks is playin' puppy dog to him again these days. Wallie's a pretty fair piece of drift to show which way the tide's settin'.'"

Homer was still unreasonably ruffled and he could not resist giving his comrade's serene self-satisfaction a shake.

"How is your wife these days?" he inquired. "Does she like the Bartlett girl as well as you do?"

The self-satisfaction vanished like a puff of pipe smoke in a gale. "Don't you let on to anybody that I ever said I liked Norma," ordered Seleucus hastily. "Don't you do it. Say, Cal," he added hurriedly, "ain't there some way you can fix it so's I'll have to stay here at the station all the time for a spell? Between Philander raggin' me about our bein' scared to go to that wreck and Jemima sailin' into me because I don't talk back to him like a man, home, sweet home is pretty toler'ble sour these days. Crimustee!"

"Well, why don't you talk back to him?"

"'Cause when I do she jibes over and takes his side and I have to talk back to the pair of 'em. That's like whistlin' for a breeze and startin' up a hurricane. Cal, if you ever do get married, don't marry a woman with relations. And don't marry one that's jealous. Don't marry a woman, any-how—that's my advice, and I don't charge nothin' for givin' it. And, look here, don't you never tell I said *that*, neither."

Kellogg drove down to Setuckit before the week ended. Homer had been expecting him, so he was not surprised. He was astonished, however, when the buggy stopped at the station door, to see Norma Bartlett on the seat beside the superintendent. It was a snowy day, but cold and windy, and the long drive had reddened her cheeks and blown her hair about. She leaped lightly to the ground and shook hands with the group of surfmen by the door. Their tanned faces were agrin as they bashfully returned her greetings.

"Isn't this a surprise party!" she exclaimed. "Of course you didn't expect to see me so soon; but you know what they say about the bad penny. How have you all been since I went away? You have been busy, I know. I read about you in the Boston paper. Why do all the exciting things happen when I am not here?"

Seleucus, who had just emerged from the mess room and to whom this last question was addressed, shuffled his feet and coughed.

"Well," he said, "I don't know's I know exactly. Maybe it's because the A'mighty figgers we couldn't stand too many kinds of excitement down here to Setuckit all to once. Ain't used to 'em, you see. Have to take the bitter separate from the sweet, I cal'late."

She laughed delightedly. "Why, that is a very pretty speech, Mr. Gammon," she declared. "You must have been practicing since I left. Thank you very much."

She and he were shaking hands as she said it. The other surfmen were smiling and their smiles broadened as, from the Jarvis shanty, came a shrill hail.

"Seleucus!" screamed Mrs. Gammon. "Seleucus, is that you? Come over here right away; I want you."

Seleucus dropped the young lady's hand as if it had bitten him and hastened to obey. A roar of laughter followed his exit.

"See him run, fellers," cackled Phinney. "He knows there's more of the sweet over home there waitin' for him."

Norma entered the mess room. There she and Calvin met. There was no sensible reason why he should have felt the least embarrassed at the meeting, yet he did, and when they shook hands he found it difficult to speak. The embarrassment may have been contagious, for she, too, hesitated momentarily. But she recovered at once and her greeting was cheery and quite matter of fact.

"Why, how do you do, Mr. Homer?" she said. "I have surprised you, just as I have all the others. And father will be the most surprised of all. Where is he?"

"He is in his room, Miss Bartlett. He'll be awfully glad to see you. Go right in."

She moved toward the door of the keeper's room, but paused, and turned back.

"Tell me," she whispered cautiously; "how is he? Is he well? He's not sick—or—or anything like that?"

"Sick? No, indeed; he's all right. What made you think he was sick?"

"Oh, I don't know. Something in his last letter—something he said—or the way he said it—worried me a little. Has there been trouble here?" Any unusual trouble, I mean?"

"No." He tried to say it promptly and in a way to carry conviction, but it was evident that the attempt was not a complete success. She was looking at him, looking him through and through with those clear eyes of hers.

"Are you sure?" she demanded.

"Why, yes—yes, of course. But how does it happen you come back so soon? We—your father didn't expect you for another three weeks at least."

"I know; but something happened there at Fairborough which made it possible for me to come now. And father's letter troubled me and—I'll tell you all about it by and by. I must see him before I say another word to anybody."

"Of course. And I'll keep Cap'n Kellogg busy for a while. Tell the skipper he needn't hurry."

"Thank you." Again she paused and looked at him. "The superintendent brought me down here," she said. "I met him up in the village. He knew me, of course—we saw a good deal of each other there at Crooked Hill while father was so ill—and he said he was coming here and offered to take me with him. Why is he coming here at this time, Mr. Homer?"

Calvin was expecting this question, or one like it, and this time he was ready.

"Oh, he comes every so often," he said carelessly. "It is part of his job. He has to inspect all the stations."

"Yes, I know, but— Oh, here he is! I'll see you all by and by."

She knocked softly at the keeper's door, and entered, closing it behind her. Homer turned to greet the superintendent.

He had dreaded the meeting, but Kellogg's manner was so good natured and casual that, after the first few minutes, he began to believe his dread unwarranted. The superintendent inquired concerning Bartlett, learned that the latter was with his daughter, and nodded comprehendingly.

"We won't disturb 'em," he said. "I shall be here the better part of the day and I'll have time enough to see him later on. Well, Calvin, how are you? How are things going nowadays; all taut and shipshape, are they?"

Calvin answered in the affirmative. He expected a sharp cross-examination, but the few questions Kellogg asked were quite general in scope.

"How is the cap'n getting on with the crew?" he wanted to know. "Do they like him better than they did at first?"

"Yes, I think they do."

"How do you like him?"

"Why—why, all right. He is queer in some ways, but he is on the job."

"Handles things pretty well, take 'em by and large, does he?"

"Yes."

"You haven't any fault to find, then?"

"No."

"I see. Well, I'm going to hang around here for three or four hours. Don't pay any attention to me. I'll see you again before I go."

That was all, and Homer was greatly relieved. He was busy with various duties and he saw the superintendent only at dinner and at brief and casual intervals during the

day. The dinner was a jolly meal, for Norma and Kellogg
were at the table and there was much joking and story-telling.
Bartlett was in better spirits than he had been since the day
of the wreck, and there were no symptoms of "queerness"
in his manner or conversation. His melancholy had vanished
and he told a story or two himself. Evidently his daughter's
arrival was the tonic he needed.

Beach drill was carried through with a snap and finish
which brought a word of commendation from the official
visitor. Homer's apprehensions concerning trouble were
pretty thoroughly dispelled by this time. Apparently the
visit was but a matter of routine, after all. Peleg Myrick's
disturbing yarns of investigations and all the rest were but
exaggerations of village gossip, nothing more; Peleg was
always a sensation monger. And the hints in Myra's letter,
and Seleucus's forebodings based upon his spiteful brother-
in-law's confidences were parts of the same magnifying of
unfounded rumor. People were bound to talk, anyhow, and
in winter there was so little to talk about. Captain Kellogg
was not the man to heed gossip; he, probably, had paid no
attention to it whatever.

But Calvin's ease of mind lasted only until four o'clock
that afternoon. Then, as he sat reading in the mess room
Kellogg came out of the keeper's room, where he had been
closeted with Benoni for a half hour or more, and laid a
hand on his shoulder.

"Cal," he said, in a low tone, "come out to the barn with
me. I want to talk with you. Better put on your sweater
and cap. It's liable to be chilly out there."

Calvin obeyed orders, so far as the sweater and cap were
concerned, and followed his superior out to the chill, shut-up
stable. The superintendent carefully closed the door behind
them and seated himself on the grain box.

"Sit down here alongside, Cal," he ordered. "Sorry I
have to lock you and me up in this God-forsaken hole, but
it seems to be the only place where we won't be disturbed.
I don't want the men to see us talking together. And I don't
want that daughter of Bartlett's to catch on, either. She's

as smart as a red-pepper plaster, that girl, and somehow or other she's tumbled to the fact that there's something going on. She asked me as much as fifty questions on the way down, and it took all my diplomatics to make her believe I was coming here to-day just because it was my regular time for coming. Even when I got through perjuring myself I doubt if she really believed it. Cal, if I was a young man, instead of a fifty-nine-year-old ruin—and thirty-five years married, at that—I'd get a line over the side for that girl. She's good to look at—no need to tell you young fellows that—and she's got something in her head besides dough. Yes, sir-ee! With a wife like her to cruise along with him the right kind of man might travel far."

He paused, chuckled, and went on. "That ain't what I towed you out here to talk about," he said, "but I just heave it in with the rest of the cargo. Now then: I want some straight-from-the-shoulder stuff out of you. No guesses and shouldn't wonders, nothing but aye, yes, or no. What about this *Rosie Cahoon* wreck? How about the yarn Alvin Crocker and his gang are telling? I want the whole truth from you, son. That's part of what I came here to get. Overboard with it."

Homer hesitated. The barn was cold and dark and gloomy. The wind wailed and rattled the windows. The horses stamped and stirred in their stalls.

"Come on," urged Kellogg. "Spin your yarn. Give me the whole of it, and don't leave out anything. Begin at the beginning. How long did you fellows wait before you started to that schooner?"

Calvin told the story. He told it as truthfully and as comprehensively as he could; how Bartlett himself had first sighted the stranded schooner, of his delay in ordering out the boat, of his expressed reasons for the delay, of the departure of the whaleboat, and then of the mad race to the wreck and the rescue of the crew. The superintendent heard him to the end, without comment. Then he nodded.

"Um-hum," he grunted. "That's just about as I got it from the other men. I don't suppose you noticed it—I didn't mean you should—but I've been at the pumps pretty steady ever since I landed here, and I've got the yarn from every one of 'em. They all bear you out, Cal. Now then, what is your idea of it all? Do you think the keeper stayed on shore because he was scared, himself, or because he really thought it was too much risk to take out a tired crew twice in a few hours, unless it was absolutely necessary . . . ? Eh? I want it straight. What do you think?"

Homer waited a moment before replying. He would have given much to evade the obligation of replying at all.

"Well, sir," he said, after the moment of consideration, "to be honest, I don't know. At first I couldn't understand. When he hung back and wouldn't give the order, I was as mad as the rest. Then—well, yes, I did think he was scared. But after he did start he soon took that idea out of my head. He wasn't scared then, you can take my word for that. I never saw a man think less about his own skin than he did. When we got that boat off he was up to his neck in the surf and didn't seem to know it. He drove us off to that shoal as if he was a steam engine. Honestly, I believe he would have jammed our bow straight through that whaleboat if they hadn't got her out of the way. If I had had any breath left I'd have given three cheers for him then."

Kellogg chuckled once more. "I'd like to have seen that," he vowed. "I understand he told Crocker where to get off, and named the port. Ho, ho! Every one of the boys took pains to tell me that part. I wish I had been there. . . . Well, that's all of that. Answer me this: Do you figure that, provided he had started sooner, you might have floated the schooner?"

Calvin had been expecting that question, and dreading it. He hesitated again before answering. There was a face before his mind's eye—not the face of Benoni Bartlett, but another.

"Why, I don't know, Cap'n Kellogg," he said again. "At first it rather seemed to me that we might. But, thinking it over since, I'm not sure about it. It was blowing a gale, and the seas were running high. They were breaking clean over her when we got there. We *might* have got her off—and then again we mightn't. It was a toss-up, I guess."

"Um-hum. But, if it had been up to you, you would have started and had a try, wouldn't you?"

"Yes. I suppose I should."

"I know plaguy well you would. Now, one more thing. Do you think Bartlett is right—right in his head, I mean?"

"I think— Well, I think he may be a little off on religious matters. He is—"

"Oh, never mind that," impatiently. "The smartest sea cap'n I ever sailed with used to read the second mate and me a chapter out of the Bible every night before he turned in. And we had prayers along with the saleratus biscuits for breakfast. But I've seen that same cap'n take the ship through an Indian Ocean typhoon and stay on deck for thirty hours running and grin and whistle a hymn tune when it looked as if every sea was going to drive all hands to the bottom. I don't care how crazy Benoni is that way. What I'm asking you is whether you think he's too crazy to be keeper at Setuckit."

"No, I don't think he is."

"And you don't think he's yellow?"

"How could I think so after seeing him head for that whaleboat?"

"Humph! That's dodging the question a little mite, isn't it? Well, never mind; you don't dodge it any more than the rest of the boys. If you were me, then, you'd let him stay on here—give him another chance?"

"Yes, I would."

"You say that prompt enough. Sure it is Bartlett and not his good-looking daughter you are giving the chance to . . . ? Well, well! you needn't bite me. Maybe I feel like giving her the chance, myself. She believes in her cranky dad, I'll say that for her. And the men are for him now. I own up that surprises me. Yes, it does."

Homer ventured to ask a question of his own.

"What does Cap'n Bartlett say about not starting sooner

for the wreck?" he asked. "Of course it isn't my business,
sir—"

"Not a mite. But I'd just as soon tell you. He talks
rational enough about it. Says he thinks maybe he should
have started; but he was so worn out and tired himself that
he felt as if he hadn't the right to order another pull like
that for the men unless he had to. Says he realizes that he
isn't quite up to the mark yet, after that Crooked Hill strain,
but he's getting better all the time and that the Lord is
helping him every day to get better yet. I don't know about
that last part—I haven't heard from the other end of the
line; 'fraid I ain't in as close touch as he thinks he is—but
I do feel inclined to make some allowances for his nerves.
That Crooked Hill smash was plain hell for any man, cracked
or whole, there's no doubt about that."

Homer made no comment. They sat in silence for some
time. Then Kellogg slid off the grain bin and stood erect.

"Cal," he said, "when I came down here, after the yarns
they're spilling up in Orham, I had about decided to give
Bartlett his walking ticket. I won't have a yellow skipper
or a yellow surfman in a station under me. But since I've
talked with all hands down here I've changed my mind. I'm
going to let him stick on a spell and see what happens.
You're all for him, I can see that, and you're all good picked
men—except Oaks, maybe, and I don't think he'll be in the
service long. If I had appointed Bartlett on my own hook
I doubt if I should be so favorable toward giving him another chance. But I didn't appoint him, you see; and if I
fire him without absolute sure cause those blasted Washington politicians will be in my wool. . . . Yes, and there's
another reason. Al Crocker and Philander Jarvis are sore
as a couple of stubbed toes because you fellows licked 'em
off yonder. They want to take out their spite on Benoni
or anybody else at Setuckit. Well, I'll see 'em in a whole
lot hotter place than this barn is just now before I help 'em
pull the nuts out of the stove. When I discharge a life-
saver it's because *I* see fit—not because somebody else does."

At the stable door he spoke again.

"Don't talk about any of this, Calvin," he said. "You won't, I know. Bartlett will be keeper here for a while yet. But—yes, I'll say it right out loud here to you—I'm still a long way from being sure that he ain't yellow underneath. I don't care if he is just crazy, so long as he is brave and up to his job. But if he is a coward—if he turns out to be— if there is any more hanging back or waiting to 'rest'—out he goes. And all the politicians from the Boston State House to Jericho won't stop his going, either."

CHAPTER XII

NORMA was planning to remain at Setuckit for a week, so she explained at supper that evening. The happening which had afforded her the unexpected opportunity to visit her father was a fire which had partially destroyed the reading room of the Fairborough library and necessitated the closing of the building to the public for a time. An overheated furnace was presumed to be the cause, and although the blaze had been discovered before great damage was done, there were repairs to be made, and it was thought best to give the carpenters and painters free scope for their work.

"So I saw my chance," she said, "and came. I have until next Monday afternoon, and I mean to make the most of it. You can't get rid of me until my time is up, you see, so you might just as well pretend you like to have a girl around here, interfering with your cooking and getting in the way."

There was a chorus of protests. Ed Bloomer voiced the opinion of the majority.

"Don't fret about the cookin'," he said. "It's Ellis's turn again this week, and what his kind of cookin' needs is to be interfered with. The more interference gets into that coffee of his the better it tastes."

"I hope this weather holds for you, Miss Norma," observed Phinney. "It's fine enough just now, and there don't seem to be any symptoms of it changin'."

The visitor announced that she did not want fair weather all the time. "I want to see a real storm," she said. "There wasn't the slightest hint of a storm while I was here before. Everything was as peaceful and serene as midsummer. I might as well have been in Fairborough as far as excitement was concerned. But the very day I left the gales began. Now I don't think that is at all polite. I must see Mr. Myrick

and try to coax him into arranging a tornado for my benefit."

Hez Rogers laughed. "Well," he said, "the last time Peleg
was down here he was prophesyin' clear and calm for a
month. That ought to encourage you a little mite, for
Peleg's prophecies generally work stern foremost."

Captain Bartlett spoke, from his place at the head of the
table.

"Don't joke about serious things, Norma," he commanded
sternly. "If the Lord is good to those that go down to the
sea in ships, and gives 'em fair winds and smooth seas, it's
our place to be thankful to Him. Don't let me hear anybody
around here wishin' for storms."

The subject was changed promptly, but the weather did
not change. Mr. Myrick was proven a true prophet, so far
as that week was concerned. Day after day was cold but
clear, and the procession of sailing craft and steamers, of
tugs and tows, moved by Setuckit unhindered by gales or
even fogs.

Norma spent a large portion of her days out-of-doors.
Muffled and wrapped against the cold, she tramped the
beaches, exploring the dunes, or visiting the lighthouse,
where the lightkeeper and his assistant endured lonely vigil,
and were in consequence glad to see visitors, particularly attractive young persons of the other sex. A few of these
excursions she made alone, but, for the most part, one or
more of the surfmen accompanied her. They pointed out
spots where famous wrecks had taken place in the past,
showed her fragments of these wrecks protruding, like skele-
tons, from the sand, told her yarn after yarn of rescues and
risks of which only the barest outlines had been printed in
the papers. And, without realizing it, they gave her details
of the life at her father's station and intimate glimpses of
their feeling toward the new keeper, glimpses which were
reassuring and tended to dispel her doubts concerning their
loyalty to the latter. As a matter of fact, the loyalty really
existed now. Bartlett had, as the crew felt, showed himself
a man. By threatening to sink the whaleboat he had won

their support—even a measure of respect—for the time. The feeling was not deep-seated as yet—it might easily be dispelled—but it was there at present. And their liking for Norma strengthened it.

They did like her, and she liked them. And, in consequence, they grew more confidential and spoke of matters personal, of their homes and families. She learned how hard it was for the Phinney's to get along on the meager wage of a surfman; how Elsie May, the oldest girl, was "cal'latin' " to help out by washing dishes at the Ocean House during the coming summer and how Joshua, next younger, had earned over eleven dollars that fall trapping muskrats and selling their skins. She heard more gossip concerning the troubled marital relations of the Gammons and agreed that what Jemima needed was to be strenuously "put in her place," wherever that place might be. And, also, she heard from man after man what a fine young fellow Calvin Homer was, how all hands liked him, swore by him, and would follow him anywhere.

"Your pa can count himself mighty lucky to have a Number One man like Cal to back him up," declared Rogers, who chanced to be escort that morning. "Some fellers would have been so sore at bein' passed over for keeper, and havin' a man from outside run in right over their heads, that they'd have laid down on the job and left the new feller to get along best he could. I don't know but I would, myself. Fact is, we was pretty sore, all hands of us, on Cal's account, but he wouldn't listen when we told him so. Said the superintendent knew what he was doin', and what was best for the service and 'twas our job to shut up growlin' and work hard for Cap'n Bartlett. That's what he said, and it's what he's done ever since the first go-off. I don't know's the skipper hardly realizes what he owes Cal Homer for smoothin' things out here at Setuckit and makin' 'em slide along right."

Hezekiah was walking a few steps in advance of his companion at the moment, and so he did not notice her manifest surprise nor the look she gave him when he first mentioned the "passing over" of Homer as keeper, and her father's appointment in his stead. When he did turn back she had stopped and was gazing at the surf as it reared and broke along the beach.

"What is it?" he asked. "See somethin' adrift there, do you?"

She shook her head. "No," she said. "I was looking at the breakers, that is all. Let's go on a little farther; I'm not a bit tired. Tell me some more about yourself and—and the other men, Mr. Rogers. Naturally you were all disappointed at Mr. Homer's losing the appointment. I understand that. But you—and he—knew, of course, why it was given to father. You don't blame father for taking the place?"

"Eh? No, no. Can't blame any man for takin' a good job when it comes his way."

"Of course not. And Mr. Homer himself was very nice about it; I agree with you there. I suppose he had counted on promotion, being Cap'n Myrick's Number One man?"

"Sure! We all thought 'twas as good as settled—Cap'n Oz and all. Kellogg did, too, I guess likely, from some things he said. But you never can tell about jobs like that. Same way with gettin' made postmaster or port collector. Just as all hands are settled down to a Democrat, there comes an election and, first thing you know, they stick in a Republican. Politics is politics; they're reg'lar vanes for switchin' round."

"Yes. Yes, of course. . . . Oh, there *is* something in the surf there ahead. What is it, Mr. Rogers?"

It was nothing but an empty box, thrown over from a passing vessel, but it served to distract attention and to change the subject. Rogers talked a good deal during the remainder of the walk, but Norma said little. She encouraged him to chat by asking an occasional question, but for the most part she was silent. Calvin Homer's name was not mentioned again that morning.

It was, however, mentioned by other surfmen during other strolls along the shore. Norma saw to that. Little by little she learned practically the whole story of the dashing of

Calvin's hopes. Each man, if accused, would have vowed that he had told her nothing she did not know before, but from each she gained the fragment which, when added to the others, helped toward the entirety.

Calvin, at the beginning of her visit, had sometimes accompanied her on her walks. And then he ceased to do so —seemed to purposely avoid her. When, after breakfast, she announced her intention of going out for what she called her "constitutional," he was always busy at some task or other. She must have noticed that these compelling duties were trivial, that they might just as easily have been done at another time, but, if she did notice it, she never commented on the fact. But, more than once, he caught her regarding him with an odd expression. It was an expression by no means disagreeable, quite the contrary, but it merely strengthened his own resolution to avoid her society. The young man was more than ever realizing that the sooner the first of March was proclaimed by the calendar the better for him. Setuickit Station had suddenly become a dangerous locality. He had dreaded the day when he must decide whether to remain in the service or leave it forever. Now Fate had made the decision for him. He must go. Loyalty to Kellogg had kept him there. Loyalty to Myra Fuller was driving him away. Loyalty! he was beginning to hate the word.

The week drew to its end. The society of his daughter had had a wonderful effect upon Benoni Bartlett. His lassitude and sullen, moody fits had disappeared. He had ceased to ask Homer questions concerning the possibility of eternal damnation as the punishment for profanity. He spent less time in his room reading the Bible. His morose nocturnal wanderings about the station ceased. He was, for him, in remarkable good spirits. He was tolerant of the jokes and horse play at meal times. Occasionally he went so far as to offer a joke himself. They were feeble antiquities, those jokes, but, coming from him, as rarities, they were enthusiastically received. Calvin was glad to remark the change in his superior, but it puzzled him. Perhaps the mental relief following Kellogg's examination was responsible; possibly Norma's companionship was the cause of her father's good humor; no doubt it was the combination of both, added to the recovery of his strength, and the rest afforded by the stretch of good weather. Whatever the reason, the change was welcome and it lifted the skipper still higher in the present favorable opinion of the men. Only Seleucus, the always contrary minded, expressed pessimism.

"Um-hum," grumbled Gammon, "I know. But it won't last—mark my words, Cal, 'twon't last. Wait till Norma's gone and then see if he don't slump back to worse 'n he ever was. He ain't right up aloft, Bologny ain't. His main topmast is sprung and, if the next gale of wind don't carry it away, there'll come one that will. He's cracked, I tell you; and I've cruised along with cracked folks afore. They're always either way down below zero or clean up to a hundred and ten in the shade. He's up now, but it won't last; he'll be down again. And some day—*some* day, Cal Homer —his whole upper rig is goin' by the board. You hear me!"

Sunday, Norma's last day at Setuckit on this visit, offered the nearest approach to bad weather she had seen. The morning sky was thickly overcast, and the Government's warnings of "For Southern New England, cloudy, followed by snow or rain" seemed likely to be fulfilled, with snow as the stronger probability. There was a high course of tides just then and, backed by three days of fresh, onshore winds, the sea was running over the beach in places, causing lengthy and provoking detours for the men on patrol at night. The days had been so clear that no patrols were necessary from sunrise to sunset.

But this Sunday morning was different. There was a heavy murk overhanging the horizon, and, as the forenoon advanced, it crept in closer and closer, until satisfactory watch from the tower became impossible. Bartlett ordered the patrolman out. It happened to be Calvin's turn, and he donned his heavy rig and prepared to start. As he emerged from the station door he was surprised to find Miss Bartlett, also wrapped and booted against the cold and wet, apparently waiting for him. He had supposed she was with her father in the latter's room.

"Do you mind company, Mr. Homer?" she asked. "I hope you don't, because this is the last beach tramp I shall have for ever so long, and father says it is almost sure to snow, and he doesn't like to have me go out alone. He was planning to go with me himself, but he is busy with his reports and papers, and I don't want to disturb him. So I am going with you, unless you tell me I shan't."

He could scarcely tell her that, yet he hesitated. He had welcomed the opportunity afforded by patrol duty because it would take him away from the station. To watch her, as she moved about, chatting, laughing, and brightening the bare, homely mess room like the sunshine of a May morning, was pleasant, but it was a pleasure in which he knew he must not indulge. Yet he watched her in spite of his resolution, just as a confirmed drunkard trying to reform might be fascinated by a bottle of liquor kept continually displayed on a shelf before his eyes. The safest procedure for the drunkard would be to run away from the room where the bottle was kept. He had tried to run away—was trying that very morning.

She noticed his hesitation and drew her own conclusions.

"Oh, it is all right," she said, quickly. "I suppose it is against the regulations. I can go alone perfectly well."

Here was his opportunity, and he should have grasped it, knew perfectly well that he should. But instead, as the drunkard might have done, when the temptation became acute he yielded to it.

"Oh, no—no!" he protested. "I shall be glad of your company, Miss Bartlett. Yes, indeed! You can come with me as well as not."

"Truly? Thanks, ever so much. Walking alone *is* stupid, on such a gloomy day as this. And, besides, I feel like talking, don't you?"

If he did he repressed his feelings. He said scarcely a dozen words for the first mile of their tramp. She talked much, however, principally about what a happy visit she had had, how she hated to leave—as she must that very afternoon—about her delight in finding her father so well, and what dear, good fellows the members of the Setuckit crew were.

"I like them all," she declared, "every one. And I feel as if I knew them now. I have had chances to be with them this time and learn to know them. They have told me all about themselves, and their families—and much more about other people. . . . Yes, I have learned a great many things this week, Mr. Homer; things which I am very glad to know—and understand."

They had reached the edge of a wet, dully shining stretch of sand which, frescoed with little rippling trickles of clear water, marked a spot where the sea at high tide had run over the beach between the grass-topped dunes. The blanket of cold, raw fog had swept in by this time, and was all about them, surrounding them as that other fog had inclosed the Jarvis catboat on the afternoon when he and she first met. Homer paused for a moment and she asked him why.

"Because I don't know whether we shouldn't turn inland here," he replied, "and go around the end of this stretch. The tide is coming in and when it is full and runs as high as it does this week, there will be some mighty cold water off there. That flat will be covered in another hour."

"What—that? Why, it is almost as dry as where we are standing this minute. I am sure we can get over without the least trouble. I have my heavy boots and rubbers on. Let's try to cross. I know you would if I weren't here. Now, wouldn't you?"

"Yes, I should. But I know just where to go and I am rigged for it."

"So am I. Come along then."

They crossed the fifty-yard stretch without much difficulty. The sand, here and there, was soft and, in one place, Homer was obliged to lift her over the deepest and wettest spot. She seemed to enjoy what she called the adventure of it, and, as for him, he had quite forgotten his good resolutions and the imminent danger of her close presence and enjoyed it, too.

When they reached the dunes at the other side she laughed gayly.

"That was fun," she declared. "Oh, how I hate to leave all this, the out-of-doors, and the sea and all the rest, and go back to that stuffy old library. I like my work, too— when I am there—but I like yours and father's better."

He shook his head. "My work doesn't amount to much," he said. "I like it, too, of course—I can't help it. But I can't stay at it much longer. I must look for something that will pay me better, and offer a chance of getting on. I don't want to settle down to being a Seleucus Gammon. Not that Seleucus isn't a fine chap, you understand; he is."

"I know. I think I understand just what you mean. What have you planned to do?"

"Oh, I haven't any real plans—yet. I may try to go to sea, mate of a steamer, perhaps. Or to get in with some ship-broking house in Boston. It will have to be something to do with salt water," he added, with a laugh. "I shouldn't be happy, I guess, unless it was."

She turned to look at him. "Then you have given up all idea of being keeper of a life-saving station?" she asked. "You did want to be one, didn't you?"

The tone of the question was so casual that he did not realize what might be behind it.

"Yes," he answered. "I did want to be cap'n of a station before I quit the service. But I don't care to go to Crooked Hill—or—"

"Or anywhere but your own station—Setuckit," she put in, quickly. "Were you *very* disappointed when father was given the place, Mr. Homer?"

It was his turn to stop and look. She met his gaze frankly and in her eyes were pity, comprehension, tenderness—something which caused him to catch his breath and look away again.

"Why—why—" he stammered; "how did you know—who told you—"

She did not wait for him to finish. "I know," she said, with a nod and smile. "I know all about it. It is one of the things I have learned since I came here a week ago. I know that you expected the appointment, that Captain Myrick and the superintendent wanted you to have it, and that the men all wanted you, too. And then father was made keeper and every one at Setuckit was bitter about it. I know all that."

He did not answer. Some one—probably several some ones—had been telling tales; telling them to her, the very person who should not have heard them.

"It is true, isn't it?" she asked. "You were disappointed —and bitter?"

He frowned. There was no use in lying; one couldn't lie to this girl. Those eyes of hers would see through any lie.

"That is all over and done with. Let's talk about something else," he suggested rather stiffly.

"No, it is what I came with you to talk about. I came for just that. . . . Do you suppose if I hadn't had a particular purpose, I should have forced my company on you as I did? I was waiting for you there at the door. You couldn't get rid of me—even though you did try very hard, Mr. Homer."

Here was another revelation of her capacity to see through pretense. It staggered him. She had seen that he was trying to get away from her. She had noticed his hesitancy when she offered to accompany him. What else had she seen—or guessed?

She answered that question herself.

"You have avoided me very carefully for some time," she went on. "Oh, yes, you have. It was plain enough. I noticed it almost the very first day I came. Or, if not the very first, then the second surely. I couldn't understand— until I found out how you felt about the appointment. Then I understood, of course."

So she did not understand at all. That was a mercy. But being misunderstood was not wholly agreeable.

"Now, Miss Bartlett," he began. Again she interrupted.

"Oh, don't pretend," she protested hastily. "We haven't time. I must leave you and go back to father very soon; I ought to go now. But I was determined to talk with you before I left, and this was my only chance. I don't blame you for feeling bitter and hard about father's being made keeper, when you had so counted upon it. And I think it is very splendid of you to be as loyal to him as you have been. I can't thank you enough for that. And he appreciates it, too, even though he doesn't know—what I know now."

He broke in sharply. "Don't you tell him," he ordered.

"Of course I shan't. I promise you that. You promised me to help him with his work and you have done it. I keep my promises, too; he doesn't know, and he shan't know, so far as I am concerned. But I have been thinking this matter over—I haven't really thought of anything else since I learned about it—and I'm afraid I am not going to be satisfied with the promise you have already given. I want another from you. I want you to be more than just loyal to my father. I want you and him to be friends."

"Why, we are friends. I don't hold any grudge against your father; if that is what you mean. I certainly don't blame him for taking the place when it came his way."

"Don't you? Are you sure? I'm afraid you do. It is natural you should."

"I don't. I did want the appointment; I may as well be honest about that. I wanted it—yes, and I expected it; but I didn't get it, that's all."

"And you realize, don't you, that father deserved it?"

"I suppose he did."

"I wish you wouldn't say 'suppose.' If he hadn't deserved it, if he hadn't earned it by his years and years in the service, risking his life over and over again—yes, and almost losing it there at the last—if he hadn't deserved it and won it fairly why was it given to him?"

He did not answer. It was on the tip of his tongue to retort that the politicians gave it to him. That they had responded, as was their habit, to newspaper sensation, and had not troubled to look into the rights and wrongs of the matter at all. He thought this, but he did not say it. He said nothing.

"You are still bitter, aren't you?" she observed regretfully. "I am awfully sorry."

"I am not bitter—against your father. I wish you would believe that."

"I should like to believe it. Will you prove it by being his friend?"

He turned toward her. "Miss Bartlett," he said, "I don't get exactly what you mean. When you went away, when you were leaving after Christmas, you told me you were glad that the skipper had one loyal friend here. You meant me, of course. I promised to do all I could to help him. I have. Now you seem to think I haven't been as friendly as I ought to have been. Why?"

"I don't think any such thing. You have been perfectly splendid."

"Then what is it you are asking me to do? What more do you want?"

"I want you to stay on here at the station for a while longer than you think of doing. You are planning to leave the first of March, aren't you?"

"Who told you I was? I haven't said so to a soul."

"You just said it to me—or what amounts to the same thing. Captain Kellogg gave me the first hint while we were driving down together. He said he didn't know whether you would be here much longer than March. He said you promised him you would stay until then. And now you yourself tell me you are going to look for another place outside of the service. It didn't need an especially brilliant mind to put the two together."

He was annoyed at Kellogg. The latter should not have mentioned the argument between them.

"Well, I was going to leave," he admitted. "I did tell you I had concluded I ought to do it before long. I didn't say anything about the first of March, and Cap'n Kellogg shouldn't have said it, either. That was supposed to be our own affair entirely."

"Then you are going then?"

"Yes. But you said you understand my reasons. I thought you agreed with them."

"I do, in a way, so far as staying in the service always is concerned. But I know perfectly well that if you, instead of my father, had been made the Setuckit keeper, you would have stayed—for some time longer. And I don't want you to leave for such a reason as that. It troubles me very much."

"It shouldn't. It isn't his fault—or yours."

"I feel as if it was. You would have stayed, wouldn't you, if it hadn't been for—for us?"

"If I had been made keeper I should have stayed for a while, I suppose. Not always."

"Won't you stay now—and wait—and see what happens?"

"I can't. Besides, what is likely to happen?"

"Oh, I don't know. Father—sometimes I think he isn't well enough to keep on here. He says he is, but I can see. If I had my way I think I should ask him to give it up—the worry and care and all—and come to Fairborough and live there with me. I don't earn a great deal, of course, but I have a little money in the bank, and we could get along, if we were careful. I have even hinted at it since I have been here this time, but he won't listen. It makes him angry and stubborn. He says he is going to stay in the life-saving work until he dies. He can't bear contradiction, and is furious if I suggest that he isn't as strong as he used to be. Perhaps he is—perhaps it is all my imagination —but there may come a time, and sooner than he expects, when he will be willing to give up and retire. Then—why then, you would have his place, and I shouldn't feel as wicked and guilty as I do now."

Her voice broke in the last sentence. He looked at her in surprise.

"Guilty!" he repeated. "You don't feel guilty on my account, do you, Norma—Miss Bartlett, I mean?"

She smiled faintly. "Oh, call me Norma," she said. "You are the only one down here who doesn't. Yes, I do feel guilty. I urged father to accept the appointment; he wouldn't have done it, if I hadn't. But I didn't realize I was helping him to take it from some one else—and—and the very one who has been the kindest, most considerate— No, I just can't bear to have you go away feeling resentful towards father and me."

"But I don't. I have told you so half a dozen times. As for having any feeling against you, that is ridiculous."

"No, it isn't. Don't you suppose I can see? At first I didn't notice, or, if I did, I paid no attention. But now, when I see how you avoid me, and understand the reason, I blame myself. I am so grateful to you for helping us as you have—a thousand times more grateful since I have learned of your disappointment, and how hard it must be for you to be so nice, or even nice at all. But I can't bear to have you give up your hopes and ambitions and feel that, even in the least, it is my fault, and that you feel that it is."

"But I don't. It is nobody's fault—nobody's here, at any rate. My quitting the service hasn't anything to do with Cap'n Bartlett or you."

"Oh, yes, it has. If it hadn't you would stay. Won't you stay, for a while longer, and wait—and see what may happen? I wish you would. It would make me feel very much better. Please say that you will."

It was the thing he could not say. For reasons quite different from those she imagined, remaining at Setuckit Station had become for him impossible. He shook his head.

"I'm afraid I can't," he said. "I must leave on March first."

"Why should you hurry? A few months more can't make much difference."

"No, I must go then."

"Father needs you so much."

"Oh, he'll be all right."

She was silent and, although he did not dare look at her, he knew she was looking at him. Then she sighed.

"I see," she said. "You are as stubborn as father. I wonder if all men are like that. I am sorry. Yes, and hurt a little, although perhaps I shouldn't be. To ask you to forget and forgive, under the circumstances, is more than I should expect, I suppose. Well, you have been a good friend, outwardly at least, and I shall always think of you as a friend. And, until you do go, you will keep on being father's friend, so far as standing by him is concerned? You will promise that once more, won't you?"

"Yes. But I—I don't want you to—you mustn't. You don't understand."

"Yes, I do. I understand everything. Well, I don't suppose I shall see you again, Mr. Homer. I hope you will be successful, and find just the sort of business opening you are looking for. Good-by."

She put out her hand. He gazed at it and at her.

"You are not going to walk any further with me?" he stammered.

"No. I'm going back to the station to pack my bag and to be with father for the little time I have left. I shall leave early this afternoon. The man from Orham is coming for me with his horse and buggy. I suppose he is on his way down now. It will be a wet, disagreeable ride. . . . Good-by. You will shake hands with me, won't you?"

He took her hand. Even then he could not realize that this was their final parting. That she was really going away, out of his life, out of his future—that although they might meet again it would be under quite different circumstances; that the intimacy, the confidences between them, were over forever. No, he did not realize this; he realized only that something was wrong—completely, absolutely wrong, and that it must not be.

"Why—why, you—you mustn't—" he stammered. She withdrew her hand.

"Oh, yes, I must," she said. "And I must hurry, too. Thank you again for all you have done. Good-by."

She turned and walked away. He took a step toward her. "Norma!" he cried.

She waved her hand. Then the heavy, cold fog came between them. His last glimpse of her was but of a slender shape, a shadow which disappeared into the grayness.

For some minutes he stood there. Then he moved slowly on down the beach in the opposite direction. He was supposed to be on patrol. He should be keenly alert to any unusual sound from the sea. Sight was impossible, the fog was so thick as to hide everything further than fifty feet from the shore, but he should be trying to look, and listening always. Incidentally he was late. His time for arriving at the halfway shanty had already passed. He ought to have hurried, but he did not, he tramped on slowly, very slowly, and his thoughts were as far removed from duty and wide-awake vigilance as they could possibly be.

Behind him the great foghorn at the lighthouse blared its mighty tremolo. From distant Orham and from the invisible ship channel other horns howled or screamed or tooted. He did not hear nor heed them. Realization was his at last. It was forcing itself upon him. He and she had said goodby, not only for the present, but for always.

He could not have it so. The thought made him desperate and savagely rebellious. He forgot that he ought to be thankful she had gone; forgot entirely that he had been doing his best to get away from the fascination of her presence; forgot the obvious fact that for a man in his position— a man betrothed to another woman and therefore bound by all that was honorable and decent—her departure was the very best thing that could happen; he forgot all this and was fiercely angry at the fate which separated them. It was not until he had tramped another half mile and was almost at the halfway shanty that reason began to return and resentment to disappear.

He opened the door of the little building and entered. His first move was to telephone the station and report that he had sighted nor heard nothing during his walk down. Phinney answered the phone and would have asked ques-

tions, but Homer did not wait to hear them; he hung up
the receiver and sat down by the stove to think for a few
moments before starting on his return trip.

There was a dash of common sense in his thinking now.
Yes—yes, perhaps it was better that she had gone. Of
course it was; better for him, certainly, and possibly better
for her. The latter possibility was remote, because, after all,
he could never have counted in the life of a girl like that,
except as what she had asked him to be—a friend. He was
a common longshoreman, nothing more, and because she
had chosen to trust him as a confidant it did not mean that
she could ever consider him an equal. And as for her thinking of him in a closer, dearer way, why—why, it was ridiculous. He laughed aloud at the insane idea; but it was not
a cheerful laugh.

And, except when she had said good-by and since, he,
himself, had never really thought of such a thing. He had
tried to avoid her company because he knew that Myra would
not have liked him to walk and talk with another girl.
Myra was waiting for him, up there in Orham, waiting and
working for him, and willing to wait, too. She was wonderful, and true, and patient—and he!— He had not been
true to her, in thought at least. He had been thinking crazy
thoughts, mean ones. He leaned back in the rickety chair
and squared his shoulders. Those thoughts were gone with
the girl who, although she was quite unaware of it and
would have been confused had she known, was their inspiration. It was a good thing for him that she had gone. It
was much better for everybody. It was all right.

Thus spoke reason and common sense. But if, for an
instant, he ceased to cling to these faculties, he was only
too conscious that it was all wrong.

The shanty door was thrown open and George Sears,
patrolman from the Orham Station, came in. They exchanged greetings. Sears observed that the fog outside was
thicker than potato soup. Calvin agreed that it was. Sears
added another item of information.

"We're goin' to have some tide to-day," he declared.

"It's runnin' acrost the beach down yonder at the marsh hole two foot deep already. I had to wade halfway up my boot laigs to get through. Have to go clear around the inside end when I go back, I cal'late. Guess likely it'll be worse up your way, Cal, 'specially there between them two high sand hills. How was it when you come down?"

"It was pretty wet in spots. The tide is coming in fast, I suppose?"

"Runnin' like a down-hill cranberry swamp ditch when the snow melts. Godfreys! I was thinkin' that it was a good thing I knew my way. A feller that didn't, in this fog—it's half snow now—might get caught out in the middle of one of them stretches and get next door to afloat. Might have to swim—don't know's he wouldn't. . . . Hey? Where you goin'? What's your hurry?"

Homer had sprung to his feet and was pulling his cap down upon his head. There was an expression on his face which caused Sears to ask another question.

"What's struck you all to once?" he demanded. "You took sick?"

"I'm all right," was the unsatisfying reply. "I must go, that's all. See you later, George."

He hurried out of the door and started, with long strides, up the shore in the direction of Setuckit. The Orham man's words had caused him to forget all that he had been thinking and remember something else. Norma! She did not know the way, along that beach, in a fog, as the surfmen did. She might not realize the rush with which the tide came in at times like these. She and he had crossed the stretch between the sand hills on the way down, but even then it was difficult. And the worst of it was that after crossing the shallow channel on the one side, the side nearer the halfway shanty, there was a comparatively dry space—almost an island—in the middle. And on the other was a second channel which, at ordinary high tide, must be waded. At this tide, such tides as were running now, it would be more than waist deep, and with a current strong enough to throw a man from his feet, to say nothing of a girl. If she attempted

to cross that stretch on her way back to the station she might
be caught by the tide. She would surely be wet through in
that icy water. She might—yes, there was even some
danger. And he, because he had not warned her, was
responsible.

Under ordinary circumstances, for any one else, he would
not have been greatly alarmed. The possibility of real
danger was remote. But for her any such possibility, the
remotest, was terrifying. He was by no means a nervous
man, and not given to unreasonable apprehending, but now,
as he strode along the shore he was thoroughly frightened.

The fog—it was now more of a sleety drizzle than a mist
—was thicker than ever, and there were occasional flurries
of snow. The wind whistled and wailed in from the sea,
whipping the dead beach grass and cutting his face with its
chilling gusts. The foghorns screeched and bellowed.

He reached the edge of the low stretch at the foot of the
high dune. The tide was pouring past, running in a frothing current, two feet deep even there. He stopped and
called her name. There was no answer. The whistle of
the wind, the boom of the surf, the gurgle of the rushing
tide, the foghorns, and the raucous screech of an invisible
gull, were the only sounds. He called again, at the top of
his voice, but received no answer.

Then it occurred to him that she might not have attempted
the crossing, after all. She might have realized that the
water was too deep, and have turned inland to go around the
end of the cut through. If she had, all was well. He
stooped and searched the sand for footprints. He found
some, but they were his, and hers—those they had left on
the way down. He walked along the edge of the channel.
The sand was loose and shifting at the higher spots and
footprints there would be vague and ill defined. It was
only at the tide edge that the marks would be plain and
unmistakable.

It was not until he had gone perhaps fifty yards further
that he found them. The marks of a feminine foot, and
leading straight out across the flat. The water was but a

few inches deep here, and it was plain to see why she had crossed at this point. She must have thought this the end— or nearly the end—of the tideway. But it was not. The other and deeper channel was beyond, barring her way. If she attempted to cross that—

He splashed through, following the footprints. On the hardpacked, wet sand at the further edge they were clearly defined, but even now the rising tide was filling the impressions. It rippled against his rubber boots as he ran. Again he called.

"Norma! Norma! Where are you?"

This time the answer came. Faint, and some distance to the left.

"Here I am! Here!" she cried.

The driving sleet prevented his seeing her, but he kept on shouting and listening for her replies. When, at last, he did sight her, she was standing in what appeared to be the middle of a shoreless sea. The current was over her shoe tops. He came splashing to her side.

"Are you—are you all right?" he gasped.

She was shivering, but she managed to smile.

"Of course," she said. "I am cold, that is all. And completely turned around. I hadn't the least idea which way to go. It all looks alike, doesn't it?"

He did not answer. All his resolution was needed to keep from saying things which must not be said.

"I was glad enough when I heard you call," she went on. "I was sure you would come pretty soon. . . . What are you doing? You mustn't try to carry me. I am too heavy."

Still he did not reply. Instead he picked her up in his arms and waded out into the rapidly deepening current. She protested.

"You can't; you mustn't," she exclaimed. "You can never do it. Gracious, how deep it is getting! Put me down, please. I can wade just as well as you can. And I can't be any wetter than I am this minute."

The partial falsity of this statement was proven before the following minute ended. The tide was pouring past

Calvin's knees, and with every step it deepened. He was midway of the channel, and almost waist deep, when a bit of wreckage, washed from its grave in the sand of the beach, was dashed against his shins with sudden violence. It caught him unawares in the middle of a stride, and threw him off his balance. Norma, also very much surprised, uttered a startled exclamation and struggled involuntarily in his arms. Her struggle was the final straw. He tottered, tried to keep his feet, and then went over with a tremendous splash. He had no time to think and his hold upon his passenger loosened. When, after a choking instant beneath the icy water, his head and shoulders emerged, his arms were empty. Norma had disappeared.

Her disappearance was but momentary. He saw her a few yards from him, stumbling and trying to stand, only to stumble and fall again. He wallowed after her, seized her with a grip that nothing short of dynamite could have loosened, and plowed madly on, through the deepest part, up the shelving shore of the cut, to the dune, to the highest point of that dune. There he stopped, still holding her in his arms. Save for that first startled "Oh!" when he stumbled, she had not spoken a word, nor had she screamed once.

He stood there, his arms about her. Her eyes were closed. The fear that she had been hurt crossed his mind.

"Norma!" he cried, anxiously. "Norma!"

She opened her eyes. "I am all right," she panted. "I shall be—in just a minute. . . . My breath—I haven't any. . . . You can put me down. . . . I am all right."

But he did not put her down. Her head was on his shoulder and her face was close to his. A disinterested person, noticing the tableau, might have found it rather funny. Both were dripping water from every thread of their garments, from their hair, from their boots, from their fingers. And still he held her close. Fortunately there were no disinterested persons present.

She looked up at him and, perhaps seeing the look in his eyes, tried to escape.

"Put me down—please," she gasped.

Instead he kissed her—kissed her again and again, murmuring all sorts of things, mad things. Myra Fuller was quite forgotten. But, even if he had remembered her, he could not have prevented himself from saying those things now. For this was real, this was different, this was—he could not have told what it was, nor wished to; it was, and that was quite enough.

As a matter of fact, he remembered nothing; honor, and brave resolutions had been swept completely from his thoughts, and he had fallen, head over heels, helplessly—just as he had gone down when the bit of wreckage struck against his legs out there in the channel. That drifting wreckage was responsible for both upsets—but this was by far the more serious.

She had reddened at his first kiss; then she had turned pale. And now, at the first opportunity, she spoke. Was it the very first? Well, perhaps not.

"Calvin," she begged. "Please! Put me down."

He obeyed, but he seized her hand, and she did not take it away. He began to stammer something, an incoherent jumble of somethings.

"Norma," he cried, breathlessly. "I—I don't know why I—I didn't mean to. . . . Oh, yes, I did! I did! I couldn't help it! Norma, I know I must be crazy to—to think you could—a girl like you—and—and a no-account fellow like me—it is—"

She interrupted. "Don't, Calvin," she said.

"But it is true, you know it is. I am no-account, and you are so wonderful. But I—I *am* crazy about you. I haven't thought of anything but you for—forever, I guess."

A remarkably short forever, and a remarkably short memory; but he believed he was speaking the truth—then.

"I didn't mean to tell you—ever," he declared. "I said to myself I mustn't—I wouldn't. But now—just now—when I thought you might be hurt, and—and it was my fault—I—I—"

Again she interrupted. "Don't, Calvin," she urged. "Because—"

"Because?"

"Why, because you mustn't say that. It wasn't your fault and, besides, I— Yes, I am very glad you did say the— the other things. I—I wanted you to."

He stared, incredulous.

"You *wanted* me to?" he gasped.

She smiled. A tremulous smile, but with a trace of mischief in it.

"Why, yes. You see, I was afraid you—you weren't going to."

"Norma! You don't—you can't mean you really love me? Love *me?*"

The smile was still there. "Of course," she said. "I don't know why you didn't see it. I was sure every one else must."

There followed another tableau. And, in the midst of it, out of the sleet-streaked dimness came a hail, a series of yells.

"Hello . . . ! Hello . . . ! Norma . . . ! Norma . . . ! Calvin . . . ! Hello!"

The tableau dissolved. Norma turned in the direction of the shouts.

"Who is it?" she asked, in a startled whisper.

"Somebody hunting for us. Seleucus, I guess. Your father must have got worried and sent him out to look for you. . . . And you're soaking wet, and you must be half frozen. And I have kept you here. . . ."

She put out her hand. "Did you think I didn't want to be kept?" she whispered. "But I *must* go now. Answer him."

So Calvin shouted in reply. A moment later the bulky form of Mr. Gammon loomed up through the sleet, a sea elephant in wet and shiny oilskins.

"Here you be, eh?" he grunted. "I've been bellowin' my head off for ye. The old man's scart to death. He thinks you've drownded or somethin'. Crimus, you look as if you was drownded! What's the trouble; been in swimmin', have ye?"

Norma answered. "I tried to cross the flats here," she explained, "and got into trouble. Mr. Homer pulled me out and got in himself. That is all."

"That's all, eh? Well, I'd say 'twas enough, too—in the middle of winter! Ain't you froze stiff?"

This was not all exaggeration; their wet garments were beginning to freeze. Norma shivered.

"I didn't realize it," she declared, with a quick glance at her fellow adventurer, "but I do believe I am."

"Yes, and you will be a whole lot more if we don't get you home in a hurry. Come on now, both of ye. Move! Run—if you can."

They could and they did. There was no more breath wasted in conversation during the rush to the station.

CHAPTER XIII

HE did not see her again for an hour, and after that only when others were present. She had changed her wet clothes for dry ones, had packed her bag, and was ready to leave for Orham before she came out of her room. Captain Bartlett, the shadow of her departure already heavy upon him, did not leave her side, and during the eleven o'clock dinner the other men were there and any chance of a private interview was precluded.

Frank Hammond, the livery stable keeper, arrived just before the meal and ate with them. He reported the weather mean enough, but the "going" not so very hard, and that the drive up along the inside—the bay side—of the beach was perfectly feasible and presented no great difficulties. He and his passenger climbed into the buggy, and the curtain and "boot" were tightly fastened about them. She shook hands with every one. When it was Calvin's turn he ventured a whisper.

"You will write?" he begged.

"Of course. And you will?"

"Yes."

"And you will be very careful of father—and yourself?"

"Yes."

"Don't tell him about—about us. It will be better for me to tell him by and by."

"Of course."

That was all, because Benoni, jealous of every last moment, crowded by to say a final farewell, and to caution Hammond about taking no chances in his driving. Norma was to stay at the Ocean House in Orham that night and to take the six o'clock train for Boston the next morning. She would arrive in Fairborough the following afternoon.

The sleet had turned to a light, fine snow, and, as the

buggy disappeared into the dimness, Seleucus uttered a prophecy.

"Settin' in for a reg'lar stretch of it," he declared. "We ain't had much snow so fur this winter, but we generally get our allowance sooner or later."

Bartlett, who had been gazing after the vehicle, turned.

"You don't figger it'll snow hard enough to bother her about gettin' to the village all right, do you?" he asked anxiously.

Gammon shook his head. "No, no," he said. "This don't amount to nothin' now. Be more flurries like this, and sleet, and the like of that, but nothin' to hurt nobody, as I judge it. What I'm tryin' to say is that I shouldn't wonder if we had some real winter from now on."

Ed Bloomer grunted. "You've been sayin' those very words ever since Thanksgivin'," he declared. "And the more you talk the finer the weather is. Just 'cause there's one or two snow squalls that don't mean we're in for a blizzard. You make a noise like Peleg. The prophet habit must be catchin'."

Seleucus regarded him with lofty contempt.

"If some things was catchin'," he observed, "I'd never have ate them cod tongues and sounds you cooked for dinner, Ed. There's enough tongue—yes, and sound, too—around where you be already without riskin' takin' aboard any more. But I do think we're in for foul weather now, or pretty soon, and I'll tell you why."

He glanced in the direction of the skipper, who had turned to enter the station, and repeated, "I'll tell you why. It's because she's gone—Norma. Long as she stops it's fine as summer, no wrecks, and we don't have nothin' to do; but just the minute she goes it thickens up and a half-dozen schooners start to run ashore. You think it over and see if 'tain't so. Crimustee! I'm beginnin' to believe it! Gettin' stooperticious, I be. Look at the old man's face—did you notice it? He's been hoppin' 'round here, spruce and lively as a sand flea. Now he's all overcast, and he was talkin' to himself when he went in that door. He'll be holdin' soli-

taire meetin' all afternoon, see if he don't. Yes, and look
at the rest of us. Don't look very chipper, do we? Course
part of that's the kind of grub we have to put under our
hatches when Ed's cook, but part of it's somethin' else.
Look at Josh there—a settled, married man, with children
enough to man a fleet of tugs. Look at Wallie, with a
wife ashore. Look at—eh? Yes, look at Calvin. Crimus,
Cal, don't cry! She may come back again. She'll come to
see me; she told me she couldn't stay away from me very
long."

Hez Rogers pricked up his ears. "Did she now!" he
drawled. "Well, well, ain't that interestin'! I'll tell Jemima.
She'll be proud to know how popular you are, Seleucus."

Calvin was grateful to Hezekiah for the distraction of
interest from himself to Mr. Gammon. He was not crying,
far from it, but he was very solemn. His feelings were curi-
ously mixed. He was happy—madly, radiantly happy. It
seemed impossible that such happiness could be his, that
Norma Bartlett really loved him. But she did—she did—
she had said so. And there was no shadow of a doubt as
to his love for her. His regard for Myra Fuller had been
merely a fancy, a delusion born of passion and impulse.
From that first evening when, after leaving her, he had
walked to the wharf to his meeting with Benoni Bartlett,
he had felt—when he permitted himself to think honestly—
like a mouse in a trap. Their next interview, that in which
they had come so near to a separation, had strengthened
this feeling. She did not see matters as he did. She was
ambitious, and to further her ambitions, she expected him
to do things he could never have done. She would always
have expected it. They never could have been happy together. She was a clever, handsome girl, but she was not
the girl for him. He did not love her. Now, when real
love had come to him, he knew that he had never loved her.

He must tell her so, and at once, there was no question
as to that. In fairness to her, to himself, and, above all,
to Norma, he must tell her and without delay. As a matter
of fact, he had delayed too long already. For weeks he

had been restless and ill at ease, and his uneasiness and dissatisfaction had reached their crisis when realization of his feeling toward Norma had been forced upon him. Not that he had meant Norma should ever know of that feeling. Bound in honor to another, as he was, even though that bond had become hateful, still he would not have spoken. Now that fate, in the shape of a bit of floating wreckage in the cut through, had overthrown—not only him—but all his brave resolutions of self-renunciation and repression, the necessity for the immediate breaking of that bond was imperative.

He must see Myra and ask her to release him from their engagement, and at the first possible moment. There was no faltering in his mind, but he dreaded the ordeal. And, although he knew it to be the only thing to do, the only honorable thing, his unreasonable conscience troubled him. He did not love Myra. Did she love him? She had said so. There had been times when he doubted if her love was strong enough to embrace the slightest element of self-sacrifice, when he had been inclined to believe that she loved herself and her own whims and ambitions first, and everything else second; but his conscience told him that this, after all, might be only surmise. She had not yielded when he told her that he could not further those schemes of hers in the way she expected; she had merely temporized and changed the subject. And her letters seemed to prove that she had not conceded anything. But she said she loved him.

He felt guilty, and disloyal—almost wicked—as he thought of her, but to hesitate or equivocate would be a thousand times more wicked. He was troubled to think that Norma did not know. He would have told her if he had had an opportunity, but she and he had not been alone together since Seleucus interrupted them there on the beach. He would tell her at once, would write her the whole story; but first he would see Myra and tell her. That "liberty day," which Bartlett had been reluctant to grant him, must not be longer postponed.

He spoke concerning it to the keeper that very afternoon.

Bartlett was, as Gammon had said, very much "overcast." His face was solemn, almost haggard. He listened absently to his subordinate's plea and Calvin noticed that the little Bible was once more upon the table. He had remained in his room ever since his daughter's departure.

"I can't spare you now, Homer," he said. "By and by I can arrange it, maybe, but not just now. I need you around here."

"But, Cap'n, I really must go. I shouldn't ask if it wasn't important. It is—very."

"Um-hum. Well, you wait a little while, a few days or so. Perhaps the first of next week."

"Cap'n Bartlett, really I don't see how I can wait as long as that."

"Can't you? Why not? What is it that's so important it can't be put off when I say I need you here?"

Calvin hesitated. "Why," he said, "it is—well, it is a personal matter that—that—"

"It ain't your turn for liberty, is it?"

"No, but I can arrange that with Rogers. It is his turn this week and I can fix it with him, I'm sure."

"I'll do the fixin' of those things, myself. I'm head of this station, I guess, although some of you fellows seem to think I ain't."

"I don't know what you mean by that."

"Don't you? No, I don't know's you do, boy. I haven't got any fault to find with you. You're all right, even though you do put your trust in things of this world more'n I wish you did. I used to myself afore—afore His great light was sent to my soul. I was just readin' the Psalm where it tells—"

Homer broke in. "Cap'n," he insisted, "I hate to keep saying it, but I wish you would let me have my day off. Perhaps half a day would be enough."

"All right, all right," testily. "You're goin' to have it, ain't you? Wait till the first of next week, and then I'll see. . . . Run along now; I want to read a spell longer."

Calvin found it hard to restrain his anger. There was no

earthly reason why he could not be spared. Bartlett spoke again.

"Boy," he said with a sigh, "I don't want you to think I'm mean, or anything like that. I just feel as if—as if somethin' was goin' to happen to me, and I want you to be on hand. That's how I feel."

Here was a new freak, or fancy. There had been enough before. Calvin did his best to seem interested, but it was hard work.

"Going to happen?" he repeated wearily. "What?"

"I don't know what. I just feel so, that's all. As if somethin' was goin' to happen—somethin' bad. I wonder if," relapsing into a sort of gloomy retrospection, "I've done anything the Lord don't like. Don't seem as if I had, I can't recollect anything, but why should He lay His hand as heavy on me, if 'twan't for some reason like that? I feel—I feel as if there was a kind of—of a great black cloud settlin' all around me. That's strange, ain't it?"

"That's easy, Cap'n. You're lonesome, that's all. Your daughter has been here. Now she has gone and you're lonesome."

"Cal'late that's it, do you? Maybe you're right. I don't know's I ought to set so much store by that girl. I don't know but it makes God kind of jealous. It says in the book that He's a jealous God; don't you remember it does?"

"I don't believe He is jealous that way."

"Think not? Seems hardly as if He would be jealous of a feller's carin' for his daughter. . . . Humph! She's an awful nice girl, Norma is. She likes it down here, likes the crew, she does; yes, and the critters, too. Notice how the cats and the dog cruise around in her wake when she's here? She likes you, too, Cal. Didn't she never tell you she does?"

The little room was rather dark and Calvin, at that moment, was thankful for the shadows.

"Why—why, she has said something—er—of that kind," he admitted.

"Um-hum. Well, she does. That's one reason why I

hate to have you go away just this time. 'You trust Mr.
Homer, papa,' she says. 'I've told him to look out for you,
and he will.' Course I told her my trust was laid on somebody higher than a Number One life-savin' man, but, all
the same, I don't like you to go on leave just now. She
wouldn't want you to; that's the way I feel."

There was no answer to be made to this. Calvin sur-
rendered for the time, but he determined to try again, and
within a day or two. He must see Myra. Writing her
would be, he felt, more than ever cowardly. He must see
her before he wrote Norma to tell the latter the story of his
unfortunate entanglement. Break that entanglement first,
and then write the whole truth to Norma. She would understand, he dared to hope, and forgive him for being such a
fool as to dream he could ever have loved any one but her.

He wrote her that very night, but in his letter he did not
mention Myra's name. It was a long letter, too—a very
long letter. And when it was sealed his conscience still
troubled him, and he was tempted to write another, telling
the whole story and begging for understanding and pardon.
Yet she *might* not understand. No, he must see Myra first.

It was the same decision he had made before; yet he
unmade and remade it again and again before morning came.
And the next day he once more sought the skipper and
asked the latter for a few hours of liberty. Bartlett's answer was still the same. Wait a little while; he could not
be spared now. Calvin gave it up in disgust. He determined
to write Myra. Writing might or might not be cowardly,
but, in any event, it was not as meanly impossible as further
postponement.

So that evening, after supper, when the skipper was in
his room, and the men off duty playing seven-up in the mess
room, he sat down at the little table in the sleeping quarters
—the only place where he could be alone—and wrote the
fateful letter. It was quite the hardest task of composition
he had ever tackled, and he tore up and rewrote many pages.
He tried to be absolutely frank, to be straightforward and
honest. He explained how the sense of their unfitness for

each other had grown upon him, had, in fact, been increasingly with him ever since the evening of their betrothal. She and he did not think alike, their ideas and aspirations were quite dissimilar. It was another sort of man entirely whom she should marry, a cleverer, more ambitious man.

"And, most of all, Myra [he wrote], is the thing that is so hard to say, but must be said because it is true. I thought at the very first that I loved you the way a fellow should love the girl he means to marry. I know now that I don't, and never did, love you like that. I ought to, of course. I realize that you are a hundred times more clever than I am, and that everybody would think, and probably be right in thinking, I was not half good enough for you. I shouldn't wonder if you really felt that way yourself, even though you haven't said so. If we were married I should be disappointing you all the time and you would be disgusted with me. If I really cared for you the way I ought to perhaps these other things wouldn't count, and I should marry you, anyhow, and take the risk. I don't—that is the truth—not enough for that. And, to be honest, I don't think you care for me in that way. I am almost sure you don't. It is better to end it now, like this, than to go on pretending, and be sorry by and by. Of course you will hate me when you read this letter and think I am everything that is mean and sneaking. But I hope that, some day, when you have thought it over, you will agree that we never were fitted for each other, and that you are well out of it. Then, maybe, you will forgive me. I hope so. I meant to see you and tell you all this, but I couldn't get the leave I asked for, and so I had to write. It was the only decent thing I could do."

He put the letter in the envelope, addressed and sealed it. Then, after a struggle with his conscience, he tore it open and added a postscript.

"I wasn't going to tell you now [he wrote], but I think I ought to. And you will have guessed it, anyway. There is some one else. Not that she makes the least difference in my deciding that I am not the right fellow for you to marry.

My mind has been made up to that for a long time, and I should have told you so when I saw you. But there is some one, that is the truth."

This time the envelope remained sealed. He took it downstairs and put it in the bag with the other letters, those which were to go to Orham whenever some one from Setuckit could take them.

Peleg Myrick, as it happened, was that some one. The hermit, in the *Wild Duck,* came to the station the next forenoon. He had just come from Orham, and was going back there, and he brought a packet of letters and papers in exchange for the one he took away. Calvin was out while he was there, and did not arrive until he had departed. There were two letters bearing Homer's name upon the mess-room table. One was from Norma. He read that first. It was short, but very satisfactory. He read it over and over again. She loved him. It seemed impossible, but there it was, in black and white. The letter was mailed in Boston—she had written it on the train. He was to take good care of her father and especially good care of himself. She had two people there at Setuckit now, so she said, to think about and dream about, and which was the more precious she wasn't going to permit herself to consider. He must write every day and tell her everything—everything. She would write again just as soon as she reached Fairborough.

The handwriting upon the other envelope was familiar and he opened it with a twinge of conscience. The twinge disappeared as he read. It was from Myra Fuller, and the young woman was in anything but a good humor. *She* had wasted no space in telling him that she loved him.

"If what people up here are saying is true [she wrote], and I guess there is no doubt that it is, I am pretty well disgusted with you. I have been waiting for you to come and see me. I expected you to come, I wrote you that it was very important you should come. But you didn't. Telling me that you couldn't get away from the station is a pretty poor excuse. Other men get away on leave, and if you wanted to very much, I imagine you could. But never mind that now. It is too late, anyway, and I am beginning not to care a great deal whether you ever come or not. If *you* don't care to see me, there are others who do, and who would come often enough if I would let them. You may as well understand that. But what makes me perfectly *furious* are the stories I hear about the things that have happened there at Setuckit. Kellogg came down there to find out about old Bartlett's cowardice when that schooner came ashore, and Alvin Crocker's crowd went off to her in their boat. According to the stories he questioned everybody, including you, and the end of it all was that Bartlett is still keeper there. Now why? That is what I want to know from you. You knew perfectly well that he was on the very edge of being discharged, that he ought to be, the cowardly old thing, and that you, by just saying a word, just the bare truth, could have had him put out of the service. Why didn't you say it? You knew there was your chance, *our* chance, and that I would count on your taking it. And you didn't take it. I hear, and it came straight from old Kellogg, that you were in favor of giving Bartlett another chance, just as the rest of the idiots there were. Oh, I am so mad I can hardly write. And I shan't write any more. It is up to you now. I have been working and planning and contriving for us, and all for your sake, of course, and when our chance comes you do the very thing you know I wouldn't want you to do. If you have any excuse, any *reasonable* one, I am willing to hear it. But I am not the kind of girl, I'll have you know, who has to *coax* and *beg* a fellow to do what she wants him to do. I am distinctly *not* that kind. And I should advise you to see me very soon—*very* soon. It is high time we had a plain talk and a complete understanding."

Whew! This was a different kind of Myra altogether, and a different kind of letter from the sweetly affectionate epistles she had written before. Calvin was surprised when he read it, but, if Myra had seen him when the reading was ended, she might have been even more so. He smiled, drew a long breath, a breath of relief, tore the letter into fragments and put them in the stove. His conscience was sufficiently salved now. He need not have worried concerning Myra's grief when she received his statement of feeling toward her. Apparently he had sent it just in time. Well, he was glad he had sent it before her letter came. She would, at least, know that her fiery ultimatum had not influenced him in writing as he did. It was all over. It was settled. He was out of the trap. And, best of all, the escape would be equally satisfactory to both parties.

He began another letter to Norma that very evening, but he did not finish it. He was in the midst of his confession, writing her the whole foolish story of Myra Fuller, and his own insane, and very brief, delirium of fancied regard for that young person, when he was interrupted. He put the unfinished letter in the drawer of his chest, and there it stayed. Many things were to happen before he saw it again.

At five o'clock that afternoon, the afternoon of the third day following Norma's departure, it had begun to blow. By nine that evening a gale had developed which, for velocity and general wickedness, had been, so far that winter, rivaled only by the November no'theaster during which Calvin, because of Captain Myrick's leaving, was in temporary command at Setuckit. It was Bartlett who interrupted Homer at his letter writing. The skipper was extremely nervous. Just as Seleucus had prophesied, the reaction on his spirits since his daughter's departure had been marked. During her stay at the station he had been an active, almost normal and cheerful man. The morning of the day of her departure he began to fidget and grow melancholy, and since then he had slumped back into his former moody, silent habit. As Phinney said, the only man he talked to was himself. With the coming of the great storm, and as it hourly increased, his eccentricities increased with it. He prowled about the station and, finding Calvin in the sleeping quarters, led him away to inspect the boat and gear, a perfectly unnecessary procedure.

The wind continued to blow, and with it came thick

snow. It stopped snowing at daybreak, but cold succeeded, a cold which forced the mercury down to the zero mark, with the gale as strong as ever. The weather bureau's warnings, sent out the day before, had cleared the ship channel of the majority of vessels; their skippers had decided to remain in port or had anchored their craft in sheltered and safe localities. As always, however, there were a few reckless adventurers who scorned such warnings. Their vessels were out there, in the thick of it, fighting the wind and tide, trying to claw away from the dangerous coast. And it was for these that the Setuckit keeper was ordered by telephone from the Orham Station—the message relayed from Superintendent Kellogg at Provincetown—to keep a sharp lookout.

Bartlett was up and about all night. His nerves were more jumpy than Calvin had known them to be, which was saying much. He paced the floor of the mess room, went to his room again and again, only to emerge a few minutes later and climb the stairs to the tower, read the barometer, peer from the windows into the snow-streaked blackness, and come down to question the men when they came in from patrol. Homer urged him to turn in and sleep, but the suggestion was gruffly, almost savagely, dismissed. By morning he was in a wretched condition, a condition which all hands noticed and commented upon.

Calvin was thoroughly alarmed. He, too, had been awake practically all night, for he was far too apprehensive concerning his superior to sleep. Remembering the so recent happening when the skipper refused to heed the call of the *Rose Cahoon* until forced into action by the whaleboat crew, he dreaded what might take place should another call come. As he lay there on his cot, he was forced to admit that he could remember no instance where Bartlett had been eager to order out the boat, or even prompt to do so. Never had he shown that keen energy, amounting almost to grim joy, with which Oswald Myrick had been wont to leap down the stairs from the tower, ordering his men into action. Benoni had shown something like it when driving the boat in pursuit of Crocker's volunteers, but that was sheer desperation. He was obliged to be desperate then or be dismissed for cowardice. And his muttered confession, made afterwards to Calvin, that he remembered very little of what he had done, was not a comforting reassurance for the future. There were times that night when Calvin was far from certain that he had done right in expressing so confidently to the superintendent his belief that Bartlett should be given another chance. It might have been better had the skipper been diplomatically forced into resigning, on the score of ill health. For, when that other chance came, who knew how he might meet it? Something infinitely worse might happen. Yes, even for Norma's sake, a resignation then might have been better. He dreaded the developments the day might bring.

At eleven o'clock, while the men were at dinner, the telephone bell rang. Orham Station reported a schooner—at that period seven eighths of the craft passing Broad Rip were schooners—in sight off the Sand Hill and plainly making a hard fight of it. Calvin answered the call and listened to the words of the Orham keeper. "She's pretty well out," the latter said, "and she may make it all right, but I thought I'd tell you to keep an eye on her. Guess likely this is the last chance we'll have to talk, because the telephone between here and town is out of kilter—poles down somewheres, I presume likely—and it's only by luck some of them between us and you ain't carried away. They're liable to be any minute, in this gale. Is it cold down to Setuckit? 'Tain't summer 'round here, I'm tellin' everybody. This is the worst we've had yet this winter. I—"

There the conversation broke off, and no amount of ringing awoke a response. In all probability the prophecy concerning the carrying away of the poles had been fulfilled.

The skipper was in his room at the moment, and to him Calvin bore the message concerning the schooner. Bartlett, pale and red eyed after his night's vigil, went immediately to the tower. Calvin accompanied him. Bearse, the lookout, reported having already sighted the schooner, but a snow flurry over that part of the sea had intervened, and she was now invisible. "Pretty well out, she was," said Bearse. "And headin' sou'west by south. She's a two-master, and heavy loaded, by the look of her. She didn't seem to be in any trouble. Long's she can keep that course she's all right. Don't you think so, Cap'n?"

Bartlett did not reply. He swept the sea with the glass and Calvin, when he had finished, followed suit; but it was still snowing off there in midchannel, and the schooner could not be seen. The skipper turned to the stairs. Homer lingered to caution Bearse.

"Watch her all the time, Sam," he ordered. "And report if there are any signs of her being in trouble."

Sam nodded. "Aye, aye," he answered, and added in a whisper, "Say, Cal, what ails the old man? Did you notice how wild he looks? Ain't gettin' another streak of the 'restin'' disease, is he? He'd have some excuse for it this time. This would sartin be one lovely day for a picnic cruise to the Sand Hill."

Calvin caught up with the skipper at the foot of the stairs. "I think she's all right, Cap'n," he said; "don't you?"

Bartlett did not seem to hear. On the threshold of his room he turned.

"Let me alone, don't bother me, boy," he said, solemnly. "I'm goin' in here to have a talk and I mustn't be disturbed."

Calvin was bewildered. The little room—he could see it through the open door—was quite empty.

"To talk?" he repeated. "To talk with one of the men, you mean?"

"No, no. Why should I talk with the men? They don't know anything."

"Then who—?"

Benoni smiled, a queerly condescending smile. He laid a hand on his companion's sleeve. He spoke as one might to an inquisitive child.

"Don't say nothin' to the rest of 'em, boy," he whispered. "They might want to peek in, or listen or somethin', and He

wouldn't like it. It's just between Him and me, you understand."

"Him? Who?"

"God. He's in there now, waitin' for me. He's goin' to
tell me what to do. Don't say anything."

With another smile, and a reassuring wink, he closed the
door behind him. For an instant Calvin remained where he
was. Then he turned away. This was sheer insanity. This
was worse than anything his misgivings of the night before
had conceived.

He walked through the mess room, where the men were
back at their everlasting game of seven-up, to the kitchen.
Wallie Oaks was there and Wallie evidently had something
to say.

"Sst—Cal," he whispered beckoning from the further
corner, "come here a minute. I want to ask you somethin'."

Calvin, his thoughts busy only with the skipper and partial
realization of what the latter's condition might mean, walked
absently across the room.

"Well, what is it?" he asked, rather impatiently.

Oaks peered cautiously over his shoulder. "Cal," he whispered, his voice trembling, "the old man ain't goin' to take
us out to-day, is he? He wouldn't try it, you don't think,
do you?"

Calvin looked at him.

"Here!" he snapped. "What the devil is the matter with
you, Wallie? What are you talking about?"

The man's fingers were twisting and untwisting.

"I'm talkin' about the old man—Bartlett," he declared.
"That schooner off yonder. The one they phoned from
Orham about. You don't think the skipper 'll try to go to
her?"

"He doesn't have to go yet. She's all right so far. When
she isn't, and if she needs us, we'll go, I suppose."

"By Godfreys, *I* won't go!"

Homer frowned. He seized Oaks by the shoulder.

"Are you drunk?" he demanded. "You talk like a fool.
. . . Oh, I see," contemptuously, "you're scared again."

"It don't make no difference whether I'm scared or not. If Bartlett orders us out a day like this he's crazy, that's all. Lots of folks think he is crazy and that would prove it. Why, it's five below zero, Cal. And blowin' worse than I ever saw it blow. We'd freeze to death, if we wasn't drownded first. We couldn't get off there anyhow. I ain't goin' to be killed to please a crazy man. Not for no sixty-five a month, I ain't. The boys won't neither, if you say not to, Cal. If he orders us out let's say we won't go. If you say it the fellows 'll stand behind you, and— Let go of me! What are you doin'?"

Homer was shaking him savagely. "Shut up, you fool!" he whispered. "Pull yourself together. Do you want the rest to hear you?"

"I don't care if they do hear me. I tell you I won't go out in that boat to-day. I'm goin' to quit this damned job, anyhow. And I'd just as soon quit it now. Aw, Cal, have some sense. . . . Stop that, will you!"

Calvin had shaken him again. This new complication, following Bartlett's weird behavior, had put his nerves on edge.

"Shut up, I tell you!" he growled. "And listen to what I say. You're going to quit the job all right. You bet you are! I'll see to that. But you won't quit it now. If you say another word about backing out or lying down, I'll knock your head through that wall. I will. . . . Now you behave yourself."

He threw the fellow away from him and walked back to the mess room. As he entered it Sam Bearse came hurrying down the stairs.

"Where's the skipper?" he demanded. "That schooner's give up tryin', I guess. She's histed distress signals. She's singin' out for us. Oh, my, what a sweet job it's goin' to be! Where's Cap'n Bartlett?"

Calvin caught him as he was about to open the door of the keeper's room.

"Wait a minute, Sam," he said. "Let me have a look at her first. Don't call the cap'n until I come down."

He ran up the stairs and bent to the telescope. The snow squall had passed and the schooner was in plain sight. Still, very far out, at least eight or nine miles from the station, she was wallowing along under a fragment of sail, and the signal for help was flying at her masthead. Calvin watched her for a moment. She seemed to be still under control, but if not—and she drifted before the gale—she might pass clear of the Sand Hill; but unless aid came very shortly she would strike upon the southern edge of the Hog's Back, or, missing that, pile up on the even more dangerous Tarpaulin. There was a possible chance of reaching her in time if they started at once. The slightest delay would eliminate that chance.

He ran down again. The men—with the exception of Oaks, who, white faced and rigid, was standing in the door-way leading to the kitchen—were already pulling on their layers of sweaters and oilskins. Homer, not stopping to knock or hail, threw open the door of the keeper's room.

"Cap'n," he called. "Cap'n Bartlett."

Benoni was sitting by the table. He turned, and rose slowly to his feet.

"Cap'n," announced Calvin, "that schooner is signaling for us. We'll have to start right off. I'll attend to every-thing while you're getting ready."

He was hurrying out when the skipper called his name. Bartlett had taken a step in his direction and was standing there, his hand raised.

"What is it?" asked Calvin.

The keeper was smiling, that same odd, reassuring smile which Homer had noticed at their parting of a few minutes before. His heart sank as he saw it. Bartlett nodded.

"It's all right, boy," he said calmly. "It's all right. We ain't goin' to that schooner."

Calvin's ears noted behind him the sudden cessation of movement as the men paused in their hurried dressing. He stared at his superior.

"You're not going—?" he repeated. "But we must go. If we don't start now we shall be too late."

Bartlett nodded again. "It's all right, it's all right," he

said once more. "We ain't goin' to start. I've had my orders and we stay here. That schooner's bein' looked after. We don't need to worry."

"Being looked after? Why—"

"Sshh! Don't worry, I tell you. God A'mighty is lookin' after her. She's in His hands. He's told me so, right here in this room. He and I had a talk about it and I—"

Calvin waited to hear no more. He swung about and faced the amazed crew.

"Get out the boat," he ordered. "Lively."

For an instant there was silence. The men looked at each other and at him. Then Seleucus spoke.

"Aye, aye, Cal," he said. "Out she comes. Come on, fellows. Sam, you and me'll attend to the horses. Come on!"

He led the way to the outer door. Bearse started to follow him, but paused. The others did not move, they were watching Bartlett.

The skipper had stepped forward, his hand upraised. The smile had left his face. He was scowling now, and his deep-set eyes were glittering.

"Stay where you are!" he growled. "Don't you move, not a man of you. Take off those oilskins and go and sit down. I'm cap'n here. Sit down."

The authority in his voice and manner had an effect. Absolute obedience was a long-established habit in this veteran crew. It was one thing to talk of mutiny. To mutiny, in fact, was quite another. The men hesitated, and as they did so, Wallie Oaks sprang to the front.

"That's the talk, Cap'n," he shouted. "That's the talk! You're boss. All of you—here, you, Josh—you stop and think what you're doin'. Didn't you hear Cap'n Bartlett say to stay ashore? He's skipper, ain't he? Tain't our business to—"

Calvin interrupted. He came running back, pushing his comrades aside. His right fist was clenched and he raised it.

"Shut up, you!" he commanded, fiercely. "Boys—Josh, Hez, all of you—this fellow is scared, that's what ails him. He was out there in the kitchen just now, almost crying,

and coaxing like a kid to make me promise we wouldn't go
to that schooner if the skipper ordered us, because it wasn't
safe and was too cold. Too cold! Think of that!"

Oaks snarled a protest. "It ain't so," he cried. "It's a
lie. I just said—"

Calvin's fist caught him on the cheek and he went backwards, over a chair, to the floor. The blow, and the crash
accompanying Wallie's upset, seemed to have a curious effect
upon the skipper. His face, which had been crimson with
rage, went white. He wrung his hands.

"Don't! Don't!" he pleaded. "You don't understand, none
of you. The Lord told me not to send a boat to that schooner.
He was in that room there, talkin' to me same as I'm talkin'
to you—talkin' right *to* me. He says, 'You and your crew
stay ashore. Those are my orders,' He says. I heard Him
say it. I—"

Homer broke in. "What are you waiting for, boys?" he
shouted. "Do you want another mess like the *Rosie Cahoon?*
You'll have a worse one if we don't start now. I'll take the
responsibility for going. Don't pay attention to *him.* Can't
you see he's crazy?"

"Crazy as a June bug," bellowed Seleucus, from the kitchen
doorway. "Cal knows what he's doin'. Come on, you darn
fools! Come on!"

They came then and wasted not another moment. Bartlett tried to stop them, but they pushed him out of the way.
Oaks remained where he was, prostrate in the corner, his
hand to his cheek. Bearse paused to say a word as he passed
on the way to the stable.

"Ain't comin', are you, Wallie?" he inquired. "All right.
Stay where you are and think about your wife to home.
You'll be with her pretty soon, and to stay there, I cal'late."

CHAPTER XIV

THE crew of the Setuckit Station had been through many trying experiences during their terms as surfmen, but if you ask one of them, even now, which, of all these experiences was the worst, he will unhesitatingly specify the trip begun that February afternoon, under Calvin Homer's leadership, to the two-masted schooner *Flyaway*, of Portland, bound west with a load of building sand. When the lifeboat left Setuckit she was short handed. Ed Bloomer, as cook, should have remained behind—was entitled to do so —but he went with the rest. Oaks was not in his place, nor was Bartlett. The whole affair was irregular, so one more breach of regulations made little difference.

The schooner was still miles out when they left the beach, but she was drifting in a diagonal direction toward Tarpaulin Shoal. She was moving rather slowly, so Homer judged an attempt had been made to anchor and that the anchor—or anchors—were dragging. He ordered the lifeboat's sail set, three-reefed, and attempted to reach to windward of the vessel. After a half hour of weary battling with the screaming gale they dropped the sail and took up the oars. The exercise was welcome, for the cold was piercing beyond belief. The flying spray froze almost as soon as it struck. The boat, inside and out, was soon coated with ice. The men's shoulders, their sou'westers, their eyebrows and eyelashes and mustaches were hung with icicles. Their mittens were armored gauntlets hooked about the oar handles. Calvin, swinging at the steering oar in the stern, was a glistening statue. The seas were so high that, in the hollows between them, the force of the wind noticeably abated and it was not until they climbed to the next crest that it struck them with the whole of its cruel force.

They made their objective at last and drew alongside the practically helpless schooner. Her load of sand brought her

low in the water and the seas were breaking across her amid-
ships at intervals. She was a mass of ice from stem to stern.
Sails, ropes, windlass and gear, everything was incased in it,
buried under the weight of shining white. She looked like
a floating berg rather than a vessel. One anchor chain was
dragging over the stern, and that, above water, was white
also.

But two figures were on her deck. One was bent over the
wheel. The other, when Seleucus threw a rope aboard,
crawled from somewhere forward of the mainmast and
seized it. This man, so they learned when they scrambled
over the rail, was the skipper.

They left the lifeboat to tow astern and set to work.
There were six men in the schooner's personnel. The two
on deck, the skipper and the hand at the wheel, were the
only ones able to be about. The rest were below, frostbitten,
helpless, and half conscious. The skipper and his companion were for abandoning ship at once and being taken
immediately ashore. They had had enough; they were
through. Save all hands and let the *Flyaway* fly to destruc-
tion, that was their advice, given whole-heartedly.

But Calvin and his men had no such idea. The *Flyaway*
could be saved and they were there to save her. She was a
dingy, forlorn old craft and when the Setuckit men had made
a hasty examination of her and her outfit they were pretty
thoroughly disgusted. Homer ordered the pumps tested and
found she was leaking but a very little, so that was a ray
of comfort. But it was the only one. The next move was
to warm his own men and the schooner's frozen crew, to
build a roaring fire in the galley and make boiling coffee,
and a great deal of it. But when this procedure was attempted, the disheartening discoveries came one after the
other.

Both anchors had been put over; but one, chain and all,
was gone. The other was dragging and they let it drag for
the time, hoping that it might eventually catch and hold.
Calvin ordered the majority of his men to chop the ice from

the ropes and windlass, to keep the schooner on a safe course down the channel, if possible, and to report if that possibility became alarmingly endangered. Then he and Gammon went to the galley to make the fires and boil the coffee.

Here they found a wretched state of affairs. The galley was a dirty, roach-infested hole. The back of the rusty cookstove was broken and was held in place by a brace of plank. A thorough search disclosed no food except four potatoes. There was no fuel, and but a gill of water. The only kerosene was that in the binnacle light. The captain of this floating ruin explained afterwards that he had intended to run into the Vineyard and refit, and, having a good wind—this was no exaggeration—had kept on with the idea of making that port the previous night. Then the storm got him and he tried to put to sea. What had happened after that was obvious.

Phinney came down with the word that the anchor had caught and seemed likely to hold—for a time, at least. He added that the gale seemed to be lessening but that it was colder than ever.

"Not that that makes much difference," he announced. "When you're froze stiff you don't care how much stiffer you get. For thunder sakes where's that coffee, Cal? We'll all die if we don't get it. Them poor fellers in the fo'castle are pretty nigh dead already."

Calvin curtly explained that coffee was out of the question. There was water, however, in the lifeboat and he ordered Phinney to get it immediately.

"Send one of the men—Bloomer, I guess—down here," he added. When Bloomer came he ordered him and Seleucus to chop wood for fires.

"Cut up some of the cabin berth boards," he said. "Fires we've got to have—or die."

He left them in the cabin, tearing the mate's berth to pieces, and went on deck. The sun was setting, its redness glimmering through the low-lying clouds, and it would be dark before long.

The anchor was still holding and the sails, what was left

of them, were down on deck. The worst of the danger, as far as the vessel was concerned, seemed to be over. Unless another storm developed they could save the schooner, provided she did not start to leak in earnest. The hold was filled with loose sand and, in that sea, there was some danger of its shifting, but he could not stop to worry about that. What did worry him were the lives of the men aboard. They would freeze to death unless warmth was provided and at once. As for taking them ashore in the lifeboat that was out of the question now. They would, some of them, surely die before that long trip could be made.

Seleucus came up with an armful of wood. In a few minutes he reported a fire in the galley and water on to boil.

"If that durn stove don't cave in," he observed, "we'll have somethin' hot to load up our bilers with. Mine's full of ice just now. I can hear the chunks clinkin' against each other. Crimustee!"

Homer ordered fires built in the cabin and in the fo'castle. He set Rogers and Badger at work rubbing the limbs of the half-frozen sailors. Then came a yell from the cabin. Josh Phinney came tumbling up.

"Ed's hurt himself, Cal," he panted. "Broke his arm, or neck, or somethin'. He's sufferin' dreadful."

What had happened was this: Bloomer had been chopping the bottom boards of a berth and had rested the end of one upon the second step of the cabin stairs. The ax, like everything else aboard the *Flyaway*, was practically good for nothing and, having hacked the board partially through, he had tried stamping upon it to break it off. An unusually heavy sea had thrown him off his balance and he was pitched headlong, striking upon and dislocating his shoulder. He was lying where he had fallen, his face white, and groaning between his set teeth. The pain was agonizing.

Calvin made a hasty examination. Then he spoke to Phinney.

"His shoulder is out," he exclaimed, "We've got to get it back somehow. Hold his other arm. Now, Ed, this is going to hurt, but it won't take long—I hope."

His hope was more genuine than his confidence. The injured man was laid flat on his back upon the floor and Homer, grasping the helpless arm by the wrist, jammed his rubber-booted foot close up under the armpit. Then he pulled with all his might.

It was a savage sort of surgery. The vessel was reeling and rocking in the seas, the loose boards and the chopped fragments of others were sliding and tumbling back and forth. The perspiration poured down Bloomer's face. He was brave enough, but he could not keep back an occasional groan, and Phinney groaned in sympathy. Homer, though equally sympathetic, was too busy to groan. He pulled with all his strength.

"Don't hold your breath, Ed," he panted. "And don't twist. Slack up. Give a little."

"You're—you're stavin' in my ribs," gasped the patient. "You're killin' me."

And then the shoulder snapped back into place. Bloomer's yell was a combination of agony and exultation.

"It's in! It's in!" he screamed. Then he fainted.

There was one berth still untouched and into it, beneath the musty blankets, Bloomer was lifted. He was whole once more, but very weak.

"It's a plaguy shame, Cal," he murmured feebly, "when you need me so. I was a fool to be so careless."

"Never mind that, Ed. You'll be all right pretty soon. Stay where you are till I tell you to turn out."

All that night the *Flyaway* rolled and wallowed. Not a man of the Setuckit crew slept for a moment. The fires in the stoves were kept going, although Seleucus vowed he cal'lated that, if he kept on, he'd have a hole chopped clean through the old hooker's broadside. The schooner's own men were all in bed now, for the captain and his only able helper had collapsed when the pressing danger was over. The live-savers took turns as watch on deck, coming down at intervals to toast their chilled bodies by the stoves and to drink scalding water by way of internal refreshment.

The morning broke as cold as ever, but clear. It was

still blowing hard. Badger came down to the cabin, to which
Calvin had descended a few minutes before to look after
his injured man. Bloomer declared that he was as fit as
a fiddle now and insisted upon getting up to do his share
of work. Homer was urging him to take it easy for a
little while longer when Badger appeared.

"'Light in the darkness, sailor,'" he quoted gleefully.
"There's a revenue cutter in sight. She sees us and she's
headed this way. Looks like the *Amgansett*. If it is, old
Ben Higgins is in command and he'll know how to handle
things. Brace up, Ed. We'll be bound back for home and
hot grub afore long. This bunch of trouble is pretty nigh
over."

But it was not entirely over. Calvin went on deck at
once, saw the cutter steaming rapidly in their direction and
recognized, with a huge sense of relief, the well-known lines
of the *Amgansett*. Higgins, her commander, was a former
towboat captain, and a man of rugged common sense and
long experience in just such jobs as the one before him.
Homer, remembering Oswald Myrick's tales of encounters
with some cutter captains—pompous young men with exalted
ideas of rank and dignity—was glad to know that Ben Higgins was here instead of one of these.

And then, just as the *Amgansett* passed slowly by, awaiting her opportunity to cast a line, the *Flyaway's* anchor chain
parted with a bang like a cannon shot. It had held bravely
all night, but to expect anything pertaining to that ancient
craft to hold longer was too much. It broke and the schooner
drove off before the gale, leaving the slowly steaming cutter
far astern.

Homer ordered all hands on deck and bade them haul the
lifeboat alongside. The boat had been riding at the end
of its towline and was now leaping and veering along behind the drifting schooner. They dragged it up to the rail
and Calvin sprang into it.

"Crimus, Cal," roared Seleucus, "come back here! 'Tain't
safe. What you doin'?"

Homer did not answer. He took up the steering oar and

pushed the boat free. That lifeboat was the property of Setuckit Station and he did not intend to have it smashed if he could help it. He set the oar in its chock over the stern and held the boat straight.

The cutter had turned and was racing in pursuit. It caught up with the *Flyaway* and slackened speed.

"Stand by for a line," roared Higgins, through his speaking trumpet. He was at the after rail, his cap pulled down on one side of his gray head, chewing the stump of a cigar, imperturbable as ever.

"Look out, you in that lifeboat," he bellowed.

The seas were more huge than ever. The time-worn description in the sea stories, of "billows mountains high," would not have been as much of an exaggeration as usual, if applied to the waves that morning. Calvin, in the boat, one moment looked down at the *Amgansett's* deck, and the next up at her stern with its threshing propeller.

"Look out! Stand by!" shouted Higgins.

A mighty sea threw the *Flyaway* high in air. It broke as it passed her and, frothing and surging, poured down and over the lifeboat. Homer had pulled in his oar and, crouching, clung to the after thwart. The water went over his head; he was buried in it. It seemed to him that he was never coming up. If the boat had not been a new one, one of the recently adopted self-bailing variety, she never would have risen again. But up she came at last, and with her occupant still there in the stern.

Gammon and the rest, watching fearfully from the *Flyaway's* rail, set up an exultant yell. A few minutes later the cutter got a line to the schooner; one hawser and then another was hauled aboard and made fast. The lifeboat, with its drenched and rapidly-freezing man, was brought alongside. They were in tow and safe. The long, wicked job was done. Now they could go home.

Calvin thawed out a bit at the cabin stove and then gave orders to start. They left the schooner's men in the bunks. They would be all right. The *Flyaway* was in charge of Captain Ben Higgins from then on. He would tow her to

Vineyard Haven. The responsibility, so far as the Setuckit life crew was concerned, was over.

But not the hardship. They had a twelve-mile journey yet to make before they could reach dry clothes and heat and food. The three-reefed sail was set and they headed for the station. It was long after noon before they beached the boat in the cove.

Calvin had been too busy since he left the station to think of anything except the work in hand. Even on the way in, his steering and the burden of responsibility had kept his mind occupied. But now, as, worn out and chilled to the bone, he staggered stiffly through the sand to the door, he began to think—and to realize. His first move, after entering, was to go straight to the skipper's room. Bartlett was there and Oaks was with him.

"Cap'n," began Calvin; but Bartlett interrupted.

"Don't talk to me," he ordered sternly. "And don't call me cap'n. I ain't your cap'n any more. You don't belong to this station. You're a mutineer and you're discharged. Now you get out."

Oaks, his cheek swollen, scowled vindictively. "Cap'n Bartlett and me have made out our reports," he announced. "Your goose is cooked, Cal Homer. . . . Here. Don't you touch me again."

Calvin had no idea of touching him. His attention was centered upon Benoni. He had expected to find the man a stark lunatic. He had certainly been something akin to that when he last saw him. Now, however, he appeared sane enough. He was pale and his eyes still showed a trace of their peculiar glitter, but he spoke quietly. Homer was hesitating, wondering whether to say more, when Josh Phinney and Rogers appeared in the doorway.

"Where's that Wallie?" demanded Josh. "Oh, there you are! We've been lookin' for you. You're goin' to get busy, did you know it? We want coffee, and grub—and plenty of both. And you're goin' to get 'em for us. Come on, you loafer! Come *on!*"

Oaks sprang to his feet. "You let me alone!" he whined.

That was all he was permitted to say. Phinney and Rogers were upon him and dragged him, profane and protesting, through the mess room to the kitchen. The sound of a brace of hearty kicks punctuated the scuffle. Calvin did not interfere, nor did he attempt further speech with the skipper. He turned and climbed painfully to the sleeping quarters. Chips of ice fell from his oilskins as he moved.

Later, after he had changed and drunk cup after cup of coffee, he tried again. But Bartlett would not talk. He gruffly ordered him from the room and, as Calvin reluctantly obeyed, he saw the keeper turn to his Bible reading. He would not talk to any of the men, Oaks excepted, nor did he issue a command or give the least attention to the routine of the station. Upon Homer, therefore, fell the responsibility which must be assumed by some one.

He was utterly worn out; fatigue, care and the loss of food and sleep were bringing their reaction and his aching muscles and tired brain refused to function clearly. Yet he knew that the other men were in the same condition and that the station work must go on. Oaks, under compulsion, was preparing supper. Assistance along that line arrived when Jemima Gammon and her brother came over from the Jarvis shanty and offered their services. Jemima, after expressing a candid opinion concerning her husband's lack of common sense in staying on a job that didn't pay anything anyhow and was just an excuse for keeping him away from home two thirds of the time and half dead the remainder, shooed all hands, Oaks included, out of the kitchen and took charge of the culinary operations.

Jarvis also volunteered to help in any way he could. His resentment at losing the race to the *Rosie Cahoon* seemed to have vanished, for the time, at least, and his offer was whole hearted. Calvin accepted it.

"We'll have to send out patrol to-night, I suppose," he said, "but there isn't a man fit to go, except Wallie, and I wouldn't trust him. You used to be in the service, Philander. If you'll go out first, I'll follow you. When I get back I'll

send some one else—Seleucus, I guess. He's pretty tough
and a few hours' sleep will fix him up. Here's hoping we
don't get another call. I don't see how we could handle it
if we did. It is clear enough now, and the glass keeps rising.
I guess we'll have a stretch of fair weather. It is due us,
I should say."

Immediately after supper—a meal in which an unbeliev-
able quantity of food was consumed and during which Mrs.
Gammon alternately urged them to eat more and made
pointed remarks concerning "pigs"—Calvin ordered the men
to their bunks. He turned in, himself, and slept like a
dead man until Philander, at midnight, shook him into something approaching wakefulness. Then he rose, donned his
clothes, and staggered out for his patrol. That tramp was
a nightmare, almost literally so, for he found himself falling
asleep whenever he paused for breath. Fortunately the wind
had gone down and the sky was clear and starlit. No vessels
were visible upon the sea. The great gale had cleared the
channel of craft, both steam and sail.

He returned at four, dragged Seleucus from his cot, and
sent him forth. Oaks he sent to the tower, with orders to
keep his eyes open unless he preferred to have them forcibly
closed. Wallie at first refused to go, but thought better of
it, and went, sullen and ugly. Homer was going to pay
for this, the man muttered; he'd find out before it was over
and done with. If there was any law anywhere he—Oaks
—would have damages for being struck in the face when
he wasn't looking.

Calvin tartly suggested that the damage would be immediate and a great deal worse if he said any more at that
moment. Having disposed of that point, he went again to the
sleeping quarters and tumbled into bed. When he awoke it
was ten o'clock in the forenoon. The crew met his angry
protests with broad grins. He needed the sleep, they declared, and they had cal'lated he should have it

Peleg Myrick's boat was in the cove and Peleg himself
was below in the mess room. His nose for news had scented
sensation and he had sailed down in the hope of finding it.

Also, he was stoutly protesting that he had known the storm was coming, and had been saying so for a week.

"Aw, go on, Peleg, go on!" cackled Rogers derisively. "Last time I saw you you was singin' out nothin' but fair weather. Said it was liable to be so calm you didn't know but what 'twould be good business to swap the sail of that catboat of yours for an extry pair of oars."

"I never neither," vowed Myrick in high indignation. "I said 'twas calm then, and 'twas too; but about last Saturday —seems to me 'twas Saturday, might have been Sunday mornin'—I got a twitch in my port laig, down in the latitudes of my ankle, that fetched me right out of bed. 'Twas a reg'lar pain, 'twas—sharp, as if somebody'd raked me with an iyster knife."

Seleucus offered a suggestion. "Probably 'twas that cat of yours raked you," he observed. "Probably the critter wanted to sharpen his claws and mistook your old tanned-up laigs for the bedposts. They're about the color of black walnut."

Calvin came in just here and interrupted to ask if Peleg was going to Orham and, if so, if he would take a message to the telegraph office. Peleg said that he would, provided the message was ready in five minutes.

"I don't know whether there's any telegrams gettin' through yet," he added, "but I can leave it to be sent soon's there is. Hurry up, that's all. I ain't got time to waste with a gang like this."

Homer wrote the message hurriedly. It was addressed to Captain Kellogg at Provincetown and urged the latter to visit Setuckit without delay. He gave no reasons for his request. The superintendent, he thought, should learn the situation from him, rather than from exaggerated gossip which might leak from the telegraph office. He cautioned Myrick to be silent.

"Don't you do any talking, Peleg," he said. "If you do I shall hear of it, and you may get into trouble."

The skipper of the *Wild Duck* promised volubly, but Calvin put little faith in his protests. Peleg was wont to be long on promise, but, under stress of temptation to act as a special news "extra," inclined to be short of fulfillment.

Bartlett was still in his room, so the men said. He had come out for breakfast, but had eaten little, and addressed no word to any one of them. He looked pretty well "shook up," as Badger described it, and his hand trembled so that he could scarcely hold his coffee cup. Oaks—but no one seemed to know exactly where Wallie was. He was keeping out of the way, they opined; perhaps he was writing to his wife ashore.

But he appeared, a few minutes later, dressed in shore-going togs and with a battered suit case in his hand. He hastened through the group in the mess room and followed Mr. Myrick to the beach. The crowd, therefore, promptly followed him. Calvin went with them.

"Here, Wallie, where are you going?" he asked. Oaks answered without stopping or turning.

"None of your business," he snarled.

"Oh, yes, it is my business. Hold on there."

Wallie threw the suit case into the Myrick dory before he spoke. He picked up an oar and shoved the dory into deep water.

"No, it ain't your business neither, Cal Homer," he declared. "It's nobody's business but Cap'n Bartlett's, and I've told him. You may think you're skipper here, but you ain't —not yet. There's a whole lot of things to be said afore you are, too. Go on, Peleg. What are you waitin' for?"

Myrick, seated at the oars, was hesitating.

"Cal," he cried, "Wallie asked me to take him up to Orham along with me. It's all right for me to take him, ain't it?"

Calvin thought for an instant. Then he nodded. "Yes, take him," he replied. "He's no use here."

And yet, as he thought more of the matter, he almost wished that he had detained Oaks, even by force, if necessary. The man, of course, was doing what he declared he meant to do, quitting the station and the life-saving service.

That was all right; he was certain to be discharged, anyway. But with him had gone all hope of keeping the story of the mutiny at Setuckit from the eager ears of Orham. Oaks would tell and what he would tell was likely to be a version not in the least creditable to him, Calvin Homer, or within a mile of the real truth. Kellogg, after all, would hear the Oaks version first. Well, it could not be helped now. It was one more straw added to the weight of trouble to come.

For the realization of how much trouble there was sure to be, was—now that he was thoroughly awake and himself once more—being driven into his mind. Bartlett had been insane when he refused to go to the *Flyaway* and babbled of his orders from the Almighty—there was no doubt whatever on that point. But his was a peculiar kind of insanity which developed acutely under anxiety and fear, but subsided when the crisis was over. Now, the average person seeing and speaking with him, might consider him rational and sensible enough. And his behavior, since the crew's return, was—Calvin was obliged to confess it—such as any man, in similar circumstances, might adopt. His authority had been defied and assumed by another. Therefore he had since refused to reassume that authority, but was waiting to tell his story to the district superintendent. Which was, to all intents and purposes, precisely what Homer himself would have done if placed in a similar position.

Calvin had hoped to see Kellogg before any one else saw him, tell the plain truth, and await the consequences, whatever they might be. He had done right—there was nothing else to be done. He and the men from Setuckit Station had saved the *Flyaway* and the lives of those aboard her. If it had to be done over again he should act in exactly the same way. The men would substantiate his story. He was not in the least fearful of the outcome. Kellogg was a man, not an office martinet, and he would understand and approve. In the very unlikely event of his refusing to excuse the extreme breach of discipline Calvin did not greatly care. His conscience was clear.

But the thought of a distorted story, a story backed by

hate and revenge, being spread from one end of the Cape
to the other, was not agreeable. It would make matters
harder for Kellogg. It would have to be referred to Washington. It might even get into the papers. Norma might
read it there. Thoughts of her had been with him since he
rose from his bed. She had left her father in his care.
She had trusted him. He must get word to her, must tell
his story to her before she heard the other.

So, while the *Wild Duck* sailed toward Orham, he sat
down at the table beside his cot to write to her. He wished
now—how he wished!—that he had sent a letter, or even a
telegram, to her by Peleg, as he had sent the message to Kellogg. But he could have told so little in a telegram, and, at
all events, it was too late for that now. He would write
and try to get his letter up to the post office that very night,
somehow.

There was the unfinished letter in his chest, the one in
which he had begun his confession concerning Myra. He
thought of it, but this new complication seemed so much
more important—for the time, at least—that he left the
former letter where it was and began another. This was
brief, but he made it as straightforward and honest as he
could. He asked her to try and understand, begged her
forgiveness, and again promised to be as fair to Benoni Bartlett as if the latter were his own father. And he asked her
to write at once—or, better, telegraph—saying that she did
understand, in order that he might know he was forgiven.

The letter he intrusted to Hez Rogers, who was to hand
it to the patrolman from the Orham Station, when they met
at the halfway shanty, and the Orham man was to get it
over to the post office by the next morning, if he could.
After Hez had gone he thought of many more things he
might have said, or said better, but it was too late. For better or worse the thing was done, and all he could do was to
wait—and hope.

The telephone lines were repaired the next day and, before noon of the day after that, Homer received a call from
the telegraph office. A message had come for him. It was

from Norma and was brief and to the point. "Am coming the moment I can get away. Take care of father." That was all. There was no mention of understanding or forgiveness. Yet she must have received his letter, otherwise how could she have learned of the trouble at Setuckit? His reason told him that she could say little in a telegram, but, nevertheless, the brevity of the message was disturbing and a little disappointing.

And, before dinner was over, his thoughts were busy with other matters. Kellogg came, and wasted no time in getting down to business. He greeted Calvin pleasantly but curtly and went immediately to the skipper's room, where he and Bartlett were closeted for more than an hour. When the district superintendent emerged he took aside and questioned one member of the crew after the other. Then, at last, he sought out Homer and led the latter to their former place of conference—the barn. They sat together once more upon the grain bin.

Kellogg produced cigars and offered one to his companion. The latter declined. He did not feel that he should enjoy smoking just then. The superintendent lighted and puffed for a moment in silence while Homer fidgeted and waited for him to speak. The wait seemed interminable. Would he never begin?

But when he did he came immediately to the point.

"Well, Mr. Homer," he observed, "there's been some considerable of a mess down here, I should judge. What have *you* got to say about it?"

Calvin glanced at him. The formality of the "Mr. Homer" was somewhat ominous.

"What do you want me to say?" he asked.

"Eh? . . . Well, I want you to say just as much and no more than will tell me the truth. That's what I want."

"That was what I intended to tell you. I guess there will be nothing you haven't heard before, from the rest of the fellows."

"I've heard a lot. But never mind that. I want to hear it from you now. Is it true that Cap'n Bartlett ordered the crew to stay in the station and not to go off to the *Fly-away?*"

"Yes, sir."

"And, in spite of those orders, you made 'em get out the boat, took charge yourself, and went on your own hook?"

"Yes, sir."

"You knew that was dead against the rules of the service?"

"Yes, sir, I knew that."

"But you did it just the same. And what's this about Wallie Oaks? Wallie says that, when he tried to stand by the keeper, as was his duty to do, you struck him when he wasn't looking, and knocked him down. Is that true?"

"Partly. Yes, sir. He was looking—but I struck him."

"I see. Well, now tell me the whole yarn—about the schooner, what you did aboard her, how things have gone since you got back here, and all the rest of it."

Calvin told the tale, omitting nothing, and excusing himself not in the least. Kellogg listened, smoking steadily. The interview so far was, to all intents and purposes, a repetition of the former session between these two in that barn. And now, as then, when the story ended the superintendent waited a minute or more before offering a comment. Then he took the stump of the cigar from his lips and knocked off the ash with his finger.

"Humph!" he grunted. "You disobeyed the keeper's orders and those of the Lord A'mighty besides, eh? Seems to me that was taking considerable on your shoulders. . . . Eh? Wasn't it?"

"Yes, sir, I guess it was."

"Um-hum. Well, now that you've had time to think it over, what excuse have you got to make?"

The answer was prompt and sharp.

"Not any, sir. If things were as they were then, I guess I should do it again. Yes, I know I should."

"And take the consequences?"

"Yes."

"Humph! Ready to hand in your resignation, are you?"

"Whenever you ask for it."

To his surprise Kellogg laughed.

"You're different from Bartlett, son," he observed. "I
hinted that he'd better get ready to hand in his and he
told me he'd see me damned first—or words to that effect.
Course he didn't say 'damn.' I'd have known better how
to answer him if he had. He told me the Almighty was
looking out for his interests and that He wasn't bothering
with understrappers like me. That's what he meant, anyhow. Well, if he's got the official papers to show for it, I
shouldn't worry, if I were he. But, meanwhile, I've given
him a little while longer to make out that resignation in."

Calvin rose to his feet.

"You've asked *him* to resign!" he exclaimed.

"I certainly have. He's crazy, Cal, just as I knew he
was. . . . Now, now, don't say any more; let me finish.
I've been busy since I got your telegram. I've heard from
the *Flyaway* cap'n. I've heard from Higgins of the *Amgansett*. By the way, son, old Higgins gave it to me straight
about how you handled that job. He praised you up to the
main truck, and when *he* praises a man that man has done
something. The *Flyaway* bunch say just as much or more.
Well, I guess likely they ought to. They'd every one of 'em
be dead—drowned and frozen, if it hadn't been for you.
All the Setuckit men say the same. So does Jarvis; I talked
with him a spell ago. The only ones who don't praise you
are Bartlett and Wallie Oaks. Wallie got after me up in
Orham before I came down here. Ho, ho!"

He rolled back and forth on the grain chest.

"Wallie didn't praise you—no," he went on, when his
laugh was finished. "But, so far as that goes, I didn't praise
Wallie much. I told him that the thing I was sorriest for
was that I wasn't here to see you black his eye. Ho, ho! I
meant it, too."

Calvin did not speak; his emotions were in a curious jumble.

"I told him," continued Kellogg, "that, even if he had anything worth saying to say, I wouldn't listen to a man who ran away from the service the way he had. And when he went on talking I told him to be careful or something would happen to his other eye. Don't worry about Wallie Oaks. He doesn't count and never did. I intended to discharge him just as soon as I could pick up a likely man to take his place. . . . Don't worry any more anyhow, Calvin. You did the right thing; the thing I would have expected you to do. I'm proud of you, son, and I'll stand back of you. That's all."

He, too, rose to his feet. Homer was still silent. The superintendent regarded him keenly.

"Well?" he queried. "What's the matter now? Haven't you got anything to say?"

Calvin drew a long breath. "Why—why, I want to thank you, sir, of course," he stammered. "I'm glad you think I did right, and—and all that. I'm ever so much obliged to you. But—"

"But you're worried about Bartlett. Eh? Is that it?"

"Why, yes, I—you see—"

"You needn't be. I have been expecting something like this to happen. The man is crazy. He is sane enough by spells; he acted sane enough when I went into his room to talk to him a little while ago. But before I left he was raving at me like a Bedlamite, quoting the Bible, and telling how the Lord came to see him that day and told him this and that—and I don't know what all. It's settled. If he won't resign, then he'll have to be discharged. He isn't fit to stay here and he shan't stay. If he does I go; that's all about that."

"But, Cap'n Kellogg, I wouldn't want you to—"

"Never mind me. I'll get along. And—just between us now, son—let me tell you that I've been getting ready for something like this for a couple of months. The department at Washington knows how matters have been going. They're prepared, and I'm willing to bet they'll stand behind me. The politicians and the newspapers have forgotten all about the Setuckit Station by this time. It's an old story with them by now. They won't interfere. And, if some of 'em did, it wouldn't make any difference. I'll have my way now, same as I'm used to having it. Yes, sir, Benoni Bartlett goes. . . . And, you come in. You're going to be what you should have been last November—keeper here at Setuckit."

Calvin spoke now and with decision. This was what he feared.

"No, sir—no," he protested. "I can't take the appointment. I thank you very much. I appreciate your thinking of me, but—well, I can't take it, that's all."

Kellogg stared in surprise. "Can't take it?" he repeated irritably. "Of course you'll take it. I want you to take it. Have wanted just that all along. And so have you. You told me so. Eh? Didn't you?"

"I told you last November that I wanted to be keeper here —yes. But I have changed my mind. You see—well, I can't tell you, Cap'n Kellogg—but—"

"But what? Are you crazy, too?"

"I hope not. But—"

"Oh, be hanged. You'll have to take the job—to help me out, if for no other reason. . . . There, there! I can't spend any more time arguing. You can think it over; there'll be time enough. And there are a few days yet before the first of March. You can't quit before then without breaking your word to me. And until then, anyhow, you'll act as keeper. You've got to. I need you."

"But—but Cap'n Bartlett will be here."

"Maybe he will, and maybe he won't. That's up to me. I'm inclined to let him down easy, mainly on his daughter's account, so I'm going to give him a few days to resign in. Resigning doesn't mean much to outsiders. A man can resign for a whole lot of different reasons. He can be fired for only a certain kind, and they are the kind that hurt. I'm going to forward my report and recommendations to Washington. He'll have until I hear from there to resign in. And I mean to write to his daughter, explaining everything, and

telling her to use her influence to get him to quit and save
a lot of talk, talk that will hurt him. I think she'll understand
and do it. . . . Meanwhile, Calvin, you're keeper here. Yes,
you've got to be. Afterwards—well, we'll see how you feel
when the time comes. . . . There! that's enough. Come on!
I'm going home."

CHAPTER XV

CALVIN'S letter to Norma Bartlett had been duly delivered to the member of the Orham Station crew at the halfway house. He took it back with him when he returned from patrol. But, when he reached the station, the mail had already gone over to the mainland and so he put the letter on the shelf in the mess room where, in the ordinary course of events, it would have been taken on the following day. But, as it happened, no one went to the village that day, or the next. There was nothing very unusual in this, for often several days elapsed before the station mail reached the post office. In this case Norma's letter did not leave Orham until the afternoon of the fourth day following that of the great storm. And that same afternoon Norma left Fairborough for Boston, on her way to Setuckit.

She had read the accounts in the newspapers of the rescue of the *Flyaway*. These accounts were brief, but in one of them was a hint of trouble at her father's station. It was but a hint, derived from a local correspondent's interview at Vineyard Haven with the *Flyaway's* skipper. The latter had learned from one of the Setuckit life-savers a little of what had happened before the lifeboat was launched, and the paper printed a distorted story made up, for the most part, of rumor and surmise. Captain Bartlett, keeper at Setuckit, had not, so it said, led his crew to the helpless schooner. Instead a man named Homer was in command, and this same Homer was, according to the reports of the *Flyaway's* men and judged by the few words vouchsafed by Captain Higgins of the revenue cutter *Amgansett,* extremely able and very much on the job. But the question as to why he, instead of Bartlett, had led the Setuckit crew that day was still a question at the time the article was written. There were rumors of dissatisfaction, culminating in open rebellion. More particulars were to follow.

This was the tale which Norma read in the Boston news-paper. It was disturbing enough and sufficiently alarming of itself. She slept but little that night and made up her mind, provided she heard nothing more next day, to telegraph to Calvin, asking for explanation and reassurance. There was not the slightest doubt in her mind of her lover's loyalty. He had promised to keep faith with her father and he would do it, she was sure of that. What she feared was that her father's health had broken, that he was ill. If so she must go to him. It would be difficult to leave her desk at the library, but those difficulties should not matter. She would go, even if it meant giving up her position there at Fair-borough.

The morning mail brought no word. The papers, when they came, contained none of the promised "particulars." She had not really expected Calvin to write; if there had been or was serious trouble he would be too busy for that. But she had hoped he might telegraph. And no telegram came.

The evening mail, however, brought a letter with the Orham postmark. The writing on the envelope was unfa-miliar; it was neither her father's nor Calvin Homer's. An awkward scrawl and her name misspelled. When she tore open the envelope her first glance was at the signature on the final page. To her great surprise the letter was signed "Walter B. Oaks." As she read her surprise increased and her alarmed forebodings changed to even more alarming certainties.

Oaks, when he left the station to board Peleg Myrick's catboat, had that letter in his pocket. He posted it in Orham that very night. He had written it partly at Benoni Bart-lett's dictation, but its phrasing and a large share of the ac-cusations and implications contained in it were his own. Bartlett, at the time, was far too agitated and irrational to think or speak connectedly. He had wailed that "she ought to know—Norma's got to know," and when Oaks volunteered to write her the offer was eagerly accepted. The letter was written that evening when Homer and the crew were aboard the *Flyaway*. Wallie sat at the table in the skipper's room, while Benoni paced the floor, alternately railing at his men, particularly Calvin, for their desertion and disobedience, and calling upon the Almighty for self-justification and aid. If Oaks had written what his superior ordered him to write, the letter would have carried with it, even to as fondly prejudiced a person as Norma, absolute conviction of her father's insanity. But the writer ignored all the incoherences, the quotations from Scriptures and revival hymns, and wrote only what his own hatred and spite inspired. These feelings, long present but suppressed, had reached their culmination that day and Wallie, to whom the task of writing an ordinary letter was drudgery, thoroughly enjoyed himself.

He overdid it a little, of course, and Norma—who had disliked and distrusted him from the first—read the spite between the lines and believed only partially. But even partial belief was dreadful. According to Oaks, there had been open mutiny at Setuckit. Her father's orders were flatly disobeyed and, so the letter said, there had been violence and blows.

"Captain Bartlett [wrote Oaks] wasn't very well and he hadn't been for two or three days, and yet Cal Homer and the rest pushed him around and would have hit him if I hadn't staved them off. Cal Homer did hit me in the face when my back was turned and knocked me down and injured me pretty bad. I shall see a Doctor soon as I can on account of it. But I don't mind that so much. I done my duty in standing by my captain which is according to rules and regulations. And your father was right in not ordering out the boat. He was looking out for his crew and that is what he is there for. But the real reeson for the trouble is way back of all that. It is part of a plan that has been going on for a long time to get your father in bad and make Cal Homer keeper. He has been working for the place all the time and doing Captain Bartlett dirt every chance he got. And pretending to the district superintendent and you to I guess likely that he is captain Bartlett's best friend. He isent and I have known it all along. He and Seleucus Gammon and

Josh Phinney are the head ones in the plan but they are all
in it. They will swear all sorts of lies but dont believe them
because what I am telling you is the truth so help me god.
I have not got nothing to gain by telling you this for I am
going to quit my job here right off. I made up my mind
to that a long spell ago. But you ought to know what is
what and how Cal Homer and them have worked underhand
against him all the time."

The letter was long and hard to read, but Norma read it
all several times. At the end of the final reading her scornful contempt for the writer was greater than ever and her
trust in Calvin still unshaken. The idea that he had offered
violence to her father was ridiculous and if he had knocked
Wallie Oaks down it was because the fellow deserved it.
But it was certain that something very serious had taken
place, that her father needed her, and that she must go to
him at once. He must be ill, otherwise he would have written
the letter himself. And, in spite of her trust in Calvin, she
could not understand his silence. He might, at least, have
telegraphed just a reassuring word. He must realize that
she was bound to hear something concerning the trouble, and
that she would be alarmed and worried.

That very evening she wired him of her intention to come
to Setuckit, and the following day she asked for leave and
obtained it. When that day, too, passed with no word from
him her anxiety began to be tinged with a shade of resentment. How could he be so neglectful of her peace of mind?
She was disappointed and hurt, and, as she brooded over
the matter during her journey to Boston her reflections concerning his remissness were not too charitable. How could
he be so thoughtless of her? The next morning Calvin's
letter reached Fairborough, but she was not there to receive
it and they held it at the library awaiting her return.

From Boston she telegraphed Hammond, the Orham hotel
proprietor and livery man, asking him to arrange for a vehicle and driver to meet her on her arrival and to convey her
to Setuckit. When she alighted at the railway station she
was surprised, and far from overjoyed, to find that the per-

son who stepped forward to greet her was not Hammond, but a deputy, and that deputy, of all persons, Wallie Oaks.

Wallie was polite to the verge of obsequiousness. He explained that Mr. Hammond had "another drivin' job on this mornin'," and therefore could not be at the depot to meet her. "He's cartin' one of them New York hat-and-cap drummers around this forenoon," went on Oaks, "and, bein' as I happened to stop in at the stable a couple of hours ago, he asked me to take the hoss 'n' team and come after you and fetch you to the Ocean House. He's goin' to drive you down to the station this afternoon, though. He's fixed that up all right for you, Norma. Frank's a dependable kind of feller. Him and me are chums, as you might say."

The young lady's reply was limited to a very brief acknowledgment of the information. Her hitherto favorable opinion of Mr. Hammond was not helped by the statement that he and Wallie Oaks were "chums." Nor was she pleased to be hailed as "Norma" by the last named gentleman. It was true that most of the members of her father's crew had fallen into the habit of dropping all formalities of address during her recent visit, but down there, somehow, it was different. And there was a certain sly implication of confidential intimacy in Wallie's use of her Christian name on the present occasion which was irritating. It made her long to slap him.

She yielded to the temptation to the extent of making her first remark a pronounced snub, but snubs meant nothing to Wallie. He led her past the loungers on the station platform with an air of solicitous protection which was provoking, and handed her into the buggy with a flourish. He did not speak, nor did she, until, as they moved away from the depot, he turned the horse's head to the right instead of the left.

"This isn't the way to the village, is it?" she asked quickly.

Wallie, beside her on the seat, turned his head and winked.

"It ain't the shortest way—no," he whispered. "But I knew you'd want to talk with me a little mite and so I thought we'd drive around by the West Main Road and come up that way. See, Norma, don't you?"

She looked at him. "I don't know that I do," she answered frigidly. "What should I want to talk with you about, in particular?"

"Eh? Why—you got my letter, didn't you?"

"Yes."

"Yes. Yes, I knew you must have. I mailed it right off the day after—after it happened, you understand."

The last sentence was accompanied by another wink and a confidential lowering of the voice. She moved impatiently on the seat.

"You needn't whisper," she said. "No one is likely to hear us. Not that I should mind if they did."

"Eh. . . ? Yes, that's so. I guess maybe you're right; only—only there ain't but a mighty few that's on to the real insides of what's been goin' on down there to Setuckit, and so I—so we have to be a little mite careful, that's all."

"Why?"

"*Why*. . . ? Say, *did* you get my letter?"

"I told you I did."

"Um-hum. Well then. . . ! Say," suddenly, as the thought seemed to strike him, "you haven't got a letter from anybody else about it, have you?"

She was on the point of saying that she had not, but she would not give him that satisfaction.

"If I have, what of it?" she asked.

"Why—why, there might be consider'ble of it. If somebody wrote you a pack of lies you might have come to believe 'em, instead of the truth. That's what I mean."

"Well," significantly, "*you* wrote me!"

"Eh? Yes, you bet I did! I and your father wrote that letter together. He was too shook up and sick to hold a pen steady and so I helped him out. He told me what to say and I said it. He—"

"Wait! You said he was sick. Is he?"

"Is he? Well, if he ain't, then he'd ought to be."

"But is he?"

"I don't know whether he is or not—now. But he was next door to it then. And no wonder, the way he'd been treated. If I hadn't been there to stand up for him there's no tellin' what that Cal Homer and the gang would have done to him."

"Did you stand up? I thought you wrote that you were knocked down."

The sarcasm was entirely wasted. Wallie's anger was boiling over at the memory of his humiliation. His tone became anything but a whisper.

"Knocked down!" he snarled. "I was struck in the eye when I wan't lookin'. If I had been lookin' there'd have been somebody else knocked down instead of me. See there," pointing to his bruised cheek. "That's what Cal Homer done to me. The sneakin' scamp! He had his gang around him or else—or else—eh? You see what he done, don't you?"

"Yes, I see that something must have happened to you."

"Well, he's goin' to pay for it. I'm goin' to see a lawyer fust chance I get. He'll spend part of his keeper's wages settlin' damages with me, that's what he'll do."

She made no answer and, turning, he became aware that she was looking at him intently. It was the first sign of interest she had shown and he was gratified by it.

"Yes, sir!" he repeated. "I'm goin' to sue him if it takes—"

"Wait! You said something about wages—keeper's wages. Mr. Homer is a Number One man, not a keeper."

"Humph! We ain't none of us too sure of that. The story goin' 'round is that he's keeper down at Setuckit Station right now, and that he's goin' to be made the reg'lar one just as soon as they fix things up to Washin'ton."

"But my father is keeper of Setuckit Station."

"Huh! He *was* keeper, but is he now? That's a question. And is he ever goin' to be again? That's another one. The story is that he ain't. It wouldn't surprise me, because—"

"Stop! Do you mean that my father has been discharged and that—that Mr. Homer has been given his place?"

"Well, he couldn't get it no other way, could he? I tell you, Norma, Cal and his bunch have been workin' and lyin' and contrivin' for it all along. Why, I wrote you that very thing in my letter. I wrote you—"

"Oh," impatiently, "I know what you wrote me! I didn't believe it, of course."

Wallie gasped. His involuntary jerk of the reins brought the horse to a walk.

"You didn't believe it!" he repeated.

"No," with scornful contempt, "of course I didn't. And I don't believe it now. Tell me, is that story of Mr. Homer's taking my father's place anything *but* a story? Do you know that it is true?"

"Well—well, I can't say as I know it just exactly, but it's bein' said. There's all sorts of yarns—"

She interrupted once more. "And they are yarns, of course," she declared. "You really *know* nothing about it."

"Well—well, I— Say, Norma, you don't seem to realize what's been goin' on down there to that station. I thought I wrote you plain enough, but it looks as if you didn't quite get a hold of it. Let me tell you. That sneakin', lyin' Cal Homer is—"

She turned on him with a swiftness that took his breath away.

"Stop!" she ordered. "I don't want you to say another word of that kind. I don't believe you. If you try to say any more I shall get out and walk the rest of the way."

"But, say—look here—Norma—"

She leaned forward and pulled at the reins. The horse —he was no fiery animal—stopped.

"Let me out," she said.

"You—you don't mean it, do you?"

"I certainly do—unless you are willing to drive me to the hotel at once and without saying another word about my father or Mr. Homer. That is precisely what I mean."

Wallie glared at her. Then he hit the horse a vicious slap with the end of the reins.

"Git dap!" he snarled, and then added, viciously, "By Godfreys, I'm beginnin' to believe you're stuck on that Homer, like a lot of other darn fool girls in this town. I swear I do!"

She did not deign a reply and the remainder of the journey to the Ocean House was made quickly and in silence.

Frank Hammond and Norma were acquainted. She had stayed overnight at the Ocean House after leaving Setuckit on her way back to Fairborough and he and his wife had done their best to make her brief sojourn pleasant. They were a kindly middle-aged couple, looked up to and respected in the town, and Hammond was a member of the Board of Selectmen and a man of substance in the community. Norma liked them both.

Mrs. Hammond, she learned, was in Boston on a visit. Her husband gave this information during dinner, a meal which he and Norma shared with Ezra Blodgett, a dapper and tiresome elderly person whom she had never before met and soon began to hope she might never meet again; Braddock, the local druggist; and a breezy young man named Thornton, who, it appeared, was the "hat-and-cap drummer" mentioned by Wallie during the drive from the railway station. Norma had hoped to learn from the Hammonds a few reliable particulars concerning the recent happenings at Setuckit, but Blodgett and the drummer, more particularly the latter, seemed to feel it their duty to entertain her and they took charge of the conversation. The young gentleman in the hat-and-cap line was so extremely attentive that he became a nuisance and she was obliged to snub him rather pointedly in order to force some realization of this fact upon his mind. At another time, and under different circumstances, she might have been more tolerant, for Mr. Thornton undoubtedly meant to be agreeable. But Norma's charity that day was not of the kind which suffers long and is kind. She was more anxious than ever and therefore inclined to be impatient. Wallie Oaks's spiteful fabrications she did not believe and had refused to hear. The little she had heard she meant to forget. But, in spite of this determination, she was troubled. What was the real truth about it all? And why—*why,* if it was as serious as it seemed, had Calvin neither written nor telegraphed? Unless his reason were very convincing she would find it hard to forgive that neglect.

Beside Mr. Hammond, on the seat of the buggy, as it rocked and shook along the deeply rutted sandy lane between the dunes, her thoughts dealt unceasingly with these questions. Even her worry concerning her father was temporarily forced into the background; she did not realize this, but it was so. The rumors in the paper, the outrageous accusations in Oaks's letter and those he had made that morning —she could not help thinking of them. After all, she knew so little of the man she loved. What did she really know —except that she did love him and that he had said he loved her? Suppose—and then she awoke to a realization of what she was thinking and hated herself for the thought. Her idea of asking her driver for particulars concerning affairs at Setuckit was abandoned. No, she would wait until Calvin himself told her. And she was on her way to him now. He and she would be together once more; he would tell her everything and she would know and understand and be happy. She was happy at that moment.

And then Hammond, who, like her, had been silent for some minutes, spoke. He turned to look at her and his expression was grave.

"Miss Bartlett," he said, "I don't know as I ought to say it, it isn't any of my business in a way, but I've been thinking not much of anything else since I got word you was coming. I suppose likely you know what's happened down at your father's station? That's why you're here, isn't it?"

She answered his look with one quite as grave. "I know something has happened there," she admitted. "I read an article in the paper, and then I got—a letter."

"I see. From your father, of course. Well, he told you, didn't he?"

She hesitated. "The letter wasn't from father," she said after a moment. "It was from Mr. Oaks."

His surprise was evident. "Oaks!" he repeated. "Wallie Oaks?"

"Yes."

"Wallie Oaks! How in the world did he come to write —you?"

She explained briefly. Oaks had written the letter because he was with her father that night and the latter was too nervous and ill to do it himself.

"At least that is what Mr. Oaks said in the letter," she added. "And he told me so again this morning."

"Humph! I shouldn't wonder. He told you a good many things, didn't he?"

"Yes, in the letter. And he would have told me many more to-day, if I had let him. I wouldn't listen. I didn't believe him, and I said so, quite plainly."

Hammond sniffed. "Wallie isn't sweet enough to feed to a decent pig," he observed. "How as smart a man as Kellogg ever let him get into the service I don't know, and I'm surprised he stayed in it as long as he did. Well, he's out of it now, and the service won't keel over and quit on that account. I was sorry I had to send him to the depot to meet you this morning, but I was busy with that drummer, and my regular driver is at home, sick. Wallie came loafing along—looking for a job, he said—so I gave him one. I beg your pardon, I do so."

She smiled. "I see," she said. "I shan't hold it against you, Mr. Hammond. I detest that Oaks man, I must admit. I think he is everything that is mean and contemptible."

"I vote yes on that. Well, he told you plenty, you say?"

"One of the things he told me was that you and he were great friends—chums, he called it."

Her driver shook his head. "Tut, tut, tut!" he observed. "And in spite of that you came down and had dinner along with me. Your appetite must have been stronger than your judgment, Miss Bartlett."

"Oh, I didn't believe that any more than I did the other things he told me."

"*That* judgment was sound, anyhow. No, Wallie's a liar three hundred and sixty-five days in any year but leap year —and even then his average don't suffer. Just now he's loaded to the rails with spite and meanness. Calvin Homer knocked him in a heap, so they say, and if Cal was runnin' for office just now he could get elected on account of it. . . . Yes, if that was all, Calvin would be the most popular man in the township limits."

The last sentence was spoken in a tone different from those preceding it. The change was slight, but she noticed it.

"Do you mean that he isn't popular?" she queried.

Hammond seemed to be troubled about something. As he did not reply she repeated the question.

"What do you mean; 'if that were all'?" she asked.

"Eh? Oh, I don't know as I meant anything in particular. . . . Yes, I did, too, but it is nothing to do with your father, Miss Bartlett. I guess Homer is popular enough, so far as that goes. There are some people who don't like him, and lately a thing has come to my notice that— But that wouldn't interest you, either."

"Anything to do with—with what has happened at father's station interests me very much. It does indeed."

"This thing I meant hasn't anything to do with what's happened down there, not really. Of course it might help to explain—it might—well, it set me to thinking when I heard it. Yes, and I've been thinking about it ever since. You know when you like a person a lot and then learn something about him that kind of shakes your faith—why, then you get kind of mistrustful when you hear other things. You begin to think up reasons, reasons you never would have thought of thinking before. You say to yourself, 'If he would play a mean trick like that on one person, mightn't he be playing mean tricks right along?' That's what you say. . . . Humph! I guess likely you're wondering what *I'm* trying to say now, don't you?"

She did not answer the question.

"So you don't like Mr. Homer," she said slowly.

"Eh? Oh, I wouldn't say that. I always used to like him, same as everybody else did. He's a smart, able young fellow. Yes, there's no doubt about that."

"But you don't like him now? You don't trust him, you said so."

"Humph! I said more than I meant to, I guess. I do hate to mistrust Calvin. Maybe I haven't got any business to. Only now, when they're saying he has been made keeper there at Setuckit— Eh? What is it?"

She had uttered a low exclamation. When he turned toward her he saw that she was regarding him intently.

"What's the matter?" he demanded. "What—"

She interrupted. "Nothing, nothing," she declared. "But, tell me, please—*has* he been made keeper?"

He was surprised. "Didn't you know?" he asked. "Didn't your father write?"

"Father hasn't written me at all. This morning Mr. Oaks said something about—about Mr. Homer's being the new keeper—and father's being—well, he said discharged; but I didn't believe him; I didn't believe anything he said. Is it true? Tell me, Mr. Hammond, please."

Hammond was disturbed. "Sho!" he exclaimed. "I thought of course you had heard from your father about it and that that was why you came."

"I came because I thought father must need me. I didn't know—but do you really know? Is it a fact? Are you certain it is true?"

He hesitated and then nodded. "It hasn't been given out from headquarters," he replied, "but—well, yes, I should say that, nine chances to one, it was true. All sorts of stories have been leaking out from Setuckit and the Orham Station, and the gist of 'em seems to be that Cap'n Bartlett isn't cap'n any more and that Homer is in command. Whether or not it's just temporary command I can't say—very likely 'tis. But, from all I hear, if it isn't permanent now, it is going to be. I'm sorry I had to be the one to tell you this, Miss Bartlett. I thought probably you knew as much or more about it than I did or I wouldn't have dropped a hint. I'm real sorry I did."

She was trying to be calm, but it was hard work. Nevertheless she made a brave attempt.

"I am glad you told me," she said. "I am glad I found it out before I saw father. He must be dreadfully sick, ever so much more so than I thought. If he were not he never would have given up his command. It meant everything to him. Now that you have told me so much, Mr. Hammond, won't you please tell me the rest—the whole story just as it happened? Then when I see father I shall be prepared. Please tell me."

So, though with reluctance, he did tell her the story, as much of it as had come to Orham. He omitted the charges of cowardice on Bartlett's part—and those charges had been at least as specific as any other part of the tale—and substituted surmises such as, "I guess your father was pretty nigh sick, same as you say." But, taken as a whole, his narrative adhered closely to the facts. Norma heard him through and, to his surprise, she seemed less troubled at the end than at the beginning.

"Father was ill and I am afraid he still is," she said. "That is it. Oh, I wish I had come sooner! But I am glad he had a man like Mr. Homer to take command during his sickness. I know father was glad, too. As for all those ridiculous and wicked—oh, lies!—they aren't anything else —about Mr. Homer's leading a mutiny and planning to get father's place as keeper, they are—I know they are not true."

The conviction in her tone was absolute. He did not contradict her, neither did he make any comment. Perhaps she noticed the omission, for when, after an interval of silence, she next spoke, it was to return to the subject which had led to his telling the story.

"You say you don't like Mr. Homer," she repeated. "I'm very sorry. I like him and so does my father. Why don't you like him?"

Hammond moved uneasily. "Oh, I wouldn't go so far

as to say I didn't like him," he said. "He's able and smart and—"

"Every one knows that. But you said you were beginning to doubt him, or suspect him—which is the same thing. You said something about a mean trick he had played which shook your faith in him. I can hardly believe that, Mr. Hammond. I think you are mistaken. He is not the kind of man to do a mean thing. I know he isn't."

"Well—well, maybe you are right. Perhaps it didn't seem so mean to him. Anyhow, it really hasn't anything to do with the fuss at Setuckit, so what's the use of our talking about it, Miss Bartlett?"

She was reflecting. "I think you believe it may have had something to do with it," she said musingly. "You spoke of its suggesting possible reasons for—for your changing your mind in regard to other matters. I wish you would tell me what Mr. Homer did that you consider mean? I may be able to show you that it wasn't. I can't conceive of his being mean to any one. Perhaps it is something I know about."

"No. No, you don't. There's only a few do know about it. And I shouldn't tell you or anybody. I'm sorry I mentioned it."

"But you did mention it. And—and Mr. Homer and I are friends, close friends. Are you going to give him a chance to explain?"

He laughed shortly. "I don't imagine he would thank me for the chance," he observed. "There, there, Miss Bartlett, let's forget it."

But she had no intention of forgetting or permitting him to do so. There was a flash in her eyes and a crispness in her voice as she asked her next question.

"Why do you think he would not thank you for the chance?" she persisted.

"Oh—oh, well," a little impatiently, "because it isn't one of those things one man would explain to another. And, if what I've heard is true, explaining would be a pretty hard job. I judge he didn't bother to do much explaining to her."

"To her?"

"Why, yes. . . . Look here, Miss Bartlett, I can see you think I'm cut a little mite on the Wallie Oaks pattern and run around spreading lies about people. That is what you do think—or about that, isn't it?"

"No, of course I don't. But I—yes, I do think you should not have hinted to me that Mr. Homer is capable of a mean action, and then refuse to explain why you think so. I shall —yes, I shall tell him you said it, and then I am sure he will ask you for the explanation, himself."

He stared. "You will tell him?" he repeated. "For the Lord sakes why should *you* tell him?"

"Because I am a friend of his—and so is father. And I try to be fair to my friends, Mr. Hammond. If any one dropped such hints about me I should be glad if a friend told me of them."

Frank Hammond whistled between his teeth. This was an unexpected development. His hint—which was merely an echo of his thought, and dropped without premeditation— had got him into trouble. She would speak to Homer concerning it; it was plain that she meant what she said. And the insinuation that he was unfair nettled him. His tone changed.

"All right," he said bluntly, "then I will tell you. I don't know as there is any good reason why I shouldn't. It is a sort of secret, in a way, but I'm not going to let you get the idea that I tell lies about people behind their backs. I did say it seemed to me that Calvin Homer had played a mean trick; I meant it. If being engaged to marry a girl and then writing her half a dozen lines saying he is sick of her and breaking the engagement isn't a mean trick, then I don't know what you would call it."

He heard her catch her breath.

"Nonsense!" she exclaimed indignantly. "Mr. Homer engaged to be married and breaking the engagement! How ridiculous! It isn't true."

"Oh, yes, it is! I ain't Wallie Oaks. I wouldn't say a thing like that if I didn't know it was true—and about a fellow I used to like as well as I did Cal Homer. He was engaged to marry—well, I won't mention any names, but the girl is a relation of mine; her mother is my first cousin by marriage. He and this girl had kept company for a good while. I knew it, so did about everybody else. Things like that are what folks, especially the women folks, talk about in a place like Orham. Only a few of us knew he was engaged to her, but he was. I saw the ring he gave her. She never showed it to me, but her mother told me about it and I've seen it on her finger."

He paused, giving his attention to the horse, which had strayed off the road. He guided the buggy back into the ruts again and then resumed his story.

"Oh, yes, they were engaged all right," he began. She interrupted.

"When was this?" she asked.

"Eh? When did they get engaged, you mean? Oh, a few months ago. I heard of it—seems to me 'twas along the first of December. The idea, so her mother told me, was not to say anything—not make any announcements, you understand—for a while, because Calvin didn't feel he was in any position to get married, and he was hoping to get a better job. What he planned to do—yes, and all hands thought it would happen—was to be made keeper at Setuckit. The pay isn't so much better, but a station keeper can have his wife with him. Besides I judge, knowing Myra, that neither he nor she would have been contented even with a keeper's job long. She, this girl I'm speaking of"—he was quite unconscious that he had mentioned her name—"is mighty clever and ambitious. She would make her husband get on in the world. Well, then Cap'n Bartlett—your father —was made keeper and that plan was knocked in the head, for a time, anyhow. I don't think 'twas given up—her mother says neither of 'em gave it up. The idea was to wait and see how Bartlett made out. If he didn't make good, why, then Cal was next in line. See?"

He waited for a reply, but she made none. After a moment he continued.

"Well, so they were engaged and she had the ring, and the girl and her mother thought it was all settled; naturally they would. I was surprised when I heard it, because, to be honest, I wouldn't have believed either of those women would have been satisfied with anything so everyday as a life-saver. They aren't that kind. Cap'n Fuller, my cousin, was an easy-going plain man enough, but his wife and daughter are different. Plain things, so I'd have said, didn't satisfy either of 'em. . . . Eh? What say?"

She had murmured something. Now she spoke aloud.

"So her name is Myra Fuller," she said. "Does she live here in Orham?"

He turned in amazement. "How did you know her name?" he demanded. "Did you know about the engagement?"

"No." She smiled wearily. "No, I didn't know. You told me her name, yourself, just now. You didn't realize it, but you did. . . . Oh, never mind! When was the engagement broken?"

"Less than a fortni't ago. Not much more than a week ago, I guess. It was after you was down here the last time. Sarepta—now I've let out so much of the names, the whole of 'em don't matter—told me about it day before yesterday. 'Cording to her tell, it was pretty mean business on Calvin's part. Myra was anxious about him, on account of the wrecks and all, but he hadn't written for weeks. And he had promised to take a liberty day and come to see her. Next to the last letter she had from him he promised that and was as sweet and loving as any girl could ask. But he didn't come, and then, next thing the Fullers knew, he sent the letter saying he was sick of it all and she could go to blazes, or what amounted to that. Now you may not call that mean treatment of a girl, Miss Bartlett, but I do."

Again he waited for her to speak, but when she did, it was far more to herself than to him. "I don't believe it," she murmured. "Oh, of course I don't believe it!"

He was angry. "All right," he snapped. "If you don't believe me go and ask Sarepta—yes, or Myra. I rather think they'd tell you.   But I'd have you understand that I'm speaking the truth."

"Yes; yes, I know you think you are.   I am sure of that. I beg your pardon, Mr. Hammond.   It was only that—that it didn't seem possible.   Mr. Homer has always seemed so—so honest, and straightforward, and—and true—that—"

"Sure!   It was pretty hard work for me to believe it myself.   But I got it straight from headquarters, so I had to believe.   Course Myra won't talk about it.   She's mighty proud and when I asked her she flew at me like a wildcat and vowed and declared 'twas she who had given Cal his walking papers, and not him her at all.   She couldn't say hard enough things about him, how she got tired to death of him, had realized her mistake long ago, and had sent him packing.   If she hadn't been so darned spiteful against him I might have believed her side of the story; but she called him too many names.   No, Sarepta's yarn is the true one; I don't think there's any doubt about that."

She was thinking.   "Myra Fuller," she said slowly. "Myra Fuller.   I used to know a girl of that name.   She was at the Bridgewater Academy when I was there.   But it couldn't be *that* girl."

"I shouldn't wonder if it was.   Myra went to Bridgewater; she studied to be a teacher up there.   Kind of a big, fine-looking girl, with sort of reddish hair and a way of looking at you with her eyes that—well, if you're a man, it kind of gets you.   They're nice eyes and she can make 'em say a whole lot.   Yes, and she knows it," with a chuckle.

"That girl!   And he was engaged to *her!"*

"Eh?   Oh, yes, he was engaged to her all right.   That much I do know for sure."

They drove on for some minutes without further conversation.   It seemed to him that having substantiated his accusation against Homer, so far as the latter's being capable of a mean trick was concerned, he had said enough.   But she, apparently, was not finished with the subject.

"Was she—was she very much in love with him?" she asked.

"Who—Myra? Why, yes, I guess so. More than she's ever been with anybody else, I'd say. She's always been a great hand with the boys, and some of her beaus wasn't exactly what you'd call boys, either. She did like Calvin a lot, though, according to Sarepta. You see, he's a fine-looking young fellow, Cal is, and Myra don't mind good looks a bit." He paused to chuckle again, and then added: "I wouldn't say her heart was broke altogether. Not so's the pieces can't be stuck together, anyhow. There's an old rooster named Blodgett—eh? Why, you saw him at the dinner table this noon; he takes his meals along with us. He's willing to help with the repair job, I judge, if she'll give him the chance. The story is that he's beginning to call on her fairly regular. He's pretty well off, and—"

She did not appear to be interested in Mr. Blodgett.

"Mr. Hammond," she broke in, "you hinted that you were beginning to believe Mr. Homer might have done what— what that horrid Wallie Oaks said he did, work against my father and plan to get himself made keeper of the station. Do you really believe that? Have you any reasons, more than you have already told me, for believing it?"

He shook his head. "No, no, no," he protested. "I haven't. And I don't say it, either. I can't think Cal would do a thing like that. As I told you, I'd have sworn he was straight as a T square if I hadn't found out how he treated Myra. That shook my confidence in him, same as 'twould anybody's. Don't you think so, Miss Bartlett?"

She drew a long breath. "Yes," she said.

"Um-hum. But, so far as his contriving and scheming against your father behind his back goes, I won't believe it —not yet. That would be *too* low-down mean. Of course Sarepta says that's what he's been doing, and so does Wallie, but they're both chock full of spite, and their testimony needs considerable salt before I'd swallow it."

He went on talking, but, if she heard, she had no comment to make. She did not speak again during the drive to Se-tuckit Station.

CHAPTER XVI

HOMER happened to be in the tower when the Hammond horse and buggy appeared among the dunes. Through the glass he saw Norma on the seat beside the driver. He was, in a way, prepared to see her; she had telegraphed that she should come soon, and when he first sighted the approaching vehicle he felt almost sure that she was there. Now, as he watched her through the telescope, his pulse quickened at the thought of seeing her again. So much had happened since they parted. The care and worry and responsibility had been wearing indeed. He had longed for her; there was so much to tell her, so much to explain; he had needed her help and understanding sympathy so greatly. Now she was here. He darted to the door and ran down the stairs.

At the closed door of the skipper's room he paused. He knew that Bartlett was in that room. Benoni had spent practically all his time there since the day of his crew's rebellion. He came out when called to meals, but at the table he said scarcely a word, and of those words not one was addressed to Calvin. He ignored the latter altogether and refused to answer if Homer spoke to him. Calvin, after several attempts, had given it up. It was evident that Bartlett did not care to have anything to do with him. So he kept out of the way of the deposed keeper and, although when they met at breakfast he always bade him a respectful good morning, he tried to avoid troubling him by sound or sight. But now, at the door, he paused, wondering whether or not he should tell him of his daughter's arrival.

As he stood there the door opened, but it was Seleucus Gammon, not Benoni Bartlett, who came out of the little room. Homer was surprised. So far as he knew no one save Kellogg had visited Bartlett in that room since the day of Wallie Oaks's leaving.

Gammon saw him standing there and raised a warning finger. He closed the door carefully behind him.

"What is it, Cal?" he asked. "What's up?"

Calvin explained. Norma Bartlett was coming, would arrive in a few minutes, and he had thought of telling her father the good news.

Seleucus shook his head. "I wouldn't if I was you," he said. "The old man is havin' one of his bad spells, seems so. He opened that door a little spell ago and sung out to me to come in; said he wanted to talk to me. It was about the first word he'd said to me for three days and I couldn't guess what he wanted, but I went in. He's in a state, I tell you. Seems he's been tryin' to write Norma a letter, tellin' her what he calls the truth about everything that's happened, and there was sheets of scribbled-on paper all over the table and on the bed and the land knows where. He wanted me to hear what he'd wrote. He read some of it to me out loud. Such a mixed-up mess you never heard. All full of talk about the Lord and his duty as a follower of the way and the light, and about bein' tempted by the Old Harry, and how the devil's agents had worked against him, and I can't tell you what. I judge you and Cap'n Kellogg are the head agents, Cal. He's down on you especial, and when I tried to put in a word on your side he jumped on me with both feet. Fact is, he got so kind of wild in his talk that I shut up. Thought 'twas good judgment, you understand. No, if I was you, I wouldn't go nigh him now. You're the last man 'twould do him any good to see."

Calvin was greatly troubled. Bartlett had been morose and gloomy since the break with the men, but he had shown no signs of violent aberration. This was most unfortunate. He dreaded the shock to Norma.

"He asked me one or two questions that kind of scared me," went on Seleucus. "Wanted to know if I'd noticed anything 'special in the noise the surf on the outer beach was makin'. Said it seemed to him to be callin' to him, singin' out, 'Benoni Bartlett, come here! Come here!' Said there was times when he felt as if he just had to go. Yes, sir, that's what he said. That meant drowndin' himself, as I figgered it. Course I told him the surf wasn't sayin' nothin' but 'Boo!' same as it always says. I tried to soothe him down best I could, but 'twas consider'ble of a job. I cal'late 'twas writin' Norma that riled up his brains so. It's a mighty good thing she's here. Maybe she can handle him. Anyhow, the rest of us couldn't, least of all you, Cal. You steer clear of him, that's my advice. . . . Hello! here comes the team now, ain't it?"

The buggy was nearing the station. The crew gathered outside the door to meet it. Homer and Phinney hastened forward to help Norma alight, but it was Josh's hand she took. She looked, so Calvin thought, white and careworn. His eager welcome she met by a look so peculiar that he stepped back aghast.

"Norma!" he cried, forgetting that none of the others knew of their intimate relation.

She turned to him, but only to ask a question. "Where is father?" she asked.

"He is in his room. Shall I—"

"I am going there. . . . No, thank you, Mr. Rogers, you needn't tell him. I'll go right in."

That was all she said; not a word of inquiry, or greeting —not a smile, nor a glance implying that she was glad to be with him again. And her tone was formal, almost coldly so. He stared after her in hurt amazement as she hurried into the station. When he entered the mess room the skipper's door was shut. She and her father were together.

She was in that room all the remainder of the afternoon. They called her and Bartlett to supper, but neither heeded the call. When Calvin knocked she told him that they were not hungry and that, if they should be later on, she would prepare the food herself. Her tone and manner then were just as coolly impersonal, and she offered no explanation nor excuse.

Hammond had driven back to Orham immediately after leaving his passenger. Homer tried to talk with him, thinking that perhaps she might have told him something con-

cerning herself, might have offered some reason, ill health
or anxiety—anything which might help to account for her
strange behavior. But the hotel proprietor's manner also was
odd. Ordinarily a cheerful, garrulous man, he was now
almost taciturn. He seemed eager to get away and did so
at the first opportunity.

It was, for Calvin Homer, a wretched afternoon and evening. All his joyful relief at seeing her had gone and the
disappointment and gloom which succeeded were crushing.
Also, with them, came a heavy sense of impending trouble.
He had had care and anxiety sufficient of late, but these he
could face, and had. Through them he had clung to the
thought of her, of her faith in him, of their love and its
wonderful happiness. Her coming had been a burst of sunlight breaking through the clouds. Now the clouds were
thicker than ever.

Something had happened, something was wrong—something—whatever it might be—had come between them. Her
first thought would be for her father—yes, he could well understand that. But why was she so cold toward him? Why
had she refused his hand and turned to take Phinney's?
Why had she looked at him—Calvin—so strangely? There
had been little of trust or love in that look.

He tried to think of possible explanations. She could not
believe that he had been a traitor to her father. He had
written her the plain, unornamented truth about that. She
must believe his story and therefore believe in his honesty
and loyalty; she would, she was so honest herself. Could it
be that she had not received his letter? He had sent it early
enough. She should have received it days before. But
perhaps she had not. She might think he had neglected her
and that would explain her attitude—partially explain it, at
least. Yes; yes, that must be the explanation, it must be.

His conscience was clear in that respect, but in another it
was not. He had not told her of his affair with Myra. The
letter in which he had begun his confession still remained,
unfinished, in his chest in the sleeping quarters. He would
have finished it had it not been for her telegram saying she

was coming to Setuckit. To tell her, rather than to write, seemed so much more satisfactory. He had planned to tell her the moment that he and she were alone. His determination to do so was unshaken. But her strange behavior toward him made the telling appear more difficult than ever. Nevertheless he must do it—and would. That she could have heard the story already, from another, did not enter his mind.

At ten the men, the patrolmen on duty excepted, went aloft to turn in. Bartlett, who had given up his own room to his daughter, had already gone to his bunk in the spare quarters. Homer lingered in the mess room, still hopeful of seeing Norma. Apparently she, too, had been waiting for that opportunity, for a few moments later she came out and joined him.

He rose to meet her and stepped forward, his hands outstretched. But she did not respond to his greeting and his eager utterance of her name she met only with a steady look of grave scrutiny.

"Norma!" he exclaimed. "Norma! What is it?"

He would have taken her in his arms, but she eluded him and, moving to the other side of the table, stood there, still regarding him, unsmiling and aloof.

"Norma!" he cried again. She motioned to a chair.

"Please sit down," she said. "I want to talk with you. I have been waiting to do it."

He took the chair she indicated. She took another, but on the opposite side of the table. Then, with her chin upon her hands, she looked at him fixedly.

"Norma," he pleaded, "what is the matter? Why do you treat me like this? What—"

She interrupted.

"Don't," she said hastily. "I am going to ask you some questions. Will you answer them—plainly and honestly?"

"Of course. Why do you say that? Did you think I would answer them in any other way?"

She did not reply, nor did she appear to heed the surprised resentment in his tone.

"First of all," she went on, "I want you to tell me the exact truth about what has happened here since I went away. . . . Oh, yes, father has told me, and so have others, but I want to hear it from you."

"But you did hear it from me. I wrote you all about it in my letter."

This statement did have an effect. She raised her head. "When did you write me?" she asked slowly.

"The day after we got back from the *Flyaway*. I wrote you a long letter, telling everything just as it happened, and I sent the letter to the office by way of the Orham Station. Do you mean that you didn't get that letter?"

She shook her head. "I have not heard a word from you since it happened," she said.

So his surmise was correct. Those careless idiots at the Orham Station were responsible. This was the reason for her coldness; she believed he had neglected her.

"That is too bad," he declared angrily. "Confound those fellows! I sent word that the letter must go right away. It is a shame, Norma dear. I'm awfully sorry. No wonder you thought—"

Again she interrupted. "Never mind," she said. "Tell me the story now."

He had expected this and was ready. He told her everything, as briefly as he could, omitting nothing of importance, offering no excuses for his own action in disobeying Bartlett's orders, but giving the reasons which had seemed imperative at the time.

"I hated to do it, Norma," he declared. "I can't tell you how I hated to, but it was that or letting that schooner drift on the shoals and drown every man on board. Your father wasn't well; you see how he is now. He was worse then. What else could I do?"

She seemed to ponder. "And you wrote me all this?" she asked. "You are sure?"

"Sure! Why, I told you I did. Don't you believe—"

"Hush, please! I don't know what I believe—now. But I must know. Are you keeper here at Setuckit?"

He hesitated. "I am a sort of keeper, I suppose," he admitted. "Superintendent Kellogg put me in charge temporarily. He came down here to investigate—that is his duty, you know—and—"

"Yes; yes, I know all that. But father says that he—the superintendent—offered him the choice of resigning or being discharged. Is that true?"

Again he hesitated; but she had demanded the truth and he must tell it. "Why—yes," he admitted. "I'm afraid it is. Cap'n Kellogg told me that was what he had done."

"And has he offered you the appointment as keeper?"

"Yes. Of course it doesn't rest altogether with him. The matter would have to be referred to Washington, and perhaps—"

"Oh, don't beat about the bush. You accepted the appointment."

"No, I didn't."

"You did not. . . . ! Why?"

"You ought to know why." Her sharp, almost contemptuous, tone and manner were having their effect, and he was finding it hard to be patient. "You ought to know why, Norma," he repeated. "Is it likely I could see your father lose his place and then take it myself? Your father! I told Kellogg I wouldn't consider the appointment for a minute."

Her manner changed then. The look in her eyes softened just a little. He pressed his advantage.

"I said I would take charge here until a regular keeper was appointed," he went on. "Cap'n Kellogg asked me to, and the men seemed to want me. I didn't like to do it. I would a lot rather have resigned myself. But some one had to do it, some one that had experience. And your father isn't—well, I am afraid he isn't sane altogether. He certainly wasn't sane that day. I hate to say it. You must know how I hate to say it to you, of all people. But it is true. . . . And I wrote you all this, all except my being put in charge here for the time—that I didn't know then."

The scornful contempt was no longer in evidence. Her eyes had lost their hardness. Now they filled with tears.

"Poor father!" she sighed. "I—I don't know what to say —or think—about him. He was in a dreadful condition when I came. He had been trying to write me and—and— oh, the way he spoke and acted frightened me. I must get him away from here. That is certain, no matter what else may be; I must take him somewhere where I can be with him, and look out for him. He is better now, and quieter. He has told me the story, himself. And he says—yes, he insists that you were the leader against him. If it hadn't been for you, he declares, the men would have obeyed his orders."

"But suppose they had? We saved that schooner, with all hands. If we had obeyed Cap'n Bartlett's orders the vessel and her crew would have gone to the bottom. And your father, Norma—did he tell you why he wouldn't order out the boat? Did he tell you about God's coming to his room there, and talking to him—and all the rest of it?"

She nodded. "He told me that," she admitted. "I'm afraid he isn't—right. Oh, it is dreadful! But, except for that, except for his religious mania—that is what it is—he talks quite rationally. And he says he knows now that you have been working against him all the time. That you were only waiting for the chance to get him into trouble, so that you might have his place. And, so he says, when that chance came you took it."

He stared at her. "You don't believe that!" he cried. "Norma, do you believe that of me?"

She shook her head. "I don't want to believe it," she said. "No, no, I don't believe it. It would be *too* contemptible. But I have heard it from others."

"What others?"

"Well, I received a letter, a letter written from this station the very day when yours—when you say yours was written. It seems odd that that letter reached me and yours did not, then nor since."

The doubt, or the hint of doubt, had come back to her voice. Calvin noticed it.

"What letter was that?" he demanded. "Who wrote it? Not your father?"

"No. Father has been in no condition to write, I am afraid."

"Then who did write? Eh? Good Lord! was it Wallie Oaks?"

She colored slightly and was confused.

"Why, yes, it was," she admitted. "But of course—"

"Wallie Oaks! You didn't believe *that* pup?"

"Of course I didn't. But his letter came. He wrote me."

"And *I* wrote you. I told you so. I'm not lying. Oh, Norma dear, how can you speak like this to me? What has changed you so?"

She was looking at him again, looking him through and through.

"Have you been absolutely truthful to me?" she asked, slowly. "Have you been loyal, in every way, to my father?"

"Yes, indeed I have."

"And to me? You have told me everything—everything?"

"Yes."

"Always?"

"Certainly."

"Then why have you never told me about Myra Fuller?"

He did not answer. He tried to do so, but he could not. The words he wanted were not at his command, then. The suddenness of her question, the knowledge that she had learned the secret from other lips than his, the overwhelming realization of what her learning it in that way might mean —all this confounded him, made speech impossible at the moment. He reddened, stammered, and stared at her aghast. In her eyes he was a picture of guilt discovered. He knew that he must be, and the thought merely rendered more acute the general paralysis of his faculties.

She was watching him intently, waiting for his reply. It did not come.

"Well?" she said, after a moment.

He caught his breath. He knew that he must say something, must explain—or attempt an explanation. It was now or never.

"Norma," he stammered, "I—I— Oh, I don't know what to say to you about that. I—I didn't know you knew. I—"

She broke in. "I can well imagine that," she observed crisply. "But I do know—a little. And I think you had better tell me the rest. Is it true that you were engaged to marry that girl?"

He nodded, overwhelmed. "Yes," he confessed. "I was. But, oh, Norma—"

"Wait. When did you and she become engaged?"

"A good while ago, months ago. But I never really meant to be. I don't know how it happened. I didn't really care for her at all. It—it just—just happened. Oh, I know that sounds foolish. Of course you wouldn't believe it, or understand, but it is the truth. I was sorry the minute afterward. I would have given anything to have been out of it. . . . Oh, but what is the use! What can I say to make you understand?"

She shook her head. "I don't know," she said. "I don't understand, I confess."

"Of course you don't. But it is true. I never did love her really. She—she—"

He broke off, the hopelessness of his attempt at justification heavy upon him. In the letter he had begun but never finished—yes, and a hundred times before and since—he had rehearsed the plea he meant to make to her. But now, when she sat there opposite him, looking at him, searching him through and through with that look, demanding the explanation which it was her right to demand—now, the confession of the whole truth, plain, absolute and without excuse—the confession which he had determined to make—seemed as hopelessly impossible of belief as the most transparent lie. How could a girl like Norma Bartlett ever believe that he, Calvin Homer, could have been attracted, even temporarily and lightly, by a girl like Myra Fuller?

Nevertheless, in his desperation, he tried again.

"Norma," he pleaded, "please try to believe me. I never

did care for her, really, at all. I didn't. I never cared for any one but you. It wasn't until I saw you that I began to understand what it meant to—to really care. I had read about it, in stories, and all that, but I thought it was all book nonsense. I never believed any one could—could love any one as I love you. You see, I—I—"

She broke in again. "Did you say these things to—Miss Fuller?" she inquired.

The chilling sarcasm of the question was like a plunge into ice water. But the plunge had the effect of restoring a little of his self-control.

"Of course I didn't," he retorted. "I tell you I didn't care for her—never did. And when I saw you I realized it."

"Yet you were engaged to her."

"I was—yes. But I had made up my mind to break it off. And I have done it."

"When did you do it?"

"A little while ago; about a week ago, I think it was. I wrote her a letter telling her I couldn't marry her, that I had found I didn't care for her in that way, and that the whole thing had been a mistake."

"That was only a week ago. And when—" she paused an instant; then, with a lift of her head, continued: "and when you spoke to me there on the beach, when you told me—what you did tell me—then, at that very time, you were engaged to another girl. Then—when you said those things to me."

He sighed. "Yes," he admitted, "I was. And I didn't intend to say them to you, Norma. I didn't, that is the truth. I had intended to write Myra, telling her just what I did tell her in the letter I wrote afterward, and then—and then, perhaps, if I was ever brave enough to do it, I meant to ask you. It didn't seem possible you could care for me, but—but I knew I must find out whether you did or not. I had to."

"But you did—say them to me then."

"Yes. When I saw you there in the channel and was afraid you—that you were drowning or—or hurt—I—well,

I said them. But I hardly knew I did. The words just came of themselves. They did."

"I see. They just happened, I suppose. As your engagement to Myra Fuller just happened. You seem to have had a number of such happenings."

"Norma!" indignantly. "How can you say that? How can you—"

"Oh, don't! Why didn't you tell me then about her? If you had, perhaps I—but never mind; you didn't."

"I couldn't. Seleucus came and you and I didn't have a word in private together before you went back to Fairborough."

"Yes. Yes, that is true. But you have written me since. I received a letter from you—not the one you say you wrote, and which I didn't receive, but another. There was no word of your other love affair—or one of those affairs—in that letter. Why wasn't there?"

He shook his head. The hopelessness of the tangle in which fate had wound him was always more and more apparent.

"There wasn't," he said, "because I didn't feel that I ought to write you until I had written her or seen her. At first I meant to go and see her and tell her. It seemed to me the squarer thing to do, to tell her how I felt instead of writing it. But your father kept putting me off when I asked for liberty and so, at last, I did write. Then came the *Flyaway* business, and the trouble here at the station—and I was so busy that—"

"That you could not write me anything as important as that. Or possibly you thought your being engaged to another girl while you were making love to me was a mere trifle in which I wouldn't be interested. I should have been, I assure you. I am not as experienced and blasé in such affairs as you seem to be."

"Norma!"

"Tell me this, then: In this second letter, the one which I never got, did you tell me of—of this Myra Fuller in that?"

"No . . . no, I didn't. You had telegraphed me you were

coming here and I thought I would wait until you came and then tell you. I meant to do it, would have done it before now if you had let me speak to you alone, if you had given me a chance. But I did begin a letter to you, telling you the whole story. I began it the afternoon before the big storm. The storm came, and all the rest of the trouble here, and afterwards you telegraphed. So the letter wasn't finished. It is upstairs now in my trunk. May I get it and show it to you?"

She shook her head. "No," she said slowly, "it is rather late now, it seems to me. That is all you have to say?"

"Why, yes . . . except that I am very sorry you found this out before I could tell you myself. I should have told you in my first letter, perhaps. I wish now I had. But waiting to break off with—with her before I told you seemed the square, honest thing to do and—"

She sprang to her feet, her eyes ablaze.

"Oh, don't—don't!" she cried. "Don't speak of honor any more. Your ideas of honor and loyalty don't seem to be mine at all, Mr. Homer. And, I may as well say this: I am beginning to doubt your loyalty to father. The stories I have heard about your pretending to be loyal to him and working against him behind his back don't seem as impossible to me as they did. I am by no means sure they aren't true."

He had risen, also. His face was white.

"Those stories are lies," he said firmly. "And you know they are lies—or will know it when you think them over by and by."

"Perhaps. And you consider that you have been loyal to me?"

"Yes. I'm sorry I didn't write you right off, after you left. But I explained why I didn't. I thought I ought to see Myra and tell her first."

"And do you think that you were loyal to—to *her?*"

"Yes. I tried to be."

"Then, as I said, your ideas of loyalty and honor are very different from mine. Good night."

She turned toward the door of the skipper's room—hers, as always, during her stay. He spoke her name.

"Norma," he said quietly. "I suppose this means the end of—of everything between you and me, doesn't it?"

She did not reply, but entered the little room and closed the door. He turned wearily away. He had had his answer.

Two days later she and her father left Setuckit. Hammond, who had been telephoned for, came for them with a two-horse vehicle, and drove them to Orham. Meanwhile Superintendent Kellogg had made another visit and the Bartletts' departure was the result of it. The district superintendent's errand was to receive from Bartlett the resignation asked for, or, failing the receipt of that, to notify him of his discharge to take effect at once. The Washington authorities had not deemed it necessary to make further investigation. The testimony forwarded by Kellogg seemed conclusive and they had left the matter in his hands.

The superintendent and Homer had only a brief interview. Its brevity was entirely due to Calvin's disinclination to talk. Kellogg told him that Bartlett flatly refused to resign, even though his daughter begged him to do so, and railed against the treason of the crew, his Number One man in particular. The tirade was interspersed with quotations from Scripture, appeals to heaven, and rambling prophecies as to the vengeance of the Almighty which was to descend upon the heads of those responsible for his downfall and disgrace.

"If there was ever any doubt about the man's being crazy," declared Kellogg, "there isn't any now. He's clean off, and even Norma had to admit as much to me. Of course she thinks that his craziness is all due to the way he's been treated since he came here, and though I tried to tell her that wasn't so, I don't think she believed me. Natural enough she shouldn't, I suppose—he's her father. But I declare I'm sorry for her. She's a mighty fine girl, and she's got an awful proposition on her hands. The old man keeps vowing and declaring he won't go; says the Lord ordered him to stay here and put this whole section of coast in his charge, or words to that effect. How he'll act when he has to go, I don't know. She don't say much, but anybody can see she realizes what she's in for. I told her I'd like to do all I could to help her through her trouble, but she wouldn't take my help. She's down on me, and I don't blame her, although the land knows I'm not to blame. If I'd had my way you'd have been keeper here at Setuckit in the first place, Cal, and all this would never have happened. I'd like to hang half a dozen politicians out here at the end of the point, as a warning to the rest of 'em to keep hands off what ain't any of their business."

He again asked Homer to take the appointment as keeper, but once more the offer was declined. The refusal was so curt that Kellogg was surprised; however, he still vowed not to accept it as final. "I'm going to wait a little spell longer, Cal," he said, "and let you think it over. The service needs you here, and, by holy, *I* need you. You'll be doing me a tremendous favor by taking the job. I've been, and am yet, a pretty good friend of yours. You can think that over, too, if you have a mind to."

The most Calvin would concede was that he would not leave at once, even though the time set—March first—had arrived. He would remain another week, possibly two, but no longer. He would not have done that were it not for Kellogg's personal plea of friendship, with its accompanying hint of obligation owed. He had no idea of staying on at Setuckit as captain. He wanted to get away from there, as far away as he could.

He saw almost nothing of Norma during the two days of her stay. He made it a point to keep out of her way, because he felt that his presence, even the sight of him, would annoy her. She and her father ate in the latter's room, for she left him scarcely at all. He slept in the spare room upstairs, and she in the room below, but she tiptoed up to peep in at him very often during the night, and her own sleep must have been fitful and scanty.

Seleucus Gammon was the only one to whom she vouchsafed the slightest intimacy or confidence. Just why Seleu-

cus was chosen nobody seemed to know. Josh Phinney
offered the surmise that it might be because he looked so
everlasting dumb that she didn't mind having him around
any more than she would a dog.

"Come to think of it," observed Josh, "Seleucus does look
like a dog. When he stares at you with them pop eyes of
his and wabbles that straw mustache up and down he puts
you in mind of one of them big poodles, the kind with
whiskers. You sort of expect him to set up on his hind
legs and say 'bow wow' for a bone, or somethin'. Probably
she used to own a dog once that looked like him. If she did
I presume likely somebody shot the critter for bein' so
homely."

Seleucus, who was, of course, within hearing when this
remark was made, bristled and blew out the big mustache.

"If they killed folks for bein' homely," he declared, "you'd
have been drownded right after you was born, Josh. It's a
wonder to me they ever let you live, anyway. Probably
thought they could make money if they saved you and showed
you off in a dime show along with the rest of the outrages
they have in them places. Norma takes to me because she
knows I've got sense. Maybe I ain't got much, but even the
least little mite is so scurse 'round here that it sticks up like
Bunker Hill monument."

To Calvin he confided his fears concerning Benoni Bartlett's condition.

"He's in an awful state, Cal," he said. "Norma called
me in there to ask if she could possibly have a little soup or
somethin' for his dinner; said he wouldn't eat much of anything at all, and she wanted to try and tempt him. I didn't
know but I might kill that old brindle hen that's been here
since Kingdom Come. The critter's too old to lay and I'm
darn sure she ain't no good for ornament. If I killed her
now and biled her all night I might get half a pint of soup
out of the ruins, don't you think? Then you could maybe
use what was left of her for somethin'—make a rubber ball
out of it, maybe. I cal'late 'twould bounce fust rate; she's
tough enough to bounce, I bet ye.

"I'd get Jemima to make the soup," he added, "only she's so prejudiced that if I told her 'twas the Bartlett girl that wanted it she'd probably flavor it up with rat pison. She gets worse and worse that way, Jemima does, seems so. And I swear I ain't never give her no cause," plaintively. "I don't care about women, Cal—never did. . . . And I care about 'em less every day, by crimus! I've got reason."

He expressed his belief that Bartlett was a pretty sick man. "I dread the time when he has to start from here," he said. "The land knows what he'll do or how he'll behave. Lay right flat down and have to be dragged out by main force, maybe. That would be tough on her, wouldn't it?"

Homer spoke without looking at him. "If anything like that should happen, Seleucus," he said, "do everything you can for her, won't you? And—and make it plain to her that she and her father needn't go until they're ready. There is no hurry at all. Just tell her that they can stay here as long as they want to. That it won't trouble us a bit. Tell her that, will you?"

Seleucus nodded. "I'll tell her you said so, Cal," he said. Then he added doubtfully, "I wish you'd say it to her yourself, but I don't suppose you'd hardly want to. Maybe 'twouldn't be best if you did. She won't talk about you at all, and she won't let me, neither. I've tried over and over again to show her that what happened that day of the *Flyaway* business wan't your fault, that you couldn't do nothin' else, and that the rest of us was in it just as much as you was. But she won't listen, don't seem to even want to hear you named, she don't. That's women's prejudice. Jemima's like that, only tuned up consider'ble more. You can't argue with 'em; all you have a chance to do is set and listen to them arguin'. Norma, she's an awful nice girl, but she's prejudiced against you, I'm afraid. Don't seem to be much doubt of it."

Calvin walked away. "Do everything you can to help her, Seleucus," he said. "And if there is anything I can do—without her knowing it, of course—call on me. Be sure you do that."

He was in the tower, looking down through the window
where he could see without being seen, when Norma and
her father came out to board the Hammond two-seater.
Benoni was quiet and docile enough. Gammon's fears of
violence and insane obstinacy had not been justified. He
seemed to be in a sort of daze, and to realize little of the
circumstances attending his departure. Norma was outwardly calm, but she was pale and looked very tired. She
shook hands with each of the men in turn and Hammond
helped her up to the back seat of the carriage. It was a
rather cold, disagreeable day, and the curtains of the vehicle
were buttoned down. Just before she closed the door she
glanced up at the tower. Calvin had, without realizing it,
moved close to the window and she saw him. Their eyes
met. She made no sign nor did he. Hammond picked up
the reins and spoke to the horses. A moment later and the
carriage moved away. She had gone—gone—and to Calvin
it seemed that everything which made life desirable, even
endurable, had gone with her.

His feelings, since their final interview there in the mess
room, had changed. Then he had been resentful, even angry.
She had misjudged him, had refused to accept his explanations, would not believe even that he spoke the truth. But,
afterward, as he thought it over—and he had thought of
nothing else—his reason told him that she had acted as any
self-respecting girl would have done. If he had been in her
place, if she had treated him as she was convinced he had
treated her, would he have believed and forgiven? He was
forced to doubt it. She thought he had been a traitor to
Myra, had played a double game with her, had been from
the first dishonorable, and, to say the least, cowardly. He
could not blame her for thinking so; appearances were
against him, his excuses must have sounded feeble indeed.
He had tried to do right, had meant to be honest and fair.
He could think now of a hundred things he might and should
have done—if he had insisted upon seeing her again that
very day when the confession of his love had been forced
from him; if he had told her then; even if he had finished

the letter he had begun; if—but what was the use of "ifs" now? It was too late. Fate, or ill luck, had been too much for him. They had beaten him; he was down and out.

He did not even speculate concerning the manner in which she had learned of his engagement to Myra Fuller. He did not care.

He tried to lose himself in the responsibilities of the station routine, but these were but ordinary just now; the weather continued fair and clear, and there were no wrecks or calls to action. Each day was like the day before, a dull monotonous round of drill and minor duties; there was no excitement, nothing to help him forget, even temporarily.

Peleg Myrick came to Setuckit with reports which the life-savers found interesting. Benoni Bartlett had collapsed entirely during the drive to Orham. He had had to be helped from the carriage into a room at the Ocean House, and he was there now, his daughter with him. There were rumors that he flatly refused to go with her to Fairborough; that he insisted the Almighty had commanded him to remain in charge of the coast, and any hint that those orders should be disobeyed threw him into a frenzy which endangered his reason, even his life, and caused the doctor to counsel pretended agreement and longer delay. In fact, Peleg heard that Norma had resigned her position as librarian, and was contemplating taking rooms, or even a small house, in Orham and living there with her father.

"You see," confided Myrick, "the yarn is that the old man is quiet and peaceable as anybody 'd ask for so long as he's let stay down here. Frank Hammond says he's pretty nigh sensible so long as they don't drop no hints about carryin' him off. The doctor thinks that his health—yes, and his mind, too—is liable to stay fairly good if they let him have his way. But if they don't—if they start any mutiny against the Lord A'mighty's orders—then he's apt to fly out to wind'ard and flap himself to pieces like a loose jib. So Norma's goin' to give up all her own plans and stick by him so long as he holds together. That's what they say, and the story is that she's been lookin' over that little five-room house of Obed Ryder's down on the hill at the lower end of the village, the fust one you sight on your port bow when you're drivin' up overland from the pint here. . . . Oh, and say, I forgot to tell you, there's a whole lot of talk about Ezra Blodgett's keepin' steady company nowadays with Myra Fuller. Course Myra's had so many beaus that all hands are a little mite doubtful—you remember there was one spell when folks cal'lated she had a line over the side for Cal Homer—but now it does look as if 'twas old Ezra that had swallowed the hook. Well, if she lands him she'll get money, but not much else except skin and bones and a red necktie. You remember the yarns they used to tell about Ez? Why, one time he—"

There was much more, as there always was when the Myrick tongue, as Josh Phinney described it, "got under way with a gale astern." The rumors, of course, reached Homer's ears, but he asked no questions concerning them. Those dealing with Miss Fuller and Mr. Blodgett interested him not in the least. The others did, far too much for his peace of mind. During the night following Peleg's visit he again made up his mind to resign from the service and go somewhere—anywhere—where forgetting was more of a possibility than he was finding it at Setuckit.

But the day after that came a southeast rain accompanied by high winds, and that night a call to a coal barge which had broken from its towline and grounded on the Hog's Back. There were three men aboard and getting to them in time to save their lives was an adventure, and a risk which came as a blessèd distraction to Calvin. His reckless daring that night caused even the old timers like Gammon and Phinney to grin and shake their heads. They admired and liked him for it, but Seleucus expressed the general opinion when he said:

"Of course doin' your best is what you're here for, Cal, and takin' risks is part of the trade, but there's some risks that's foolish. You done everything to-night but walk on the water, and even Saint Peter couldn't get away with that, they tell me. You acted as if you thought 'twas up to you to get them coal heavers off all by yourself even if you drownded doin' it. It wan't; there was a whole boatload of us there to help you, and, besides, they wasn't wuth drowndin' for. Two of 'em was drunk and the other would have been if the whisky had held out. Take it a little easy, Cal. We've had one crazy skipper here and that's a plenty."

Homer laughed. He was tired, actually so tired that he believed he could sleep a little. Sleep, with no dreams, and a few hours from the torture of bitter self-disgust and un-availing regrets, were worth all the fatigue they had cost. From the time the boat was launched until it had landed on the beach he had been too busy to think of Norma Bart-lett. There were some compensations, other than the extra ten dollars a month pay, in the keeper's job at Setuckit Station.

And when Kellogg came down the next forenoon and again urged him to accept that position as a permanency, he hesitated. After all, why not? He liked the work, had al-ways liked it. He liked the crew and they liked him. Norma would, of course, consider her judgment justified, would feel sure that he had been disloyal to her father, and was now reaping the reward of successful treason. But she could not think worse of him than she did already; she had said she believed him a liar and a traitor. What did it matter? What did anything matter—now?

He drew a long breath.

"All right, Cap'n Kellogg," he said. "I'll take the job."

CHAPTER XVII

THE district superintendent brought with him the news of the enlistment of two new men to fill the ranks of the Setuckit crew, short handed since the departure of Oaks and Bartlett. Both of these were veterans in the service and one, James Poundberry, was a South Orham man whom Homer had known since boyhood. The other, Baxter Cahoon, was a transfer from the Wellmouth Hollow Station. Both were certain to prove valuable additions to the Setuckit group and their selection was pleasing to Calvin. They reported for duty the next day and Philander Jarvis went back to his preparation for the spring fishing, a work which his partner, Alvin Crocker, had carried on at the shanty up the beach.

The weather was good. The March winds were in evidence, and the blown sand made patrol duty rather uncomfortable, but the sky was clear and traffic over the shoals and past the rips uninterrupted. Homer, striving to keep busy, found himself almost wishing that another storm might come. So long as he had plenty to do his mind was occupied. But the days were long and, although he tried to keep his thoughts from dwelling upon the wreck of his hopes and their cause, he could not do so. He dreaded the idle monotony of the summer to come. July was certain to be a long, miserable month for him. The other men were already looking forward to it and planning what they should do during their four weeks' furlough, but he, as keeper, would be obliged to remain there at Setuckit, with no one to talk to except the occasional boatloads of summer visitors, and they would expect him to talk far too much. Well, he had yielded to Kellogg's urging and was keeper now. He could not go back on his word; but already he was sorry that he had not obeyed his first impulse, and gone away perhaps to Boston or New York. Yet he knew perfectly well that, wherever he might be, forgetfulness would not go with him. Norma's face was in his dreams, her eyes looked at him from the darkness when he blew out his lamp at night. Every corner of the skipper's room, his own room now, was redolent of her. He realized that all this was quite unavailing, that he must forget, and face the future as if the past had never been. Work, hard work, was his only cure and he tried to find it.

Every detail of routine was strictly looked out for under his régime. Drills were performed exactly on time, and with no toleration of slackness. The few calls to active duty were answered the instant they came, and from the moment the men were ordered to their posts until the boat was back again in the station, he drove his crew like the old-time master of a tea clipper. They didn't mind. There was no grumbling. They liked it. If he did not spare them he certainly spared himself less. But they noticed that his appetite was poor, that he was growing thin.

Seleucus spoke to him about it.

"Cal," he said, "you're makin' yourself sick. There's no sense in it. That three-master we went to yesterday didn't need us no more than Peleg Myrick's cat needs an extry set of claws. All ailed her skipper was that he got lost in the fog and sung out like a young one for mother to come and lead him home by the hand. You know that, but you went after him as if you *was* his mother and he was your only kid. And then, when we got back here at one o'clock in the mornin', you set up till four makin' out your report. What's the good of it? Reports 'll keep. You won't, if you don't sleep once in a while. Why don't you take a liberty day yourself—you ain't had one since afore Christmas— and have a cruise up to town and enjoy yourself? Play a game of pool, or go to a dance, or somethin' reckless. Say, Hez tells me there's an Uncle Tom show comin' to the town hall Tuesday night. One of them big ones with two Topsies and three or four bloodhounds and a live jackass, and I don't know what all. Why don't you go to that? It will do you good to see that Lawyer Marks and—what's his name?—Gumption Cute—and the rest of 'em cut up. I've seen 'em myself so often I know every blessèd thing they'll do and say next, but I enjoy it just the same. I'd go quick enough if I had the chance."

Calvin smiled. "Well, why don't you go?" he suggested. "We can spare you all right."

Seleucus sighed. "I don't go," he retorted, "for the same reason a hen don't do much flyin', 'cause what I get out of it ain't wuth all the fuss. If I hint at such a thing my wife begins heavin' out talk about my not takin' any liberty in a thousand years when she was up to the village, but sence she got here, she says, I'm always hankerin' to take it. . . . Ah hum. . . . ! But say, Cal, you ain't married; you can do what you want to. Go—and have a change. See the girls and have a good time. Only see a lot of 'em to once; they ain't any risk in that."

Calvin laughed, or tried to. But he did not accept the suggestion. Shore liberty in Orham was the least appealing of all things to him.

The other men took their allowance of liberty, however, and they brought back all the village news. The rumor that Norma Bartlett had hired the Ryder cottage, furnished, and was living there with her father, was confirmed. There had been a consultation of doctors, so the story went, and they had recommended Benoni Bartlett's being committed to some sanitarium or institution. But at the slightest hint of leaving the Cape, or even Orham, the patient's mental condition became so alarming that Norma refused to consider the idea. Taking the Ryder cottage was the alternative and that she had done. She was there alone with her father during the days and at night Elsie May—Joshua Phinney's oldest girl —came in to stay with her. It was from Josh that this authentic bit of news was learned. He had more to tell.

"Elsie May says," declared Josh, "that Bologny's real quiet and sensible most of the time. He ain't well; fact is, he's gettin' kind of feeble. The doctors say his general health's breakin' up, whatever that means—cal'late maybe they don't know themselves. Elsie May says he don't give no trouble at all, night or day, so long's the weather's good. But when there's a gale or a storm, even a little one same as we had t'other night, it seems to sort of froth up his brains, and he's all for startin' out and doin' all sorts of things. Seems to cal'late he must order out the lifeboat, and go to save somethin' or somebody. He's still got that loony notion that God's put him in command of all alongshore in these latitudes, and he must get right on the job. T'other night, Elsie says, he tiptoed past her, and was all but out-door afore she noticed him. She was settin' up, too, and on the lookout while Norma tried to get a little sleep. Yes sir-ee! He'd have been out in that pourin'-down rainstorm with nothin' on but his nightshirt and a sou'wester if she hadn't grabbed him and hollered for Norma. Pretty tough on his daughter, ain't it? She had a nice well-payin' job at Fairborough, they tell me, and she had to write 'em and give it up. Well, I guess the old feller won't live very long, and that's a good thing, when you think about it sensible. Say, Ed, how's Cal been while I was off? He don't look fust rate. More peaked and thin than ever, seems to me. What do you cal'late ails him, anyhow?"

There were many things "ailing" Calvin just then. The mental and physical strain under which he had been since the day of the meeting, and the shock and agony attending and following the wreck of his love affair, had brought the reaction which might have been expected. The harder he worked to forget, the greater the strain upon his nerves. He was in what Cape Codder's call a "run-down" condition, and therefore, the wet and exposure to which he had been subjected when leading his crew to a three-master in the fog, had given him a slight cold which he, so far, had not been able to throw off. In fact, it grew daily worse, and one thick, threatening morning he awoke from a troubled sleep to find himself shaking with a chill.

The chill was followed by fever fits, not severe but uncomfortable. Seleucus—now Number One man by official appointment—tried hard to keep his superior in bed, but

Calvin refused to heed his advice. He insisted upon getting up, and he remained up all day, trying to attend to his work, and succeeding after a fashion. By night, however, he was worse and, at last, he was obliged to admit that, if he wished to avoid real illness, he must turn in and stay there for a while, at least. The wind had risen, and it was then blowing steadily, sweeping before it a fine wet drizzle which Seleucus called a "caow storm," a combination of fog and rain, which made it hard to see for any distance. The barometer, however, was reassuring, nor had the bulletins of the weather bureau indicated any protracted or alarming disturbance.

He slept heavily, a sleep filled with dreams, in which he and Norma were again together, and she refused to listen while he explained and explained, over and over, each explanation more weird and futile than the one preceding.

He awoke to find Gammon standing by the bed. Seleucus was wearing oilskins, rubber boots and sou'wester. The dim light of a wet, early April dawn shone faintly through the window. The panes of that window were streaming with water. Calvin started and attempted to rise, but Seleucus's big hand held him down.

"Steady, Cal, steady," ordered Gammon. "No, you ain't goin' to get up; you're goin' to be sensible and stay right where you be. Listen to what I'm sayin'. There's a two-master off back of the Sand Hill signalin' us to come to her. Poundberry sighted her fifteen minutes ago, when the drizzle blowed clear a little mite. She ain't in no danger, nigh as we can make out; in deep water off in the channel, and gettin' along all right, seems so. Probably there's somebody sick aboard, or the skipper's lost his bearin's or somethin'. Anyhow, they're signalin' for us, and we're goin' off to her. . . . No, you ain't goin'. There's no need of it at all. The wind ain't much more 'n moderate, and a ten-year-old kid could handle the job. It's wet and raw and no kind of weather for a sick man to take chances in. You stay right where you be, and leave the rest to me and the boys. If I can't take care of it, with a crew of old timers like this one

to help, then I'm goin' to quit life-savin' and take to cro-
chetin' pillow shams. You go to sleep again. We'll be back
in a couple of hours. Lay down and sleep, I tell you."

Homer, of course, refused to lie down. He insisted upon
getting up, climbing to the tower, and inspecting the schooner
through the telescope. She, as Gammon had said, appeared
to be in no danger whatever, yet the call for help was flying.
He looked out at the soaking miserableness cloaking sea and
land and sky, and another chill set his teeth chattering.
Seleucus noticed his condition and pulled him toward the
stairs.

"You come down and turn in again," he commanded.
"You're sick now, and if you go off yonder you'll be dead.
A dead skipper ain't no good to anybody but the undertaker.
Come on, Cal, come on! Don't worry. It's a kid's job, and
I'm the spryest young one this mornin' ever you see. You
turn in and leave it to me. There's no use arguin', because
you ain't goin'. The boys are all agreed on that; they'll tie
you in bed afore they let you. Use your sense, Cal. You
don't want another mutiny here at Setuckit, do ye?"

The chill had been succeeded by a flash of fever. Calvin
gave it up. He would be no help aboard the lifeboat, and
it was likely to be an easy job.

"All right," he muttered reluctantly. "Go ahead then. But
take all hands with you. You may need them, and I certainly don't need any one here with me."

"You sure? It's Phinney's cook week, and he's got the
right to stay ashore, you know."

"Right or not, he's got to go, if I don't. And I guess it's
as you say, Seleucus; I should hinder more than I helped.
Hurry now! Get her out. Good luck to you."

"Don't you cal'late I'd better telephone for the doctor?"

"Don't be foolish. Clear out—and hurry."

He waited there in the tower until he saw the lifeboat leave
the shore and swing off over the lines of surf. Then he
stumbled down the stairs and, partially dressed as he was—
for he had donned some of his clothes before leaving the
room—tumbled into bed once more. This time he did not

sleep, but lay there, watching the dim light brighten the window, and worrying about the safety of the schooner and his own men. It seemed as if he should have gone—but how could he?

The telephone bell rang. It rang again. He crawled from the bed, and, going into the mess room, took down the receiver. It was Nelson, keeper of the Orham Station, who was calling. He had news.

"Who is it?" he asked. "Oh, that you, Cal? Why ain't you off with the crew? I saw the boat leave a spell ago and, of course— Oh yes, yes! I see. Sorry to hear it. This ain't any day for a sick man to be out in, that's a fact. And I don't cal'late there's much the matter with that schooner. Cap'n's got the toothache or has run out of chewin' tobacco or somethin'. . . . Yes, I was goin' to tell you. We've just had word from Orham that Benoni Bartlett's run off somewheres in the night. Eh? Yes, run off is what I said. You've heard how the least little mite of wind or rough weather kind of goes to his head, and makes him wild . . . ? Um-hum. Well, seems he began to act funny last evenin' when it commenced to breeze on and rain. Norma—that's his daughter—she was worried and she stayed up with him till two o'clock or so and then, as he'd turned in and seemed to be sound asleep, she took a little nap herself, in her own room, you understand. She left the Phinney girl—that one of Josh's—to set up and keep watch in the settin' room. Well, seems the young one dozed off, and when she woke Benoni'd gone. . . . Eh? No, they don't know where. He'd put on his ileskins and boots and sou'wester, so they figger he might have got the notion of cruisin' down the beach here somewheres, to Setuckit, maybe. You know he still hangs to the idea that the Lord's ordered him to look after everything up and down the shore or in the channel. They phoned for us to watch out for him and notify you folks. . . . You ain't seen anything of him, 'tain't likely, have you, Cal?"

Homer had quite forgotten his chills and fever flashes. The aches in his head and limbs had gone. The thought of

Norma—her frightful anxiety and dread and fear; she alone there, while her crazed and sick father was wandering in the cold and rain, no one knew where and upon no one knew what insane errand—these thoughts had driven all others from his mind and all pains and discomfort from his body. He poured question after question into the telephone. Nelson did his best to answer.

"No, they ain't found a trace of him so far," he declared. "He don't seem to be anywheres around his part of the town. He's either trampin' the beach, they think, down this way or back towards Trumet; or else he may be out in a boat. . . . Eh? Yes, boat's what I said. There's a chance he's done that. There's half a dozen catboats and a dozen dories down there by the wharf and, crazy as he is, he may have took one of them. No tellin' what a loony will take it into his head to do, that's a fact. Cooper, he went up to the tower when he come in from patrol, to see how you folks was gettin' along with that schooner, and he see a sailboat off in the bay, headed down, with what looked to be one man aboard. He couldn't see plain, but he took it for granted 'twas Philander or Alvin Crocker gettin' an early start. It thickened up right off and since then it's been so thick you can't see nothin' on the bay side from here. You better take a look yourself; you'd ought to be able to see better from where you are. Anyhow, I'd keep my eye peeled. Let me know if you do see anything looks suspicious. . . . Yes; sure I'll keep you posted."

Homer waited to hear no more. He dropped the receiver into its socket and hastened to the tower. The hurry of his ascent caused his head to swim giddily, but he clung to the door jamb until the dizziness became less acute and then, whirling the telescope toward the windows facing the bay, opened one of those windows, and peered through the glass.

Rain—fine, thick, and driving at a steady slant—with gray water showing dimly through it, this was all he saw at first. He swung the outer end of the glass as far as possible to the west, and then moved it slowly back, searching the bay —or the little he could see of it—for a boat.

The rain was so heavy and close that, looking through it, especially at that early hour, was as unsatisfactory as trying to look through a succession of gauze curtains. The beach and cove showed plainly enough, but out, beyond them, the dimness increased with every rod. There was nothing to the west, or southwest, so far as he could see. Nothing afloat on the rips at the end of the point. Yet if Bartlett had left Orham as early as two, or even three, he should, with that wind, have been well out into the bay by now. If it was Setuckit he was making for he should be almost at his destination. Of course it was possible—even most probable—that he had not taken a boat at all. Calvin devoutly hoped he had not.

He moved the end of the glass in its half circle until, through it, he glimpsed the blotch of white water which indicated the outer edge of the Scallop Flat, the shoal a mile or so out in the bay to the northwest of Peleg Myrick's shanty, and perhaps three miles in a direct line from the Setuckit Station. At low tide the Scallop Flat was dry, but at high water the larger part of it was navigable for the average sailboat, and the waves, breaking along the outer boundary, marked the danger line. It was just past high water now; the tide was beginning to ebb.

And in the midst of that white and troubled water he did see a boat. A catboat she looked to be, and aground on the edge of the flat. Her reefed sail was swung off to leeward, apparently at the end of a loose sheet, and she was heeled down against the high bar at the edge of the shoal. He could not make out whether or not there was any one aboard. If there was he was not moving, was not making any apparent effort to get his craft afloat. Calvin gazed intently. Then a squall drove a thicker curtain of rain across the view and he could see her no longer.

Nor did he wait to see. He had little doubt that the stranded boat was the one in which Benoni Bartlett had left Orham. She was in no great danger as she lay, and if she was as firmly aground as she appeared to be, the ebbing tide would soon leave her high and dry. But there was a possibility that the increasing strength of that tide, with the wind to back it, might swing her off again into deep water. There she would be in real danger, she might career and sink. Bartlett—if he was aboard her—was certainly doing nothing to help himself or to insure the boat's safety. In all probability, if he was there, his exertions had already been too much for him and he was prostrated. A sick man, an insane man, helpless, in that drenching rain! And that man was Norma Bartlett's father!

Calvin, his own brain spinning in giddy circles, ran down the stairs to his room. There were certain obvious things to be done, and, had he been his normal self, he would have done them. He would have telephoned the Orham Station, told Nelson what he had seen, and a squad from that station would have started immediately to the rescue. He might have gone to the Jarvis shanty and enlisted Philander's aid. But Homer, just then, was far from normal. The fever was blazing in his veins, and thinking and acting clearly and sensibly were beyond his capabilities. Norma's father was out there in that boat, alone, helpless, and in danger; these were the essential facts, and the only ones he seemed able to grasp.

He donned his wet-weather rig—he had sufficient common sense for that—but even this was done automatically and afterward he could not remember doing it. He ran out of the station and down to the shore of the cove where, hauled up on the beach, were two or three dories, Philander Jarvis's among them.

Launching that dory was an amazingly hard struggle. There was no reason why it should be, for the beach had an easy slope, and the tide was high. But it seemed to him that he would never get her afloat, that she fought against him with the obstinacy of a living thing, and spun around and around—always around and around—instead of going ahead. But she was afloat at last, and he scrambled, or fell, aboard, took up the oars, and began to row. He headed down the beach, keeping close to land. The wind was off-shore, and the shoal water was scarcely rippled.

At first the exertion of rowing seemed to clear his brain, and he began to realize more clearly what he was doing, and what must be done. The first mile he covered at a good clip, rowing the short, deep strokes always used by one accustomed to the idiosyncrasies of that touchy, but dependable craft, the fisherman's dory. Then the rowing became harder, his shoulders were shot with pain, there was a pain in his chest, each breath hurt, and his brain again became a sort of merry-go-round. He set his teeth and pulled and pulled and pulled.

He saw, just ahead of him, the lines of tumbling water which indicated the inshore edge of the Scallop Flat. At this stage of the tide, however, there was more than depth enough to float the dory, so he kept on over what, a few hours later, would be stretches of white sand. Then he turned and rowed out toward the bay. Another quarter of a mile, and the growl and surge of the breakers on the bar sounded near at hand and, peering through the rain ahead, he saw the stranded catboat. She was there, just where he had seen her through the glass. She had not gone adrift.

As he drew near to her on the windward side, he shouted. There was no answer, and as shouting caused the pain in his chest to become more acute, he gave it up. He gave a final stroke, then drew in the oars and, as the dory shot alongside the upturned rail of the catboat, he seized the rail and held fast. He shouted again, but no one answered.

He picked up the rope which, coiled in the dory's bow, was attached to her anchor, and, with the loop of rope in his hand, scrambled over the rail into the catboat. He pulled the anchor aboard after him. The dory, of course, swung away at the end of the line, but the anchor in the larger craft held her fast; she could not get away.

There was a man lying on the floor of the catboat's cockpit. His feet were toward the wheel, and his body stretched between the centerboard box and the thwart, on the starboard side. That side was lower than the other and she had shipped some water. The man was lying in a pool. The rain was driving down upon him. He was dressed in oilskins, and the strap of a black sou'wester was buttoned beneath his chin. Calvin, bracing himself by the centerboard, stooped over the figure and pulled back the brim of the sou'wester. The man lying there, his beard in the water, was Benoni Bartlett. Calvin was not surprised; he had been practically certain of it from the first.

He grasped his former skipper by the arm and dragged him a little way out of the puddle of salt water. Then he tried to shake him into consciousness.

"Cap'n Bartlett!" he shouted. "Cap'n Bartlett!"

For at least a minute his shouts and shakings had no effect. Then Bartlett stirred and groaned. Homer gasped in relief. There was life there; the man was not dead.

"Cap'n!" shouted Calvin. "Cap'n Bartlett! Here! Get up! You must get up!"

Bartlett's eyes opened, he rolled over on his back, leaning against Calvin's knee.

"Aye, aye, sir!" he muttered. "Comin'. On deck in a minute."

Calvin put his hands under the other's armpits and, exerting all his strength, dragged him from behind the centerboard box until his shoulders rested against the closed lower half of the cabin hatch. Then, holding him steady, he strove to awaken him to full consciousness.

"Cap'n Bartlett," he urged. "Wake up! Wake up and listen to me. You're all right now, aren't you? You aren't hurt?"

Benoni moved again, tried to rise.

"Who said I was hurt?" he demanded feebly. "I'm all right. What are you standin' here for? Turn out the crew. Get out the boat. Don't you hear me? Get her out!"

Homer, his own brain almost as queerly muddled as that of his companion, still had sufficient comprehension of the situation to try and humor him. "All right, skipper," he said cheerfully. "The crew are getting her out all right. Now you want to hurry or you'll keep 'em waiting. Can you stand up? Sure you aren't hurt?"

Bartlett could not have stood alone, but with Homer's

arm about him and clinging to the rail, he managed to do
so. His wanderings took a new turn.

"Got all hands off her, boy?" he queried. "Saved all of
'em, have you? That's good! that's good! That's accordin'
to the Lord's orders. He says to me, 'Benoni,' He says—
that's how He calls me, by my first name; that shows how
I stand along of Him—'Benoni,' says He to me, 'here's another call for you. You save that bark,' He says. 'Turn
out and go off to her.' I did it, too. I didn't let Norma
know. She don't know I started, but—eh? Where is
Norma? Ain't she to the station?"

"Yes, yes; of course she is. You've saved everybody,
Cap'n. Now you sit down on that thwart a minute and
then we'll get aboard the lifeboat. . . . That's it. Sit down
and wait—just a minute."

He forced Bartlett down upon the bench bordering the
upper edge of the tilted cockpit. It required little force. A
hand upon his shoulder and the rescued man's knees gave
way, and he sank in a huddled heap by the rail, his chin
upon his breast, muttering disjointedly. Calvin crawled forward, loosened the halyards, and let the sail go by the run.
It fell into the water, but he did not heed that. Somehow
he felt an extraordinary responsibility for that catboat. He
must make sure of her safety before he left her. That catboat—but was she a catboat? Cap'n Bartlett had said she
was a bark. Well, it did not make any difference, he must
make sure she did not get adrift again. He found the anchor,
cast it loose, and threw it overboard. She would hold. And
now he must get Bartlett ashore.

He drew the dory alongside and held it there. Then followed a long, tangled argument. Which side of that argument was the more insane it would have been hard to say.
Benoni was babbling about the bark and the bark's crew,
of his responsibility to the Almighty, and his doubt concerning Norma's whereabouts. Homer answered all his questions, and agreed with him whenever possible. The one
point upon which he insisted was that they must get aboard
the lifeboat—that is, the dory. And, at last, his insistence

prevailed. Bartlett climbed over the rail, Calvin holding him tightly by the arm, and sank down in the dory's stern. His rescuer, the anchor of the smaller craft in his hand, followed him. Then he took up the oars and rowed toward the beach.

The tide had ebbed somewhat, of course, but there was still water enough on the flat. The row in was a long one, but, to Calvin, it seemed to last forever. He swung back and forth automatically, the pains in his chest and shoulders causing him agony; and wondering why they had not been seen from the Orham Station before this and help sent. Had he been able to think clearly he would have understood. The rain—Gammon's "cow storm"—had ceased to fall, and had left in its place a fog so thick that objects a hundred yards off were invisible. Nelson and his men had been watching from the tower, but they could not see even the bay shore, to say nothing of the Scallop Flat.

Calvin tugged at the oars. He had lost all ideas of time and place, and was conscious only that he must row and keep on rowing. Consequently the dory's bow struck the beach with such force as to throw him backwards, off the thwart, and into the bottom of the dory. Bartlett, too, had been upset, but he did not seem to be aware of it. He lay where he had fallen, muttering, and singing a verse of a hymn. Homer got to his feet, climbed wearily over the boat's side and pulled her as far up the shore as his depleted strength would allow. Then, after a struggle, and more argument, he managed to get his passenger out of the dory. Benoni could walk, but scarcely that; Calvin's arm supported him, and his weight leaned heavily upon the latter's shoulders.

It was obvious, even to Homer's cloudy brain, that to attempt the long, circuitous tramp over the dunes and through the sand to Setuckit was out of the question. Bartlett could not walk so far, nor could Calvin carry him, for the support amounted to that. The Orham Station was, perhaps, a little nearer, but it, also, was too far. Calvin, desperately trying to consider possibilities, remembered Peleg Myrick's hut. That was a long mile down the beach, but one mile

was better than two—or four. And Peleg would look out
for them, if he was at home. If he was not the shanty was
certain to be unlocked, and they could get in and find rest
and warmth.

So, down the beach toward the hermit's shanty the pair
started. Bartlett leaned more and more heavily as they
walked and appeared to be oblivious of what was going on.
At first he had muttered or shouted orders to the crew he
evidently imagined himself leading, but soon he ceased to
do even that. Calvin, alarmed by his silence, and his labored
breathing, spoke to him occasionally, but received no reply.

The hermit's shanty loomed through the gray fog, a spark
of yellow lamplight in its window. Evidently Peleg was up
and stirring. Calvin pantingly staggered up the slope of the
beach, his companion's head bumping against his shoulder.
He turned the corner of the little building and, seizing the
latch of the weather-beaten door, shook it.

"Peleg," he gasped. "Peleg."

Inside the shanty a chair was pushed back. An instant
later the door was opened. Mr. Myrick, in a state of extremely careless negligée, his scanty hair tumbled, blinked
at them.

"For thunder mighty sake!" exclaimed Peleg. "What—"

Homer interrupted. "Help me with him—quick," he
ordered. "Get him in there. I—I can't hold him up much
longer."

Between them Benoni Bartlett was assisted into the shanty.
They put him in a chair, removed his boots and hat and
oilskins. Then they carried him into the adjoining, and only
other, room and laid him on the bed. He made no objec-
tion; his eyes were closed and he did not speak. If it had
not been for his stertorous breathing Myrick declared he
would have thought him dead.

"But where'd he come from, Cal?" Peleg demanded,
"How'd you get aholt of him? What's it all about?"

Calvin's explanation was as brief as it could possibly be.
A cup of the hermit's horrible coffee, already prepared for
breakfast, had in a measure warmed his chilled interior and

cleared his swimming brain. The pains in his chest and shoulders and limbs were as severe as ever.

"Don't ask me any more questions," he ordered irritably. "Give him some of that hot coffee, if you can make him swallow it, and cover him up warm. Then you hustle across to the Orham Station and tell Nelson you've picked him up, and that he's here and needs to be looked after. Tell them to get word to Norma right off. Now don't talk any more. Go!"

"But what you cal'late to do, Cal? Say, you look mighty well beat out yourself. Hadn't you better turn in, too? I can fix up a shakedown for you on the floor, and a—"

"No, no, no! I've got to get back to my own station. The boat's out and I ought to be there this minute. I'm going now. But you do as I tell you. Be sure they get word to Norma."

"I'll see to that. But, Cal—"

"Be still, can't you? You tell them that. . . . But—but don't you let them tell her anything about me. No, and don't you tell *them* either. There is no need of it. Tell them you saw that catboat—it's Taylor Gould's, I guess, by the look of it—tell 'em you were the one who sighted her off on the flat, and went off and picked Cap'n Bartlett up. Tell them you did it, and don't mention my name at all. That's what I want you to do. Understand?"

"But I never picked him up, Cal. You done it. What should I tell all that pack of lies for?"

"Because I tell you to. I want you to. See here, Peleg, you leave me out of this. You've got to. I don't want anybody but you to know I was mixed up with Benoni Bartlett. There has been enough talk about me already—too much."

"But—but he'll tell 'em himself, won't he?"

"I'm afraid he'll never tell any one much of anything after this. And, if he should, no one would pay any attention; he is out of his head. You say you found him and brought him here, Peleg. You've *got* to promise me you'll tell everybody that; do you hear?"

"There, there, Cal, don't fly up this way. You look half crazy, yourself, I declare if you don't. Course I'll tell 'em if you say so. But I don't see why. 'Tain't nothin' to be ashamed of, as I see it. More t'other way 'round. And as for talk about you and Benoni, why—"

"Shut up!" Oh, why did this idiot persist in opposing his every suggestion? "Don't you see?" he demanded. "I've left my station all alone. I don't want any one to know I did it. That's it—that's the reason. Now you get it, don't you? Be a good fellow, Peleg, and don't say a word about me."

Peleg nodded. "Oh, now I cal'late I do get you, Cal," he said. "I don't believe anybody'd find much fault on account of your leavin', considerin' what made you leave. . . . But there, there! don't fly up again. I'll tell all the lies you want, if it suits you better. I'm a pretty fair average liar when I set my mind to it. But have you got to go right now? Won't you have some more coffee? Won't you—"

But Homer had gone. He was already plowing through the sand, on his way back to Setuckit. When he entered the hermit's shanty he had had no idea of forbidding its owner to tell of his part in the rescue of Benoni Bartlett. The conviction had come upon him suddenly, out of the whirl of queer thoughts in his fever-stricken brain. It was a brilliant thought, too—he was certain of that, and proud of it. And the real reason prompting it had nothing whatever to do with his leaving the station unguarded. That was a trifle of no importance. The important thing—yes, that was it, the important thing—was to prevent Norma from hearing his own name; she must not again be troubled with any thought of him. He had troubled her enough. She was trying to forget him, probably had forgotten him already and must not be reminded. He was a traitor—and disloyal—and—and— It was hard to remember what he was, hard to remember anything at that moment—even the way to Setuckit—and he must remember that.

He did remember it somehow and staggered into the mess room to the accompaniment of a tinkling of bells. It was queer that they should ring the dinner bell so early in the morning. And queerer still considering that there was no dinner bell in the station. But the bell continued to ring and, after a while, he decided it must be the telephone bell. It was, and Nelson was speaking from the Orham Station.

"Hello, Cal!" hailed Nelson. "That you finally? Asleep, I presume likely. Sorry I turned you out. Hope you're feelin' better. I just thought you'd like to know the news. Peleg Myrick's been here, and he's got Benoni Bartlett over to his shanty. The old feller was aground in somebody's catboat on the Scallop Flat and Peleg sighted him and went off in the dory and fetched him in. We've telephoned and they'll get word to Norma. Some of the men have gone across to Peleg's already and I'm goin' in a minute. Benoni's in pretty bad shape, so Myrick says, but it's a mercy he isn't at the bottom of the bay. Good thing old Peleg was awake and had his eyes open. . . . Yes. . . . Yes, I told you we'd sent word to his daughter. I'll let you know how things go with 'em. Take care of yourself and—"

Calvin had hung up the receiver. He scarcely knew that he did it. The door to his room looked a long way off, but he reached it, and threw it open. When, an hour later, the crew returned from an entirely unnecessary trip to the two-masted schooner, Gammon found his skipper lying upon the bed in that room, dressed in dripping oilskins and boots, groaning with pain and delirious.

CHAPTER XVIII

RHEUMATIC fever—that is what the old-fashioned doctors used to call it—is not a cheerful disease. They give it another name nowadays, but the change does not make it less painful. Calvin Homer was a sick man and a sick man he remained for weeks. Seleucus, Phinney, and Hez Rogers held a consultation that morning, and, as a result of it, Doctor Palmer, the Orham physician, was telephoned for, and he drove to Setuckit that afternoon. Calvin was not dangerously ill, so the doctor declared—that is, there was no immediate danger to be apprehended—but he must be kept in bed, and he should have constant attention and care. His removal to Orham was out of the question.

"He ought to have some one with him all the time, night and day," declared the doctor, "and who that somebody will be I'm sure I don't know. There is a good deal of sickness up in the village, and about every available woman who goes out nursing is busy. I might get a nurse from Boston, but it will take some coaxing to find one who will come down and stay at a place like this."

"Couldn't you get a man that would do?" inquired Phinney.

Doctor Palmer shook his head.

"I can't think of one," he said. "Can you? Old Henry Pepper is the only one who does that sort of work, and he is sick, himself. Besides, the last patient of mine that Pepper took care of swore he had rather be alone. It was Cap'n Tom Doane. Henry is deaf, you know, and Cap'n Tom vowed that the exertion of yelling every time he wanted anything made him sicker than going without that thing. And, so the cap'n said, Pepper had a habit of dropping asleep on watch, and once asleep no amount of yelling would wake him. Then Cap'n Tom had to climb out of bed, and go

344

and shake him and howl into his ear what it was he needed. 'He makes me so darned mad, Doc,' says the cap'n, 'that, if I wasn't so weak, I'd have killed him afore now. Then you'd have been called into court to swear 'twas justifiable suicide.' He meant homicide, of course; he's a dry old chap, Doane is. But I had to admit that Pepper, as a nurse, was a little worse than nobody. And, even if he was good for anything, he is out of the question now. Isn't there some one down here you could get?"

Rogers suggested Peleg Myrick. Seleucus expressed doubt.

"I don't believe Peleg would take the job," he observed. "He's independent as an eel in a grass channel, and he'll do what he cal'lates to do and nothin' else. Besides, the season for clammin' and quahaugin' is just openin' up and that's when he makes what little money he needs. Oh, yes, yes, I know he could make maybe as much by nursin' Cal, but that wouldn't be any argument with Peleg. He'd say no to begin with, and after that he'd stick to it just out of stubbornness, same as he sticks to his weather prophesyin'. He'll come down here, with the sun shinin', and swear it's a howlin' snowstorm only we ain't got sense enough to find it out."

Phinney grinned. "Yes," he agreed, "and if he did come he'd want to fetch that fiddle of his and his old Sou'west cat, and then there'd be the Old Harry to pay. His cat wouldn't get along with our cats, and between cat fights and that fiddle squeakin' poor Cal would wish he was dead, even if he lived through it. No, my vote goes in against Peleg— hard."

"We'll think it over, Doctor," said Rogers. "And, while we're thinkin', we'll take turns lookin' out for Cal. It's comin' spring, so we ain't likely to be very busy."

Doctor Palmer said he would come again next day, and would telephone that evening. He left medicine and directions for the care of the patient. He must hurry now, he declared, to the Orham Station and Benoni Bartlett. He had stopped there on the way down. Asked concerning Bartlett's condition, he looked grave.

"He is in bad shape," he admitted. "Doesn't seem to know much of what is going on and I am inclined to think he may have had a slight shock. His daughter came down with me. We are going to try and take her father back with us when we go; that is, if he is in a condition to stand the trip."

After the doctor's departure the entire crew discussed the situation. No one had a satisfactory suggestion to make as to a possible nurse for Homer. But when Seleucus next went over to the Jarvis shanty his wife offered one very much to the point.

"What's the matter with me?" she asked tartly. "I don't set up to be any trained nurse, as I know of, but I guess likely I could do as well as old Henry Pepper. If I couldn't I'd sell out cheap."

Her husband, much surprised, pulled at his mustache. "Why—why, I never thought of you, Jemima," he admitted.

"No, 'tain't likely you would. I'm the last one you think of. If I was Olive Myrick or that Norma Bartlett—if I was anybody else but your own married wife, you'd think of me. I know that."

"Eh? Now, Jemima, don't talk foolish. You're always thinkin' I'm thinkin' about other women. That's silly, that is. Look at me! Crimustee, *look* at me! What do you cal'late a woman's liable to see in me?"

"I don't know, I'm sure. *I* must have seen somethin' in you or I wouldn't have married you. That was a long spell ago, though, and my eyesight was always poor. But I can take care of Calvin Homer, and whatever the pay for doin' is I can find ways to use it. Besides, I'd just as soon spend my time over in that station as not. There must be somethin' turrible attractive about it, or you'd leave it oftener than you do. I have to use main strength afore you'll come home long enough to split me a mess of kindlin' wood. . . . Yes, and while you're strainin' your brains thinkin' up reasons why I shouldn't take the nursin' job, you can be splittin' some right now."

Mr. Gammon, obediently chopping, did venture one or two

possible objections. They were not weighty—the weighty ones were so intimately personal that he kept them to himself. He wished to know who would look after Philander's cooking and housework if she took up residence at the station. Jemima soon disposed of that. Her brother, she declared, would be at the weir shanty most of the time. "And, besides," she added, "Philander is used to lookin' out for himself. He ain't so helpless as some folks. He can get along without a woman to wait on him; yes, or one to tag around after, either."

Seleucus, badgered into silence at home, reluctantly carried the news of his wife's offer to Phinney and the others. They accepted it with enthusiasm. "Fine!" "First rate!" Why had they not thought of it themselves?

"Good stuff!" exclaimed Josh. "A woman is the only kind of a nurse that's good for much and Jemima's right here on deck. Besides," with a wink over his shoulder, "it'll be such a nice thing for you, Seleucus, to have her with you every minute of the time. All the comforts of home, as you might say."

So that very evening Mrs. Gammon came to the station and took charge of the sick man. Hers were no light duties. Calvin's pain was incessant and agonizing, his fever made him delirious, and he groaned and muttered. When, in his delirium, he attempted to turn in bed, he shrieked with pain. Several times that night Seleucus was called by his wife to come and help her with the patient. His own temper was severely frayed by each successive summons, but Jemima's was so much worse that he swallowed his wrath and meekly obeyed orders.

"Kind of hard work, ain't it, Jemima?" he said with a sigh.

Mrs. Gammon sniffed. "Hard!" she repeated. " 'Twouldn't be so hard if you was like some husbands, and was willin' to set up and do a little of it yourself. But all you want to do is sleep."

"But I never got to sleep till after twelve. I was out on patrol."

"Yes, and if I'd set up as late as that I'd just as soon stay up the rest of the night. I'd be used to it by then."

"Well, you *was* up, wan't ye? I heard you up when I come in."

"Oh, don't talk so foolish! Course I was up. I've been up all night, ain't I?"

"Um-hum. I suppose you have. But you said somethin' about bein' up till twelve makin' you used to it. Seems to me—"

"Oh, mercy on us, do go to bed again! I don't know what they'll pay me for doin' this, but whatever 'tis I'll earn it."

She was a faithful nurse, and never neglectful of her duties, although the exacting nature of those duties rendered her a difficult problem for the life-savers to contend with. One or the other of the men relieved her during the hours in the middle of the day when she went back to the Jarvis shanty for a scanty measure of rest and sleep. Doctor Palmer came regularly, rain or shine. The journey down and back was a hard one, but a country general practitioner, in those pre-automobile days, was accustomed to hard journeys.

The doctor pronounced Homer's condition satisfactory. There was little to do except ease his pain as much as possible, keep careful watch, and let the disease take its course. Calvin was young and strong and, barring accidents—that is, provided his heart was not affected—he was, so Palmer said, almost sure to come out all right. The days and nights passed, with their round of fever, pain and delirium. Superintendent Kellogg visited Setuckit, inquired solicitously concerning Homer, and placed Seleucus in temporary charge of things at the station until the regular keeper should again be fit.

These visitors—and Peleg Myrick, when he came—brought news from Orham. Benoni Bartlett was still alive, but little more than that. The doctor's surmise that he had suffered a slight paralytic stroke was confirmed. They had taken him back to the little Ryder cottage, where he now lay, attended by Norma, the Phinney girl, and occasional volunteers among the kindly neighbors. He was conscious only at rare intervals and then only partially so.

"He may slip off any minute," Doctor Palmer confided to Seleucus. "That is the truth. And, for his own sake, not to mention Norma's, the sooner he does the better. His mind is gone, and he is paralyzed. Who could want him to live in that condition? That girl of his is a wonder. She shows what she has been through, but she doesn't complain and won't talk about herself. She's spunky—by George! she is!"

This statement was made at the door of the sick room, just as the doctor was leaving. Jemima, in the room with Calvin, heard it. She tiptoed forward and asked a question.

"Have you told her about"—with a motion of her hand toward the bed—"about *him* bein' so sick?" she asked eagerly. Something in her tone caused her husband to glance at her in surprise. Doctor Palmer, however, noticed nothing unusual.

"Oh, yes, I told her that first day when we took Cap'n Bartlett back to town," he replied.

"I see. Um-hum. Kind of interested, was she?"

"Yes. Of course she was. As much as any one in her position just then was likely to be. Her father was almost dead and most of her thoughts were taken up with him. But she was interested, I guess. She asked a good many questions about Homer."

"Um-hum. Asked some since, has she?"

"Yes. I always tell her how he is getting on when I go there. But everybody is interested. The whole business is keeping Orham talking nowadays. By the way, has anybody found out what Calvin was doing after you fellows left him here at the station that morning? Where he went —and why he went? You left here, you say, Seleucus; and, when you came back he had evidently been out in the rain, for he was wet through. Have you any idea what got him up and out-of-doors—a sick man, in such weather?"

Seleucus shook his head. Those were questions over

which he and his fellow surfmen had puzzled and speculated much.

"No," he admitted. "Cap'n Nelson, down to the Orham Station, says that soon as they got word to him that Bologny —Cap'n Bartlett, I mean—had got loose and might be trampin' the beach or adrift in the bay, he telephoned here. He says Cal answered the phone. Cal told Nelson he was sick and we'd had to go to the schooner without him, and seemed to be dreadful interested about Bartlett. After Peleg had fetched Bologny ashore to his shanty and had left there and hustled over to the Orham Station, Nelson telephoned again. Cal answered that time, too, but Nelson said he couldn't get much out of him, or make much sense of what he said. When we found Cal he had his ileskins and boots on, and the water from 'em had run all over the floor. We sort of figger—we fellers here—that he might have been down to the shore maybe, trying to see if he could catch sight of Bologny, or a loose boat or somethin'. That sounds the most reasonable of anything we can think of. Of course we ain't asked him about it. He's out of his head a lot of the time and when he ain't he's too weak to bother with questions. Ain't said nothin' to you about it, has he, Jemima?"

Mrs. Gammon's answer was prompt.

"No," she declared. "He says enough, land knows. He's jabberin' away half the time, but it's mostly about—well, 'tain't about that."

Palmer smiled. "Peleg Myrick has made a hit without knowing it," he observed. "His sighting the Gould boat and getting off to it right away were the saving of Bartlett's life, for the time, anyhow. The man would have died from exposure in a little while, there is no doubt about that. Old Peleg is quite a hero. Did you read the piece in this week's *Item* about him? And there was a story in one of the Boston papers, too. The hermit business will be good this summer, I imagine, and Peleg will grow fat on it. He dearly loves to show off before the summer people."

Seleucus laughed. "I bet you!" he agreed. "Crimus! how he will strut and lie! The yarns he'll tell will grow and spread like the green hay tree in the Bible. By the end of next August he'll have saved half of Cape Cod and only just missed savin' the other half. Funny thing he won't talk to us about it. He's down here every other day to ask how Cal's gettin' along. He's took a turrible shine to Cal, seems so. We've asked him a lot of questions about how 'twas he come to be up and sight the boat, but he shies every time. Preach his head off about his fool weather prophesyin', and name over every bone and jint he's got aboard himself; but he won't talk about pullin' Bologny out of the drink. Savin' that up for the city folks, I guess likely."

After the doctor had gone Seleucus asked his wife what she meant by asking if Norma had seemed interested in Homer's condition. She smiled—a knowing smile, it seemed to him—but refused to give him any satisfaction.

"Maybe I didn't mean anything," she said. "And, then again, maybe I did. Anyhow, it ain't any of your affairs, as I know of."

"But you did mean somethin', Jemima. I could tell you did. I've lived along with you enough to tell when you've got somethin' up your sleeve."

Mrs. Gammon sniffed. "Most of the time you've been livin' with me," she observed, "you've been doin' your best to keep away from me. Just now you want to hang around. You trot off and attend to some of that work you're forever tellin' me about. *I* don't need you. I ain't Olive Myrick, nor the Bartlett girl, nor any of the rest of 'em. I'm just your wife and I'm used to doin' without you."

So Seleucus went, but, as he went, he thought. And, although he did not mention his thoughts to any one, he continued to think. His provoking better half certainly had some reason for her coupling of Calvin Homer's name with that of Benoni Bartlett's daughter. As he told her, he had lived with her a long time, and that air of sly triumph and smug satisfaction meant something. She had learned some-

thing which he and the others did not know. And it must
be something concerning Calvin and Norma.

Mr. Gammon had heard, as had all Orham and its neighborhood, the rumors of Homer's "keeping company" with
Myra Fuller. He did not approve of the match, for although every Setuckit life-saver, married or single, was
willing to agree that Myra was "some girl" and a "pippin,"
her name was usually mentioned with a grin and a wink.
If Calvin was cal'latin' to marry her, they opined, he was
in for a lively and watchful future. They hoped, for his
sake, that she might not get him. And now it appeared that
she had given up any idea of getting him. Ezra Blodgett
was reported to be the latest candidate for Miss Fuller's
favor and a successful one. In fact, Cooper, of the Orham
Station, had told Ed Bloomer that his wife heard from
some one else, who had learned it from another some one,
that Ezra and Myra were engaged.

But Seleucus had never seriously dreamed of the possibility of a love affair between Calvin and Norma. Those
two had known each other but a little while, and that only
during her visits to Setuckit. She had at first seemed to
like him, but, for that matter, every one—Oaks and Bartlett excepted—liked him. She had asked questions about
him; she had talked with Seleucus about him, or, rather,
had led Seleucus to talk. And, that foggy afternoon, when
Bartlett had sent the latter out in search of his daughter,
and he had come upon the pair at the edge of the cut through,
for just a moment his suspicions had been aroused. They
had seemed a little embarrassed or confused, Calvin especially. Yes, then, and for a short time thereafter, Mr.
Gammon had wondered and speculated, although he had
kept his speculations to himself.

But the idea that Calvin Homer and Norma Bartlett might
be keeping company—Seleucus never, even in his thoughts,
designated the relation in any other way—did not last long.
Norma's behavior on the occasion of her final visit to Setuckit settled that, he believed, conclusively. She was very
cool to Calvin; she had kept out of his way, had not talked

with him, nor would she permit Seleucus to talk about him. As he told Homer, she seemed prejudiced against him, and, greatly as Seleucus regretted the prejudice, nothing he could say changed her attitude. He had been forced to believe she shared her father's mistaken conviction that Calvin was at least partially responsible for Bartlett's disgrace and the loss of his position.

Therefore any surmise of attachment between those two seemed ridiculous and impossible; but it was the only explanation he could think of to account for his wife's peculiar questions and manner. She must know something, but, if she did, he would be the last one she would take into confidence.

But the very next day he learned the secret himself. Jemima had gone to the Jarvis shanty for her midday allowance of sleep and Seleucus took her place as watcher in the skipper's room, by Calvin's bedside.

Of late, and as a usual thing, Calvin's days were comparatively quiet. Any one who has endured the long torment of the disease from which he was suffering knows that the daylight hours are, for the patient, the comparatively easy ones. The sunshine and the movement in the room, the sense of safety and watchful care which they bring, tend to lull the tortured nerves and quiet the fevered fancies. Calvin dozed much during the day and, when awake, was very weak, but usually rational. It was at night that he moaned and muttered and talked aloud in his delirium.

This day, however, it was different. He had passed a more comfortable night, and was awake when Mrs. Gammon left him. Then he dozed again and from the doze awoke to call a name and to carry on a long conversation with some one whom he fancied to be present. He was making a plea, an earnest, agitated plea for forgiveness for some wrong he had done. He made it over and over again, in a half-dozen different ways, and Seleucus, listening, began to comprehend. He had found the answer to the riddle. He was learning what, he was sure, his wife had learned already.

He turned, to find Jemima standing in the doorway. She nodded, a grim smile on her thin face.

"Humph!" she sniffed. "So you're gettin' it, too, be you? Well, it's a wonder to me you, or some of the rest of 'em, haven't picked it up long afore this. If you'd been here with him nights, same as I have, you'd have got it long ago. This is the way he's been about every night since I come with him. Talkin' about her all the time, ain't he?"

Her husband nodded. "Yes," he answered. "He was sleepin' quiet as you'd ask for, and I guess likely I was half asleep myself. All to once he sung out 'Norma! Norma!' and I jumped as if a crab had nabbed hold of me. . . . Shut that door, Jemima, won't ye? We don't want anybody else to hear. He wouldn't want 'em to, that's sartin."

Mrs. Gammon, obedient for once, closed the door. She crossed to the bed and proceeded to give the patient a dose of the quieting medicine left by the doctor.

"It's the aches and pains that starts him goin'," she declared. "They come on to him by spasms. I don't know what this doctor stuff is, but it generally soothes him down and gets him to sleep again. Some kind of morphine or such dratted trash, I presume likely. Well, 'tain't none of my business, but I tell you this, if 'twas *you* I wouldn't give it to you. I don't believe in dopin' sick folks. No, sir, you'd have to groan it out."

Seleucus shuddered. "I'm darn glad it ain't me," he announced fervently. "You sure that door's shut tight? I wouldn't want none of the boys to hear the kind of talk he's been firin' off. Say, you don't cal'late any of 'em have heard it, do you?"

His wife tossed her head. "It's a wonder they ain't," she said, "but I guess they haven't. If they had they'd be talkin' about it. They're like you and about every other man I ever run acrost. You can't any one of you keep a thing to yourself. It takes a woman to keep her mouth shut, and her ears open. I've been sittin' here listenin' and learnin' and if folks in Orham knew what I know there'd be tongues awaggin', now I tell you."

"But what do you know, Jemima?"

"I know that he's plumb crazy about that Bartlett girl, and that there's been things goin' on between 'em that nobody ever suspected. As nigh as I can find out she was as gone on him as he was on her—for a spell, anyhow. And then they had a rumpus and she gave him his walkin' papers. Just why I ain't quite sure, but I am almost. 'Twas somethin' to do with Myra Fuller."

"Myra Fuller! What on earth could she have to do with it? How you talk, Jemima!"

"Humph! You ought to hear *him* talk when he gets goin'. There's been nights here, when he was the worst, that he just chattered, chattered, chattered till I thought the top of my head would come off. I guess 'twould if I hadn't been so interested. Nigh's I can get at the truth from his crazy jabber he and Myra Fuller was goin' 'round together and was engaged to be married."

"Jemima, how you do talk!"

"Mercy on us, do stop tellin' me that! I know how I talk and what I'm talkin' about. He and Myra was engaged or what amounted to that. And I judge that when this Norma come along he forgot all about Myra and took up with her. But he didn't tell her about Myra; there was where the trouble come in. And, somehow or other, she—the Norma one—found it out from somebody else. That settled Mr. Calvin, and no wonder. Tryin' to keep two strings to his bow. Humph! that sort of trick is always found out, sooner or later—and generally sooner."

"But—but, Jemima, did Cal tell you all this?"

"He didn't know he was tellin' it, of course, and he didn't tell it right straight along. I had to pick it up a little bit here and there, and piece it together, same as a body might string rags for a mat. She won't have anything to do with him, nigh's I can find out, but he is as gone on her as he ever was. Keeps beggin' her to forgive him and listen to what he's tryin' to tell, how it happened he never told her about Myra afore, and the like of that. Such a lot of mushy, soft-soapy talk *I* never heard. I declare there's been times when I've been glad I was blessed with a strong stomach. All that sugar and syrup is enough to upset anybody's appetite for their meals. And over a stuck-up, highfalutin' chit like that Norma Bartlett, too. My soul!"

"Why—why now, Jemima! Norma ain't stuck up. She's a real nice everyday kind of girl. Everybody thinks so."

"Oh, I know *you* think so. She ain't your wife, so of course she's lovely. You ought to be ashamed of yourself. I'm ashamed for you. Now don't you tell a soul I've told you this. If you do I'll—I don't know what I'll do to you."

"Eh? Why, of course I won't tell. 'Tain't likely I would, is it? Crimus! it makes me kind of ashamed to think I let you tell it to me. 'Tain't a thing I ought to have heard— no, nor you either. I—I 'most wish you hadn't heard it, Jemima."

"What! You do, eh? I want to know! Well, I'm glad I heard it. It's kept me from dyin' of the fidgets those long lonesome nights. I have heard it, and I mean to hear more. There is more. Somethin' about a letter he started to write her, tellin' her the whole yarn, and never finished. There's spells when he gets goin' about that letter and goes on and goes on. He must finish it—he's got to finish it; that's what he keeps sayin'. He's got that letter somewheres, I'll bet you. I wish I knew where it was. If I could read that letter then I *would* know what was what for sure."

Seleucus jumped from his chair. "Jemima Gammon!" he cried, aghast. "You—you wouldn't read that letter, would you? Course you wouldn't! You're foolin'."

"Foolin'? Why? Why shouldn't I read it? I'd read it quick enough if I got the chance. 'Twould be mighty interestin', I guess. . . . And he'd never know I read it; I'd take care of that."

For the first time her husband showed signs of rebellion —active, open rebellion.

"Don't you read that letter," he commanded. "Don't you dast to read it! That letter ain't any of your business. How'd you like to have anybody else read your letters?"

"Humph! If it was one of your letters to me it wouldn't

take long to read. And the letters you write me are so scurse that a person wouldn't be able to find more than one or two in a lifetime. Don't you talk to me like that, either. Tellin' me what I dast to do! The idea! You get right out of here now, and if you whisper a single word about what I've just told you I'll—oh, you'll see what I'll do! You go right along."

The rebellion was crushed in its infancy. Mr. Gammon sighed. "I didn't mean to order you around, Jemima," he explained, with unconscious humor. "I'm sorry I spoke so. But when you told me you was cal'latin' to read a letter that —that Cal here wrote to his girl, I—I—well, of course I know you don't mean it."

"Never you mind what I mean. I'm sorry I told you as much as I did. And," triumphantly, "I haven't told you the whole, either. There's somethin' else, somethin' about that night when Benoni Bartlett got adrift in the bay. You'd give your head—if it was worth anything and anybody'd take it—to know what I'm findin' out about that, too. . . . No, I shan't tell you a word. You get out of this room. You— a married man—tellin' your poor wife she don't dast to do this or that! Ain't you *ashamed* of yourself?"

Seleucus, as usual, obeyed orders. He left the skipper's room under fire. But during the weeks which followed his newly acquired habit of thinking grew upon him. What he had heard from his wife explained much. He was tremendously fond of Calvin Homer. He liked him, admired him, and was grateful to him for his own advance in the service. These feelings had grown and deepened during their comradeship at the station. And he liked Norma Bartlett. If marriage was a necessary, although disagreeable, part of life —and it did appear to be—then Norma was the sort of girl a man like Calvin ought to marry. And Myra Fuller, whom he had never liked—she had a superior way of patronizing and poking fun which he resented—was not the right sort at all. It troubled him to think that Myra had come between his two friends. He devoutly wished there might be some way in which he could help them. But he could not think

of any. He tried several times to learn more particulars
from his wife—to find out if she had learned more—but she
would not vouchsafe another word on the subject. She
seemed to regret having told him anything.

April went and May came. Good weather almost every
day, and few calls from the sea for the help of the Setuckit
life-saving crew. These few were of little consequence; the
season for severe storms and serious disasters was passing—
had practically passed already. Calvin began to improve and
to regain strength. His fever left him, and he began to sit
up and develop an appetite. Doctor Palmer told Phinney
that his recovery would be much more rapid if his spirits
were better.

"He doesn't seem to take much interest in anything," confided the doctor; "not even in getting well. He used to be
good-natured and cheerful enough, but now he doesn't seem
to care whether school keeps or not. What has happened to
put him so far into the dumps? Does anybody know?"

Seleucus knew, but he could not tell. Jemima knew, but
she merely looked wise and there was an air of malicious
triumph about her which her husband noticed and distrusted.
That letter of Calvin's—had she found and read it? He
could scarcely believe she would do such a thing, but experience had taught him that if there was one thing in the world
which his wife loved it was to burrow into the intimate details of other people's affairs. She did not gossip more, nor
perhaps as much, as some of her Orham acquaintances. She
seemed to find the keenest satisfaction in knowing things
which others did not know, hiding them in her thin bosom,
and gloating over them like a crow over a hoard of glittering
odds and ends.

By the middle of May Calvin was strong enough to get
out-of-doors and sit in the sunshine for short periods on
pleasant days. An important item of news had come to
Setuckit, an item which the men, at Gammon's suggestion,
did not impart to their commander. Benoni Bartlett was
dead. He had never recovered from the night of exposure
and the paralysis which followed. He grew gradually

weaker, spoke scarcely at all, and never naturally, and at last died, quietly and without suffering. He was buried in the Trumet cemetery beside his wife. Norma, after the burial, came back to Orham, but she was not going to remain there. Her former position in the Fairborough library had been offered to her and, after a week of rest—for she was very tired—she would, so people said, close the Ryder cottage and go away for good.

One morning, two days after the Bartlett funeral, Seleucus and Peleg Myrick had an interview which developed consequences. Peleg had been up to town early and, taking advantage of a good breeze, sailed down to Setuckit in the *Wild Duck*. He was freighted with the Orham gossip, the rumors concerning Norma, the village guesses as to the amount of Benoni's life insurance, and the news that Wallie Oaks and his wife had had a violent disagreement, and that she had gone over to her mother's at Denboro—people said, never to return.

"Nobody blames her much," declared Mr. Myrick. "Wallie ain't done a real lick of work since he quit life-savin', and I guess likely she got tired of takin' in washin' so's he could eat three square meals a day, and sleep and talk between times. Him and Cap'n Kellogg run afoul of each other at the post office, and the superintendent told him a few things about himself that made all hands happy—all hands but Wallie, I mean. Obed Halleck says he never heard anybody get such a goin' over as Wallie got from the cap'n. Says 'twas more fun than the Uncle Tom show, and the whole post-office crowd was invited free. Dear, dear! I wished I'd been there."

His wish was shared by the station men. Peleg delivered his usual consignment of prognostications concerning the weather, but he seemed to have something even more important on his mind. He inquired particularly about Mr. Gammon. "Where's Seleucus?" he wished to know. "I want to see him a minute."

Seleucus, as it happened just then, was over at the Jarvis shanty. He and his wife were concluding an argument based upon the question of his going to Orham. There were certain station errands to be done in the village and Homer, not yet strong enough for the trip, had suggested his Number One man's making it in his stead. Seleucus was willing, but Jemima was not. Her patient was now able to get on without her care during the day, although she still spent her nights at the station.

"No, you ain't goin'," she told her husband. "Let Josh Phinney or Hez Rogers or some of the rest of 'em go, if somebody's got to. You stay right here where you belong. When I was up there you could find excuses enough to keep from comin' to see me, but now you're crazy to get away. What for? That's what I want to know. What for?"

"I told you what for, Jemima," pleaded Seleucus. "Cal asked me to go, and he's my boss, ain't he?"

"He ain't *my* boss, and I say you shan't. You're altogether too anxious. Want to cruise around and see how your precious Norma's gettin' along, I presume likely. That's one place you was goin', wasn't it?"

Seleucus tried hard not to appear confused, but the attempt was a failure. He stammered and hesitated.

"Why, I was cal'latin' to stop there just a minute," he admitted. "The boys wanted me to. Her father's dead, and she's goin' away, and it did seem as if some one of us had ought to say good-by, and tell her how sorry for her we all was, or—or somethin'."

"Yes," sarcastically. "I knew that was it. You can't fool me, Seleucus Gammon. You'll stay right here, that's what you'll do."

"But what'll I tell Cap'n Cal?"

"Tell him—well, you needn't tell him anything. . . . Say," suspiciously, *"he* hasn't given you any message to take to that Bartlett girl, has he?"

"No, course he ain't."

"Hasn't finished that precious letter he started to write so long ago?"

"I don't know whether he has or not. Why should I?"

Mrs. Gammon chuckled. *"I* know he hasn't," she observed. "Not that one, anyhow. Tell me," she added quickly, "has he said anything to you about—about missin' anything? Anything out of his trunk—or anywheres?"

Seleucus stared at her. "Missin' anything?" he repeated. "What do you mean? What would he be likely to miss?"

"Oh, nothin'—nothin' at all. If there is anything missin' he'll find it again pretty soon, I shouldn't wonder. . . . Now don't stand there with your mouth open like a codfish. Clear out. I'm busy."

But her husband still continued to stand and stare.

"Jemima," he said slowly, "what is it you're talkin' about? You don't mean to tell me that *you* took anything out of Cal Homer's trunk? . . . Jemima, you didn't take—"

He was interrupted by a strident hail from without the shanty. It was Peleg Myrick, who shouted his name. Mrs. Gammon seized the opportunity to end the interview. She opened the door.

"There, there!" she called to the hermit. "Don't holler any more, he's here." Then, turning to her husband, she ordered, "Go out and see what he wants, why don't you?"

Seleucus went. Mr. Myrick greeted him with an air of relief, but also with a certain air of embarrassment and secrecy.

"Seleucus," he whispered, "are you busy just now? I've got to be startin' home right off. Got to make another trip to Orham, I have, and I wanted to talk with you a little spell afore I went."

Gammon sniffed. Whatever Peleg had to talk about was not likely to be important, and he was in a troubled state of mind.

"All right, here I be," he said rather impatiently. "Go ahead, get it off your mind."

But Myrick still hesitated. "It's—it's kind of—er—what you might call a secret," he whispered. "I wouldn't want nobody else to hear it. I ain't sure as I'd ought to tell even you, but seems 's if I'd got to tell somebody. It's about— about Cap'n Cal, and I know you're about the best friend he's got down here. Can't we—well, walk acrost the beach a little ways while I tell it to you?"

Seleucus's interest was aroused. He took the hermit by the arm. "Come on," he ordered. "We'll walk over towards the outer beach, and you can talk while we're doin' it. What about Cap'n Cal?"

Peleg glanced over his right shoulder, then over his left. "I snum I don't know's I ought to tell you," he confided. "He made me swear I'd never tell anybody. . . . I ain't so far."

Gammon's patience had been much tried that morning. "And it don't look as if you was liable to tell *me* in this lifetime," he observed tartly. "Come on, come on! *If* you're goin' to tell—tell. What is it all about, anyway?"

His companion breathed heavily. "It's about my goin' off to Taylor Gould's catboat that mornin' and fetchin' Benoni Bartlett up to my shanty," he said. "You see—you see, Seleucus, I never done that."

Seleucus stopped short and gazed down into the leathery face at his shoulder.

"*You* never done it!" he repeated. "Then who did?"

"Cal Homer done it. . . . Yes, he did. 'Twas him that took Philander's dory and rowed off to the Scallop Flat and got Benoni. The first I knew of the whole mess was when Cal pounded on my shanty door, and I went there and see him holdin' Bartlett up. I cal'late Benoni'd have fell down flat if Cal hadn't been holdin' him by main strength. They was both of 'em all in—I could see that—but, afterwards, when Cal made me promise I'd never tell 'twas him done it, I didn't realize he was sick and kind of out of his head. Since then I've thought of it and thought of it, and—"

Gammon stopped the flow of words with a shake. "Never mind what you thought," he commanded. "Begin at the beginnin' and tell me the whole yarn. The whole of it. Crimus . . . ! Crimustee . . . ! This makes it plain where Cal had been that mornin'. Nobody knew, and we ain't dared mention it to him. . . . Well, heave ahead! Go on!"

Myrick told his story, rambling and commenting and protesting, but dragged back to essentials by Seleucus's shakes and orders to hurry up.

"So I kept my word to Cal," concluded Peleg, "and ain't told anybody. When all hands was praisin' me up for bein' so smart and findin' Benoni when nobody else could, I felt consider'ble mean and foolish, but I never said a word. But yesterday afternoon Norma Bartlett, she run acrost me up on the Main Road, and *she* commenced to praise me up, and tell me how thankful she was to me for savin' her poor pa from dyin' off there in the cold and wet. I declare, Seleucus, I felt as if I'd been caught stealin' hens' aigs! I did so! And she was in mournin', you know, and looked so sort of white and—and sorry, that—that—well, by Godfreys, the more I thought of it the meaner I felt. Thinks I, 'When I go to Setuckit to-morrer I'll tell the whole yarn to Seleucus and see what he says.' Course I could have kept it to myself; 'twas kind of nice when they printed them things about me in the newspapers and all; but—but—" he paused, and then added ingenuously, "I realized that some day they might find out I never done it, and then 'twouldn't be so nice, you see. That's how 'twas, Seleucus. Of course I promised Cap'n Cal, and—"

But Seleucus had heard enough, quite enough.

"Sshh!" he ordered. "Hush, be still! Let me think, can't you . . . ? You say Norma don't know a thing about this? She thinks 'twas you saved her father that time?"

"Why, course she does! Why wouldn't she?"

"She don't know that 'twas Cal, and she's goin' away, to stay, believin' that— By crimus! she's *got* to know! She has, somehow. Say, Peleg, are you startin' right back to Orham?"

"Just soon's I can get to the *Wild Duck*."

"All right, you get aboard. But don't you start till you hear from me. Get sail on to her, if you want to, but don't you haul anchor till I give the word. Understand that?"

"Hey? Sartin I understand. . . . What you goin' to do? Where you goin'?"

Seleucus was not exactly sure what he was going to do,

but he intended to do something. And, at that moment, he was on his way to find Calvin Homer. What he should say to the latter when he did find him was another matter. He had not thought as far as that.

He strode across the eighth of a mile of sand which he and Myrick had traversed in their walk and hurried in at the side door of the station. Calvin was, at that moment, strolling along the edge of the outer beach, faithfully carrying out the doctor's orders concerning daily exercise. This Seleucus did not know. He hastened through the mess room and, without knocking, opened the door of the skipper's room and entered.

Homer was not there, but some one else was. Mrs. Gammon was there. She was kneeling on the floor before the trunk, or chest, which belonged to Calvin and in which he kept his spare clothes and personal property. Jemima was kneeling before that trunk and fitting a key into the lock. Beside her, on the floor, lay several sheets of note paper with writing upon them.

When her husband made his hurried entry she started violently, sprang to her feet, and leaned against the wall in the corner behind the trunk. She was pale and during their long and tempestuous married life Seleucus had never seen her as taken aback or at a loss for words.

"Eh?" he exclaimed. "What are you doin' in here all alone? What makes you look like that? What ails you?"

Jemima did not answer. A look of relief came to her face. Evidently she had not expected to see her husband, but had expected—and feared—to see some one else. She was still pale and agitated, however. A thief, caught in the act, could not have looked more guilty. She did not speak and Seleucus suddenly transferred his stare from her countenance to the trunk and then to the sheets of paper beside it. Upon the upper sheet—it had never been folded—he could read from where he stood the words, "My own dearest Norma." And he recognized the handwriting. An inkling of the truth flashed to his brain.

"Crimus!" he cried. "My crimustee! That letter of Calvin's! You was—you was takin' it out of his chest!"

The color came back to Jemima's face, came with a rush. Her voice returned also.

"I was not," she retorted shrilly. "I wasn't. I was puttin' it back. Don't you tell him I took it. Don't you tell him I ever saw it. Don't you dare! Get right out of here!"

She made a dive for the letter, but her husband dived in the same direction. Her hand seized the letter first, but Seleucus's huge paw clutched her wrist and held it tight.

"Let go of me!" she cried, twisting and struggling. "You—you oh, you let go of me!"

But he did not let go. Instead, holding her wrist with his right hand, he bent her fingers back with his left, and took the letter from them. Then, clutching it, he turned to the door. Frantic, she sprang after him and caught him by the arm.

"You give me that! You give me that!" she shrieked.

Seleucus swung about and picked her up in his arms. It was the first time he had ever dared to assert himself in his dealings with his wife, and, so far as is known, he never so dared again—but the assertion, although short and temporary, was complete. He bore her, struggling and kicking, across the room and deposited her forcibly upon the bed.

"You stay where you be," he ordered. Then he ran from the room.

The mess room was untenanted at the time, for the men were all down at the shore, amusing themselves by teasing Peleg. Rogers and Cahoon had pulled his dory up on the beach during his absence, and the crowd was enjoying itself watching his struggles to get it afloat unaided. He had at last succeeded, however, and now, with oars in place, paused a stroke or two from the shore, to express his candid opinion of his tormentors.

The first hint of disturbance at the station was brought to the group by Seleucus himself, who came plunging toward them like a charging rhinoceros. They demanded to know what was the matter, but he neither stopped nor answered. He was wearing, not rubber boots, but a thin pair of canvas shoes of the variety called "sneakers." In spite of this he dashed into the cold water, waded above his knees to the dory and clambered, heedless of Myrick's frantic pleadings to "look out," over her side.

"Lay to it," he panted. "Row!"

Peleg began rowing toward his anchored catboat. Then, from the doorway of the life-saving station came a series of shrieks in a shrill and angry female voice. The men heard them and turned to look. Peleg heard them, too, and might have ceased rowing if his passenger had permitted.

"Go on!" roared Seleucus. "Go on, or I'll heave you overboard! Faster! Lay to it!"

The *Wild Duck* was reached and boarded. Myrick sprang to the halyards, Gammon to the anchor rope. The sail rose, so did the anchor.

From the beach came a shout.

"Hi, Seleucus! Seleucus!" bellowed Bloomer. "Your wife wants you. She says for you to come back."

And then Mr. Gammon gave utterance to an answer which was destined to be added, one of the choicest gems in the collection, to the history and traditions of Setuckit Station.

"She can go to hell!" roared Seleucus. Then he went to Orham.

CHAPTER XIX

SELEUCUS returned late that evening. Myrick brought him down as far as his—the hermit's—hut on the beach, and he had walked the rest of the way. The members of the crew were already in bed when he entered the station. Calvin was in his room and asleep. Mrs. Gammon, for the first time, was not sitting in that room—nor, as she had since his convalescence, in the mess room, awaiting a possible call from him. Her attendance was no longer really necessary and, even if it had been, he would have been obliged to do without it that night. Jemima, after her husband's hurried departure, went straight to her brother's shanty, and there she stayed. The men, after watching the *Wild Duck* sail away, found the lady gone when they came up to the station. They were loaded with curiosity and dying to ask questions, but she was not there to hear or answer them. They talked about her, however. Her husband's amazing performance, and his final order, the shouted suggestion that she might journey to a distant and tropical port, were topics which prevented that evening from dragging. The exclamations of delight and the roars of laughter must have been heard at the Jarvis dwelling, but, if they were, the occupant of that dwelling made no sign. Philander was away, down at the weir shanty, but a lamp burned in his sister's room, and was still burning when the Setuckit crew went aloft to turn in.

"She's settin' up for him," announced Phinney, peering out at the light. "She's there waitin' for him. . . . Oh, my! oh, my! And when he does come home—Whew!"

Bloomer, looking over Josh's shoulder, hummed a verse of a sentimental ballad.

"'There's a light in the window
Burns brightly for me'"

he sang. "Humph! Do you suppose he'll *ever* come home? I wouldn't if I was him. No sir! If it was me that told Jemima Gammon to go to Tophet I'd go there myself afore I'd come back where she was. 'Twouldn't be any hotter one place than the other, and I'd ruther face the Old Harry than that woman. What did he do it for? Was he drunk? Was he crazy? Has *he* caught the fever, now Cal's got rid of it, and gone off his head?"

Calvin himself had offered a reason for Seleucus's going with Myrick to Orham. He had asked him to go there because there were certain errands to be done. This might explain the going, but it did not explain the manner of Mr. Gammon's departure, nor his public defiance of his wife. Nothing explained that.

"If I hadn't heard it with my own ears I wouldn't have believed it," declared Hez Rogers. "No, and I don't believe it yet. I've been dreamin'. Pinch me, somebody, so's I'll wake up. . . . Ow! Consarn you, Josh, you needn't pinch so hard!"

Phinney paused at the skipper's door on his way to the stairs. He opened the door and peeped cautiously in. Homer heard him and stirred. Josh was conscience stricken.

"There now!" he exclaimed remorsefully, "we've been makin' so much noise you couldn't sleep, Cap'n. I'm sorry. We ought to had more sense. But since Seleucus blew up and went loony I cal'late it sort of touched the rest of us in the head. I'm sorry enough. You all right? Anything we can get you?"

Calvin declared he was perfectly all right, and would probably fall asleep soon. He asked questions about the weather, told Phinney to call him if anything happened and bade the latter good night. He was all right, so far as his bodily health was concerned; although still weak, he was quite free from pain, and was traveling back to normal at a satisfactory rate. But as for sleeping—that was not easy. The doctor had told him that he must, that sleep was the finest tonic in the world, and he did try to obtain that tonic. But, while trying, he invariably fell to thinking, and his thoughts were dreary and pessimistic. He must do his best to get well, completely well; he supposed it was his duty to do so. But, facing the situation, there alone with his thoughts, he realized that he cared little what happened to him.

He was still awake when Mr. Gammon tiptoed into the mess room. Seleucus meant to be very careful, but in his nervousness he bumped against a chair and Calvin heard him and called. Seleucus opened the door and fearfully thrust in his head.

"Eh?" he queried. "That you, Cap'n Cal. . . ? Oh!" with a sigh, apparently of relief, "you're all alone, ain't ye? She—Jemima, I mean—she ain't here?"

Homer informed him that his wife had not been there since his departure. "I think she is over at the shanty," he added. "You'll go over, I suppose? You aren't on duty to-night."

"No-o. No, I ain't. Unless," hopefully, "there's somebody that—that ain't feelin' well—or—or somethin'. Then I could go on patrol for 'em. I'd just as soon as not."

"No, all hands are first rate. You go and see your wife. She must be expecting you. . . . I hear you left in a hurry."

"Eh. . . ? Um-hum. Yes, I did. Er—you see—well, Peleg was goin' up to the village and—and I thought maybe I'd better go along with him. Didn't know when I'd get another chance, you see."

"I see. Well, what did you do up there?"

"Eh? . . . Oh, I done the errands all right. I don't think I forgot nothin'. The stuff from the store 'll be down to-morrer or next day. Peleg's got some of it aboard his boat right now, and he'll fetch it to-morrer—I mean this afternoon; it's after twelve, ain't it? There was a little mail, and I've got that in my pocket. Nothin' for you, Cal. . . . Well, I guess that's all. I—I presume likely I might's well go up aloft and turn in. . . . Eh?"

"Wait a minute. Did you hear any news up there?"

"News. . . ? Why, no, I guess not. . . . I'll be gettin' on now. . . . Good night."

"Wait. Who did you see up there? Where did you go?"

Mr. Gammon uneasily shifted his feet. He was thankful that the room was dark.

"Oh, I just went—er—around," he said vaguely. "Just kind of 'round and—and around. I see the fellers at the store and the post office, of course."

"Didn't you go anywhere else?"

"Who? Me. . . . ? Why, where was there to go? There ain't anything stirrin' up to the village, no town-hall time nor nothin'. . . . Well, I guess I'll go aloft. That is, unless, you bein' sick, you'd like to have me stay here and keep watch."

"I'm not sick. And it's a fine clear night. You'd better go over to the shanty and see your wife. She'll be expecting you. Tell her all the Orham news."

"There ain't no news—that is, none she don't know already."

"Well, go and see her, anyway."

Seleucus shifted his feet again. "It seems too bad to—er—disturb her, don't it?" he stammered. "She—she don't like to be waked up, you know."

"She probably is awake now. She'll be glad to know you're back. Go and see her."

"We-ll," doubtfully, "if you think I better. I suppose—Say, sure you don't need me to set up along with you? Give you your medicine or somethin'?"

"Of course not. I'm not taking any medicine to speak of. And, if I do, I don't need any one to give it to me. Go on. I must get some sleep."

The door slowly closed. Seleucus, alone in the mess room, sighed. Then he pulled at his mustache, looked at the clock, and sighed again. Sighing did not help matters. He walked to the window and looked out. The lamp in the Jarvis shanty burned brightly. Mr. Gammon's next sigh was accompanied by a shiver. He tightened his belt, groaned aloud, and went out into the night. A minute later he entered the Jarvis living room. Jemima was there, waiting for him.

The patrolman—Baxter Cahoon—returning after midnight saw the Jarvis window still illumined. From behind the drawn shade the sound of a voice, a shrill, animated voice, drifted across the stillness. It was Mrs. Gammon's voice. Cahoon, lingering at the corner of the station to listen, could not hear what she was saying. Her husband, apparently, was saying nothing.

And yet Seleucus did say something, something which came to him in the nature of an inspiration, and which, like a life preserver thrown to a man who had fallen overboard, was destined to keep him afloat for many days to come in the stormy seas of his life as Jemima Gammon's husband. Whenever those seas threatened to go over his head and drown him, he took a firm grip on that life preserver and the fury of Jemima's wrath was thwarted for the time.

He had listened silently and hopelessly to the tirade with which she greeted his appearance in the Jarvis living room. He bore her reproaches meekly, acknowledged that maybe he had been a "little mite rough" when he threw her down upon the bed in Homer's room at the station; he was "dreadful sorry" for that, he confessed and for consigning her to perdition when aboard the *Wild Duck* at the moment of departure. "I guess likely I hadn't ought to said that, Jemima," he admitted, abjectly "but, you see, I was all sort of het up. Peleg had just told me somethin' that—that upset me—and then when I see you with Cal's letter, it—it just—"

She interrupted. "Where is that letter?" she demanded. "You give me that letter this minute."

"Why—why, Jemima, you see—"

"Give it to me! Hand it right over, do you hear?"

Seleucus groaned. "I can't," he confessed. "I ain't got it. I—I give it to—to somebody else."

She sprang from her chair. "You—you give it to somebody else!" she repeated. "You give it to— *What!* Seleucus Gammon, did you give that letter to—to *her?*"

Mr. Gammon nodded. "That's what I done, Jemima," he said, in complete surrender. "You see, 'twas her letter—

Cal was writin' it to her and—and, bein' as she was goin'
away so soon—for good—I—I—well, I went right up to
where she lives soon's I got ashore and give it to her. . . .
Whether 'twas the thing to do or not don't make any difference now. We can't change it; Norma's got the letter."

His wife's face had been crimson; now it turned
white.

"Did you—did you tell her how you got it?" she cried.
"Did you tell her about—about *me?*"

Seleucus shook his head. "I never mentioned your name,
Jemima," he declared. "Course I didn't. She don't know
you ever see it. She thinks I—I found it on the floor in
Cal's room. That's what she thinks."

Jemima caught her breath.

"She—she better think so," she declared, with savage emphasis. "If you ever let her think anything else—if you
ever tell one soul that I took that letter out of Cal Homer's
trunk, I'll—I'll— O-o-oh, if you ever do!"

And it was here that inspiration came to Seleucus. He
raised his head; there was a new note in his voice.

"I shan't, Jemima," he said, slowly; "I shan't tell, never—
unless—"

"Unless! Unless what?"

"Why, unless you make me desperate, same as you done
over there this morn. If you keep on pitchin' into me and
—and layin' me out same as you're doin' now, if you get me
all worked up and—and reckless—why, you can't tell what
I might do. You couldn't tell what any man might do if
he was drove half crazy. So long's you treat me—er—kind
of decent and—and reasonable I'll never tell a soul, you
can bet on it. But if—if I get where I can't stand it any
longer, I—I"—with earnest solemnity—"I might blow up
and tell all hands. I wouldn't swear I wouldn't. A desperate man ain't responsible for what he does or says in them
cases. You'll have to be—er—kind of—well, considerate
of me, Jemima."

Mrs. Gammon's face was crimson again, and now, as she
struggled with her emotions, it became purple. She choked,

panted, and stared at her husband. Seleucus remained silent, but there was determination in his look and attitude.

Jemima's clutching fingers slowly straightened

"Oh, go to bed!" she gasped. "Go to bed!"

Mr. Gammon gratefully obeyed the order, but he hugged the life preserver to his breast. It could be used again— even, perhaps, again and again.

A weary and silent Seleucus Gammon appeared in the mess room at breakfast time. He was warmly greeted. His comrades were very glad to see him back, they said so. They said many things, but Seleucus was noncommunicative. He would not talk, but apparently would have been quite willing to fight. In fact, his manner became so truculent, and his few remarks so personal, that the men, acting upon a hint from the keeper, let him alone.

"He's had trouble enough, boys," said Homer. "And he is a good fellow. Don't nag him into punching somebody. We've had all the trouble down here we need. I have, at any rate. Let him alone."

So, for the time, they did let him alone; but the surcease was but temporary. As long as he remained in the service he was destined to be favored with casual reminders of his one assumption of power as head of his household.

"Now—now—now, Seleucus!" one man or another would protest. "Don't get up on your high horse. Don't try to bully the rest of us around the way you do that poor little wife of yours. We can't stand it; we're scared of you. Be easy on us as you can. Save your bullyraggin' and cussin' for Jemima."

Seleucus pretended to ignore these jocularities and bore them with fortitude. There were times when, in spite of the life preserver, he almost wished he had been less energtic, certainly less public, in his one outbreak against petticoat tyranny. But there were other moments when the memory of the uprising was pleasant to dwell upon. It had been wonderfully comforting while it lasted.

Spring, real and genuine, came to Setuckit a few days

later. One morning the sun rose in a sky unsmirched by
the smallest cloud. The wind, blowing lazily from the south,
was almost warm. The great sea gulls, their wings glistening
in the light, dipped and sailed and circled above their fishing
grounds along the edge of the point rip. Where the long
sand flat thrust a yellow fringe out into the cove the terns—
"mackerel gulls" or "kyaks," the life-savers called them—
were clustered in bunches that, from a distance, looked like
banks of snow. The roofs and steeples of Orham rose in
clean-cut outline above the eastward horizon. The entire
crescent of sea, from Broad Rip back to the Crow Ledge,
was dotted with white sails or black tugs and scows.

"She's come, boys," declared Ellis Badger, stretching himself luxuriously before the door of the station. "Here she
is. Reg'lar spring weather and no make-believe. No more
no'theasters for a long spell. No more icicles on your eye-
winkers when you go for a little cruise off yonder in the
channel."

"Not till next winter, anyhow," agreed Josh Phinney.
"Well, it's time we had it fair and smooth. We've earned a
rest, we fellows here at Setuckit. We've hauled the old boat
through a whole lot of mighty rugged water since last fall."

"It's pretty nigh time," went on Badger, "to think about
plantin' garden up home. My wife's cal'latin' to pick consider'ble many strawberries this season. She done pretty
well last year, but the bed'll be better now. Strawberries and
cream! How's that notion set on your digestion, eh, old
salt-hay mustache?" smiting Mr. Gammon a mighty thump
on the back.

Calvin went out after dinner that forenoon for a walk
along the outer beach. Doctor Palmer had examined him
the day before and pronounced him well. "I shan't come
again unless you send for me," said the doctor. "All you
need now is to keep out-of-doors in good weather and inside
when it is bad. Eat—or try to eat. And don't let the station work fret you. The busy season is over; there won't
be any storms to amount to anything, and if a vessel should
get into trouble, let Gammon handle the boat. Another

month, and you can do it yourself; but what you need now is strength. I've told Cap'n Kellogg that and he told me that those were his orders to you. He is coming down to see you pretty soon, and he'll give them to you himself. And, one other thing! Cheer up! Get hold of your nerves. Grin once in a while. You've got a lot to be thankful for. Don't go around looking as if you'd lost your last friend. You haven't, you know."

To Calvin, however, it seemed that he had done just that. The one friend that counted—who had been so much more than friend—had left him and her leaving was his fault. He wondered what she was doing, how she was getting on with her sick father. The tidings of Bartlett's death and burial had been carefully kept from his ears. "Don't tell him yet awhile," commanded the doctor. "This rumpus down here was, more than anything else, responsible for his getting into the condition where he was ready for any sort of sickness that came along. He worries over it. I think he is afraid people may say he put Bartlett out so as to get the keeper's place. Everybody knows he didn't—every one worth while, that is—but don't tell him Benoni is dead. Wait until his nerves are stronger."

Seleucus, too, was very insistent on that point. "Cal thought consider'ble of the old man," he declared. "Yes, he did, even if he did stand up against him when he had to. If we tell him Bologny's petered out he'll figger he helped kill him. We'll break it to him by and by, when he is better. Maybe Kellogg'll tell him when he comes; Kellogg or—or somebody."

So Calvin remained in ignorance of this additional blow which had befallen Norma. His memories of the strenuous morning when he rescued his former captain from the stranded catboat on the Scallop Flat were still rather vague, almost as foggy as that morning had been, but they were coming back to him. He remembered forcing Peleg Myrick into promising to keep silent concerning the fact that it was he who had brought Bartlett ashore. As he thought of it now he wondered why he had been so stubborn in that matter. There was no essential, sensible reason why Norma should not have known that he found and saved her father. Nevertheless, he was glad she did not know. It would only remind her of him, and she would not wish to be reminded. Yes, he had used common sense even when half crazy. Strange, for he could, even now, remember next to nothing of what had happened after he left the hermit's door. The telephone message by which Captain Nelson informed him that Peleg had reported Benoni's presence at the shanty he had forgotten altogether. And yet he had taken down the receiver and listened to that message.

He walked on, by the water's edge, in the glorious sunshine of that May morning, thinking these thoughts and others, until he reached the end of the point. Then he turned up the beach and sat down upon the sand at the foot of a high bank, which—the lightly waving beach grass fringing its top—shut him from view from the station, even from the tower. There was no intention in his mind of getting out of sight; the bank cut off the breeze, that was all, and the sunlight was warmer there.

He sat there for some time. If he had not been so lost in his thoughts, none of them too agreeable, he would have heard the rattle of a vehicle approaching over the rutted road leading between the dunes to the station. He did not hear it and it was only when he chanced to look up and glance down the beach that he became aware some one was walking toward him, following the footprints he had left in the moist sand just below high-tide mark. He looked— and looked—not believing the evidence of his eyes. Then he sprang to his feet.

The person walking toward him, now only a little way off, was the one person whom he had never expected to see again—Norma Bartlett.

She saw him, too, and waved her hand. He stood there, weak and pale and trembling, his newly and partially regained strength scarce proof against the shock. Norma! She was here—at Setuckit! Why had she come? What could her coming mean?

And, as she drew nearer, he noticed something strange, something different, in her appearance. She was in black— a small black hat, a black shirt, a white shirt waist. Not a touch of color about her anywhere. Why, she was—she must be in mourning! And then the truth came to him. Her father must be dead. Bartlett must have died while he, Homer, was sick, and, because he was sick, they had not told him.

The realization of this obvious truth and of the grief she must be suffering, made him forget even the tremendous surprise at seeing her there; he ceased to wonder why she had come. He stepped toward her, holding out his hands.

"Norma!" he cried. "Norma! Oh, I'm so sorry! So sorry for you. It—it is your father, isn't it? He—"

She took his hands. Her acceptance of them was, of itself, something quite different from what he might have expected—would have expected if he had had time to think clearly. He looked into her face and she into his.

"Oh, how white and—and tired you look!" he exclaimed.

She smiled bravely. Yet, as she looked at him, her eyes grew wet.

"You are so white and thin," she said. "And you have been so sick, haven't you?"

"Oh, I'm all right now. Yes, I am all right. But you— it is your father, of course? When—"

"A week—yes, nearly ten days ago. But I thought you didn't know. They said no one had told you."

"No one had. But when I saw you—dressed like this— I guessed. I knew it must be. I am so sorry. You believe that, don't you? It. . . . I think perhaps I had better sit down again. I am a little shaky on my pins still, and this— this seems to—"

She put her hand upon his arm. "Yes, sit down," she urged. "Please sit down."

He hesitated. "But you—you won't go—"

"No, I will sit beside you. . . . You are all right now? You are not going to—to faint, or anything?"

He laughed, weakly, at the idea. "Faint!" he repeated.

"I never did faint and I never saw any one do it but once. That was when Ed Bloomer keeled over after we pulled his shoulder into place. No, I shan't faint. I was dizzy, that's all. That confounded rheumatism took it out of me, I suppose, and that is why I am acting like a kid. . . . But you? You have been through all that and I didn't know! Why didn't they tell me? They ought to have told me!"

He flushed angrily at the thought. She saw his agitation, and, sitting beside him, put her hand upon his.

"I am very glad they didn't tell you," she said gently. "It would only have worried you and you have had worry and trouble enough on our account—poor father's and mine. Calvin, I came here to-day to ask your forgiveness. Can you forgive me?"

He gazed at her. "Forgive you!" he repeated. "*I* forgive *you*. . . ! Norma, why—why—"

"Hush! Don't look like that. You frighten me. I shall think you are going to be ill again. Listen, please. I have so much to tell you."

"Yes—yes, I'll listen, of course. But, Norma, why did you come? How did you get here? What—?"

"Please be quiet and listen. Please! I'll tell you all about it. Captain Kellogg brought me. I rode down with him. Mr. Gammon said you were walking here at the point and I came, as soon as he told me, to find you. Captain Kellogg has been very, very kind to me. He has been a wonderful friend when I needed friends so much. And he is your friend, too. So is Mr. Gammon. We both have good friends, Calvin. And oh, how much we owe to them!"

She had called him Calvin again. And her tone, her look, her manner toward him! Why— He seized her hand in both of his.

"Norma!" he cried once more.

"Hush! Remember you promised to listen. And there is so much to tell. Calvin, I have treated you dreadfully. I realized it—I think I began to realize it almost that very day after father and I went away from here. But I wouldn't admit it, even to myself. You see, I—well, I was jealous,

I suppose. Yes, I know I was. I couldn't understand how you could ever possibly have cared for that Fuller girl. I— I never liked her and—oh, she isn't nice! I—but there, we won't talk about her, will we?"

He colored and looked away. "I don't wonder you can't understand that," he said. "I don't understand it, myself, now. She—she—well, what I told you was the truth. I never did care for her really, and—oh, I am ashamed of it all. . . ! But there! it was all my fault. You did the right thing in getting rid of me. I have never blamed you in the least. Any decent girl would have given up a fellow who treated her as I did you. And then, when I wasn't man enough to tell you—"

She leaned toward him. "Don't!" she pleaded. "You mustn't say that. You did tell me. You tried to tell me."

"Yes, after you found it out from some one else."

"No, before that. In the letter you wrote me. Calvin, I have read that letter."

He turned and stared. "Which letter?" he asked.

"Both of them. The letter you wrote to me at Fairborough; they forwarded it to me afterward."

"But there was nothing about—about her in that."

"No. But there were ever so many other things, about father and your reasons for taking out the boat when he told you not to. Everything you told me you had written. I was almost happy when I read that letter; or I should have been if I had not been so ashamed of myself. I—you know I had doubted whether you ever wrote it. I had."

"I don't wonder you did. You had reason enough to doubt my doing anything decent and honest."

"No. No, I hadn't. I should have known—for I knew you. But I was jealous and hateful and generally wicked just then. But I thought and thought—and grew more sensible, I hope, and when they told me how ill you were, I —well, I think I should have come to you even then, if it had not been for father. . . . And then, when I got the other letter—"

"Other letter! What letter?"

"The one you began to write me and never finished. The one in which you told me the whole truth about—about her. When I got that—"

"But wait—wait! I didn't send you that letter. It was in my trunk. I was writing it the night before your father —before the trouble happened. You couldn't have got *that* letter."

She smiled. "Yes, I did," she said. "Mr. Gammon brought it to me three days ago. He came to the cottage with it. He said he had found it on the floor of your room and saw my name at the beginning of it and brought it to me."

"But—but it wasn't on the floor of my room. It couldn't have been. It was locked up in my trunk. How could he have got it?"

"Hush! hush! You mustn't excite yourself so. Never mind how he got it. I think, myself, there is some mystery about his getting it; he was very much fussed and behaved queerly enough when he was there. But what does it matter? Why should we care about that? I read it as soon as he had gone, and I have read it I can't tell you how many times since. . . . And that wasn't all he came to see me about. He told me that it was you, and not Peleg Myrick, who went out in that storm, as sick as you were, and found father and brought him to the shore. . . . Oh, what is it? Are you feeling badly? Shall I call some one?"

She would have risen but he held her hand and prevented her doing so.

"No—no!" he protested. "I'm all right. These things are coming pretty fast, that's all. They make my head swim. . . . Let me get it straight. Seleucus told you that I—Seleucus told you that?"

"Yes. He told me all about it."

"But how did he know? No one knew that but Peleg, and Peleg promised me he wouldn't tell. He must have told, though. Confound him, of course he did!"

"Yes, he did, he told Mr. Gammon. Oh, you mustn't blame him. He didn't tell for ever so long, but when, so Seleucus says, I met him on the street in Orham and thanked him for saving father, he couldn't keep it to himself any longer. His conscience troubled him."

"Humph! Conscience! I guess the real reason was he was afraid some one might find it out, and he would get into trouble. Well, he is in trouble now. Wait until I see him, that's all. And Seleucus, too."

"Hush! You mustn't say that. Can't you understand how grateful I am to both of them? Suppose I had found it out, afterwards. Long afterwards, after I had gone away. Suppose I never found it out, any of it, but had gone away thinking—what I did think. . . . Calvin, why didn't you want me to know? Tell me, please."

He did not answer. It was something else she had said which caught his attention.

"Going away," he said, slowly. "Where are you going?"

"I am going back to Fairborough. They have offered me my position—the one I used to have—in the library. I must go, you know. I must earn something. Father's sickness, and all the rest, have taken almost all the money I had saved. I must get back to work at once."

He did not speak. She was watching him intently, and she saw his expression change.

"I shan't try to thank you for—for doing that for father," she said. "You were ill, and—and you risked your own life. . . . Don't say you didn't. I know you did. Of course you did. And, because you did, you—you almost lost it."

She paused. Then, after a moment, she continued.

"But why did you make Mr. Myrick promise not to tell?" she asked. "Calvin, why didn't you want any one to know? Tell me that, please."

He was not looking at her, and he stirred uneasily.

"Oh, it was just a crazy notion of mine," he muttered. "I guess I must have been half crazy that morning, anyway."

"But you had some reason, you must have had. What was it?"

He smiled, rather bitterly. "Well," he confessed, "I thought—I suppose I thought you had had trouble enough on my account. You wanted to forget me, and you should, of course. If you heard I was mixed up with finding your father it would remind you of me again, and only make more trouble for you. You might think you ought to thank me, perhaps—think it was something you had to do. I didn't want you to feel that way."

He heard her draw a quick breath. "Thank you!" she exclaimed. "Surely you couldn't believe I wouldn't want to thank you!"

"There is no reason why you should. Looking after people and boats that have gone adrift is part of my job, that's all. That's what they pay me my seventy-five a month for. Don't say any more about it, Norma. And you shouldn't have come way down here for that."

She, too, was silent, for an instant. Then she said quietly, "But I didn't. That wasn't why I came. I think—yes, I am almost sure I should have come even if Mr. Gammon had never brought me your letter or told me of your saving father. I think I should have come, anyway. Or, perhaps, written you to come to Orham and see me."

He looked at her now. The color came to her cheeks as he did so, but her eyes met his, brave and unfaltering.

"Why?" he demanded.

"Can't you imagine why? I should think it was plain enough."

He did not try to imagine.

"Why did you come?" he insisted.

"I came because—oh, because I was ashamed of myself! And I wanted you to know it. I don't believe I could have gone away without telling you so. I—"

But now he interrupted. He put his arms about her, quickly, almost roughly, and drew her to him.

"Norma!" he cried, "Norma, do you mean—do you care for me now? Do you? Do you?"

She looked up at him, then down.

"I should think that was almost apparent," she said. "This looks as if I did, doesn't it?"

There was an interval here, a rather long interval. She

was the first to speak; perhaps she would have spoken sooner if she could, if he had permitted it.

"Calvin dear," she said, "don't you think you had better go back to the station now? You have been out here a long while. And you have been sick, you know."

Sick! He laughed aloud. "I'm better this minute than I've ever been before since I was here," he declared. "And I'm not going yet. Why, I've got a million things to say to you, and that I want you to say to me. . . . Did you—did you *really* come way down here just to tell me that you were willing to forgive me? Did you?"

"No, of course I didn't. I came to tell you how ashamed I was of myself, and how proud I was of you—and some other things, perhaps, although I rather hoped you might tell them to me first."

He told them then; as a matter of fact, he had been telling them over and over again for five minutes or more. She, however, seemed willing to listen to the repetitions. But, at last, she insisted upon their discussing other, although less important, matters.

"We have so much to say," she declared, "and such a little time to say it in. You must go back to the station—you must. They will be coming to look for you pretty soon."

He looked at his watch. "Yes," he admitted reluctantly, "I suppose I must. It is almost drill time—and Kellogg is there, isn't he? But we've got a few minutes yet. Norma, you believe I never really cared at all for Myra Fuller, don't you?"

She put her hand to his lips. "Hush!" she said. "You and I are not going to mention that person's name again— *ever*. Are we?"

"You bet we aren't!" he declared, and meant it.

"No. And now we must be very sensible and talk about ourselves and our plans. I am going to Fairborough day after to-morrow. . . . Oh, yes, I must! And you must stay here, and do your work, of course. We will write each other every day and, perhaps, see each other once in a while. And we must work very hard and save all we can, because—well, you know why, don't you, dear?"

He nodded. "I'll work, you may be sure of that," he declared. "But I'm not going to be satisfied with this kind of work long. I'm going ahead now; I've got something to work for. Life-saving is the best fun on earth, for me, anyhow—but I'll get fun enough out of something with a better future and that pays better. I shall stick here until Kellogg can find another keeper. I hope he'll give the chance to Seleucus; he is a good fellow, and an able man, although his reports might be hard to read. I shall stay at Setuckit as long as the superintendent feels he can't do without me. I owe him that much. But, while I'm here, I shall be putting over my lines for something worth while. Why, he told me, himself—Cap'n Kellogg did—that, if I really wanted it, he guessed he could place me with one of the Boston and Savannah steamship lines. It might not be so much of a job to start with, but I'll make it more in a hurry. You watch me, Norma. With you to work for, if I don't earn money and get ahead, then—"

She laughed happily. "Hush! hush!" she said. "Goodness, how excited you are! Of course you will get ahead. There isn't a bit of doubt about that. And as for the money, I shall earn some myself. And, after all, what does all that matter to you and me—now? It doesn't seem to me that anything really matters now—except this. . . . And we *must* go back to the station."

He rose to his feet. She, too, rose and stood beside him. He drew a long breath. She was right, absolutely right. With her beside him he could—and would—get on in the world. He was young and, therefore, for him that world was full of opportunities. The harder the fight the better he should like it. And it would be for her that he fought. They would be together. That was the essential thing, the only thing that really mattered.

He squared his shoulders, and, figuratively speaking, snapped his fingers at the future. He, Calvin Homer, twenty-six years old, and, at present, keeper of the Setuckit

Life-Saving Station at a wage of seventy-five dollars a month and found, had that future conquered, or as good as conquered, already. Twenty-six, and the girl he loved beside him! Why—it was easy!

He pulled his cap down upon his head.

"Now watch me handle that boat drill," he announced triumphantly.

(¹)

THE END